Atlas Rising

By Blake Severson

Book One of the Divine Genesis Series

The group wound through multiple hallways before finally coming into an enormous space. Tiers of flooring rose from the sides, giving the appearance of movie theater seating. Ten pods rested on each of the flat platforms. The line of people filtered up the steps and groups split to each tier to stand beside their respective pods. Atlas reached his floor, and they directed him down the line. When he finally stood by the pod, he marveled at the design.

The egg-shaped contraption had a glass top, and the padded inside looked like a fluffy cloud. A helmet rested in the space with a large tube extending from it and into the back of the pod. The device itself rested on a small, circular platform that kept it from sitting directly on the ground.

As Atlas approached, the glass front swung open. A female technician stood near the pod with a clipboard and a smile. She gestured for him to enter and he slipped into the confines. The seat was comfortable, and the fabric breathed well. His original fear was the bulky material would make him sweat horribly.

"What's your name, sir?" the attendant asked.

"Atlas, Atlas Remere."

Chapter 1

The Gaming Center

Atlas Remere stood on his toes and peered over the crowd. The line into Gaia Corporation's newest gaming center stretched over a hundred yards. With a heavy sigh, he dropped back down. *I'll have to wait forever to get in*, he sulked.

Gaia Corporation made a name for themselves with the most innovative Virtual Reality Massive Multiplayer Online games in the last decade. Their last game, Destiny Fall, still boasted a record number of players with its haptic feedback system and patented Full Motion suit. It was the first true VRMMO to allow one-for-one movement in a suspended mobility system.

Atlas turned to face his best friend, Keenan.

"You know what you want to play as yet?" Atlas asked in excitement.

"Not sure. They've been so vague on the game details it's hard to decide. We don't even know how the combat system works yet. Gaia told us a handful of the races but even they said it wasn't the full list."

"But just think about it! A true full immersion VRMMO with no more suits. They even made it sword and sorcery style gameplay. It can't get much better than that!" Atlas rattled on, the anticipation killing him.

"I'll have to reserve judgment until we hear more," Keenan told him cautiously.

Atlas heard a commotion and glanced to the front of the line. The center doors opened and people moved forward, visibly excited as they quickly shuffled through.

Atlas and Keenan followed the line and edged forward. He kept expecting the line to stop as the building filled, but he couldn't have been more wrong. The line never stopped its flow and before long, they stood at the doors of the colossal structure.

The sleek lines and bright silver metal shone in the sunlight as they passed the enormous glass doors and walked into an amphitheater style entryway. Fine works of art hung from the ceiling in displays of crystal. It took Atlas a few minutes for them to resolve in his mind.

"Keenan, those are crystal sculptures of some of the greatest champions in Destiny Fall," he blurted as he grabbed his friend's shoulder.

He spun him and pointed at the figure of a large orc hanging from the ceiling near the entry, "That's Farr Drot. The number one player and highest ranking orc chief in the entire game. I heard he killed an entire tribe of humans by himself in a legendary quest."

"Ooh, ooh, and that one's Darlana Windstrider. She led the coup of the elven city of Gladenspring last fall," Atlas squeaked.

"Geez," Keenan whispered as he pushed Atlas' hand from his shoulder, "Don't nerd out so hard in front of people. There are actually ladies here. You know I was never a big fan of Destiny Fall, anyway."

Atlas stared into his friend's brown eyes and stuck his tongue out, but fought to calm himself. He managed some success but still bounced around as they continued through the room. Every statue in the area resembled something from gaming history, and every picture on the walls shone with vivid scenes of historic battles in his favorite VRMMO games.

The two filtered through with the crowd when Atlas noticed the line split as everyone approached. Eight massive freight elevators sat at the end of the hall. Each looked to hold well over a hundred people at once. The attendant at the front of the line addressed them as soon as they approached.

"You, the one with the short brown hair, to elevator four. You, with the long dreads, elevator six."

"But sir, we want to go to the same place so we can play together," Atlas said.

"That's not how this game works. Everyone spawns in a unique location. Even if you sit side by side in pods, you still may be on the other side of the world in the game. No matter what, you'll have to search for your friend," the man said as he motioned for them to continue forward.

Atlas turned to Keenan and shook his head, "Oh well, we'll find each other in game. Good luck, man."

They bumped fists and then walked to their assigned elevators. Atlas looked around at the eager faces, and his hesitation about leaving Keenan quickly faded. The building excitement from those around him was infectious, and he found himself with the familiar flash of eagerness again.

It took another fifteen minutes for the elevator to fill to capacity, then the operator motioned for everyone to back away from the entrance. Large steel doors slid closed with an eerie silence and the elevator hopped before descending. The trip down felt like an eternity. Atlas couldn't begin to guess how far they'd traveled beneath the surface.

Their elevator came to a halt, and the doors swung open to reveal an auditorium with rows of seating. A raised platform with a podium stood at the front, along with two men in white lab coats that waited for their arrival. Everyone neatly filed into the room and grabbed the closest chair. The elevator doors clicked shut and all the attendants sat waiting.

A man in a lab coat approached the podium. He stood a little under six feet tall and had short black hair, streaked with gray. His walk was a little stiff, like he had hip problems, but he trudged his way to stand in front of the small microphone.

A few taps on the mic with his hand confirmed it was live, and he started his speech, "Welcome to Gaia Corp! I'm Kevin Ingram. I'm the Director for Immersion Pod Facility Z, and one developer of the new Limitless VR interface you will experience in our new game. I know you're all excited to get into the game and experience it for yourself, but I ask that you bear with me for just a little while longer."

Mr. Ingram looked around the room and remained silent until the murmur of excitement settled back down and the room was mostly quiet, "We are supremely happy that you've chosen to come play this new game with so little information available. Destiny Fall was a tremendous leap in video game technology, and we've done everything possible to keep this one a secret. It's with great pleasure I finally announce the name of the game you will soon enter," he said with flair as he picked up a small wireless device and pressed a button.

An enormous banner unfurled from the ceiling and fell to cover the entire wall. Atlas stared in wonder at the assortment of characters shown on the banner. Twenty distinct races of people adorned the banner. Elves, Dwarves, and even Beastkin appeared on the large canvas and each held a wide assortment of weapons. He spotted everything from knives and swords, to bows and staves. He even swore he saw a musket in the mix. All wore an equally diverse set of armor and clothing. Fabrics, leathers, metals, and even many others he couldn't identify stood displayed on the characters. The top of the banner was the exciting part. After a year of hype and development, he finally laid eyes on the name of what he was positive would become his new obsession. Divine Genesis.

Cheers rang through the room as everyone took in the sight. Atlas watched as random people high-fived around the room in excitement. Mr. Ingram called for everyone to settle down so he could continue.

"We want our players to discover most aspects of the game on their own, so we will only provide small snippets of information to help you. Tutorials won't be offered and most of the mechanics you need to investigate yourself. I'll only stress that you can do anything you put your mind to in this game. Since it's a full integration with your mind, there are no physical limits to what you can achieve. Craft anything you want, cast spells, swing swords, sit around all day and carve wooden figures. You can do whatever you put your mind to," he explained to the looks of shock around the room.

Atlas turned toward the young woman on his right. She had an asymmetrical bob hairstyle that came to her jawline. Her hazel eyes turned to regard him with the same look of disbelief he felt.

"Did I hear him say no tutorial? No guidance?" Atlas asked.

"I think so. Unless we're both hearing things," she responded with a grin.

"We won't send you in completely blind, though. I will tell you basic details of the game. You will enter and choose a class and race. These details will decide the general area you will start. It also decides your base abilities and bonuses. Choose carefully here because you'll never be able to change this. You also can't create alternate characters. The neural link for the Limitless VR will tie directly into your mind so you can't integrate alts."

Grumbling echoed around the room as people protested at the idea. *I love playing alts.* Atlas complained as he slouched forward and rested his chin on his hands.

"Also, I'll stress there are no limits on your skills," Mr. Ingram reassured them. "You won't need alts to spread your skills across. No matter your class or race you can learn any weapons skill, any armor skill, or any craft. Certain combinations carry penalties based on specific criteria. For instance, a wizard trying to wear plate may encounter difficulties and spell penalties unless you get certain items."

Atlas perked up at that. *What items could allow people to overcome specific downfalls like those? Can it have something to do with specialized classes?*

"And now, the cherry, or in this case cherries, on top. Players in the game can earn the chance to become company executives at Gaia Corporation," he announced and the entire crowd turned silent. Everyone stared at him as though he'd gone insane.

All at once, multiple voices rang across the room, peppering the man with questions. Some announced loudly how they would be the next executives, while others proclaimed someone at the company must've gone insane.

"Everybody, calm down!" Mr. Ingram yelled into the microphone. The volume of his yell caused the speakers to buzz and screech slightly from the feedback.

"We will not reveal any details about that program, but the next announcement might interest you even more. We have worked over the last year to solidify market agreements, and currency in the game will have direct value in the actual world. Retailers will begin rolling out Divine Coin purchases in their businesses. The prices will fluctuate slightly with the market, but we've striven to make the conversion simple. Each copper coin is roughly one cent. One hundred coppers equal a silver and one hundred silver equal a gold. For those mathematically challenged, a gold coin is worth an average of one-hundred dollars. You can cash out your in game currency with us directly to convert it to standard money or spend it with the supporting retailers." Mr. Ingram said before another explosion of sound rocked the room.

Cheers and hollering echoed off the walls, and Atlas had to cover his ears because of the volume. The room went pitch black for a few moments and fell silent. When the light returned, a smiling woman in a lab coat walked away from the light controls near the edge of the room. *How does that always work?*

"Be careful here because you can die in the game. You will respawn, but there are consequences. With that last warning, let's get you guys into the Limitless rigs," he told them all as multiple security guards in uniforms directed people through a door in the large room. Everyone filed through and Atlas diligently followed behind.

"Good to meet you, Atlas. I'll be the one starting the interface for you. It's a quick procedure. I need you to sign these release forms first," she said as she handed him the clipboard. Atlas glanced at the first page and saw what looked like a standard Terms of Service agreement. Common on every game and piece of software he'd ever seen and scrolled through and accepted faster than the computer itself could usually acknowledge. The second page worried him for a moment. The title on it showed Medical Release.

"What's the medical release for?" he asked.

"When you go into suspension, we will insert intravenous lines into your body to keep it hydrated and healthy. This release merely asserts we won't administer any medicines or chemicals of any kind unless in an extreme emergency and directed to do so by a board certified doctor."

Atlas reflected on that. *Kinda scary. I guess they have to keep our bodies going somehow.*

"How long can we stay in at a time?" Atlas asked.

"We allow a maximum immersion of two days. After that you're not allowed to re-enter for at least twelve hours."

"Holy crap! I can stay in the game for two days before I have to leave?"

"Sure can," she said with a smile. "Questions?"

"Uh, how do I go to the bathroom while stuck in there?" He asked as he nodded toward the pod.

She giggled at the question before responding, "We equipped the pods with nanotechnology that allows them to slow down the metabolic rate of your body. It almost freezes time for your physical body as you stay in the game. Because of this, you won't have to take care of those specific functions. I will tell you a trip to the bathroom will definitely be one of the first things you do as soon as you log out."

Atlas thought about the situation and just shrugged. *They are obviously smarter than me, so I guess I should just enjoy the game.*

"Then I can't think of anything else," he told her.

She walked up and placed the helmet over his head. The inside appeared to be lined with something resembling microfiber, and it felt like millions of tiny hairs as the device slipped on. The woman moved and adjusted it until it fit just the way she wanted and stepped back.

"As soon as the interface finishes, I'll insert the intravenous lines and then close your pod. When you log out, someone will be here to help you out of the pod. Enjoy your time in Divine Genesis," she told him with one last wave as she walked to the side of the pod and pressed a series of buttons on a small control panel.

Lights flared to life around the pod and Atlas squinted his eyes at their brightness. A low humming noise filled his mind before his vision went black.

Chapter 2

Divine Genesis

Atlas watched a kaleidoscope of colors swirl in his vision before the space turned a solid gray and a screen popped up in front of him. He looked at the screen carefully as it floated in the space.

Welcome to Divine Genesis. Please proceed to the portal on your left to choose a class.

As soon as he finished reading the text, a portal of blue energy with streaks of silver lightning appeared to his left. With a shrug, Atlas stepped through. He entered a room that looked like a walk-in closet. Arrayed in front of him were a large assortment of people, but all stood with an eerie stillness. All twenty of the races were visible in this room, and there was a male and female variant of each. Their forms lined the area from shortest to tallest. A glance at the short side of the line showed him some familiar sights. Two sets of dwarves and what looked like some kind of vulpine character sat near the end with their short stature. Out of curiosity, he walked to the first set of dwarves and a box appeared.

```
Mountain Dwarves
```

<table>
<tr><td>

Racial Abilities:

    5% increased
chance to find
items when mining.
Endurance -
Stamina drains 15%
slower when doing
strenuous
activities.

</td><td>

Description: Mountain
Dwarves live
underground in
mountain ranges and
are known throughout
the world for their
skill in harvesting
ore and gemstones.
Their smithing skills
are typically better
than almost any other
race in terms of
craftsmanship.

</td></tr>
</table>

Neat! So each race has specific bonuses to them. Atlas looked at the next set of dwarves and saw it listed them as Hill Dwarves. While being a dwarf would be cool, his mind floated back to the researcher's warning. Whatever he chose, he could never change. Such a small frame would clash with his senses. He wasn't quite six foot tall as he stood now, but shrinking down to their height permanently would seriously mess with his perception. It'd also be an odd thing to transition to and from when he left the game.

The next race in the line was the fox looking one. The humanoid style body had a smooth stomach with very short hair while the back, arms, and legs consisted of longer fur. The face had a humanoid appearance but the mouth and nose elongated similar to a fox. Large pointed ears stood from the top of the head. There was no way Atlas could imagine himself stuck in that body, as fun as it may be, but he looked at the information for it as he approached.

Vulpine

Racial Abilities:	Description: Vulpines live in forested regions and live in harmony with nature. They hunt and forage for their own supplies but are known to trade with neighboring kingdoms.
Able to detect low sounds up to 40 feet away. Swiftness - Like their common mammal counterparts, Vulpine are incredibly fast and have a base Agility of 8. Their compact frame also allows them to increase their speed by 15% every 10 minutes. This effect only lasts for 30 seconds.	

Atlas knew exactly what the next creature in line was without even looking at its description. The small, ugly, green-skinned monster stood barely taller than the previous ones but was far scrawnier. Its jagged teeth looked intimidating, but Atlas would never consider playing a goblin. In the past, he'd played his fair share of bad guys in games, but this wouldn't be one of them. He quickly passed the little beast and moved to the next race.

The next figure in line was a fantasy of many anime fan boys. The creatures looked human for most of their body, but they had the tall soft ears of a cat and a long fuzzy tail. Tufts of fur covered their sides and back. Atlas checked their information.

Beastkin	
Racial Abilities: Able to detect faint smells up to 40 feet away. Acrobatic - Beastkin can leap up to 10 feet in the air. They also have a 15% natural boost to climbing.	Description: Beastkin roam the land as wanderers. They frequent cities of most of the kingdoms and are often bounty hunters. Their love of adventure keeps them on the move.

As awesome as that'd be, I don't think I could get used to turning into a furry person. His gaze continued down the line. The next three races were human. One was a darker skinned race, the second appeared to be someone of Asian origins, and the final one was of Caucasian descent. A quick look at them showed similarities. They all shared the same first ability of tenacity, giving them a 15% increased resistance to physical damage. Their second abilities differed. Atlas didn't dig in too far since he didn't plan on playing as a human. The point of playing a game was to do something different. He walked further down the line.

The next race intrigued him. The lithe figure and pointed ears of an elf greeted him. Two others just like this one stood next to it further down the line. This first one wore leather armor and stood with long braided hair. Vines wove through the man's hair while flowers decorated the woman's. A quick glance at their information intrigued him.

Wood Elf	
Racial Abilities: Receives a 10% boost to stealth in wooded areas. Harmony - Wood elves have a 15% bonus to Life and Nature Magic.	Description: Wood elves live in the forests of the world. They strive to maintain balance in nature.

Atlas had a good feeling about the race but wanted to look at the other options. The next in line was a dark-skinned elf. They labeled it a Drow while the final was a regal-looking elf in fancy robes, listed as a High Elf. They had similar characteristics, but their racial abilities differed. Drow were more geared toward stealth, while High Elves focused on magic almost exclusively. Atlas wanted to be a mixture of both, so Wood Elf seemed the better choice.

Something blue caught his eye as he looked down the line. He walked closer to it and saw another towering figure. It was a muscular being, standing a full seven-feet tall. Broad shoulders and a wide, somewhat flat nose stood out the most. The hair on its head looked slick, almost like the old greased back style. Intrigued, Atlas investigated this one as well.

Ar'naen	
Racial Abilities: Reduces magical and physical damage taken by 50%. Regeneration – regenerates health when damaged at a rate of 10 HP/minute.	Description: The Ar'naen are the ultimate warriors of the universe. They are steadfastly loyal to their empire as they travel the cosmos and crush worlds that oppose them.

Holy shit! That class has overpowered written all over it in permanent marker. How could they offer something so unbalanced? Atlas almost selected the race out of pure instinct before his consciousness caught up with what it said. Their description clearly marked them as a bad guy. He'd already resolved not to play one in this game. *Great, now I know one of the toughest challenges in the game,* he moped to himself.

He looked up and down the line, and his gaze always stopped on the Wood Elf. Further down the line he saw other familiar forms of all shapes and sizes. A werewolf, a kobold, even a fae littered the lineup. Atlas merely shook his head and walked back to the male Wood Elf. With this game being so realistic, he wasn't fond of the idea of trying a female character. He reached out and touched the elf and a prompt appeared.

Do you wish to choose Wood Elf as your Race? Keep in mind, this choice is final. Yes/No.

Atlas mentally selected *Yes*, and the room shifted. Everything disappeared, and he stood alone in a sea of gray with the male elf. Swirling blue energy appeared below his feet and rose to surround them both. The power closed in and pushed the two of them together until their forms touched. A flash of light blinded him, and when he opened his eyes, the elf was gone. He looked down at his hands only to notice they weren't his anymore.

A mirror shimmered into view in front of him, and he saw the reflection of the Wood Elf.

Do you wish to alter your default appearance? Yes/No.

Atlas selected *Yes*. Small slider bars appeared near many of his features in the mirror. It reminded him of the customization options in many of the old school MMO games where the player could adjust the size of different body parts. He selected the slider that stretched the length of his body and mentally slid it higher. As he did, he noticeably grew taller. With glee he slid the slider as far as it would go, and he rose to a little over seven feet tall. It was an odd feeling as he shifted his feet, trying to gauge his new balance.

He slid it back down and settled for a height just a little over six feet instead. A few tweaks to his ears, eyes, mouth, and forehead allowed him to make the face he sought. High cheekbones accentuated his face and the long, pointed ears stood out. Satisfied, he nodded at his new form and looked around in confusion. *What do I do now?*

He took three steps away from the mirror
when a box popped up again.

*Are you finished with your customization?
You can't change this appearance once you
leave. Yes/No.*

Yet again, he selected *Yes* and another
portal of blue sprung to life.

*Congratulations adventurer. Proceed through
the portal to choose your starting class.*

Atlas hopped through and appeared in
another room. It was like the last, but not as
many forms stood in the place. The people
swirled with energy and power. Many bristled
with weapons sticking out all over them. Atlas
was both amused and a little scared to see
another musket. *Damn. It's going to suck
dodging gunfire in this game.*
Most of the figures he could figure out by
sight. A Gladiator and a Warrior stood side by
side. One wore what looked more like Roman
style armor, while the other had a full suit
of medieval plate armor. An archer stood
nearby in her leather armor. Near her was
another figure that confused him. The man
stood in leather armor but stood with his arms
to the side and green energy swirling around
his hands.
Atlas walked forward and examined him. The
box labeled him as a Druid, but there was
almost no information other than that. Unlike
the races, the classes showed nothing more
than the class name and the hints at what the
person wore.

He looked further along the line and saw a Wizard. Close by was another figure dressed in robes but with swirling purple energy. A quick inspection of him showed this was a Warlock. Directly beside him was another figure with purple energy, but flashes of black lightning showed in the magic. The man looked pale as a ghost, and Atlas understood as soon as he saw the title. Necromancer. *For fuck's sake. Undead too?*

An assassin dressed in dark leather crouched to the side of the group. His small blades and black clothing made his profession obvious. Atlas also swore he saw a green liquid dripping from the blades.

The selection bummed him out. He truly expected there to be far more options with the extensive selection of races they had. Mr. Ingram's words about there being special items to unlock other skills reverberated in his mind, though. It must be possible to make hybrid classes with some special items found in the game. That would explain the lack of some classes he'd expect to see. A Paladin was a prime example of that. They were essentially warriors with divine magic.

With the options on display, he walked back over to the Druid. Reaching out, he touched the man and the prompt he expected showed up.

Do you wish to take the Druid class? Yes/No.

Atlas selected *Yes,* and the figure in front of him moved. The druid lowered its arms and stared directly at him before speaking.

"Well met. I'm Zephyr Longstride, Master Druid of the order of Ancients. What is your name?" the druid asked.

Frozen in shock for a moment, Atlas's mind struggled to comprehend what was happening before his eyes. *A name? Makes sense. Need to figure out a name.* He thought as he lifted his hand to his chin. I've used tons of names through the different games I've played before.

"I've used many names over the years, Sir Longstride, but call me Atlas," he told him with finality. *This place already feels far more real than anything I've ever played before, so why not keep my name real as well?*

"Well met, Atlas. Find me in the town of Kilthan. I'll instruct you in the ways of the druid upon your arrival," the man finished before turning and walking away. The Master Druid faded from view as he left the area. Atlas looked around in confusion for a few seconds until he spotted another swirling blue portal behind him. In eager anticipation, he jumped into it.

Swirls of color assaulted his mind until he finally stood in a small wooded area. Tall trees rose high around him, and the underbrush in the area low and clear. The scent of the fresh breeze filled the air with a hint of pine. He walked to the nearest tree and placed his hand on it. The familiar warmth of the trees reached out to him and he almost felt like he could speak to it.

The sensation surprised him. This was truly a game on a whole new level. No clunky devices, no peeks of your surroundings from the sides of your glasses to throw you out of the simulation. Just pure interaction. To see the depth of it, he reached over and pinched his arm.

Damn, that hurt. He thought to himself as he rubbed at the affected area. His olive skin even flushed a slight shade of red where he'd pinched. *That could be a problem.* Realistic feelings of pain would certainly suck, but it would also make him play the game more carefully.

Atlas liked the occasional game of race in and kill everything you could, but those games only really worked because nothing stopped you until you died. It was a totally different story when pain interfered with your actions and forced you to stop.

A quick surveillance of the area showed trees in all directions. A narrow path wound through the forest in front of him. Looking behind him confirmed it went both directions. He would have to trust the game and follow the path in the direction he faced upon arrival. Hopefully the game oriented him in the direction he needed to go.

As he walked, he noticed his footsteps were lighter than he expected. Then he remembered he was no longer a clunky human. With a few quick bounces, he tried to get a feel for his new body. The realism of the way he moved astounded him. He could jump and spin with ease while dashing around much faster than he could as a human. With the thrill of his new form, he raced down the path.

He hopped low bushes and danced along the edge of the path without a care for his surroundings. The trees thinned out and the forest floor took over more of the space. Tufts of grass sprouted in places and gradually grew thicker as he continued his trek until he burst through the last of the trees and faced an enormous grassy clearing.

A small town sat in the center, and Atlas watched as puffs of smoke rose from the buildings. With nervous anticipation, he approached cautiously. He didn't want to race toward the village in a dash and startle anyone guarding the place. If his first act in the game was to be shot and killed by a guard, he'd never live down the shame. Hopefully, an Artificial Intelligence kept them from that behavior, but this place was so realistic he didn't want to bank on that.

The elves on the edge of the town looked up at his approach. A few wore looks of curiosity, while others merely returned to their work. None rose to greet him as he entered. Atlas walked to a male elf with a bow slung over his shoulder.

"Hi, I'm looking for Master Longstride of Kilthan," Atlas announced.

The elf shook his head before returning his gaze, "Master Longstride is in the longhouse at the end of this main road. Good luck in your trials."

"Uh, thanks." Atlas replied, confused by his comment about trials.

He traveled down the path and surveyed the buildings as he passed. They made each of meticulously woven strands of wood. The strips fit so closely that he doubted water could get through them. They also had the general shape of normal domed-style houses. Most intriguing of all were the different appearances.

As his journey continued, he noticed the houses all looked similar, but some of them appeared to be made from unique wood. The grain styles differed from house to house and the colors varied. It looked like natural, unfinished wood, so he didn't think they stained them to look different.

The longhouse at the end of the road was unmistakable. The gigantic building stretched at least one-hundred feet and was at least half that width, if not more. Double doors with an arched doorway sealed the building on the front. Two elves with bows on their shoulders and a dagger on their belt stood guard at the door. Atlas waved to them as he approached.

"Hey guys, I'm Atlas. I'm here to meet with Master Longstride," he said as they stared forward without saying a word. Neither turned nor made a noise, so he continued, "He told me to find him here."

The two remained motionless in complete silence and never even glanced in his direction. He considered walking over and prodding one to make sure they were real, but the doors swung open.

"Ah, Atlas. It's good to see you again. Please come in," Master Longstride said as he gestured for him to enter.

"Thank you Master," Atlas told him with a slight bow. He was unfamiliar with this world and wanted to make a good impression.

"So you're to be our newest druid candidate? I guess you'll do. Few wish to take that specific lifestyle."

"I'm eager to begin. Where do we start?" Atlas anxiously replied, his voice tinged with excitement.

The master merely raised an eyebrow before leading him to a secluded room. A beautifully carved wooden desk rested in the center with legs made from woven rods of wood. The desktop showed the live edge on all four sides, and it shone with a smooth coat of what Atlas could only assume was some kind of lacquer. Two chairs with matching wooden legs sat on each side of the desk.

Master Longstride sat in the one behind the desk and motioned for Atlas to take the other. The master clasped his hands together on the desk and looked at him.

"Druids work with the elements of life and nature. Life is something that is taught as you advance further, but we will work on your training for Nature Magic. A druid relies on three basic spells. Nature's Wrath, Entangle, and Nurture. Nature's Wrath will be the first one I teach you," Master Longstride said as he reached over and grabbed onto Atlas' arm. A surge of power passed between them and images flooded his mind. Atlas felt the power draw through his body from the ground and build in his hands. The ball of swirling green power solidified and he could almost grab it. Right before he took hold and launched it, the power stopped and a notification filled his mind.

You have learned the Druid Spell: Nature's Wrath.

Druid Spell - Nature's Wrath	

Requirements
    Druid Class
    Level 1
	Description: Summons a ball of raw nature energy to launch at your target.
	
	Damage: 3-5 HP
	Mana cost: 15 MP

That was lackluster. *Fifteen mana for something that does such a tiny amount of damage? Surely this spell is bugged? I wonder if there's a way to report bugs in this game.* Atlas thought to himself as he searched in all directions for any hint of a help button or menus.

His gaze returned to Master Longstride, only to see the druid staring at him as though he'd lost his mind.

"Something interesting in my office?" Longstride asked.

"No. Thought I saw something. Must be my imagination," Atlas spurted quickly.

The master merely waved his hand and continued, "Your other two spells must wait. Entangle requires you to reach level 3, while Nurture requires level 5 before I can teach it. In the meantime, you can run quests in the surrounding area to level up."

"Sweet! Do I get to fight monsters? Go hunting? Subject evil to my magical wrath?" Atlas asked with glee.

"Uh, no," Master Longstride answered, "I need you to gather ten bundles of Haeyna Sprig."

As soon as the words left the master's mouth, a notification popped up.

<table>
<tr><td colspan="2" align="center">Quest - Haeyna Sprig</td></tr>
<tr>
<td>Requirements:
   Level 1

Quest Rarity: Common

Quest Reward: 50 experience, 5 copper coins, 1 Minor Healing Potion.</td>
<td>Description: Master Zephyr Longstride has tasked you with finding 10 Haeyna Sprig's.</td>
</tr>
<tr><td colspan="2" align="center">Do you wish to accept this quest? Yes/No.</td></tr>
</table>

Atlas selected *Yes*, and the druid smiled. Master Longstride reached down behind his desk, grabbed a small pouch, and handed it to Atlas. He immediately took the bag and opened it.

"Inside are the bare essentials you'll need in the forest. Anything better, you'll have to work for. You may find others in the village who have need of your services as well."

"How do I know how much experience I need to level or how my skills level up?" Atlas asked.

"Think the words Personal Information in your mind. Your character information will appear for you," Longstride replied, although his voice sounded more monotone and computer-like than before.

"Thanks. Do you need me for anything else or am I free to go?"

Master Longstride didn't bother with words and just shooed him away with his hand. Atlas walked out of the building while continuing to dig through the bag. His hand nudged something sharp, and the pinprick of pain caused him to withdraw it from the bag. A small line of blood welled from the end of his index finger and he opened the top of the bag large enough to peek inside. A metal glimmer filled his view, and he carefully reached into the bag.

His hand wrapped around the smooth end of the object and carefully withdrew it from the bag. The item was a short knife with a coppery hue to it. He stared at it in confusion for a moment before remembering the druid's words. If his personal information required him to think of a command, this may as well. His first thought was *Identify*. After picturing the word in his mind, nothing happened. *Maybe that doesn't work because it's typically a magical spell name?* Instead, he just tried *Item*. This time a box popped open in front of him.

Item - Bronze Knife	
Requirements: Level 1 **Rarity:** Common **Quality:** Poor	**Attack:** 1 **Durability:** 15/15 **Weight:** 1 lb. **Slot:** Main-Hand/Off-Hand **Traits:** A basic knife made of bronze.

So this is gonna be one of those games? Everything starts off with low HP and gradually climbs. Atlas checked his personal information to see where his base stats stood.

Name: Atlas **Class**: Druid **Level**: 1 **HP**: 49/50 **Mana**: 50/50 **Experience**: 0/100	**Agility**: 2 **Constitution**: 3 **Intellect**: 3 **Strength**: 2 **Spirit**: 3
Combat Skills: None	**Magic Skills:** **Nature Magic:** Nature's Fury - Rank 1
Crafting Skills: None	**Artifacts:** None

Well, at least there aren't any of the stupid stats like Luck or Charisma to waste points on.

The bag also contained some meat that registered as *Dried Venison* when he examined it. He pulled out a small hide container with a wooden screw top on it. A quick shake confirmed it was a water skin. He considered tying the dagger to his pants, only to realize they weren't his normal blue-jean style pants with pockets and belt loops. These were coarse fabric and offered no way to tie anything to them, so he tossed the blade back into the bag to join the rest of the items. Wrapping the string tight around the top, he carried the bag as he traversed through town.

Atlas was every bit of a noob in this situation and had no money of any kind. He resolved to take the master's advice and search out more quests before he ventured to the woods. A sign with a plant leaf on it drew his attention, so he ducked into the building.

"Welcome to Zaina's Herb Emporium," a young elven woman greeted from behind the desk. "Is there anything I can help you with?"

"Hi, I'm Atlas and am new to the town," he
said with a wave.

"Well, Atlas, I could guess as much since
I've never seen you here," she replied with a
sweet smile.

"Uh, yeah," he said sheepishly, "I was
checking to see if you have any quests
available?"

"Hm," she mumbled as she lifted her finger
to her chin, "I am running short on a couple
different herbs. They are common to the area.
Are you familiar with Zanth Root and Weer
Bloom?"

Atlas could've sworn she spoke another
language for a moment, but realized that they
were the names of the odd plants.

"No, I'm afraid I don't know them. Do you
have a picture of them?" he asked.

"A picture? What's that? I have a drawing
of them. Would that help?" the woman asked,
confused.

Atlas felt like a fool. *Cameras probably
don't exist here, so she won't know what a
picture is.*

"That should do nicely." He agreed.

She turned toward the bookshelf behind her
and began rummaging around. Atlas took that
time to get a good look around the place.
She'd engaged him in conversation as soon as
he entered. Shelving lined the walls to his
sides. Small jars filled each shelf with tags
in writing below them. Some contained seeds,
others petals of flowers, while more contained
large sections of roots.

More decorated the wall behind the counter,
but these looked far more important. Some
harbored living plants in soil, all vibrant
with life. One row contained only vials, each
with oddly colored liquids in them.

The woman turned back to him with a dusty leather-bound book in her hands. She walked to the counter and plopped it down with a slight puff of dust. Brushing the cover off with the back of her hand, she carefully grabbed the edge and flipped it open. A quick shuffle through the pages and she stopped and flipped the book around toward him.

Atlas walked closer and examined the page. A drawing of a plant with a single stem, decorated with four large leaves, showed on the page. The illustration contained enough detail to even show the way the roots appeared beneath the soil. The thick tubes wound into a loose ball the size of a baseball.

"This plant is the Zanth Root. Look for the unique leaf style and it's easy to spot. It's difficult to get them out of the ground without damaging the roots because of how they wind," the woman warned before flipping the pages again and stopping, "and this one is a Weer Bloom."

The illustration showed a small plant with a large bulbous top. What Atlas assumed was the bloom itself looked like a fat bottomed vase and tapered into a thin neck with a flared opening. The most distinct aspect was the blue and white swirl pattern on it.

"These are also in the area. Can you find five of each of these for me?" she asked.

<table>
<tr><td colspan="2">Quest – Supplying the Herbalist</td></tr>
<tr><td>Requirements:
  Level 1

Quest Rarity: Common

Quest Reward: 50 experience, 5 copper coins, 1 Minor Mana Potion.</td><td>Description: The Herbalist has asked you to retrieve Zanth Root x5 and Weer Bloom x5.</td></tr>
<tr><td colspan="2">Do you wish to accept this quest? Yes/No.</td></tr>
</table>

Atlas merely shrugged and selected *Yes*.

"Fantastic. I look forward to your return."

He turned to leave but paused. He quickly realized he didn't know what the Haeyna Sprig looked like.

"Before I go, can you show me the drawing for a Haeyna Sprig? I have another quest to find some of those and don't know what they look like."

She flipped through the pages again before stopping at another drawing. This one showed a vine-like plant with small red flowers.

"That's what you seek. Those can be tricky to harvest, so I wish you luck."

"Why's that?" Atlas asked with a look of confusion.

She gave him an odd look, "Guess you're not familiar with Herbalism, huh?"

"Actually, I'm just starting out," Atlas admitted.

"That plant has small thorns that are annoying to deal with," she explained while pointing to the picture, "the toughest part is you can't just pull them up. If you don't carefully dig them out, you're guaranteed to damage the roots and render the plant unusable."

"Well, damn." Atlas muttered.

The young woman reached behind the desk and pulled out a small tool. She walked over and handed him the item.

Item - Herbalist Trowel	
Requirements: Level 1 **Rarity**: Common **Quality**: Poor	**Durability**: 15/15 **Weight**: 1 lb. **Slot**: Main-Hand/Off-Hand **Traits**: A basic trowel made of bronze. Increases the user's chance to harvest low level herbs by 5%.

"Thank you. What's your name?" Atlas asked.

"Why Zaina, of course," she told him with a laugh, "It's my shop after all."

"Well, until we meet again, Zaina," he told her with a wave as he walked out the door.

Once outside, his resolve sat in. *It's time to search for some plants.*

Chapter 3

The First Excursion

Atlas strolled from the shop and looked around the town. He wanted to pick a direction, but also needed to make sure he didn't get lost. Using the sun as a guide, he walked in the direction he assumed was east. When he reached the last building, a thought occurred to him.

Most of these games have a minimap. This one should as well.

He focused inward and pictured *minimap*. A small floating map showed in the corner of his vision. He saw the buildings clearly marked on the map and even noticed a trail that led from the town. That trail and the town itself were the only visible pieces on the map.

It must only show places I've been. Would explain the trail I ran to get here.

No longer worrying about getting lost, he strolled with confidence into the surrounding forest. His trek continued until he crossed a game trail and he turned to follow it in a southeastern direction. The ground was a clear path ahead on the trail, but to either side sat a carpet of grass.

Atlas glanced at his feet. *I'll never find herbs on the game trail itself. I'll have to go dig through the grass and around the trees.*

Changing directions, he headed into the wooded area. The trees in this area provided plenty of shade and blocked out a fair amount of the sunlight. Most of the grasses were of the broad-leaf variety. The soft squish of the grass under his boot helped calm him. Smells of the surrounding woods amazed his senses. *It's truly hard to believe this is a game.*

Movement interrupted his walk as he noticed the grass near one tree swayed in erratic movements. Atlas carefully reached into his bag and pulled out the small Bronze Knife. The creature scurried into a clear part of the path, and he identified it as a squirrel. He mentally thought *abilities*, and the only thing that appeared was one attack. Double Slash (Rank 1). Atlas charged for the little creature and when he closed, the distance received a message.

You have entered combat!

So it gives you some warning, huh? He shook off the message and mentally activated Double Slash. What he saw made little sense. A ghostly image of a knife raced from his own weapon and hit the animal in the side. He continued his original swing despite the weird image, and his dagger hit the squirrel in the back leg.

You dealt 1 HP damage to Squirrel.

He attempted to pull back, to thrust again, but his hand froze. Standing up straight, he watched the squirrel in confusion. It spun to look directly at him before. Atlas saw that same silhouette from earlier, but this time it showed his arm lifting and his dagger facing an upward position. Contrary to the image, Atlas just freaked out and threw up his hands. A sharp pain stung his arm.

A furry faced stared at him with beady eyes over the edge of his forearm. The squirrel released its bite and scurried up his arm. The ghostly image returned and showed an arm swinging across his own, into the path of the squirrel. Atlas swung his other arm in the general direction the image showed, but it breezed past and didn't stop the creature. Teeth dug into his bicep and the sharp pain returned. This process repeated one more time until the creature took a bite of his shoulder and then jumped back to the ground.

Squirrel dealt 3 HP damage to you with Triple Bite.

That's not possible. Is this thing higher level than me? He looked down at his skin and saw no marks left from the bites. The squirrel had one small blood spot on it from his attack. Atlas concentrated on the little animal and a small bar appeared over its head. The bar showed a small missing section that accounted for a little less than a quarter of its health missing. Beside the bar was a number 1.

So it's level 1, but somehow did three times more damage than me?

Atlas shifted and realized his arm moved again, so he took another stab at the animal. The image swung in a wide arc, but Atlas performed a straight thrust. The blade bit into the creature's side, but then he froze in place again before standing back up.

What the hell is going on? The image must be important or I wouldn't keep seeing it. Maybe I should try to mimic it?

The furry animal leaped toward him again, and Atlas waited for the ghostly motion to appear. As soon as he saw it, he swung his arm directly through the image at the approaching monster. His arm flew forward and his knife found empty air. He tried to swat at the incoming enemy with his other hand, but it wouldn't move. The little guy landed on him a moment after, and its teeth dug into flesh. It scurried up his arm in the same motion as before and bit him three total times as he flailed uselessly at the tiny monster.

Squirrel dealt 3 HP damage to you with Triple Bite.

Frustration set in and his anger rose. Atlas couldn't figure out how a level 1 Squirrel was besting him. *It shouldn't be possible. Is the game bugged?* He gritted his teeth and swung his knife at the animal again. This time, when the image appeared, he carefully shifted the path of his own knife to move in time with the image. To his surprise, it struck the enemy without fail and he could still move. The image appeared again, and he tried to match it. The second strike was a sideways slash, and he was close to right on track. The squirrel collapsed and an unexpected message greeted him.

You dealt 3 HP damage to Squirrel with Double Slash.
Squirrel died.
You gained 5 experience.

Whoa. An addition? So this whole combat system works on mimicking movements? Interesting. Atlas walked to the corpse and reached down to grab it. A box popped into his view and showed him the items available.

Loot - Squirrel (Level 1)
Raw Squirrel Hide
Raw Squirrel Meat

So, some meat and fur, huh? No coins magically appearing or anything? Atlas selected both items, and a rolled up bundle of fur and a chunk of meat on a tiny bone appeared in his hands. Hair from the hide littered the surface of the meat, and he looked at his surroundings. One of the nearby plants was a broadleaf variety, and he pulled two of its leaves and wrapped the meat in it before stowing the items in his small bag.

A glance toward the ground showed the body of the squirrel already gone. With a shrug, Atlas continued his trip. It took him another ten minutes of walking before he finally spotted a cluster of small plants near a large rock. The blue and white streaks over the plant drew him closer. When the vase-like shape resolved, he knew he was in luck. He looked at the plant for a moment before the name, *Weer Bloom*, appeared over it.

Atlas reached down and grabbed the base of the nearest plant. With a quick heave, he ripped it free from the ground. He held the plant in his outstretched hand and waited until it identified. *Destroyed Weer Bloom* appeared over the now wilting plant.

"What the hell!" Atlas yelled as the plant slowly withered and disintegrated in his hand. Before the entire plant faded into dust, he noticed a broken section on the main root stem. *Is it really so picky I have to harvest the entire plant intact?*

With a frustrated sigh, he dug through his bag until he found the small trowel Zaina gave him. He knelt near the next plant and thrust it toward the ground. His hand froze in midair as he spotted the increasingly familiar ghostly image. He watched the illusion as it dug into the ground a few inches from the edge of the plant. With careful precision, he tried to mimic the movement. His movement didn't align perfectly, but it must have been close since the image changed to show him putting pressure on the handle to pop up some dirt. The actions shifted again and showed him placing the trowel in a new spot. He gingerly copied the movements until the ground around the plant popped up. Cupping the dirt in his hands, he lifted the plant and watched as the excess soil fell from the roots, leaving only a perfectly preserved plant.

You learned the skill, Herbalism.

<table>
<tr><td colspan="2" align="center">Item - Weer Bloom</td></tr>
<tr><td>Requirements: None
Rarity: Common
Quality: Poor</td><td>Durability: 10/10
Weight: 1 lb
Slot: Crafting

Traits: A vase-shaped plant with blue and white streaks.

Uses: To unlock this section you must advance your Herbalism skill or learn recipes using this plant.</td></tr>
</table>

One down, four more to go. Atlas spent another twenty minutes and only ended up with three intact Weer Blooms in his bag. On one attempt he slipped while digging and the trowel dug into the base of the plant, killing it.

With all three packed away, he surveyed his surroundings. Nothing stood out, so he consulted his minimap and walked in a random unexplored direction. After a brief stint of travel, a noise caused him to freeze.

The thick bush on the trail in front of him shook slightly. He crept forward until he was only a few steps away. A furry little creature hopped from the foliage and onto the clear path. Atlas stood up tall and smiled. An examination identified it as *Rabbit - Level 1.*

"Scared me for a second little guy."

He crouched down and stared at the fuzzy little animal. Its ears perked up and its eyes locked onto his own. Atlas reached out to touch the creature, but it looked back toward the bush it emerged from and darted off in the opposite direction at a run. Its actions confused him until he heard more rustling in the leaves.

To his surprise, a cat like form exited the bush and came to a halt in front of him. It crouched down as though it would pounce. The tag for *Bobcat - Level 3* appeared over its head. *Two levels isn't a terrible difference.*

You have entered combat!

Atlas slowly reached into the bag at his side while the bobcat shifted its weight to its tall hind legs to prepare for its jump. His blade came free at the same time the cat leaped into the air, and he watched the shadowy form of his blade move in his vision. He partially panicked when he noticed the claws of the bobcat extended and pointed toward his face.

Instead of following the motion, he reacted on instinct and threw both arms up and crossed them in front of his face. A sharp pain exploded from his forearms and a tearing feeling entered his mind as the weight of the creature drug it down his arms. His relief was short-lived as the cat used its claws to jump farther up his arm and it sunk its teeth into his left shoulder.

Bobcat dealt 4 HP damage with Biting Claw.

The little monster fell back to the ground and stared at him in anticipation of his attack. Atlas almost dove forward with his dagger before he remembered he now had a magic spell. With a feral grin, he mentally activated Nature's Fury. A rush of power filled his arms but, to his dismay, images of his arms moving danced in his view. He stared at them in confusion until the power left him and he saw an unwelcome notification.

You failed to cast Nature's Fury. There was no spell backlash.

I have to do these motions for spells as well? How the hell am I expected to do that during combat?

A growl interrupted his thoughts as the bobcat attacked again. This time, Atlas maintained his composure and followed the movements as closely as he could. His arm matched the ghostly image and his blade scored a shallow cut on the side of the cat in midair. The attack knocked its jump off course and it flew slightly to his left as the feline hissed in pain.

You dealt 1 HP damage to Bobcat with Deflect.

Hey, I'm getting the hang of this. He activated his Double Slash ability and leaped forward in time with the visualization. His blade wavered in and out of the image as it flew, but maintained a general pace with the copy. An angry bobcat marked the end of the trail as the knife continued and hit its side.

Instead of seeing the next attack, his vision flashed red for a moment and then the cat leaped for him again. The ghostly image showed a defensive slash across his body, so he attempted to follow. Off balance from his attack and the unexpected follow up attack, he stumbled and his defensive swipe flew wide of the indicated path. Instead of the teeth of the cat, Atlas received a swipe of claws as searing pain ran down his forearm and his movement froze again.

You dealt 1 HP damage to Bobcat with Double Slash. (Interrupted)
Bobcat dealt 2 HP damage to you with Counter.

So the creatures can counter attacks? That could make things interesting.
The bobcat attacked again, and he matched the movements, knocking it off balance. An idea struck him and he tried to activate Double Slash as soon as he successfully countered. It worked, and the image of his attack appeared immediately. He followed the movements and struck both times without being interrupted.

You dealt 3 HP damage to Bobcat with Double Slash.

This combat system seems to be almost turn based. If I mess up an attack or miss a counter, it stops my movements until the opponent can strike.

He circled to his right, and the cat
crouched down and slowly circled with him. It
stayed low to the ground and crept forward as
though stalking prey, never taking its eyes
off of him. The bobcat dashed forward and
Atlas jumped to the side. The animal flew
past, and he spun to watch it land and turn
toward him. It froze in place with a snarl.

Time to try a spell again. Atlas slipped
his dagger in the waist of his pants and
activated Nature's Fury, bracing himself for
the onslaught of images. As soon as they
appeared, he frantically followed the
movements. His right arm spun one full circle
in a clockwise motion, while his left did the
same in a counter-clockwise pattern. When both
completed their rotation, he brought them
together with his palms touching, as though in
prayer, and then pushed both out at the same
time. His excitement rose when a ball of green
energy formed in his outstretched hands and
shot forward toward the bobcat. The orb of
power hit the animal on the side and it
stumbled backward.

*You dealt 4 HP damage to Bobcat with
Nature's Fury.*

Woo Hoo! Finally managed a spell.
The Bobcat cut short his internal
celebration as it jumped for him, mouth open.
His glee from casting a spell caused him to
stumble as he tried to get his dagger back in
his hand. He missed the counter swipe and
ended up with two more spots of burning pain.

*Bobcat dealt 4 HP damage to you with Biting
Claw.*

I'm not about to die to a stupid cat. Need the experience to level up.

Atlas grit his teeth and squeezed the handle of his knife. *Time to finish this.*

He activated Double Slash again and followed the ghostly image. His blade sliced into the creature's side and then swung back the other way and caught it in the neck.

You dealt 3 HP damage to Bobcat with Double Slash.
Bobcat died.
You gained 15 experience.

The small animal collapsed, and Atlas walked to the corpse. The loot box appeared when he reached for it.

Loot – Bobcat (Level 3)
Rough Feline Claw x 3
Raw Bobcat Hide x 1

Nothing super special, but I'm sure the hide will fetch a decent price. He accepted both of the items and the claws dropped into his hand. A soft hide appeared immediately after, rolled up the same as the squirrel's had been.

Atlas looked around to see if the rabbit was nearby but saw nothing. He checked himself and didn't see any wounds anywhere. A quick thought showed his HP at 33. His health didn't seem to regenerate on its own. He was still missing the 1 HP from stabbing himself with his own dagger in the bag.

If health doesn't regenerate here, I'll need to find out what can restore it and keep it in stock.

An enormous boulder stood out in the distance, drawing his curiosity, so Atlas headed through the trees in its direction. Flowers carpeted the ground in a small clearing and the boulder sat directly in the center. The oddly serene area stopped him in his tracks. Something akin to a stillness settled over him and a feeling of peace filled him. Even the air felt suddenly fresher.

Out-of-place stuff like this always has something bad in it. He turned away from the clearing when something caught his eye. Vines covered in small red flowers crawled along the side of the boulder. *Of course they would be in this weird place.*

He let out a heavy sigh and turned his attention to the plants. A quick glance showed nothing in the immediate area, so he walked into the clearing. As soon as his foot brushed against the first flower, a chittering sound echoed through the space. Soft brown fur sprouted from the tall grass near the boulder and a large bushy tail emerged behind it. The small animal stood on its back feet and stared at Atlas.

Another squirrel! Perfect practice for my combat. His spell work needed the most practice, so he activated Nature's Fury.

You have entered combat!

The movements were easier this time as he followed the same pattern as before. *I hope the spell's pattern always stays the same. It will make it much easier to remember.* Matching the movements, the spell sped forward and hit the squirrel. It squeaked and rolled to its side.

You dealt 5 HP damage to Squirrel.
Squirrel died.
You gained 5 experience.

Arthur jogged to the animal and looked at the loot. It was the same hide and meat as the previous squirrel, so he selected both. They fell into his hands and then quickly dropped into his bag. He took one step before a message appeared that sent chills down his spine.

You defiled a sanctuary. Your life is forfeit!

Branches creaked and leaves rustled as Atlas quickly spun around and checked his surroundings. Sweat beaded along his forehead as the message sunk in and fear gripped him. A rustling noise caught his attention near the edge of the clearing, and he jumped at the sound out of fear. He crouched down and trembled at the thought of a grotesque monster appearing from the underbrush. With his knife in hand, he waited for the beast to arrive.

A grayish blur leaped from the underbrush, and the insignificant creature came to a halt. A look of fiery fury reflected in its eyes as it stared at Atlas. He felt foolish and almost laughed at the scenario. The oh-so-scary monster he feared was nothing more than a larger squirrel with gray fur. This one was the size of a husky house cat. An examination of it confused him. *It has a name? Guardian Reil - Level 5.*

You have entered combat!

Crap! Level 5 and a named creature? The oversized squirrel charged for him, so Atlas ran directly at it. He activated Double Slash. His blade flew forward, but no image appeared. The reason was quickly apparent as the animal jumped to the side and dove in for a bite on Atlas' leg. It jumped up and latched claws into his side and then jumped once more and bit into his shoulder. The movements were so fast Atlas flailed like a wild man trying to counter to no avail.

Guardian Reil dodged your Double Slash.
Guardian Reil dealt 6 HP damage to you with Triple Threat.

Atlas panicked and tried to run from the clearing. No matter how quickly he ran, his feet seemed to run in place. A message popped up in his view.

You failed to Flee.

Failed? How do you fail at running away short of falling on your face and being eaten?
An intense pain interrupted his thoughts as the animal latched onto his leg. The guardian jumped and bit him two more times before Atlas spun to watch his attacker.

Guardian Reil dealt 6 HP damage to you with Triple Threat.

In a panic, Atlas frantically screamed into his mind *Status*. A small box appeared, showing him the information he wanted to see.

HP: 21/50	
Mana: 15/50	

I've got to do something fast. I can't take many more of those attacks before I'm a goner. My health won't regenerate naturally, but luckily my mana has a little.

With no other abilities to rely on, he jumped toward the animal and activated Double Slash again. The fire returned to his eyes as the ghostly image appeared and he mirrored their attack pattern. The bright flash of red lit his vision after the first attack landed, but Atlas was ready. He deftly shifted his weight and swung the blade at a backward angle as the image showed, catching the monster on its side and sending its counterattack off course.

Capitalizing on his successful deflection, he activated Double Slash and followed the attacks shown to complete his ability.

You dealt 1 HP damage to Guardian Reil with Deflect.

You dealt 3 HP damage to Guardian Reil with Double Slash.

Feeling smug about his success, he gave the little animal a grin. It quickly morphed to a feeling of dread when he noticed its health bar hadn't moved and still looked full. He wasn't sure, but he would swear the little squirrel smiled back before it leaped toward him again.

He frantically tried to dodge as before but failed in the attempt and received three more hits for his trouble.

Guardian Reil dealt 6 HP damage to you with Triple Threat.

Desperate to escape, he tried to flee
again, only to be rooted in place after a few
steps as the same message appeared in his
vision. It took only moments for the agony of
the creature's bite to return.

*Guardian Reil dealt 6 HP damage to you with
Triple Threat.*

Resigned to his fate, he did the only thing
he could think of and turned to face the tiny
thing. With the rest of his mana, he cast
Nature's Fury. He followed the movements and
spun his hands as the power built. When the
circling motion finished, a stinging sensation
in his left arm broke his concentration and
caused him to focus on the small squirrel now
holding on to his arm by its teeth. The image
continued moving, and he failed to follow
while the guardian finished the last two bites
of its attack. The power building in his arms
manifested into a ball of energy in front of
his chest and then detonated. He flew backward
and landed on his back. Blackness filled his
view as a disturbing message drifted to his
mind.

*Guardian Reil dealt 6 HP damage to you with
Triple Threat.*
*You failed to cast Nature's Fury. You took
3 HP damage from the spell backlash.*
You have died.

Chapter 4

Redemption

Dead? From an overgrown squirrel? That's flat out embarrassing.

You will respawn at your designated bind spot in three hours.

Error: Bind location not set. You will bind at the closest population center.

Since you were under level 5, no death penalties take effect.

Death penalties? Why didn't my druid trainer tell me about this? Why didn't he let me know I needed to set a bind location?

The darkness shifted, and he was sitting in a recliner in a modern style room. A large television hung on the wall directly opposite him. The screen came to life, and a message popped up.

Sorry, but you died. You can either take this time to log out and return after the three-hour respawn timer is up, or you can stay here and play some classic games while you wait. Please make a choice.

Atlas looked didn't want to log out, so he chose the *Classic Games* button. A controller materialized in his hands and the screen changed its picture. A list of classic consoles filled the screen. He selected one of the arcade style emulators and the complete list of titles for it showed up. He spent his three-hour hiatus from the game on a nostalgia trip.

His anxiety rose as the clock neared zero. When the coveted number finally arrived, his vision shifted from an empty gray expanse to the vibrant colors of the forest. The smell of wood smoke caught in his nose and he spun to see the town of Kilthan.

With both a sigh of relief and a groan of realization, he trudged back toward the master druid's home. He arrived in nothing but the standard clothing he'd started the game with. His bag and belongings were noticeably absent. In a flash of insight, he looked at his minimap and spotted a small skull and crossbones icon on his map.

I guess my belongings are still where I died. He followed the familiar path back to the residence of Master Longstride.

"Ah, welcome back Atlas. Finish up that quest?" called the voice of Longstride as he entered.

He spun to face the druid and the man's face shifted.

"I guess that's a no. Judging by your appearance and lack of a bag, I'd guess you met an unfortunate demise? You Reborn sure have a habit of dying," the druid said with a shake of his head.

"We need to talk, Master," Atlas said with a grimace, "Why in the world didn't you also teach me the motions for the spell casting of Nature's Fury?"

"Uh, you didn't ask me to," Longstride said carefully, "I offered to teach you the ability, and you accepted. You never once asked me to show you how to cast it. Why? Didn't you run outside and immediately try it out like all the others of your kind?"

The thought hit Atlas like a lightning bolt. *Why didn't I try it out? You'd think I'd be stoked to test out a magical spell in this hyper realistic game?*

"Well, why didn't you remind me to bind my spawn point here?" Atlas asked as he changed the subject.

The druid adopted a deep frown before he glared at Atlas, "I'm not your parent nor your babysitter. I'm willing to help and instruct but don't blame me because you don't know the correct questions to ask."

Atlas gulped at the look and carefully reminded himself this man was much stronger than him. With a sigh of resignation and knowing the man was right, he relaxed his stance and faced the druid.

"My apologies, Master Longstride. I know it isn't your fault. I'm just frustrated with the turn of events. Would you be willing to tell me how I can set a bind point?"

Longstride's eyes bore into Atlas for a few moments before an enormous grin split his face, "That's more like it. Setting a bind point is simple. Go to the inn and talk to the innkeeper. Just tell them you want to set your bind point there and they will be happy to help. That is the best option until you find a Spawn Beacon."

Atlas' eyebrows rose, "What's a Spawn Beacon?"

"You're bound to see one as you get higher level, but they are portable spawning locations tied directly to you. They are pretty costly, and only specific artisans can even make them. They can be invaluable to guilds though, since they allow you to set your spawn location anywhere, including a secret base," Longstride said with a wink.

That sounds fantastic. I'll definitely need to invest in one of those in the future. I imagine I'm in for a shock when I see the sticker price on one of those bad boys.

"Can you elaborate on the combat system here? I've discovered my physical addition and figured out how to cast Nature's Fury. I've also discovered the very unfortunate side effect of failing a spell mid-cast. How does the counter system work and what are the combat rules?" Atlas asked.

"Well, I can't answer all of that. I can only discuss your class specific elements. You're rewarded for following the movements. What you may not know yet, is that you can increase the levels of spells as you gain levels. When they increase in level, they sometimes change the pattern for their casting sequence. Often, this decreases their cast time. If you are supremely lucky, and become one with the spell and cast it with perfect movement mirroring, it unlocks auto casting for the ability. This allows you to trigger the cast without worry for the movements or failure."

"That sounds great. Do you know how to do it or is it just luck?" Atlas asked, intrigued.

"Only rumors," Longstride said with a wave, "just the normal 'inner peace' and 'be one with yourself' that is always tossed around for solutions."

"So, how do I learn more about the hand-to-hand and weapon combat?"

"The Weaponmaster in the village can teach you those things. He is in the large practice yard on your right as you head back down the road. Get him to teach you those skills."

"Thank you for the help. I need to go talk to the Weaponmaster so I can get back to my gear."

"Ah, the ever so fun gravestone run of the Reborn. Good luck, Atlas," Longstride called as Atlas turned and exited the building.

He walked down the path toward the main section of the village and spotted the large practice yard. Three men stood in a loose formation while two others sparred nearby. Atlas approached the group of two fighting and observed the action.

Unlike when he fought, he couldn't see the triggers or movements either men had to follow. The ghostly images were absent and none of the warning flashes were present. He noticed the combatants occasionally froze during their fighting, and Atlas assumed they finished the attack or missed the motions as he had.

When the two finished their fight, both stood straight and then performed a bow. When they rose, they walked back toward the group of three nearby. The older gentleman with gray-streaked hair addressed them.

"And that is why your counterattacks are so important. An advanced fighter can string together far more abilities than a newer one. If you can't interrupt them, they could kill you before you even have a turn to strike at them. Just make sure you practice. Always remember, if you miss a counter then they get another free attack on you after their current finishes. It essentially bounces your next initiative."

The group all nodded and the older man called out, "Dismissed." The area cleared out quickly as each went on their way until only the older man remained.

"Hello, Sir. My name is Atlas. Are you the Weaponmaster here?"

The man turned to look at Atlas. A scar stretched from the base of his eye to the bottom of his jaw on the left side.

"Another Reborn. What can I do for you, Atlas?"

"Another? I've seen no others yet," he said confused as he searched his surroundings.

"You won't, so don't bother searching. None of your kind can see each other in this area. There is a magic spell that cloaks this entire place. When you move to the next destination, you'll see your people."

Makes sense. Bet it's to keep out griefers from camping new players.

"How did you know I was a Reborn?"

"Only a Reborn would be in the middle of the forest without so much as a knife to his name," the man said as he nodded his head toward Atlas' empty waistband.

"Had an unfortunate incident with a squirrel," Atlas told him sheepishly.

"A squirrel? You let a squirrel kill you?" the man asked before belting out a hearty laugh.

"It had a name," Atlas grumbled.

"You found a named squirrel? Not too many of those in the forest. Surely you weren't stupid enough to confront Reil?" the Weaponmaster asked with a raised eyebrow.

Atlas stared at the ground and kicked at a clump of dirt. He didn't want to answer that question and make things even worse.

"Not only did you stumble into one of the few sanctuaries in the area, but you defiled it and got killed by the guardian. You must have some horrible luck or are incredibly foolish."

"How about we just chalk it up to foolishness," Atlas said. "I was hoping I could ask you about combat."

"Fine, fine," the Weaponmaster said with a wave, "What can I help you with?"

"Are you able to teach me new abilities and show me how this combat system works? I've stumbled through some of it, but I'd appreciate a professional's training for this."

"That depends. It costs money for training. I have a certain number of skills to train and each has an associated cost. I do have the basic Counter I can teach for free, which is an essential skill. It becomes far more important as you learn further abilities to combo with it. I guess you only have the basic Double Slash?" the Weaponmaster asked.

"That's it. I'd like to take you up on that offer for the Counter ability though."

"Good. Come over here for a minute."

Atlas walked toward the instructor and when he was within five feet of the man, a warning popped up in his vision.

You have entered combat!

What the hell, was his thought before he watched the image of his arm moving across his body to intercept an incoming punch. He panicked and swung hard to the side, barely catching up to the movement. His forearm connected with the Weaponmaster's hand and knocked it away.

"Very good. You're already picking up the visual commands nicely."

"Maybe some warning next time!" Atlas complained as he stepped back from the man. "Now, why didn't I learn the Counter ability? I just countered your punch?"

"No, you didn't. Do you know why not?"

"If I did, we wouldn't be having this conversation."

"What you just did was deflect my attack. There are three methods of physical damage negation that are the most common. One is dodging attacks, the second is parrying or deflecting attacks, and the final one is blocking the attack. None of those amounts to a Counter. Any of those can trigger a Counter, though. A Counter requires a return strike that does damage. For instance, had you knocked my arm to the side and immediately followed with a punch that struck a solid blow that would be considered a Counter."

Atlas hit himself on the forehead with an open palm. *Of course, I need to actually counterattack, not just block it.*

"Care to try again?" The Weaponmaster asked.

Atlas only nodded. This time, the image that showed up in his vision differed from anything he'd ever seen. The Weaponmaster had crouched down low and kicked out with a sweeping leg. Atlas' image showed him spreading the base of his legs and bracing his weight on his left leg to take the hit. Atlas shifted his weight and waited.

The leg struck and his knee buckled, sweeping him off his feet and causing him to fall in a heap.

You failed to block Leg Sweep.
Weaponmaster dealt 1 HP damage to you with Leg Sweep.

"I followed the movement and still fell flat. What was that about?" Atlas asked in confusion as he slowly rose back to his feet and dusted himself off.

"I'm glad you asked. We must teach every one of you Reborn this lesson. The image tracing system will only show you ways to block or deflect. It doesn't actually show you maneuvers to dodge attacks. You can still dodge any attack that comes your way with enough speed and combat knowledge, though. That attack would've been simple for you to leap over and avoid the blow, leaving me in an off-balance position and prime for a Counter."

"So I can dodge any attack then?" Atlas asked in excitement.

"Yes, and no. Some attacks you must dodge. If your opponent is much stronger than you, it's possible for them to break your blocks and deflects. That's what happened on my Leg Sweep. I'm at a higher level and far stronger than you. There was no way you could withstand that attack. As you progress, make sure you remember that. Powerful attacks can break through your defense. I've seen many a man take a sword through the skull from an overhand chop they thought they could block."

"Sound advice. I'll keep it in mind," Atlas agreed.

"Also be wary of Area of Effect attacks. Anything made to attack a large space can be very difficult to block or even dodge. Magic can also be very difficult to dodge, but you'll have to discuss ways to prepare for that with your class trainer."

"I'll talk to Master Longstride about it. You mentioned having other abilities you can train? Can I see what they are?"

The Weaponmaster eyed him up and down, "I can tell you have absolutely no coin on you, but I'm sure you'll be able to find some in the future. Let me teach you the proper form for a Counter and unlock the ability for it and then I'll show you the list of abilities. You can come back and find me later to learn more."

"Thank you, sir. Actually, what's your name?"

"I'm Leo Swiftstrike. Now let's get to work."

Leo showed him the movements in slow motion for him to learn the Counter ability. He quickly discovered that he only needed to learn the ability one time with a successful counter and then he could activate it on command. Leo showed him how to counter the punch he originally threw, and after four tries, Atlas finally succeeded.

You have learned the ability: Counter.
You deal 1 HP damage to Leo Swiftstrike with Counter.

"Now that you have the ability, you can counter any type of strike, not just that specific one. Dodge, block, or deflect the attack and the activate Counter. It will show you what to do."

"I'm still surprised I never learned this before. I've dealt damage to creatures before when deflecting attacks," Atlas said quietly.

"All about the intent young man. Dealing damage to a creature during a deflection because your weapon grazes them is just a byproduct of the deflection itself. Following it with the attack is the true Counter. If you get good with deflection techniques, you can increase your damage, allowing you to hit them during the deflection and then hit them again with Counter."

"Sweet. Can I see those abilities you mentioned before I leave, Master Swiftstrike?"

"Since you understand your manners and all, sure."

The Weaponmaster waved his hand and gestured toward Atlas. A menu popped up in his vision.

Weaponmaster Leo Swiftstrike	
Ability	Description
Blade Chase Requirements: Level 3 Cost: 5 Silver	A 3 hit addition. Only useable following a successful Counter.
Fallback Requirements: Level 3 Cost: 8 Silver	A retreating jump. Only useable following a Dodge. Increases the chance you can Flee from a battle.
Charge Requirements: Level 4 Cost: 10 Silver	A dash to close the distance and disrupt spell casting. Rank 1 combo skill.

"I've got some leveling to do so I can take you up on those skills."

"Yes. You do. Now get to work and come find me if you have more questions." Leo told him with a dismissive gesture.

Atlas gave a slight bow and turned toward the forest. He checked his map and tried to find the most direct path back to his body. Not wanting to beg for supplies, he raced to his gear so he could pick up what he lost. Hopefully, he could get there before being attacked by anything.

He inhaled deeply and stared toward his goal in trepidation. The looming trees of the forest made him uneasy after dying at the paws of a squirrel.

Damn, it's a game. I can't let it win. He dashed full speed into the trees and wove through the brush. With no way to defend himself the direct path seemed like the best choice so he merely ignored all the crisscrossing game paths as he charged ahead. When he neared the sanctuary, he slowed his pace.

Peering into the clearing, he carefully searched for dangers. There was no way he could tell if the sanctuary was still hostile to him. Looking toward the location of his death, he saw a small gravestone sticking up from the grass. His foot crossed the threshold of the tree line and gently settled into the grass. Holding his breath, he waited for the dreaded message from before as he squeezed his eyes closed. After a few seconds, he visibly relaxed and opened his eyes. The calmness of the clearing settled back over him again and nothing tried to attack him. He took a few more cautious steps before his nerves settled and he returned to a normal walk.

The gravestone was a standard shape for most of those seen in cemeteries, but he had to admit it was an incredibly creepy feeling seeing his name on the object. Chills ran down his spine as he reached forward and touched it.

You have found the Gravestone of Atlas. Do you wish to take the contents? Yes/No.

Atlas mentally said *Yes* and the contents of the gravestone fell to the ground in a heap as the stone dissolved. He wasted no time and slung the bag back over his shoulder while grabbing his weapon. Checking the contents, he found everything was still intact. With his belongings restored, his attention turned to the Haeyna Sprig plants on the boulder.

It took him a solid hour of time, but he methodically dug up the plants. Seven intact Haeyna Sprigs dropped into his bag while he discarded two he damaged. He grimaced at the pain from the work.

Haeyna Sprig dealt 8 HP damage to you with Thorn.

Zaina wasn't lying when she said those could be a pain to harvest. Glad I only pricked myself eight times. I don't have enough health to do a lot of that.

Nothing else of interest was visible in the clearing, so Atlas examined his minimap. He didn't want to venture too far from Kilthan when he was such a low level. Dismissing his map, he turned east and walked back into the forest. It took him four more hours of traveling and another ten failed attempts before he finally gathered the herbs he needed.

Armed with the new knowledge from the Weaponmaster, he quickly dispatched another ten squirrels and added their meat and fur to his bag. Luckily, he had lost no experience when he died, so he was only 25 short of his next level. He hadn't escaped the fights unscathed and checked his status.

HP: 36/50
Mana: 18/50

I can stay out here and grind away the rest of the experience or go back to town and claim the quests. The decision warred in his mind until a message appeared.

You have 4 hours of game time left for this session.

Decision taken from him, he nodded to himself and checked his minimap. He picked the direct path for the town and ran through the trees.

That respawn I had to wait for really dug into my game time. I also spent too much time screwing around in town and playing with my character selection.

He wasn't far from Kilthan, so the trip lasted less than half an hour. A light push and the door swung open. The bubbly voice of Zaina greeted him as he entered.

"Welcome to Zaina's Herb Emporium," she started before seeing who entered. "Oh, Atlas! Welcome back. Took you longer than I expected to get back, but good to see you here. Do you have the herbs?"

"I do," Atlas said carefully before latching on to what she'd said. "Zaina, those things can be a hassle to find. They don't exactly hang out near the beaten path."

The young woman shook her head from side to side, "They are common in this area but can be tricky to find. You must've run into trouble since it took you longer than normal."

"Had a minor accident. Took some time to recover from it." Atlas told her.

Her face adopted a deep frown before she examined him carefully, "You're a Reborn, right?"

"Yea."

"Did you die?"

Atlas nodded slowly in response.

"That explains it. Guess you had to wait out the respawn?"

"Sadly, I did. Learned a valuable lesson about choosing my targets carefully."

Zaina giggled at the answer, "That can happen. The respawn timer is an essential thing to keep Reborn from causing havoc with Spawn Beacons. One Reborn could wipe out an entire village if he could drop a beacon and immediately respawn when he died. It'd carry harsh penalties for his deaths, but he could also own the city. The same would apply for Dungeons and Treasure Caches. There is a spawn time to prevent this."

"Is the respawn timer always that long?" Atlas mumbled.

"I'm afraid so. Luckily, you're low enough level, there shouldn't have been penalties."

"What penalties are there when I get higher level?"

"I'm not really sure. I recall one Reborn saying they lost all their experience for the level they were working on and another told me he got a debuff to his attributes for a while. I can't tell you much more than that." Zaina said with a note of pity in her voice.

"I appreciate the information, Zaina. Let me get those herbs out for you," Atlas said as he walked to the counter and fished in his bag. He placed the five Weer Bloom and Zanth Plants on the counter and she examined them.

"Great work! I hope you didn't destroy too many of them while harvesting."

"Following your advice, I avoided damaging too many. Thank you for that. I would've never harvested them all without your instruction."

She directed a warm smile at him and waved a hand in the air. She twisted the hand, and it looked like she punched on an unseen menu with her finger before her arm twisted again and extended toward Atlas. A message popped up in front of him.

<table>
<tr><td colspan="2" align="center">Quest - Supplying the Herbalist</td></tr>
<tr><td>Requirements
  Level 1

Quest Rarity: Common

Quest Reward: 50 experience, 30 copper coins, 1 Minor Mana Potion.</td><td>Description: You've returned with 5 intact Zanth Root and Weer Bloom plants.</td></tr>
<tr><td colspan="2" align="center">Do you wish to complete this quest? Yes/No.</td></tr>
</table>

Atlas pictured *Yes* in his mind and waited. The box disappeared and a small, squat vial of bluish liquid plopped onto the counter. A bag followed with a *clink*. The sound of chimes accompanied the noise on the counter and a message appeared.

Success! You've reached Level 2.

Attribute points, huh? What do I want to play as in this game? I'm a druid, so I think that means I can be pretty flexible. I don't want to be a jack-of-all-trades, though. Those are passable at everything, but not very good at anything specific.

His thoughts turned to his real world job, and he smiled. *I haven't played a healer in a long time!* A glance of his character sheet showed his stats. He used the free points and assigned one to Intellect and the other to Constitution. *I'm still a little too squishy for my taste.*

The increase in stats bumped his HP and Mana both up to 60. *Looks like Intellect and Constitution both give a ten point boost.*

"That got me to my next level. Thanks." Atlas told Zaina.

"Hey, you helped me out, so it's only fair."

Atlas turned to leave the shop before a thought struck him.

"Zaina, how do you heal yourself here? I've noticed my mana regenerates but my health doesn't."

"There are many ways. Eating food will help your body replenish some of your health, but the regeneration is slow since it takes your body time to process it. Potions and bandages work, but they are usually more costly and only used for emergencies. Resting in a bed at an inn will also restore you to full health. You don't have to stay long. Just pay for the room and lay down. You can immediately get right back up with full health. You Reborn are actually quite fascinating with your ability to function with little sleep."

"Do you teach how to make healing potions?"

"I teach basic Alchemy but it isn't cheap. It costs ten silver to learn the skill itself. Minor health and mana potions are two of the starting potions you learn, though. I'd be happy to teach you if you can gather the money."

Damn, everything here is so expensive.

"Would you be interested in buying more herbs? I found more than what you needed while I was exploring."

"What do you have?" Zaina asked as she swiped her hands in the air and the menu reappeared. This one said Selling at the top and listed the herbs he had. Each showed a price next to them. He could get 8 copper coins for each Weer Bloom and 12 copper coins for each Zanth Root. He sold the three Weer Blooms and three Zanth Root he had, netting him 60 copper.

With a wave, he dismissed the menu. "Thanks again. I'll let you know if I find more."

She bid him farewell as he left the building. *Time to go turn in my other quest.*

Chapter 5

Back to the Toil

Atlas exited the herbalist shop and turned toward Master Longstride's house. The scent of flowers near a few houses drifted to his senses on the wind, and he took a deep breath to calm himself.

This game will take some time to get through and the skills are pretty expensive to get. Probably going to have to focus on the long game.

His steps brought him to his destination, and he gently pushed into the building. A deep, earthy scent assaulted him and he spotted the master druid seated in the corner at a table.

"Back again, young Atlas? Hopefully, this time under better circumstances?"

Atlas smiled at the jovial manner of the druid before responding, "This time was a success. I have the Haeyna Sprig's you requested."

He walked to the table and pulled ten plants from his bag. The herbs fell from his hand and he shuffled them around on the table so the master could count them. The older man glanced at them and then returned his gaze to Atlas.

"Great job. Here you go," Master Longstride said, and a box appeared in Atlas' view.

Quest - Haeyna Sprig	
Requirements Level 1 Quest Rarity: Common Quest Reward: 50 experience, 40 copper coins, 1 Minor Healing Potion.	Description: You've successfully gathered all the required Haeyna Sprigs.
Do you wish to complete this quest? Yes/No.	

Atlas selected *Yes,* and a small pile of coins appeared on the table. They clinked against a glass vial filled with a red liquid. He reached out and scooped the contents into his bag.

"Thanks Master Longstride. Do you have any more quests for me?"

The druid leaned back in his chair and looked toward the ceiling, "I have nothing I think you can handle at your current level. Try back when you've gotten stronger. Until then. Check around town. There should be more people who could use help."

A thought occurred to Atlas, "Is it possible to learn other magical spells that aren't specifically class related?"

Longstride sighed, "It's possible but expensive. You can only do it through magical scrolls. Some spells are impossible to transcribe. Most of those are class specific. There are some useful spells you could learn. Things as simple as lighting a campfire or purifying water are examples of those."

"Thanks! I'll keep an eye out for them."

"They don't come cheap, so expect to pay a hefty amount for them if you find one. Speaking of," he said as he eyed Atlas up and down, "invest some of your recent money in new gear. Your small knife isn't a well-suited weapon for your class. Keep an eye out for a usable staff and some leather. If all else fails, make some of your own leather."

"I would but the skills are far too expensive to learn one now. I'll have to wait to stock up on money to train a trade skill."

"Who told you that?" Longstride asked.

"I saw the cost of training Alchemy at Zaina's."

The druid chuckled, "Every class has specific trade skills you're allowed to learn for free. It'd be damnably difficult to make a living and survive without skills early on. The options for a druid are Leatherworking and Woodworking. Keep in mind, only the first one is free. After that, you must pay for the second at the normal rate."

Atlas' eyes lit up at that. *If I can learn a skill, that'll help me make money even faster. If I take Leatherworking, I'll also have a use for the hides I have and be able to make myself armor. I haven't checked prices, but I'm sure armor is expensive for someone in my financial situation.*

"Another great detail to know. It'd be nice if you gave us this information from the start," Atlas grumbled.

"You Reborn are always a handful. We are naturally born with this basic knowledge. Good luck in your travels and return when ready for more training," Master Longstride told him with one last wave.

Atlas turned and walked for the door. As he stepped outside, the cool breeze hit his skin, and he felt invigorated. His mind spun as he thought about all the little things he needed to do.

Need to find more quests.
Need to learn Leatherworking.
Need to make more money.
Need to find more gear.

All the thoughts built, one upon another, until a message popped up on his screen.

You have 1 new message forwarded from your phone.

They tied my phone into this game too? I guess I would still need to get messages while logged in.

A mailbox style screen appeared in his view. The subject and sender of the message made him audibly groan.

Not Kathryn, surely they don't need me to pick up another shift.

She marked the message with a red urgent flag and, dreading what he'd find, he opened it.

Atlas,

Quentin got sick and can't make it in to work today. I need you to cover his shift. You're all the reserve pool we have right now. Everyone else is out of town at a conference. Shift starts at 7PM.

"Son of a…" Atlas huffed.

Can't even enjoy a game without work calling me back in. He pictured the time in his mind and the external clock appeared. It said it was 7AM in the actual world.

I guess now is as good a time as any to log off. I don't have a lot of time left in here anyway before I'm forced to log off.

With the decision made, he turned and headed directly for the inn. No point in delaying the choice. If he tried to procrastinate, he was sure he'd end up being forced out of the game at an inopportune spot.

The tall building grew in size as he approached. It was easily the largest building in town and stood three stories tall. They made the building of a sturdy wood Atlas couldn't identify. The handle twisted smoothly and silently as he opened the door.

A clean and welcoming entertaining area greeted him. Tables decorated the room and a small stage took up the back corner. Directly ahead of him, an enormous staircase rose to the upper levels. The bar looked well stocked and bottles of all shapes and sizes covered the wooden display. The cleanliness of the place astonished him. Atlas could swear this place was as clean as one of their trauma rooms.

An elf in an apron stood behind the bar, dutifully shining a pewter looking mug with a rag.

"Greetings. Can I help you with anything?" The innkeeper asked.

"I'm looking for a room."

"Have plenty available. Any preference?"

"Not really. Just need somewhere to rest for a couple days."

The innkeeper gave a quizzical look, but Atlas approached and waited for his key. The man shuffled around items under the bar until his hand rose, holding a metal key about the size of Atlas' middle finger. When he reached out and touched it, the innkeeper smiled.

"Ah, that makes more sense. You're a Reborn. I guess you'll be traveling to your world for a few days?"

"Uh, yeah…"

"No worries. You're perfectly safe in your room. As long as you lock it before you go to sleep, no one can disturb the room while you're gone."

That's a relief. It would suck to log back in and find someone killed me while I was gone.

"Thanks. I'll see you in a few days." Atlas said.

Atlas clutched the key in his hand and headed for the stairs. He gripped it tightly and felt raised sections of the metal against his palm. An inspection showed it had the number 304 on it.

Trudging up the stairs, he headed for the third floor. The sturdy wood didn't creak as he ascended. *They must have fine artisans to make a wooden staircase that is so quiet.* A landing appeared for the second floor and he turned around the banister to continue to the next. Weariness crept over him as he came closer to his room.

The key slid into the lock with perfect precision and a sharp click echoed as he turned it. Entering with a light push led him to a respectable room. The wooden floors were clean and even looked polished. Sturdy and comfortable furniture greeted him. Nothing fancy, but welcoming. A chest sat at the end of the bed and a small table stood near the head of the bed with a pitcher on it.

He remembered what the innkeeper said and turned and locked the door behind him. With no thought to it, he walked to the bed and collapsed face first with his arms to the side. His bag slipped from his hand and the blade inside made a metallic clink as it landed. His eyes closed, and a message appeared in the blackness.

Do you wish to log off? Yes/No.

With a grumble, Atlas reluctantly selected *Yes*.

***

Whirring, buzzing and beeping flooded his mind. Atlas opened his eyes to a familiar face. The woman's long black hair hung down to frame her face as she scrutinized the panel outside of the glass dome. Her fingers flew across the small device and noises echoed through the pod. Atlas felt something akin to snakes crawling on him as tubes and devices slid around him. He looked up to see the tubes retracting into a small compartment above and behind his head.

That is a really creepy feeling.

His attention on the tubes shattered when the dome popped open and the cheerful voice of the technician brought him back.

"Welcome back, Atlas. I notice you came out earlier than expected. I hope you enjoyed your time!"

"Thanks. I loved it. Unfortunately, work called me in unexpectedly, so I need to get cleaned up and head in. I appreciate the help. Forgot to ask, what's your name?"

She smirked at him, "I'm Jean. I think you might be the first player in this entire place to ask any of us our name. I may have just won the office pool on that."

Atlas grimaced as he climbed out of the machine, "Sorry. I forget proper manners sometimes. Where do I need to go from here?"

She turned and pointed toward the, "Follow the stairs back down, through the doors, and into the hallway on your right. There will be someone who can instruct you further."

As soon as she finished talking, she picked up a spray bottle and starting soaking the entire pod in it.

"Such a high-tech machine and it can't even clean itself?" Atlas asked with a smirk.

"Oh, it does. Think of it as a pre-soak treatment. It goes through a quick wash cycle when I close it and activate the process. Who doesn't love the smell of bleach, though? You better head out. Clock's ticking."

Atlas turned toward the stairs and took one step. The moment he did, an ungodly feeling of pain hit his lower stomach. His eyes watered uncontrollably, and he took off in a half waddle, half dead run toward the stairs. He faintly heard the technician call out behind him, "There's a bathroom where I told you to go. Better hurry before it's too late."

The hint of glee in her voice didn't amuse Atlas at all, but he also figured he deserved it. His feet thumped along as he shimmied down the stairs, trying to hold the contents of his bladder. When he hit the bottom landing, he made a beeline for the hallway and spotted the person she mentioned.

Thoughts of talking to the person immediately faded as he saw the sign for the men's restroom directly behind him. Atlas dashed past him as the man sputtered and tried to talk to him. He made the bathroom with no time to spare and quickly released the floodgates. Relief flooded him and he could breathe normally again. A quick shiver down his spine let him know he'd come to the end.

"That was a hell of a tremor. Must've been a fantastic piss," a man said as he walked up to the sink.

"May have been the best one ever. Definitely top three," Atlas told him with a grin.

With everything in the world back in good order again, he walked back outside to talk to the man he'd ran past. The attendant watched him approach with an enormous grin on his face.

"Guess you couldn't hold it any longer?"

"Not a chance. Where do I need to go from here?"

"No worries. You're definitely not the first I've had do that, but I'm sure as more wake up and go back to their lives I'll see that same reaction more frequently. At least you made it. One other wasn't so lucky," the attendant said as he pointed toward the side of the passage. Another man in coveralls mopped up a small area on the ground.

"From here you'll proceed until you reach an arched door. On the right there is an elevator that will take you to the ground floor as soon as you enter. Once there, follow the exit signs to leave. You'll exit on the side of the building near the parking garage."

"Thanks so much. Catch ya next time," Atlas told him as he walked away. The floor was a dark composite material layered in a coat of wax to protect it and make it glimmer. The walls looked like standard sheetrock with white paint. Fluorescent lighting buzzed as he walked down the narrow passage. The elevator bay was easy to identify, and he pressed the button on it.

The ding of the machine marked its arrival, and the doors slid open. He shuffled inside and turned to press a button when the doors closed and it rose on its own. *He said it would take me to the ground floor. Guess it's the only option when returning.*

Sunlight hit his face through the windows. The room he walked into was similar in style to the entrance but didn't have the opulent decorations and all the gaming memorabilia. A glass front let the light through and he spotted the door marked Exit. He pushed out of the door and stepped onto a large sidewalk. A small sign on a supporting concrete column told him the parking structure was to the right, so he followed the indicated direction.

It didn't take him long to spot the six story parking garages. Atlas had parked in the one closest to his current position. He rose to the 5th floor in the elevator and sunk into the driver's seat of his beat up Honda Civic. The car had gone through hell, but it was as reliable as ever and got great mileage. A twist of the key caused the tiny engine to fire right up and he put it in gear.

The trip back to his apartment studio was less than twenty minutes and he walked through the door. He passed the tiny couch and TV in his living room and the small kitchenette. He rarely cooked anything more extensive than Ramen noodles, anyway. Down the hall, he ignored his bedroom on the right and ducked straight into the bathroom on the left. After a quick wash down, he donned his scrubs and snatched his badge from his dresser. A glance at his phone told him he had a little less than an hour until work.

Traveling back to his car, he hopped in and fired it up. The local Mexican food restaurant drew his attention, and he got a quick burrito before work. The spice hit his stomach, and it grumbled in satisfaction. *That might come back to haunt me later.*

Atlas pulled up to the front of the medical clinic. He worked in a small urgent care facility. They combined it with an emergency room, but it wasn't a full size hospital. As a nurse, he spent his time helping with the never ending ailments of those who entered. Most days it was just people coming in for standard coughs and colds. The occasional UTI or flu would drop in as well. Occasionally you would see a laceration or something equally fun.

"Good Morning Atlas!" Kathryn said in a cheery tone. Her strawberry blonde hair bouncing in a ring of curls. Abundant eye shadow drew far more attention to her face than it should have. *Guess the boss can do whatever she wants and doesn't need to worry about the dress code.*

"Morning Kat. Quentin going to be okay?"

"Hope so. He didn't sound too hot on the phone but let's be honest, this is Quentin, it's possible he's just hung over and didn't want to come to work."

"That's true," Atlas grumbled, "The man has a bit of a lazy streak in him."

"Sorry I had to call you in early. I know you were hyped up about playing that new game. Did you have time to play?" Kathryn asked.

Atlas' eyes lit up at the mention of Divine Genesis, "Yeah. It was amazing. Had to leave a little earlier than I intended, but it was a great time while it lasted. I was almost due to get out of the game anyway, so no big deal. You do anything interesting while I was out?"

"Not really. I actually got called into a few meetings over my days off. The company is concerned with the numbers for the clinic. We aren't getting as many patients as they'd like daily."

"Can't exactly walk around and make people get sick, now can we?" Atlas said with a chuckle.

Kathryn took on a pensive look as her brow creased. She seemed to wrestle with herself for a few moments before she nodded slowly.

"Atlas, you didn't hear any of this from me but you may want to polish up your résumé. The grumbling from the higher ups sounds like they may consider shutting down the clinic."

"Close this place? Where will the people go? The main hospital is an hour from here depending on traffic. Hell, there isn't another clinic closer to the hospital that offers half the services we can. I think you may be stressing about this too much."

Kathryn seemed to turn that idea over in her head for a while before she smiled, "Maybe you're right. I might be worried for no reason. I hadn't considered the problem with access to healthcare around here."

She looked to the clock on the wall and quickly nodded. Rising to her feet, she lifted her bag and slung it over her shoulder, "My time's done. I'll catch ya later. Kevin is due to take over after your shift. You're working tomorrow as well, right? If so, I think I'm working with you."

"Yep, see ya tomorrow. Have fun," Atlas told her with a wave.

She walked out, and he turned his attention to the computer screen. Their program didn't show anyone waiting in the lobby, so he had some free time to spare. He pulled out his phone and swiped the screen to unlock it. A tap on Keenan's name and the phone started ringing. It wasn't long before it went straight to voicemail.

Damn. Guess he's still in game. He must be playing the full two days' worth so he won't get out for at least another few hours.

Atlas looked through his phone and a couple of news announcements caught his attention. He followed a few gaming blogs and news sites and got push notifications on major articles. Every one of them had massive articles talking about Divine Genesis. Now that they officially announced the name, the NDA protecting the details no longer applied. News sites flooded everything with articles talking about how impressive the game was. He skimmed through most of them and couldn't disagree with their points. A few of the sites complained about the lack of guidance and whined about the difficulty because of that, but that was the part Atlas enjoyed the most. He grew tired of the boring games that walked you through it. Most of these seemed more like kids' games to him.

Mr. Ingram said they tied Divine Genesis into the real world economy.

A general search took him to their main website. The home page looked similar to the lobby of the building, with achievements and testimonies everywhere. There was a small button to download the app for the game on your phone, so he clicked on it and quickly opened the app.

He logged into his account and saw the status of his character. It even displayed the money he had. 1 silver and 30 copper showed on the screen. All of which were recent rewards from his two quests and the coins he received from selling the herbs. He could also see the different animal skins and meat in his inventory. Next to his money was a button that said Redeem. Out of curiosity, he pressed it.

The app opened to a new page titled Global Market and the exchange rate showed on it. Atlas' eyes bulged a little when he saw it. Mr. Ingram was telling the truth. Every gold coin was worth $100, while a silver coin was worth $5 and each copper was around 5 cents. *This game will be lucrative for some of those gold farmers. Hell, with that kind of money flying around, I may want to figure out ways to make more money myself. I'll definitely need to get my leatherworking started when I log back in.*

Atlas grumbled at that thought as he remembered he had three back to back twelve-hour shifts. He wouldn't be able to play again until after that. With his fate resigned to work, he buckled down and waited for the torture of the days to pass.

Chapter 6

Moving Forward

Atlas opened his eyes to the room in the inn. The pitcher still rested on the table near the bed and looked untouched. He sat up and spotted his bag on the ground where he'd dropped it. Popping out of bed, he scooped up the bag and walked downstairs.

"Welcome back, Atlas. How fared your journey?" Juul called to him.

His mind reeled at the question before he remembered their lore around the Reborn. "Everything went well. Wish I could've come back sooner. Anything interesting going on around here?"

"Not really. The guards subdued a wild boar that tried to rampage through town. That was the most eventful thing to happen while you were gone."

"Sounds thrilling. Can you point me in the direction of the leatherworker's shop?" Atlas asked.

"Of course. Turn left when you exit and travel to the third building on the right. Old Ramma will probably have some hides stretched outside that will give the place away."

"Thanks. Take care," Atlas said with a wave and walked through the door. He followed the innkeeper's directions and walked to the building in question. Juul was correct and there were two large hides stretched on wooden racks in the back of the building and numerous small hides hung from different places on their own miniature racks.

Burned into the door was a large symbol that looked like a stretched hide. Atlas pushed lightly, and it swung open with ease.

"Hello!" "Anyone here?" he asked as he looked around the room. A pile of small pieces of wood sat in the corner. Atlas noticed they looked like the pieces of the racks he'd seen outside. A few rolled up hides, tied with string rested along a shelf on his right. A sharp, acrid smell hit his nose and Atlas assumed they must use urine in some of their work.

Muffled speech that sounded like cursing echoed from the back room, and he heard stomping feet plodding toward the front of the building. A short man with a burly chest emerged from the back. Atlas fought to hold back a laugh at the man's appearance. In almost every story he'd ever seen, elves rarely had much facial hair, if any at all. This elf sported one of the largest and scruffiest beards he'd ever seen. The facial hair, combined with the hair on his head, made it hard to see any of his other features.

"What do you want," the ball of hair grumbled.

"My name's Atlas. I'm looking for Leatherworker Ramma. I'm interested in training as a leatherworker."

A grunt issued from the smaller man, "I'm Ramma. You have the coin to learn the skill?"

Atlas wasn't sure how to answer. Master Longstride told him his first skill was free, so he played that route. *Better make sure he knows I'm a Reborn.*

"I'm here to claim my free skill as a Reborn," Atlas told him with confidence.

The smaller elf looked him up and down before crooking his finger and motioning for Atlas to come closer. He hesitantly moved closer, not sure what to expect from the surly man. The leatherworker's hand extended out with his palm flat and stared at Atlas. Unsure what to do, he lifted his hand and placed it onto the elf's hand. A quick tingling sensation passed through him before the elf dropped his hand and huffed.

"Fine. Damn Reborn just waltzing in thinking the world runs on their schedule. Here," Ramma said with a dismissive flick and a menu popped into his field of view. Atlas spotted the *Buy* title at the top and scanned through the list. It looked like a list of different hides and their prices. He glanced at them and then looked toward the shelf he noted when he entered. The items were the ones from the shelf. Dropping to the bottom of the list, he saw an item called *Learn Leatherworking*. Next to it was a price of 10 silver, but a line crossed it out and said *Free* over it. He selected the option, and a box appeared in his vision.

Do you wish to claim the trade skill of Leatherworking as your free skill? This decision can't be changed. Yes/No.

Atlas selected *Yes* and messages hit him.

You have learned the trade skill: Leatherworking.
You have learned the Leatherworking ability: Cure Light Hide.
You have learned the Leatherworking ability: Create Leather Sinew Thread.
You have learned the Leatherworking ability: Create Basic Leather Gloves.
You have learned the Leatherworking ability: Create Basic Leather Boots.
You have received Leatherworker's Tool Bag.

Sweet. Finally, some skills I can use.

Atlas turned to regard the trainer as he rummaged behind the counter.

"How do I learn to make additional items with Leatherworking, Master Ramma?"

The fuzzy head popped back above the counter as he responded, "Just return after you've leveled up. You unlock new patterns as you gain skill levels. You'll breeze through the first few levels pretty quick once you find hides. The new patterns are relatively cheap to learn. You can also purchase Salt from me, which you'll need to use the Cure Light Hide Ability. You should have the small knife and the needle you need for the other patterns in your Tool Bag."

Atlas selected the Cure Light Hide Ability and examined the box that popped up.

Leatherworking - Cure Light Hide	
Requirements Leatherworking Level 1 Rarity: Common Requirements: 1 pinch of Salt	Description: Turn smaller animal hides into a Cured Light Hide. Cured Light Hides are used for entry level Leatherworking patterns.

His mind turned over the options, and he dug through his regular bag. His bag held twelve hides from the squirrels and the bobcat, all rolled up tight.

"Master Ramma, can I see your inventory again?" Atlas asked.

This time the elf didn't even bother lifting his head from where he searched. Instead, Atlas just watched as a hand rose above the counter and dismissively flicked toward him. Atlas smirked as the menu popped back up. He looked through the list and spotted Salt. It cost 2 copper per pinch. He quickly pressed the tiny arrow next to quantity and selected twelve. When he pressed the Purchase button, a small bag fell onto the counter nearby and he dropped it into his larger bag.

Unsure of what to do, Atlas looked at his skill screen and selected the Cure Light Hide skill. He clicked on the Craft button on the bottom right of the menu, but a message popped up.

Insufficient Materials. Please select and hold the materials you wish to use.

Atlas reached in and grabbed a squirrel hide and the bag of salt. He held one in each hand and selected craft again. His eyes bulged as his hands and body moved on their own at incredible speed. Sinking to a knee, he rolled the skin out flat on the ground and sprinkled salt across the raw side. His hands rapidly rubbed in the salt before he fished out the small knife in his bag. The blade swept across the skin in swift strokes and layers of the fat on the back of the hide peeled away. With the hide freshly cleaned, he sprinkled more salt on the skin and rolled it tightly one more time. The tools and salt dropped back into his bag before he took the hide in both hands and twisted it as if wringing out a towel. A low ding sounded in his head.

You created Cured Light Hide.
You received 25xp in Leatherworking.

Atlas looked at the piece in amazement and took the rolled up hide in one hand. He snapped his wrist and the piece unrolled to show a smooth skin. The entire process took roughly thirty seconds with the speed his body completed the task. Smiling at the leather, he checked his patterns. He noticed the gloves took two hides to make, and the boots needed three. They also each required 2 Sinew Threads. Checking the Sinew Threads pattern, it used 1 Cured Light Hide and made 14 strands of Sinew Thread.

He held his newly cured hide in hand and selected his Create Leather Sinew Thread ability. Selecting the *Craft* button, his body exploded into motion again. This time he spread the hide on the floor with the hair side up and his knife popped back into his hand. The knife carefully slid across the surface and delicately removed the hair while leaving the underlying cured skin intact.

With the hair removed, he sliced the remaining hide into long thin strips. When finished, he had fourteen neat strands of leather that looked like thick strips of thread.

You created Leather Sinew Thread x 14.
You received 30xp in Leatherworking.

Atlas spent some time curing the other eleven hides he had. When it was complete, he was happy with his notifications.

You received 275xp in Leatherworking.
Success! You've reached levels 2 and 3 in Leatherworking.

Pleased with some tangible progress, he
held up two of the hides and two of the
threads. He brought up his Create Basic
Leather Gloves ability and hit *Craft*. His body
went into overdrive as it slung out the hides
and began cutting them into pieces resembling
a glove. When four pieces were complete, he
paired them together and fished a punch out of
his tool bag. The punch neatly cut holes into
the leather. With the holes complete, he began
weaving the thread through the openings around
the borders. He finished them by turning them
right side out and running a nice trim line
near the wrist. An item description box popped
up.

You created Basic Leather Gloves.
You received 45xp in Leatherworking.

Item - Basic Leather Gloves	
Requirements: Level 1 **Rarity:** Common **Quality:** Poor	**Defense:** 1 **Durability:** 15/15 **Weight:** 0.8 lb. **Slot:** Hands **Traits:** A set of gloves made from low-quality leather. Provides minimal protection for the hands.

Not that great, but better than nothing. At
least I'll have a little protection on my
hands. Atlas slipped them on and found that
they fit perfectly. They were nice and snug
while smelling of fresh leather. He repeated
the same process for the boots, and the
crafting action was similar. Two chunks of
leather made the sole, while one layer created
the sides of the boot. The pattern took longer
to punch and sew up, but he was happy with
what he had.

He'd entered the game with a pair of boots
on, but looking at the stats on them just
showed a plain gray item with no stats. They
were just labeled as Beginner Boots. This new
set offered some protection, like the gloves,
even if it wasn't much.

You created Basic Leather Boots.
You received 60xp in Leatherworking.

Item - Basic Leather Boots	
Requirements: Level 1 **Rarity**: Common **Quality**: Poor	**Defense**: 2 **Durability**: 25/25 **Weight**: 1.5 lbs. **Slot**: Feet **Traits**: A set of boots made from low-quality leather. Provides minimal protection for the feet.

Atlas struggled with the idea of what to make with his remaining pieces before he remembered Ramma's words about learning new patterns. Making the two items took him almost ten minutes, with the extreme speed that his body completed the motions. This left him plenty of time to do some more crafting before he went in search of quests.

"Hey, Master Ramma? Can I trouble you to teach me some new patterns?" Atlas called through the building.

"What?" the elf called through the building as Atlas heard wood rattling around.

"I wanted to learn more patterns."

"Hell, you haven't even left yet. What could you possibly have to learn?" the leatherworker complained as he came back into the room. "I don't put up with people wasting my time young man."

"I got my leatherworking to level three and wanted to learn the new patterns," Atlas explained.

The leatherworker looked at Atlas and then looked to the floor before frowning, "Since you're obviously new around here, I'm going to cut you a break this time. But, if you ever make a mess like that on my floor again, my next hide I tan will be yours. Clean up that mess and I'll show you the new skills."

Atlas grimaced as he looked down and noticed all the scraps of leather and tufts of hair littering the floor. "Sorry bout that. I'll get this cleaned up right away."

The elf merely grunted and walked to the back again. Atlas shuffled along the floor and picked up the scraps of leather. He also used a few of the larger scraps like a broom and dustpan, sweeping the fur onto the pieces and tossing it outside. Unsure of what to do with the scraps of leather, he opted to put them back in his bag. There was no way to know if they could be useful later. *The pieces themselves register as items called Leather Scraps, so surely I can use them somewhere?*

"Ramma, I finished up cleaning the place. You still around?" Atlas called into the back. The diminutive man walked out of the back and examined the room. He glanced around and finally nodded.

"Well done. Just remember to do your work outside next time," Ramma told him before gesturing. Atlas looked at the menu and found the section for trade skill abilities. Two new options appeared on the list. Create Basic Leather Jerkin and Create Basic Leather Pants were the two new options. They each cost 10 copper pieces to learn.

Wincing at the cost, he bought both and watched 20 copper siphon from his bag. Atlas turned and walked to the door.

"Thank you Master Ramma," Atlas yelled to the back room as he left.

Once outside, he examined the two new abilities and found that both the jerkin and pants required five hides a piece. *Damn. Don't have enough for both.* Considering his options, he opted for the jerkin. In the end, he was more likely to be hit in the chest than in the legs by normal attacks.

He pulled out five hides and six strands of
the sinew and hit *Craft*. His body took over
and began cutting out the pieces and slowly
sewing them together. The jerkin was a little
more complicated, so it took him a little over
a minute to make the piece but, when finished,
he beheld his new chestpiece.

You created Basic Leather Jerkin.
You received 75xp in Leatherworking.

Item - Basic Leather Jerkin	
Requirements: Level 1 **Rarity:** Common **Quality:** Poor	**Defense:** 3 **Durability:** 45/45 **Weight:** 2.0 lbs. **Slot:** Chest **Traits:** A jerkin made from low-quality leather. Provides minimal protection for the upper body.

Slipping the piece over his head, he
considered his options. *I don't have enough
money to learn any new skills and don't have
enough leather to make anything. I guess it's
back to the grind.*
Atlas made a trip around the town and
talked to the people. He found two quests. The
first one was from the Captain of the Guard,
Rilmael.

Quest - Deal with the Predators	
Requirements Level 1 Quest Rarity: Common Quest Reward: 50 experience, 30 copper coins.	Description: Rilamel wants you to eliminate 5 bobcats in the surrounding area.
Do you wish to accept this quest? Yes/No.	

Apparently, the meddling cats were killing some of their domesticated chickens. A woman in the village named Qua gave him the second quest.

Quest - A Quick Errand	
Requirements Level 1 Quest Rarity: Common Quest Reward: 70 experience, 40 copper coins.	Description: Qua asked you to find her husband, Tillo, in the forest. She said he entered the forest north of the city in search of a special plant.
Do you wish to accept this quest? Yes/No.	

The second quest was pretty vague, but knowing what Atlas did about these kinds of games, he was willing to bet he'd find the man trapped by a monster. While he was searching for quests, he ended up in the woodworkers shop. While it hurt him to spend more money, he knew he needed to spend some money to make money, so he bought a Basic Wood Staff so he could get some more reach. The staff cost 30 copper and had interesting stats on it.

Item – Basic Wood Staff	
Requirements: Level 1 **Rarity:** Common **Quality:** Fair	**Attack:** 3 **Defense:** 2 **Durability:** 55/55 **Weight:** 6.0 lbs. **Slot:** 2H Weapon **Traits:** A staff made of basic wood. It can be used to attack or defend.

Atlas hadn't considered a staff would be a dual purpose weapon, but it made sense. The longer reach would be instrumental in his fighting. New staff in hand and his bag slung across his back, he walked into the northern part of the forest. Atlas went on a small killing spree as he finished every little animal he found that had fur. Four squirrels fell to his new weapon. The new combo felt more natural than those of the knife. His movements were smoother and crisper as he thrust the wooden weapon and used it to bat the creature out of the air. The counters also flowed smoothly now that he had the extra reach and momentum of the swinging staff.

Three bobcats also fell to his attacks before he came across a small clearing. A soft growling noise caused the hair on the back of his neck to rise. He crouched down low and crept through the underbrush as he approached. Grunting echoed through the clearing, and it sounded like a person and not a monster. A cry of pain followed and Atlas dashed into the open space.

An elf stood on a large boulder and was
kicking at three leopards. Atlas examined the
closest one and saw it listed as *Leopard –
Level 3*. *Well, think I found Tillo.*

He charged toward the nearest cat and
followed the illusionary thrust pattern as the
image formed in his vision. The weapon thumped
solidly against the leopard and he followed it
with its combo swing.

You dealt 7 HP damage to Leopard.

The creature emitted a loud noise that
almost sounded like someone sawing on wood
before it leaped toward him. He interposed his
staff into the path of the attack, and the
cat's jaws closed over the haft of the weapon.
A push dislodged the animal, and it landed a
short distance away on its feet.

He aimed his next attack for the creature's
head and the swing connected, causing it to
roll onto its side. Atlas tried to take
advantage of the situation and dove for
another attack at the helpless animal. Before
he reached the leopard, his vision flashed
red, and he saw the image of his staff shift.
In a panic he followed the new pattern, unsure
of what happened. His staff continued its new
path and slammed into the side of one of the
other creatures that was diving for him, jaws
open. The leopard launched away and Atlas
stumbled as he landed off balance.

*You dealt 3 HP damage to Leopard with
Double Slash. (Interrupted)*
*You dealt 3 HP damage to Leopard with
Counter.*

The delay as he regained his footing allowed the initial leopard to return to its feet. Atlas stared at two different animals as they attempted to circle him. Instead of diving in for an attack, he played the defensive. One dove for him and he swept his staff to the side, grazing it and knocking it off course. The red flash from before hit his vision, but no image showed for him to counter.

Before his mind could comprehend that issue, a searing pain tore into his back as it felt like claws ripping through his flesh and tearing downward.

You dealt 1 HP damage to Leopard with Deflect.
Leopard dealt 4 HP damage to you with Rend.

Atlas swung around as the weight left his back and shifted his hands to one end of the staff. He reared back and cocked his shoulder before his attack unfurled and the five-foot chunk of wood whipped around and hit the leopard with a full force home-run swing to the face.

You dealt 12 HP damage to Leopard with Attack. (Critical Hit)
Leopard (Level 2) died.
You gained 10 experience.

The poor creature landed in a crumpled mess. Atlas heaved a breath and snapped his hands back into position on the staff. *One down and two to go.* He jumped forward to catch the other cat. His attack landed solidly, and he cleanly followed with the combo strike.

You dealt 7 HP damage to Leopard with Double Slash.
Leopard died.
You gained 15 experience.

A mewling noise drifted to his ears. Atlas swung around to see Tillo over the last leopard with a small blade in his hand. The elf looked ragged, and the leopards had shredded his pants during their encounter.

"Tillo?" Atlas asked.

"Yes. Thanks. For. Your. Help," the man panted out. He leaned forward with his hands on his knees.

"Qua asked me to find you. I guess she thought you may need help."

Tillo stood straight and sucked in a deep breath of air to steady himself.

"Bless that woman. She really is too good for me. How can I ever thank you?" Tillo asked.

"Just walking by and thought you needed the help. Qua gave me a quest for it, anyway. I'll collect the reward when I get back to Kilthan. Get back to her. Sure she's worried about you."

Tillo walked to the leopard he killed and collected a bundle of fur and meat. He approached Atlas and handed them over.

"I know it's not much, but my life is worth far more than a few coins and some experience. I have little to offer, so at least take the spoils of the battle."

Atlas accepted the gift with a nod.

"I'll see you back in town," Tillo told him as he left the clearing with a wave. Atlas watched as he jogged out of sight.

With nothing else pressing to attend to, Atlas continued his hunting. He picked off more squirrels and bobcats in the area. His travels also netted him some herbs. It took time to extract them and keep the plants intact, but he knew they'd be worth it in the end. The last bunch he sold were worth a decent amount of money. Oddly enough, the Herbalism skill would never show him experience gains, but he advanced it. *Need to ask someone about that.*

The day he spent in the game brought back haunting memories of grinding MMORPGs. He accomplished a lot, but it was such tedious work that his mind almost shut off. The pattern was predictable as he walked to town and turned in the quest only to find two more of the same style. Some more killing and herbalism finished those, only to return and get a couple more. This pattern continued for the entire day, and he slowly watched his experience and wealth climb.

During the time in town, he crafted items with the new furs. Since he focused on hunting the smaller game animals, it gave him plenty of hide to work with. Luckily, Ramma seemed to have a near infinite supply of the salt he needed to cure with. This led him to a quick discovery of the local economy.

As he'd leveled, he learned a few more patterns. He could now make a belt with a built in storage pouch. This allowed him to discard his old bag and was much easier to carry around. A leather coif adorned his head for a small amount of added protection, and a set of leather bracers rounded out the ensemble. Now fully equipped, his focus shifted to selling off the excess. This led to a quick influx of coins.

The prices he received for the pieces of armor astonished him. The first Basic Leather Jerkin he sold went for 1 silver and 40 copper. It sounded insane to him at first. The hides weren't that expensive. As a matter of fact, he could buy all the materials required to make the armor from Ramma for 70 copper. The profit margin made no sense to him with the short time he could finish it.

The situation clarified itself as he watched the townspeople do their work. They couldn't make items the way he did. They had to do the entire process in the traditional manner. That also explained why Ramma bothered to stretch hides on racks. His crafting speed gave him a distinct advantage, and he quickly saw how much a Reborn could change a town.

The prices fell with every piece he made, though. Supply and demand must've played a part in this. He'd sell a few pieces and then go back out on hunting missions. When he returned, he'd see his armor on a guard or a townsman. They were investing and buying them from Ramma almost as fast as he sold them. Eventually, there would be no more demand.

Atlas finished one final squirrel and looked at his notifications for the day.

You gained 345 experience.
You gained 460 experience from 7 quests.
Success! You've reached Levels 3, 4, and 5.
You gained 1190xp in Leatherworking.
Success! You've reached levels 4, 5, and 6 in Leatherworking.
Success! You've reached levels 2, and 3 in Herbalism.

It took plenty of work, but he'd hit level 5. He tried to focus on the casting aspect of his class, even though he relied on his staff more than his magic. Atlas assigned the 6 points as he received them. The first two went into Constitution and Intellect. The second two into Intellect and Spirit. The last two he dropped into Constitution and Spirit, bringing all three stats up 2 points. This also bumped up his HP and Mana pools to 80.

Atlas scoured the town but couldn't find any more quests, and Ramma had no more patterns he could learn. His crafting work left him with a hefty 8 silver and 10 copper. This was after he spent the money he needed for supplies, and he even learned Blade Chase and Charge from Leo. He didn't learn Fallback yet. Wanted to save some money. Charge had been invaluable for him to get a quick shot on the enemy. Best yet, after he used it, he could immediately transition into a two hit combo since it was an opening move. Blade Chase he had used little. The monsters were so weak compared to him now that they usually died too fast for him to counter. It also meant he was getting tiny amounts of experience for monster kills now compared to what he needed to advance levels.

All things considered, it was time for him to move zones. He strode into Master Longstride's building and found the druid.

"Greetings Master Longstride."

"Welcome back, Atlas. How fares the hunting? Looks like you've done well and reached level 5."

"It's been going smoothly. I think it's time for me to move on though. I'm not getting much experience for monster kills and can't find any more quests in town," Atlas told him.

"I'd imagine so. The experience just can't keep up as the requirements get higher. Quest zones are also designed for levels and this one caps at level 5. You could stay here and grind animals all day but you'd never learn anymore new skills and it would take damnably long. Looks like you need to make the trek to Lairthyn. Would you like to learn Entangle and Nurture before you go? A healing spell could be very useful."

"Of course. Thank you for reminding me," Atlas told him. He felt foolish that he forgot about his class spells.

Master Longstride waved a hand in his direction, and the menu popped up. He selected Entangle and Nurture and hit Learn. The surge of magical power filled him, and his body felt light and rejuvenated.

You have learned Druid Spell: Entangle.

Druid Spell - Entangle	

Requirements
   Druid Class
   Level 3
	Description: Thorns erupt from the ground and encircle the target's legs.
	
	Damage: 1 HP/ 3 seconds
	Mana cost: 10 MP

You have learned Druid Spell: Nurture.

Druid Spell - Nurture	

Requirements
   Druid Class
   Level 5
	Description: Infuses the target with the healing magic of nature.
	
	HP Restored: 15 HP
	Mana cost: 10 MP

Finally, a healing spell.

"What's the best way to get to Lairthyn?" Atlas asked.

"Northwest of here you'll find a worn path that leads directly to it. No doubt you've crossed it while exploring and hunting around town."

"Sounds familiar," Atlas said as he searched his minimap for the road in question, "Thank you Master Longstride. Hopefully, we'll meet again."

"I'm sure we will. I do like to travel from time to time," he said as he walked over to a small desk in the corner and rummaged through the drawers, "I figured this day was coming soon so I wrote an introduction letter for you to Master Proth. Deliver this to him in Lairthyn."

Atlas took the letter and tucked it into his bag. He dropped into a shallow bow and left the building. Tapping his staff on the ground, he took off for the road at a brisk pace.

Chapter 7

New City, New Problems

Atlas strode toward the city of Lairthyn without a care in the world. His trip was nothing more than a leisurely stroll through the forest. No animals disturbed him and nothing attacked him. When he finally left the edge of the forest and caught sight of the city, he staggered to a halt.

The place was easily five times the size of Kilthan, and that was judging by what he could see. A small wall rose around the perimeter and a gate stood in the middle of the pathway he traveled. From this distance, he could see a small stream of people entering and leaving.

His pace increased with the anticipation of exploring somewhere new. The distance melted away, and he stood in a short line to enter the city. The guards at the gate took one look at him and just ushered him through without so much as a question.

Buildings lined both sides of the road, and he checked the signs. Most of those near him looked like inns, and he remembered the advice from Master Longstride. He walked up to the door on one establishment called The Plucky Goose and pushed through. A crowd filled the room and Atlas got his first glimpse at something he'd been missing. Other real-world people dotted the room.

It was pretty obvious for most of them. Many wore mismatched pieces of armor and looked relatively new. A lot of them had odd names reminiscent of a video game player. Most of them were between levels 5 and 8.

Atlas approached the innkeeper and immediately asked to set his Bind Point at the inn. The innkeeper only nodded and dug behind the counter. The husky man pulled out a small black box with an orange gem embedded into the surface. The innkeeper's hazel eyes glanced from Atlas to the gem a few times until Atlas realized he wanted him to touch it.

Atlas extended his hand and touched the gem with his palm.

Do you wish to bind to The Plucky Goose? Yes/No.

He selected *Yes,* and a shiver of cold traveled down his spine. The innkeeper watched him squirm with a knowing look and grinned.

"First time binding? Odd experience isn't it?"

"Definitely an odd feeling. What's your name?" Atlas asked.

"Harold. Anything else I can get for you, Reborn?"

"I'm Atlas, by the way. You know anyone around here that has quests available?"

"You could try by the stables nearby. I'd heard there were a few quests available in that area but don't know for sure," Harold said as he looked at the state of Atlas' attire, "Judging by the layer of dust on you, I'd say you just arrived. If that's the case, I suggest you go by your class trainer's place first. No point in running off in search of action before then."

"Have every intention to do just that. I'm sure I'll see you again," Atlas told him as he turned to leave.

As he left the building, he looked around the area. *I need to find a guard or someone who can point me to Master Proth's place.*

He spotted two people in armor wearing tabards with a matching symbol. Atlas wasn't sure what the local heraldry looked like, but he doubted any players would wear them. They also displayed normal fantasy style names.

"Excuse me, guys. Do either of you know where I can find Master Proth?"

The guard on the left stood a good foot taller than the other and wore a sword on his hip. His plate armor fit him well, and a scruffy mustache poked out through the opening in the faceplate.

"Master Proth? That's the druid master here in town, right?"

"Yes sir," Atlas confirmed.

"Take this road into town and turn right at the second intersection. He's the seventh house down the way. His place has pillars on the front that are living trees. Hard to miss," the guard assured him.

"Thank you. Take care guys."

Atlas waved as he left and followed their directions. His interest peaked when he spotted a leatherworking shop on the way. Figuring he could spare a little time, he turned and examined the sign. Trailia's Hides. The scent of leather assaulted him as he walked through the door. It reminded him of walking into a western-wear store.

A lanky woman stood behind the counter and eyed him as he entered.

"Welcome traveler. I'm Trailia. Can I help you?"

"Hi Trailia, name's Atlas. I'm here to see what you offer in terms of Leatherworking training," Atlas told her with a smile.

Her stern gaze worried him, so he tried his best to exude confidence. The more she stared, the more he felt his resolve crumbling to dust.

"I don't train newbies. You have to be at least level 5 before I'd even consider working with you. Who did you train under before?"

"I trained under Master Ramma. I'm currently level six in Leatherworking."

She grunted in response, "Suppose I can work with you. That old scoundrel knows his business. Here's what I have for you."

Are all leatherworkers grumpy?

Her hand flicked toward him, and the menu settled into his sight. There were two abilities he could learn. Hide Patch was the first while the second one was Basic Reinforced Leather Gloves. They each cost 20 copper, so he purchased both.

Leatherworking - Hide Patch	
Requirements Leatherworking Level 5 Rarity: Common Requirements: 1 Cured Light Hide, 1 Leather Sinew Thread	Description: Create a small patch of leather that can be applied to existing leather armor. Anyone can use this patch. Use: Seal holes in armor and restore 10 durability.

Leatherworking - Basic Reinforced Leather Gloves	
Requirements Leatherworking Level 6 Rarity: Common Requirements: 3 Cured Light Hide, 3 Leather Sinew Thread	Description: Create a set of reinforced leather gloves. These have higher defense and durability than the basic gloves.

Looking at the stats on the reinforced gloves, Atlas saw they had 1 extra defense and 10 extra durability. Not shabby for just one extra hide and sinew. Another thing that caught Atlas' eye was the hides. Trailia had 12 Raw Hides of varying animals available, but prices in town must be really low. Each of them only cost 5 copper. *I guess others figured out what I have and have been buying up raw materials and flooding the market to drive down prices.*

Atlas decided it was worth the investment to his skill experience alone for that low of a price and bought all 12 hides. He'd stocked up on salt before he left Ramma's so he had plenty to cure all 12.

"You have a work space I can use here or do I need to find somewhere outside?" he asked Trailia.

"I have one in the back you can use. Follow me."

They walked toward the rear and passed a
room full of skins in varied states of curing
on racks. Two rooms sat against the back wall
behind this one. They headed for the one on
the right and it looked to have nothing more
than a sturdy and plain table and a large
wooden bucket.

While passing by, he caught a brief glimpse
of the other room. Pieces of armor in
different states of completion sat on wooden
mannequins, and a variety of fancier tools
filled the space.

"You can use this room as long as you clean
up when finished."

"Thanks," Atlas said with a nod.

She left him to his work, and he heard her
walk to the other room and close the door.
Atlas wasted no time and immediately cured the
12 new hides. Those combined with the surplus
he already had brought him to 22 total hides.
The first hide he made more sinew thread with,
and then he made two of the Hide Patches. *May
need those for repairs in the future.* Five
sets of reinforced gloves followed.

*You received 300xp in Leatherworking for
Cured Light Hide x 12.*

*You received 60xp in Leatherworking for
Hide Patch x2.*

*You received 450xp in Leatherworking for
Basic Reinforced Leather Gloves x 5.*

*Success! You've reached level 7 in
Leatherworking.*

With only four hides left, Atlas called it a day on the crafting. He still needed to find Master Proth. His first item on the agenda involved him slipping off his Basic Leather Gloves and putting on the reinforced version instead. Walking over to Master Trailia's workspace, he knocked on the door. The sound of footfalls echoed through the room and the door swung open.

"What ya want?"

"Wanted to sell some stuff I made," Atlas said slowly. The fire in her eyes still made him nervous.

She looked into his very soul with her piercing gaze as she waved her hand again. The menu blissfully took over his vision and blocked his view of her. *Let's see how badly they drove down prices.* Selecting his Basic Leather Gloves, he winced as he hit the *Sell* button. Their price was down to 10 copper. *Looks like I was right and people are flooding the market with this basic gear.*

When he selected the first of his reinforced gloves, his eyes nearly bulged out of his head. One set of gloves was worth 2 silver and 80 copper. That was an astronomical price for such low-level gear. *There must be no one high enough level to make this yet in this village. People must've chosen other skills. I missed a few days from work, so they should be plenty far ahead of me.*

Selling all four of his sets of gloves added a pleasant 10 silver and 90 copper. The price of each set of gloves only dropped 5 copper per pair sold. This left him with 18 silver and 10 copper. Two more patterns were available as well. The first was Basic Reinforced Leather Boots, and the second was Basic Reinforced Leather Pants. He learned both for 20 copper a piece. They both added 1 Defense and 10 Durability to their respective patterns. Each of these also came at the price of one additional thread and one additional Cured Light Leather.

With his last four hides, Atlas made one set of the Reinforced Boots and swapped out his current set. The extra padding in the new boots showed him the importance of quickly upgrading his armor. He hadn't noticed just how much he could feel while walking until he put more padding between his feet and the rough ground. His old set of boots sold for a measly 15 copper, but he was positive when he found more hides he'd make plenty of money to make up for it.

You received 100xp in Leatherworking for Basic Reinforced Leather Boots.

Atlas cleaned up his work area and tossed the scraps in the bucket. With the place back in order, he walked back to the door to Master Trailia's workspace. The leatherworker opened the door with her usual charm.

"What?"

"Just wanted to say thanks for letting me use the room. I have it cleaned up. Wasn't sure if you wanted me to dump the bucket out somewhere, so left it there."

"That's fine. I'll take care of that later. Come back by when you have more hides to work with."

Before Atlas could respond, the door swung closed with a thump.

Figures. Oh well. Off to go find Master Proth.

His surroundings shifted from fragrant leather to dirty streets in an instant as he walked from the shop. Refuse littered the streets as he walked down the road. The sight of it made him sad. The nagging feeling that it was part of the 'Reborn' problem resonated with him. *Some people just don't care.*

Atlas passed another sign that intrigued him. The picture showed a small knife whittling away at a shaft of wood. Figuring this must be the woodworking place, he ducked inside. The smell of sawdust hit him, and aromatic lengths of log lined shelves around the room. Some longer pieces looked destined to be staves, while others looked like tool handles or even short wands.

"Can I help you, stranger?" the older man behind the counter asked.

"Of course. I'm Atlas and I'd like to learn Woodworking."

"I suppose I could teach you that if you have the coin. Take a look at what I offer," the man said before flicking his hand toward Atlas. The window popped open, and he saw the long list of different wood. Some of them were terribly expensive. Toward the end of the list was the item he needed. Learn Woodworking. With a cost of 10 silver. He quickly purchased the skill and the list of abilities filled his vision.

You have learned the trade skill Woodworking.

You have learned the Woodworking ability: Wood Cutting.

You have learned the Woodworking ability: Create Rough Wood Log.

You have learned the Woodworking ability: Create Basic Wood Handle.

You have learned the Woodworking ability: Create Basic Wood Rods.

You have received Woodworker's Tool Bag.

"Wood Cutting? That's a skill of woodworking?" Atlas asked, confused.

"Well, of course, young man. How else are you going to get the wood you need to craft with?"

"I figured Wood Cutting was its own skill, and I'd need to learn that as well."

"I guess I can see that. But woodworking is nothing but constantly cutting and carving wood. Have to know how to cut it to work with it so it all fits under the same skill. If you need anything in the future, let me know."

Atlas examined the skills and saw how it worked. He needed to use Wood Cutting to get the pieces of wood. Create Rough Wood Log would trim those pieces and create the rough log he needed, and the rest of the abilities turned that rough log into an item.

The store interface was still open, and he
noticed Rough Wood Logs sold for a mere 8
copper a piece. Wanting to get a little of a
head start, he bought 20 of them and 1 silver
and 60 copper drained from him. He walked to a
small room on the side of the building and
activated Create Basic Wood Rod. Sliding the
small carving knife from his tool bag, Atlas
began furiously carving away at the chunk of
wood until only a handful of thin wooden rods
remained. Five Rough Logs turned into a small
stack of Basic Wood Rods.

*You gained 100 experience in Woodworking.
Success! You've reached level 2 in
Woodworking.*

A quick chat with the woodworking trainer
let him learn another ability for Create Basic
Wood Wand. It only cost him 10 copper. This
ability created two small wands per use, and
Atlas looked at the weapons.

Item – Basic Wood Wand	
Requirements: Level 1 **Rarity:** Common **Quality:** Poor	**Attack:** 1 **Magical Attack:** 3 **Durability:** 55/55 **Weight:** 0.8 lbs. **Slot:** 1H Weapon **Traits:** A wand made of basic wood. While physically weak, this weapon can increase your magical damage slightly.

So there are magic specific weapons? That explains how I increase my magic damage for my spells. He created six sets of the Basic Wood Wands.

You gained 150 experience in Woodworking. Success! You've reached level 3 in Woodworking.

The next ability he received was Create Basic Wood Staff. This ability he used his last ten pieces of wood for and made ten staves. They very much resembled his staff, but slightly weaker. They only had 2 attack and 1 defense.

You gained 350 experience in Woodworking. Success! You've reached level 4 in Woodworking.

His next skill surprised him. It was Create Basic Wood Buttons. *I guess the trade skills do need to help each other here. I bet Tailors need these.*

With nothing left to make, he sold off the recently made items. None of them held any value to him, and he only made them for the experience. Inferior quality woodworking pieces also sold for low prices. The twenty rods, twelve wands, and ten staves only fetched 80 copper.

Out of wood, he bade the older man farewell and continued on his original trek in search of Master Proth. *I've got to stop chasing squirrels and stick to the plan.*

The guard was spot on with his assessment of the Master Druid's residence. As soon as he laid eyes on it, the place practically screamed a druid lived there. Living trees formed the pillars in front of the building and a porch awning connected to them. The smell of cedar hit Atlas as soon as he stepped on the porch. The sensation confused him because he didn't see any cedar in the construction. Brushing off the thought, he knocked on the door.

"Who is it?"

"My name is Atlas. I'm looking for Master Proth."

A chair scraped across wood behind the door, and the plodding of footsteps drew closer. The door opened to reveal a tall and slender figure. He looked to be in his thirties, but Atlas wasn't sure he could accurately judge the age of an elf. A robe made from the hide of a bear hung heavily from his shoulders. It looked far too heavy to wear with comfort or during combat, but Atlas spotted the bare arms and neck of the man and noticed a defined and muscular physique. His shaggy brown hair hung to his brow and the deep green eyes appraised Atlas.

"I'm Proth. What can I do for you, Atlas?"

"I have a letter of introduction from Master Longstride," Atlas began as he fished the document from his belt pouch. He handed the paper to the druid, and the man immediately opened it and scanned the contents.

"Well, Atlas. Welcome to Lairthyn. Come in," the druid said as he stepped aside and held the door open.

Atlas walked through with a nod and looked around. The inside looked like a log cabin. All the walls were solid logs from trees and not the standard boards seen in so many other buildings. Most of the furniture appeared made from one piece of wood, almost as if grown instead of carved.

Master Proth closed the door and motioned for him to follow. He led Atlas out of the back of the house and into a yard surrounded by a stone wall. The landscape itself was completely empty save for short grass.

"How's Longstride?"

"Doing good as far as I can tell. I wasn't there long before moving here, so didn't get to know him very well."

"I figured as much. Reborn move around at a fast pace. The successful ones advance quickly and bounce from place to place, picking up new skills. Did you learn all three abilities Master Longstride offered?"

"Yes, I did."

"Can you show me Nature's Wrath?" Master Proth asked, "You can cast it toward that stone wall in front of us. It won't damage the wall."

The request confused Atlas, but he did as commanded. He lifted his staff and followed the hand motions. The staff made it more difficult to move in the precise pattern, but he got it close enough for the cast to complete.

"New to the staff?" Master Proth asked.

"Yeah. Bought it recently and had minimal fighting with it."

"No problem. How about Entangle? Target this," the druid said and walked to the side of the building and picked up a solitary stone. He tossed it toward the middle of the clearing.

Once again Atlas cast his spell and, as before, it resolved and vines rose from the ground to wrap around the rock. Master Proth asked him to demonstrate his Nurture spell as well. This one was new, and he hadn't tried it out yet.

Atlas targeted himself and began the casting. A tingling sensation flooded his arms as he followed the motions. The spell consisted of wide, flowing motions with his arms and reminded him of someone doing Tai Chi. The last motion of the move required him to run both of his hands across each other on the palms but in opposite directions as his arms came back to center. The magic coalesced and the cloud of energy soaked into him.

"Well done. You can cast all three," Master Proth said as he began walking around Atlas and looking him up and down.

"I assume you picked up leatherworking by the appearance of your armor. I'll say I'm impressed at how far you've advanced in it already. Your staff is an excellent choice for combat, but you use it terribly inefficiently. We can work on that later, but I can see by how you hold it you use it as more of a club than anything else."

Well, he's not wrong.

"You're definitely in better shape than most of the druids I am sent. I don't train just anyone, though. You must complete a quest first to see if you're worthy of advancing among the druids."

A quest? They gatekeep the class training between trainers with quests? Well, not the craziest thing I've seen in a game.

"What's the quest?"

The druid flicked his wrist toward Atlas and a box appeared.

Quest - Druidic Ritual	
Requirements Level 5 Quest Rarity: Common Quest Reward: 110 experience, 50 copper coins.	Description: Venture to The Standing Stones and meditate upon the central platform to confront yourself.
Do you wish to accept this quest? Yes/No.	

Atlas accepted the quest and turned to Master Proth, "Where are The Standing Stones?"

"You can find them northwest of the city. It's about a mile from here. I'll mark the general area on your map."

"I'll be back soon then."

Atlas trudged back through the house and exited through the front door. Checking his minimap, he could see the layout of the entire place. He followed the main thoroughfare north to the gate in the wall. The size of the city made it difficult for him to maneuver, and it took much longer than he expected to exit.

When he finally left the confines of the city, a sprawling field of green greeted him. A narrow road led north and ran into the forest ahead.

Looks like The Standing Stones are somewhere near that road.

With the map confirming the location, he
followed the road. The smooth, hard-packed
dirt made for quick travel and he reached the
tree line in thirty minutes. The path was
clean cut, and no underbrush dotted the road.
The canopy of the trees intertwined above the
road and shaded the path as it wound deeper
into the forest.

Atlas followed the trail and kept an eye
out for dangers. He discovered pretty quickly
that his leveling would be rough. During his
travel, he found four animals to fight. Two of
them were level 5 foxes, one was a level 5
coyote, and the last was a level 5 badger.

Defeating all four wasn't terrible, but it
took a while for each. His damage wasn't very
high in melee combat with his staff. He
finished the fights without too much
difficulty, but the time it took meant he'd be
grinding here for a long while to get the
experience he needed.

You gained 90 experience.

It also netted him more meat and four more
hides to work with. *I should really find
someone to teach me cooking. That or sell off
these bundles of meat I keep getting.*

A large stone structure near the road interrupted his musings. He followed a game trail through the trees toward the rock face. When he stumbled through the last shrub, he stood in a large clearing with what looked like a miniature version of Stonehenge in it. Large rectangular bricks stood in a circle, arranged in an indiscernible pattern. Atlas walked up to the nearest one and ran his hand along the surface. The stone felt coarse and almost had a sandy feel to it as his skin drug against the surface.

In the center of the monument was a large stone disc with a swirling Celtic knot. Atlas cautiously approached the symbol and looked around. *This is a quest, after all. There has to be something here to fight or some puzzle to solve.*

After carefully circling the ring of stone and not spotting anything, Atlas sat and meditated as the quest told him. He dropped into a cross leg position and laid his arms on his knees. It took him some time to drown out his surrounding noise. The chirp of birds and the rustle of leaves on the wind drew his attention away and continually disrupted his focus.

Eventually, his mind calmed and the turmoil of his surroundings faded. He felt adrift on the wind as his mind hovered in peaceful serenity. The feeling didn't last long because a voice broke him out of his reverie.

"You're a pathetic excuse for a druid. Out here meditating when you should be fighting and getting stronger. No wonder you take so long to kill stuff."

The voice sounded both odd and familiar at the same time. He felt like he knew the person who spoke but couldn't remember from where. When his eyes cracked open and glimpsed the figure, they immediately burst open the rest of the way. He stared at a mirror image of himself, yet it was his body from the actual world and not the one in the game.

"How?"

"I can't be this dense. Video game remember?"

Atlas felt foolish for a moment before his focus returned to his copycat and he stood from the ground, "Why are you here then?"

"Your test, of course. This is about facing yourself, in this case, quite literally."

A dagger appeared in his reflection's hand as a sadistic grin adorned his face.

"Time to see what you can really do," the copy said as he dove toward Atlas.

No combat image appeared to show him his movements. The blade continued directly for his chest and, at the last minute, he twisted to the side, causing the blade to skid off a rib and pain to flare through his chest.

Hopping backward, he clutched at the spot on his chest. Red blood seeped through his fingers and into his leather armor. He dragged his hand back and examined the wound. A gash bled in a slow, continuous trickle. The bright red fluid covered his hands and the rivulets of blood flowed down his hand and slid down his wrist as he watched.

This isn't right. The wounds don't normally bleed this much. I also didn't see any of the combat motions.

Before his mind could process that any farther, a glimmer of light reflected from his copy's blade and flashed across his eye. Out of sheer instinct, he dove to his right. He rolled back to his feet and turned to see a blade stabbed into the space he just vacated. Gritting his teeth, he rose to his feet and held his staff out in front of him.

"Fine, if I have to do this without the combat images, then so be it."

The copycat dove for him again, but Atlas noticed he'd done the exact same motion as the first time. Believing he'd seen a key to the fight, he stepped to the side and swung hard with the lower end of the staff. The wood rose and thumped against the meaty section of the duplicate's arm. It yelped in pain and dropped the dagger. Atlas stepped in and swung the staff in the other direction to catch him in the temple. The impact knocked the opponent down in a crumpled mess.

"That won't work again," Atlas said, confidence returning.

This is a video game, after all. He must have a specific set of abilities he can use.

The simulacrum of himself looked at him with that eerie smile again before returning to his feet.

"Fine, druid," he said with a sneer, "try this!"

Almost too fast to see, the figure's hand reached behind his back and flung a small knife at Atlas. The speed of the flight startled him, but he turned at the last minute and a shallow cut along his bicep was the only damage.

"That all you got?" Atlas started before his eyes blurred and he swayed on his feet. He blinked in rapid succession before he steadied himself again and his vision returned to normal. An inspection of the wound caused Atlas' brow to furrow in concern. The cut just happened, but the skin was bright red and swollen already. *Poison!*

"Tick tock," the image of himself said as he pointed at an imaginary watch on his wrist, "now what will you do?"

"I'm grow tired of this nonsense," Atlas yelled, "time for you to die once and for all."

Atlas leaped forward and brought the staff around in a two-handed swing. His copy ducked below the weapon and rolled to the side. He tried to stop the motion of the staff and bring it back toward his target, but the wave of dizziness hit him again and he stumbled to the side. His grip on the staff involuntarily loosened, and he struggled to keep from dropping it.

Damn. If I can't keep my balance, I won't be able to win. My strength is fading faster than I hoped.

Leaning on his staff, he squinted through blurry eyes at his copy and saw nothing but a foot heading for him. The kick hit him directly in his chest and he stumbled backward. *I need to recover health or I'm done for.* He tried to pull up his stats to see his HP and Mana, but nothing showed and the damage notifications weren't working. *Surely my magic works, right?*

With a thought, he triggered Nurture. As with before, the images didn't show up, but he felt the power course through his body. He'd only cast this spell a few times since learning it, but he'd gotten the general pattern down. Instead of relying on the images, he mimicked the motions himself. The power built along his arms as he completed the gestures and the spell finished with his hands sliding across each other from side to side. The ball of green energy formed by the spell leaped into the air and then showered him in a cascade of green sparks. Strength returned to his muscles and his balance steadied. The blur faded from his vision and he looked toward the copy of himself.

"Round two," Atlas said with a wry grin of his own, "Fight!"

Atlas ran forward as the copy scrambled around the ground, trying to grab a hold of the knife Atlas knocked free earlier. His hand finally found purchase as Atlas closed in and the copy's blade swept in a wide arc toward him. He merely grinned and planted the butt of his staff into the ground in front of the copy and vaulted over his head. Since the fake him was still low to the ground, he didn't have to jump very high, but he landed gracefully.

His opponent turned, but it was too late. Atlas grabbed the staff with both hands and gave a hearty home run swing to his double's back. A sharp crack echoed through the clearing as his doppelganger flew almost ten feet and landed on his back, air bursting from his lungs. He walked over to the copy and stared into his own face. The feeling was surreal as he watched himself gulp for air and struggle mightily.

"You've lost. Now stay in your own world. This one is mine," Atlas punctuated before slamming the end of his staff directly into the throat of his reflection. A crunch signaled the end of the fighter as his body went limp.

Well done, Druid. You've faced your inner turmoil and come out victorious. This will allow you to advance in your druid skills unabated. Return to Master Proth to receive your reward.

The calm serenity returned to the clearing and the body of his slain doppelganger was nowhere to be found. A scan of the area showed nothing out of the ordinary, so Atlas left the ring of stones and walked back toward the city. On the way back, he detoured a few times to fight some animals and harvest skins.

You gained 180 experience.

Truth be told, he wanted to see if the combat images returned more than anything else. To his relief, they were back as normal. His path led him back to the city, and he headed directly for the druid master's house. *This place sure is strange.*

Chapter 8

The Folly of Friends

Atlas entered Master Proth's house to the sight of the druid working on a hide. The soft fur was a dull gray color, but he couldn't quite place the animal it belonged to. The deft hands of the master slid a blade along the edges, and thin strips of leathery skin and fur dropped to a neat pile below the table.

"Greetings Master Proth," Atlas called.

The druid looked up from his work and grinned, "Welcome back Atlas. How fared the trial?"

"Bested myself and live to tell about it. Sure was an odd sensation. Any idea why the combat system didn't work during the trial?"

"The combat system is designed for struggles in this word. Yours was an internal struggle."

"Internal struggle my ass. The asshole sliced open my ribs and poisoned me. I crushed his windpipe with my staff. How is that internal?"

"The fight happened in your consciousness. That's why the combat system didn't take over. It seemed perfectly real to you."

Atlas considered that before asking another question, "What would've happened if I lost?"

"Oh, you would've died and respawned back here. There's a slight chance it may have damaged some of your mind, but that rarely ever happens," the druid said as he waved away the thought.

"Great… this place worries me sometimes. Anyway, I'm here to turn in my quest."

The druid motioned with his hand and the box appeared in his vision.

Quest - Druidic Ritual	
Requirements Level 5 Quest Rarity: Common Quest Reward: 110 experience, 50 copper coins.	Description: You defeated yourself and claimed victory.
Do you wish to turn in this quest? Yes/No.	

Atlas selected *Yes*, and the coins appeared in a bag in his hand. He checked his experience and saw he now was at 395/600.

"What skills can you teach and what levels are they available?" Atlas asked.

"I teach three skills here. The first is Barkskin at level 6, the second is Harmony at level 8, and the last is Resurgence at level 10."

"I can guess what Barkskin does, but what do Harmony and Resurgence do?"

"Harmony allows you to call upon the energy of nature and focus it on a target. The power of nature will slowly heal that target for a set amount of time. Resurgence allows you to resurrect recently slain people. I'll warn you, Resurgence requires a quest to learn it."

"Good to know. Sounds like Harmonize is a good old fashioned Heal-Over-Time spell. Those are always great in a pinch. Is there anything I can do to help me kill stuff faster? I noticed it takes ages to grind animals in the woods."

Proth shook his head, "Not really. Without a combat subclass, you're stuck as a healer with little damage potential. If you could strengthen your magic, then your Nature's Wrath spell would do more damage. The downfall of that is less mana to heal with. Increasing the rank of the ability would help with that. You could also work on your additions and try to master your first. That would help you move to the next."

"Wait? I have to master my first to learn more? The weaponmaster taught me some already. Do they not keep teaching them to you?"

"Weaponmasters only teach counters and special types of moves. Mastering your current additions teaches you the next. That's why your standard attack is only a two-hit attack. Once you master it, you can move to a three-hit one."

"Well that's good to know." Atlas wanted to go back and yell at the weaponmaster for not telling him that but he knew he'd get the standard response of 'you didn't ask about it.'

"Do you know how to master them?"

"Both magical spells and additions are mastered in the same way. You must follow the movements of the spells or abilities perfectly. Your movement can't be off in the slightest. You spells or weapons must land in the precise spot, at the exact angle. As for how to do it, I'm not sure. It seems to deal with a component of luck or chance. I've heard some say they have more success when they let their instincts guide them through the movements instead of actively trying to follow them."

So it needs to feel natural then? That makes sense. You'd need to train your body to move as it should on its own. Must be like warriors of old training to keep their muscle memory for combat.

"Thanks, Master Proth. You don't have any quests for me, do you?"

"Sorry Atlas. I can't give you a quest until level six. You can return then. I'd suggest finding some people to party with. That should help with the slow speed of your killing."

"That should work! There an inn around here where I might find some help?"

"You can try The Blushing Fairy. It's down the street two blocks on the left. I'm sure the sign will give it away. They attract many types of people. Just be careful what you get mixed up in," Proth warned.

"I'll do just that," Atlas said as he left out the door with a final thanks.

Atlas followed the druid's directions and headed directly for The Blushing Fairy. The sign outside showed a humorous depiction of a fairy woman in a Marilyn Monroe pose holding her skirt or flowers down. A rosy red color filled her cheeks.

He was right. Pretty obvious. Atlas chuckled to himself.

Pushing through the door, the smell of wood smoke and a sour tinge assaulted his nose. The sour smell he couldn't quite place, but judging by the lack of cleaning evident in the room, he assumed it was from soured alcohol.

Atlas scanned the room and spotted two people with names that stood out sitting together. One was a level 6 person named Skullcrusher, and the other was a level 6 named Hercules. *Not very creative on the names, but don't seem like names from the game itself.*

He approached their table and waved as they looked at him.

"Hey guys. You questing here as well?"

They looked at each other and then the one named Skullcrusher answered.

"Sure are. Haven't seen many others from the real world yet. You just get here?"

"Sure did. You two are the first outsiders I've talked to. How you liking the game?"

"Lots of fun. They are a little stingy with the gear and weapons, though. The cost of everything makes it difficult to move fast. That's some nice gear for such a low level. Where'd you get it?" Hercules asked.

"Made it. I'm a Leatherworker."

"How in the world did you save up money for that? I'm not even halfway to a profession yet," Skullcrusher grumbled.

Atlas opened his mouth to tell them about the free profession thing, but decided against it. *I don't know these guys, so I'll keep that to myself. These games always become competitions and if I can keep hold of the market in town for longer, I'll be set.*

"I spent a lot of time grinding before coming here. Didn't do a lot of quests and leveled the hard way. Gave me plenty of stuff to sell. Now it just takes too long to kill stuff. You guys need a healer to run quests with? I can make you guys some armor with stuff we kill. Seems like a good tradeoff?"

The two shared a look again before both smiled and Skullcrusher answered, "That sounds great. You have any open quests right now? We have two fetch quests. One is for panther fur and the other is for Hippoblooms."

"Haven't searched the city for quests yet. Think you can share them if we are in a party?" Atlas asked.

"Yeah. We do it all the time. We split up and each gather quests in different parts of town and then share them. Sit down and get some food with us and we can go grind out these quests," Hercules told him.

Atlas agreed and sat for a meal. He ordered roast, and a barmaid brought out a mug of yellowish liquid and a chunk of meat on a wooden platter. The drink itself was very bitter and after the initial coughing spell, Atlas couldn't imagine drinking anymore of it. The roast wasn't bad, but it had a stringy texture to it. He decided he didn't want to know what animal it came from. The food gave him a small buff though.

You gain 1 Stamina for the next hour due to Pleasingly Full buff.

So food gives unique benefits. Definitely need to invest in the cooking skill.

Each paid for their respective meals and Atlas followed them from the inn. They traveled toward the northern end of the city. The path they chose was almost identical to his earlier passage. When they reached the wall, one guard turned to examine them. His brows creased in concentration as he examined Skullcrusher and Hercules, but when he spotted Atlas, he hurried over to him.

"Well met druid. Can I trouble you for assistance?"

"Sure. What can I help you with?" Atlas asked.

Before the guard responded Hercules chimed in, "He's going to ask you to kill foxes for him. Think it was eight of them, wasn't it?" he asked as he turned to Skullcrusher for confirmation.

The other man merely nodded in agreement. The guard picked up as though they hadn't spoken.

"Some nearby farmers have been complaining about foxes stealing all their chickens and eggs. Can you help us thin the menace and kill some?"

Quest – Cock Thieves	
Requirements Level 5 Quest Rarity: Common Quest Reward: 80 experience, 40 copper coins.	Description: A guard in Lairthyn asked you to eliminate foxes pestering the farmers. Kill 8 foxes to complete the quest.
Do you wish to accept this quest? Yes/No.	

Atlas selected *Yes* and turned to the others.

"You were right. It's eight."

"Thought so. Oh before we forget, let's party up so we can share our quests," Hercules said. The fighter stared ahead into nothing for a few moments as his hands danced in the air. It looked like he was pressing buttons on a menu.

You have been invited to join Hercules' party. Do you wish to join the party? Yes/No.

Atlas selected *Yes* and looked at the two players. He could now see one labeled as a Warrior and the other showed to be an Assassin. When he focused on them, a small icon appeared in his vision and showed him the amount of HP and Mana they had available. *Nice. I bet that's how I target them for spells.*

He looked up and saw Hercules still moving his hands, and more messages showed up.

Hercules shared the quest Blooming Giants.
Hercules shared the quest Feline Stalkers.

Both quest boxes popped up, and he accepted both. They needed six of the Hippoblooms and eight Panther Fur.

"Thanks guys. Let's get this show on the road."

It didn't take Atlas long to figure out they were leaps and bounds ahead of him in combat prowess. Well, at least in terms of combat damage. They fought in a very methodical fashion, and each of their strikes usually dealt at least 12 damage in a two-hit combo. Atlas was lucky to hit 8 on a good crit.

Where they lacked was in technique. They didn't know how to counter properly and Atlas never saw them use anything other than their class skills and the two-hit combo. *I guess they never bought the extra skills from the weapon master.*

They found three of the Hippoblooms and scrounged up four of the Panther Fur. Luckily, Atlas had more luck with the foxes and they killed all eight of those. The panthers were harder to find and most of them they'd actually had to lure out of trees. One almost killed him when it dropped on his head from above, and none of them expected it.

The trip allowed him to get in plenty of practice with his healing magic. Not only did the two fighters do a fair amount of damage, but they took more damage than Atlas was comfortable with. He watched them not even attempt to block attacks more often than not. They just waited for the animal to bite or scratch them and then immediately dashed forward with another two-hit attack.

As they collected hides, Atlas cured them and then used them to make pieces for the other two fighters. They both chose the belts with pouches for their first piece and then Hercules chose a jerkin while Skullcrusher chose pants. Atlas felt generous and made each a pair of gloves and boots with the skins he got.

You gained 210 experience.
You received 550xp in Leatherworking

"Hey, Atlas. You make good money with your Leatherworking?" Hercules asked him as they walked through the trees in search of more of the panthers.

"A fair amount. Nothing all that great but I'm hoping if I can level it up more I can use it to make good money," he answered hesitantly.

"That's a shame. See, Herc and I are out here as mercenaries and have decided you're going to give us all your stuff. Judging by your full set of armor we know you must've made a pretty hefty profit since you arrived in game and we aren't interested in slogging through the money grind anymore," Skullcrusher said as they both came to a halt and turned to face him. Seditious grins covered their faces.

"And if I refuse? I doubt you'll be able to attack me since we are in a party and I'm sure once we get back to the city the guards will take my side if you try anything there."

"That's true, but you also forgot who the party leader is. They have the neat ability to kick anyone they choose. Since we didn't sign any kind of contract, we can do whatever we want to you out here. So choose. Hand over everything, or we kill you and take it all anyway," Hercules told him.

Crap, Crap, Crap. Atlas looked around the area for any way to escape the situation. He knew these guys seemed off but just figured it was normal awkwardness from gamers. Now he realized it was because they were asshole player killers. With nowhere to run, he gulped before responding.

"I won't hand anything over to cowardly player killers. Looks like you'll just have to take it."

Atlas lifted his staff up to guard and slid his right leg back to widen his stance and balance himself. Skullcrusher slid his short sword free while Hercules pulled out his two daggers. The images appeared at once as the two figures rushed. Unfortunately, they were conflicting and didn't line up. If he followed one, he would certainly take the attack from the other. He couldn't think of another option, so he followed the motion to block the attack from Hercules. The assassin class surely had nasty surprises that would do crippling damage or give bad debuffs.

His staff twisted in his hands and knocked both of the daggers off course. A small feeling of accomplishment took over before a searing pain lanced through his side. Skullcrusher's short sword hit a glancing blow. The movement he performed to block the assassin's attack pulled him out of the direct path for the warrior, and he hadn't compensated for the difference.

Skullcrusher dealt 8 HP damage to you. (Glancing Blow)

The sword slid free from his side as the fighter pulled it back for another strike. He forced himself to keep fighting and advanced toward Hercules. The assassin looked surprised as the staff swung for his head in a high arc. His blades almost came up high enough to deflect the attack, but he was too slow and the solid thump of the wooden weapon rattled him.

Hercules stumbled to the side, and Atlas continued to the second part of the attack. The red flash lit up his vision, and he followed the change in the image. Twisting his body, he redirected the momentum of the weapon and barely caught the descending blade of the warrior.

The power of the attack rocked him back a step, but he still triggered his Counter ability. Surprise lit up the warrior's eyes, and Atlas assumed he just saw the unnerving red flash. He brought the weapon around in a low spin and cracked the man in the knee, buckling his left leg and causing him to fall to a crouch.

Atlas followed this by activating Blade Chase. A new combo series popped up in his vision and he stepped forward with a thrust directly at the man's chest with the top of the staff. The tip cracked into his sternum and Atlas heard an audible crunch as the warrior cried out in pain. The image led him into the second attack as the staff pivoted and clipped the fighter in his temple. The last strike was interesting as it required him to spin the staff one full rotation before coming back down onto the man's shoulder. It made little sense at first until the attack landed.

The added speed from the rotation caused the staff to hit with significant force and the warrior crumpled to the ground, clutching his arm.

You dealt 3 HP damage to Hercules with Double Slash. (Interrupted)
You countered Skullcrusher for 3 HP damage.
You dealt 16 HP damage to Skullcrusher with Blade Chase. (Critical)

"How dare you," hissed the assassin as pain
erupted in Atlas' back. He spun to see the
fighter back on his feet with his daggers in
hand.

*Hercules dealt 8 HP damage to you with
Shiv.*

"I don't know how you managed that long
combo on Skull, but I won't sit around while
you cheat the system. Looks like I have to
take you out quick."
"That's rich. A worthless player killer
blaming me for being a cheater. Maybe if you
learned the game instead of trying to screw
people over, you wouldn't be in this
predicament."
Atlas made a move before Hercules could. He
dashed forward with his Double Slash. The
first attack landed a solid hit to his side,
but the assassin deflected the second attack.

*You dealt 3 HP damage to Hercules with
Double Slash. (Interrupted)*

With a grin, he charged back at Atlas. The
evil gleam in the man's eye took him off guard
and caused him to step backward. His mind
caught up with him and watched the image
moving to counter the blow, but he couldn't
match the speed with his delay. The first
dagger plunged into his stomach, causing him
to buckle forward and grasp his belly in pain.
Hercules never slowed and spun to lodge the
other blade into his kidney while pulling his
first blade free.

Atlas swung his staff around and Hercules
jumped backward to avoid the hit. A warm
feeling trickled down his back and Atlas
reached back to touch the spot. His hand came
forward with a bright splotch of red blood.
*Damn. Damage over time effect can be nasty. On
the bright side, that means healing them
closed should stop the bleed.*

He needed to cast a healing spell, but he
didn't want Hercules to attack while he
attempted it. Instead, he chose Entangle to
lock the fighter in place. Entangle was also
faster to cast than the healing spell.

Activating the ability, he concentrated on
the power as it rose in him. He followed the
quick, swirling motions and finished the spell
by pointing both hands at his target. Vines
burst from the ground and caught Hercules as
he dashed toward Atlas. They twisted around
his legs and rose all the way to his waist.
Thorny protrusions stabbed into the assassin's
legs and he grimaced. With a small sigh of
relief, Atlas turned to his Nurture spell.

The power flooded into him, and he
concentrated on the motions. The spell
completed with no problems and the magic
soaked into him.

Great. Now to finish this assassin. He took a step forward to attack the trapped fighter when the hair on the back of his neck stood on end and a chill permeated his being. *The warrior!*

The thought hit him too late as a blade smashed into his shoulder. The sword dug in deep and pain like molten fire burned through his arm. The sword ripped free, and another strike followed in a sweeping side slash, digging into his side. Ribs cracked and crunched as the blade punched through and the force caused him to trip backward. He twisted with the fall and jabbed the end of his staff into the ground to halt his motion. Sliding his feet back under him, he steadied himself and looked toward the fighter.

Skullcrusher dealt 18 HP damage to you with Furious Rush. (Critical)

The warrior looked enraged and a red coloring flushed his face. Atlas swore he saw a literal red tinge around the man's irises. A chopping sound caused him to look toward Hercules and he watched the man methodically cutting the vines away from himself. I have to keep them separated to have a chance at this. A glance at his status didn't comfort him.

| **HP:** 44 |
| **Mana:** 60 |

If I can Entangle the warrior, I should be able to get another heal spell in before the assassin gets free.

He activated the ability, but the warrior didn't wait. Skullcrusher dashed at him again, and Atlas continued his spell. The furious look on the fighter's face worried him, and he almost made the mistake of trying to move faster than the spell required. The short sword arced for his side again, but his spell wasn't complete. Knowing this was going to be unpleasant, Atlas closed his eyes.

The blade sunk into his side with a meaty thump, and his teeth ground in pain. Luckily, his focus paid off as the spell completed a moment later. Opening his eyes, he saw the vines fly from the soil and wrap around Skullcrusher's legs. This also allowed him to see the image he needed to counter the second swing. With a force of will, he lifted his staff and deflected the second attack.

Rage fueling his reaction, he activated Counter again. Instead of following the image he saw pop up, Atlas changed it up. He dropped to his favorite hold and gripped two hands along the bottom of the staff. The rage-filled baseball swing that followed would've made a MLB player proud as the end of his staff smashed into the man's jaw and caused him to crumble over backward, legs still trapped by vines.

You discovered Heavy Counter!
You dealt 9 HP damage to Skullcrusher with Heavy Counter.

The anger of the situation fueled him further, and he activated Blade Chase again. Skullcrusher struggled back to a knee and held his jaw tenderly with one hand. He never even saw the first attack as Atlas' staff connected with his chest. The spinning staff then clipped his shoulder before the final blow hit him in the neck.

You dealt 12 HP damage to Skullcrusher with Blade Chase.

"You're going to pay for that," screeched Hercules and Atlas turned to see him cutting free from the last of the vines. With no time to waste, he activated Nurture again and began the spell cast. The last vine fell free and Hercules dashed forward. *He can't get to me before I finish this spell. Will just have to make sure I block his attack.*
The assassin blurred in his vision as a slight haze covered his body and he sprung forward at tremendous speed. The distance between them narrowed in a heartbeat, and Atlas tried the same trick as last time. With blades heading for him, he closed his eyes and tried to cast the spell by memory.
Instead of the piercing pain he expected, a solid thump hit him in the chest and his spell fizzled. The built up magic backlashed into Atlas and it felt like his head would explode for a few moments.

Hercules dealt 3 HP damage to you with Kick.
Hercules interrupted your Nurture cast with Kick. Spell backlash dealt 4 damage to you.

Atlas opened his eyes and scrambled to deflect the incoming attack. He was slightly off and the assassin's blades cut a shallow glancing blow. His staff knocked the follow up combo attack away, and he activated Counter. The image led his swing and Hercules whimpered as the staff hit his side.

Blade Chase followed, and the crunch of Hercules' sternum sent a smile across Atlas' face. *Worthless PKers get what they deserve.* The two follow up attacks cracked across his face and he fell to the ground.

Hercules dealt 3 HP damage to you with Double Slash. (Glancing)
You dealt 3 HP damage to Hercules with Counter.
You dealt 12 HP damage to Hercules with Blade Chase.

Hercules slowly rose back to his feet, and Atlas heard scuffling in the dirt behind him. He turned and watched as Skullcrusher broke through the last of the vines and stood straight. *This is hopeless. I know Skullcrusher has 100 total health and Hercules' max health is 80. I haven't even taken half of either of their health yet and I'm below half.*

"Let's finish him, Skull. He can't have much more health left. Attack at the same time. Doesn't look like he can use his trickery on both of us at once."

The warrior nodded, and they both ran at Atlas. He followed the images and deflected the assassin's attack, but took the full force of the short sword. He stepped backward, but the second swing was already heading for him from each. Deflecting the warrior's attack, the assassin's blades punched into his side. *Can't let them complete a combo or they get the bonus damage.*

Skullcrusher dealt 7 damage to you with Furious Rush. (Interrupted)
Hercules dealt 5 damage to you with Double Slash. (Interrupted)

The two turned smiles at each other seeing the damage they inflicted and charged in again. Atlas sighed. *Well, if I'm going to die. I might as well get a little satisfaction out of it.*
Both fighters launched their attacks again, but this time, Atlas focused on Hercules and deflected his attack. Ignoring the pain from Skullcrusher's attack, he activated Heavy Counter and dropped his grip on the staff. The home-run swing caught the small assassin in the jaw and sent him flying. Not wanting to waste this moment of satisfaction, he followed the move with Blade Chase and grinned when the last attack landed a solid crack into his nose. The second combo attack of Skullcrusher landed as he closed the distance, and he winced at the pain.

You dealt 9 damage to Hercules with Heavy Counter.
You dealt 12 damage to Hercules with Blade Chase.

Skullcrusher dealt 14 damage to you with Furious Rush.

"For fuck's sake, kill him already," Hercules squealed through his hands as he rolled on the ground clutching his nose.

Atlas charged toward Skullcrusher while his buddy was down and activated his Double Slash. The first blow flew toward his face, and the clumsy warrior missed the block.

"You guys will win this fight, but I promise if we meet again, I'll kill you both. You won't be able to hide from me anywhere," Atlas spat as he moved to his second swing.

The threat must've unnerved Skullcrusher because he froze on the second attack and took the hit directly to the stomach. The air burst from the warrior with an audible *whoosh*. He readied himself to attack again when a stabbing pain hit his back. Turning to see what happened, he saw the face of Hercules and watched his blades raise and fall again for the second attack. They slid into his back and the quick burst of pain turned into a dull ache as his body collapsed. His vision dimmed until nothing but blackness remained.

Hercules dealt 12 damage to you with Double Slash.
You died.

Chapter 9

Starting Over

The comfy lounge chair and large TV appeared to him again as the countdown timer for his respawn started. Instead of logging out, Atlas fumed for a few minutes at the fight.

I will get those guys back.

While waiting, Atlas played another classic game. Giant fighting frogs entertained him as he beat up bad guys. The timer finally counted to zero and his vision faded again. Atlas sat up in a rush and looked around.

You lost 208 experience because of your death. (35% of current level at level 5)

He groaned to himself as the fight came back to him. The starting clothes he arrived in greeted him when he looked at himself. The small table near the bed held two bags he recognized. His Woodworking Tool Bag and Leatherworking Tool Bag. *They must stay with me since you need the skill to use them. Guess they are soulbound objects.*

A buzzing noise sounded, and he looked around the room. Nothing in the area looked out of place and he focused inward. A small red icon lit up on the edge of his view and he selected it.

You only have 5 minutes of game time left before you must log out.

Damn respawn timer! Guess I have to start over again next time I log in. Atlas walked to the door and checked to make sure it was locked before falling back on the bed. He closed his eyes and the message he expected popped up.

Do you wish to log off? Yes/No.

Selecting *Yes*, he felt a pull on his mind before he woke to whirring noises and flashing lights. Tubes slipped back into the top of the capsule behind his head. The helmet gently retracted, and the capsule popped open. Jean stared at him with a big smile plastered on her face.

"Good to see you again. How've you been the last couple days?" Atlas asked.

"Not too bad. Been busy keeping up with all the gamers here, but luckily you all have spread out pretty reasonably with your logouts. There are a few times it gets hectic when multiple want to jump out all at once, but we manage. Have a good time in the game?"

"Was having a great time until a couple losers killed me. Oh well, that's a downfall of a game like this. Always people who are assholes no matter what world you're in. You going to be here in two days? I'll be back on Thursday morning to go back in. My last shift ends Wednesday night."

"Yep! I probably won't be here when you log off, though. I have Saturday off. What do you do, if you don't mind me asking?"

"I'm a nurse at a medical clinic. Not the most glamorous job, but someone has to do it," he told her with a smile.

"That's so sweet. As much as I'd like to stay and chat, I have another person waking up in less than an hour and I think you better head down to check out before you have to make a mad dash again like last time," she told him with a chuckle.

His face flushed red knowing she'd seen that embarrassing race to the bathroom, and he agreed. A quick wave and a goodbye and he was off down the stairs. The attendant near the hallway waved him through when he confirmed he knew the way, and Atlas headed straight to the bathroom.

Finally relieved and ready to go, he hopped in the elevator and ascended back to the main floor. The entire trip to the parking garage, he formulated plans to get back on his feet when he logged in. Luckily for him, he had two professions to lean on. He just needed to get a few things so he could get started.

Firing up his car, he stopped and got a burger on the way home. The couch beckoned to him when he entered his apartment, but he caught a whiff of his funk and redirected his path to the shower. The warm water felt heavenly as he scrubbed off God only knew what chemicals were on his skin. His sweat seemed to have a wicked odor from the machine regulating his body in the pod. He tossed on a pair of basketball shorts and a t-shirt. Making sure he set his alarm for work in the morning, he sat on the couch and turned on a rerun of one of his favorite shows.

* * *

Incessant beeping noise filled his mind and jolted him awake. Atlas looked around in confusion while his eyes tried to focus. The colorful screen of the TV was the first sight that registered to him. The gang had just unmasked their latest villain, and he was blaming the meddling kids for foiling his plan.

Patting his hand around him, he finally located the source of his noise as he gripped his phone and brought it to his face. It was 6:00 in the morning and his alarm wanted to make sure he made it to work on time.

"Must've fallen asleep watching TV," he grumbled as he ran a hand over his face. A flick of his finger silenced the alarm, and he got up and dressed in his scrubs.

The refrigerator looked like a barren desert when he opened it. It was usually too much hassle to stock food. With only him there, he never needed to cook. There was a soda in the door that he grabbed. Coffee wasn't his thing, so his caffeine fix usually came from the sugary drinks.

He grabbed his keys and headed out the door, deciding he'd grab some fast food for breakfast on the way to work. The line was fast, and he zoomed through the drive through before pulling up at work. His morning was slow and their patient load was small.

During his lunch break, he tried to call Keenan but got his voicemail. *Must still be in the game. We are almost on exactly opposite schedules.* Atlas left him a message to call when he got out and told him he wasn't logging back in until Thursday morning.

Flipping through his phone screen, he searched for Divine Genesis. Countless articles popped up. Most of them talked about how fast the game was growing and how the marketplace was already ripe for investment. Atlas altered his search and added forum to the end. The first result was a site called Divine Genesis Fanatics.

He clicked on it and it brought him to a standard forum site filled with categories. Many of them were common, such as general discussion and recommendations for similar games. The one that intrigued Atlas the most was the Tutorials section. Tapping on it, he found a plethora of articles, all with different guides. There was a standard guide for each class. A few of them talked about the Addition system.

He tapped on one called Mastering Additions and saw a post from a person named Ladygamer1224. Her write up was good and covered many of the details he already knew. This player must've talked to the NPCs as well. She described how you could get new additions by mastering the previous one. Supposedly, there were up to 7-hit combos available in the game, but you needed to master each rank to attain it. The post even said to master the additions you needed to line up the motions it showed for the ability perfectly. Mastering it would also help your body react naturally to the attack and make minor adjustments as needed on its own.

The idea that someone was so forthcoming with information that could prove game changing at later levels inspired him. In the spirit of the game, he registered to the site as AtlDruid25 and replied to the post. He added the details that Master Proth had given him. The process was arduous to describe, but he did his best. Outlining the idea of completing the move subconsciously might help someone else reach the limit they needed to find. When he hit that final reply button, he sat back in his chair with a smile on his face. It felt good to help people, even though other players just screwed him over.

"Atlas! We need you in exam room three to help with this procedure," Doctor Sako called.

With a sigh, he put his phone away and returned to work.

***

The lights were out in his apartment, and only the dim glow of the TV illuminated the space. Atlas was close to dozing off when a buzzing noise startled him, and he frantically patted along the couch to find the source. Looking at the screen on his phone, he saw Keenan's name pop up and smiled. A quick swipe answered the call.

"What's up, Keenan?"

"Not much, man. Just leaving the Gaia building and listened to your voicemail. Wanted to call and reach out before I passed out for the night. Sure I'll still be asleep when you head off to login in the morning."

"How's the game treating you so far? What level did you get to?" Atlas asked.

"After those hints you told me it's been a breeze. I immediately found a trainer and learned Alchemy. I've made a handful of bomb ass potions and the few I didn't keep sold really well. I also picked up the Counter ability and even bought one additional skill from the local weaponmaster. All-in-all, I'm at level 7 and moving steadily forward."

"Damn, that's nice. I was doing fantastic myself and moved to the second city. Picked up Woodworking in addition to my Leatherworking. The more advanced gear from Leatherworking that I unlocked in my second city sells for very good prices. I teamed up with two other players and we went to complete a few quests, but the asshats betrayed me and attacked me. They ended up killing me, but I got in decent damage on them first. Now I get to start over on my armor and weapons. Luckily I can make everything I need so just have to grind."

"Ah, that's whack. I've only come across a few other players, but they were more interested in grinding or crafting and didn't want to team up. Why would you party up at such a low level, anyway?"

"Takes me too long to kill stuff by myself. At least it did until I figured out the best way to combo counters with one skill I learned from the weaponmaster. If I incorporate it into the fights like I did with the two players, I should be able to speed up my grinding. When they pissed me off, my anger reminded me of the abilities."

"Well, at least you have a game plan. The death penalty wasn't too bad, was it?"

"Took thirty-five percent of the current level's experience. It seems to get worse because that was just the level five penalty. Better than losing all the experience for the level, though."

"No doubt. Have you mastered your first addition yet?"

"Not yet. One of the NPCs I talked to me gave me a hint and I'm going to try it out while grinding. You essentially have to clear your mind and let your body do it naturally if you want to match the strike perfectly. I think it's like the old saying about warriors and their muscle memory taking over. Not sure if it works or not, but I'll let you know if it does."

"Why didn't you enter a contract before you left town with those PKer's?" Keenan asked.

"A contract? What are you talking about?"

"Well, well, I finally get to teach the almighty Atlas something about the game. I was asking questions around my second city when I found out about contracts. When you party up with people you can find contract makers at the local adventurer's guild or registrar's office. These contracts can have any language you choose in them, such as loot rules or criteria for leaving the party. It also has the added benefit of distinctly forbidding attacking each other. Most people choose that option with some wording for loot rules and then make it where the people can't drop the party before returning to the safety of the town."

"Well, son of a bitch. That must've been why they acted odd as we left town and then didn't invite me to the party until we walked out of the gate. They wanted to see if I would ask for a contract first to see if I knew any better," Atlas said as he slapped his forehead. "Now I feel like an idiot for not asking around as I preach to you. I just rushed into a party without looking into it."

"Can't even follow your own advice, huh?" Keenan asked with a chuckle, "Oh well, I bet you won't make that mistake again. Knowing you, you'll bounce back from that death without a problem. You want to hurry because I heard rumor of an event going down in a few days. Supposed to be a decent prize that was awarding gold."

"Gold? That stuff is worth a decent amount of money in real world currency right now. I may have to play this game full time to pay the bills if things pan out just right. I've always joked about playing games for a living, but with this game it may truly be possible."

"I could see myself doing it as well. I actually have work for the next two days so I won't be logging in until later. I'm headed to bed since I have to get up early. Hit me up when you get out of the game and let me know how things went. If I'm logged in, just leave me a message so I'll know." Keenan said.

"Sounds good. Talk to ya later." Atlas told him and hung up.

A look at the clock told him it was only 8:00PM, and he stretched out on the couch. Hunger hit him as he remembered he skipped dinner. He struggled to finish waking up as he stared at his phone screen.

"You win this time, stomach," he grumbled as he tapped on the contact and placed his call.

Thirty minutes later a knock sounded on his door and he pulled himself from the couch. The smell of melted cheese assaulted him as he opened the door and saw a pizza box thrust in his face. He paid the delivery guy and scarfed down a few pieces before wandering off to the bathroom and cleaning up. Hair still partially damp, he fell to the bed and closed his eyes.

* * *

The morning dawned earlier than Atlas normally cared for but, since it meant he was heading back to Gaia to jump into the game, he grudgingly got out of bed. Scarfing down a few pieces of cold pizza was the only task he accomplished before dashing out of the door and straight for his car.

Traffic was light, making the trip fly by, and before he knew it, he was walking back through the glass doors into the gaming auditorium at Gaia. A quick check-in at the desk near the elevators and they ushered him down to the pods.

"Hi Jean," he called as he walked to his assigned pod and saw the technician waiting for him.

"Oh, Atlas. I guess it really is Thursday already." she said as she tapped the button on the side of her watch for the display to light up, "Time really flies sometimes."

"How've you been?" Atlas asked while she checked over the pod and inspected the cable harness near the top.

"Busy as usual but as you can tell, it sure makes the day go by quick. How was work for you? You still going to be logging off early Saturday?"

"Work was the same old boring stuff. A stuffy nose here, a cut there, nothing too wild this time. I still plan on logging off on Saturday unless something comes up."

"Well, that's a bummer. Guess I really won't see you when you log off. Maybe I'll catch you when you come back in. Let's get you hooked up and back in the game. You have some catching up to do if I remember correctly. I believe some losers ganged up and killed you. Time to get you back on your feet."

She ushered him into the pod and settled the helmet on his head. A few button presses on the control panel and Atlas watched the lid close and seal the pod. A few more taps on the pad before she looked to Atlas, and a muffled "Good luck" echoed through the pod before his vision faded to blackness.

***

Atlas opened his eyes to the room at the inn. A quick glance around showed everything in the place it had been when he logged off. The door was still firmly locked and his tool bags were still nearby. Sitting up, he grabbed the bags and tied them to his waist.

With a heft, he stood up and walked downstairs. The innkeeper sent an appraising look his way before shrugging and returning to his work. Atlas wasn't sure if the look was because of his clothing change or confusion on how he ended up back upstairs without ever passing by the innkeeper himself.

When he exited the inn and entered the streets, his mind started turning over his problems. He needed to decide on where to go, so he ran the list through his head.

I need to get a weapon.

I need to make more armor.

Those were his two primary goals to get back on his feet. Gaining levels and things would happen naturally if he could make those two happen. Since he had Woodworking now, all he needed to find was some usable wood. That should be easy. *There is a forest nearby, after all.* Finding something he could use before a monster found him might not be possible.

Armor might be a problem. Assuming he could find a weapon or kill animals with his bare hands, he didn't have any salt to cure the hides. He had all the tools he needed for everything else.

I guess I have to do it the hard way and grind a few mobs without armor to sell their meat. That should give me enough to buy some salt. That'll definitely depend on me making a weapon before finding hostile animals.

An inspection of his status showed him something he'd forgotten. Before they betrayed him, he completed a quest for the guard at the gate. Checking the quest, he saw it offered 60 copper as a reward. *Not a lot, but definitely enough to buy a surplus of salt.*

Atlas followed the roads on his map to the gate he'd exited on his ill-fated journey. It took him a few minutes, but he found the guard that gave him the quest and turned it in.

Quest - Cock Thieves	
Requirements Level 5 Quest Rarity: Common Quest Reward: 80 experience, 60 copper coins.	Description: You killed 8 foxes, as requested. Turn it in to the guards.

A quick trip to the leatherworking shop showed him Master Trailia's perplexed expression. He didn't wear it long as Atlas guessed he figured out he died and lost his stuff.

"Looks like you ran afoul of some trouble," the leatherworker finally said with the closest thing Atlas ever heard to mirth from the woman.

"You could say that. Was ambushed out in the forest. Now starting back over."

"Ambushed? Bandits out in the forest again?" the leatherworker asked with concern.

"Of the Reborn variety. I doubt they'll bother merchant operations. They just wanted my gear and coins."

"Well, that's unfortunate. What can I do for you?"

"Just need to buy some salt before I go out and hunt for more hides."

Master Trailia merely nodded and waved her hand, causing the menu to appear in Atlas' view. He spent all 60 copper to buy 30 pinches of salt. At first, he considered only buying a handful and then buying a cheap weapon, but he overruled that thought. Having to scrap an inferior weapon later was more hassle. Finding one piece of wood should be pretty easy. A small wand would work for him to start.

Tying the small bag of salt to his pants, he waved goodbye and left the shop. His minimap showed the explored area they quested in before they betrayed him, and Atlas decided he wanted to start in familiar territory. Hopefully, the two betrayers moved from the zone. Deciding to stay close to the town, he scoured the nearby forest in search of anything he could use.

With the surrounding area being predominantly forest, he figured finding wood to use would be a breeze. He quickly found out that wasn't the case. Most of the trees he couldn't do anything with. There was a small hatchet in his tool bag for woodworking, but when he tried to use it on the larger trees or their branches, it bounced off without a scratch and he received a message.

Unable to harvest wood from this source.

The lack of information was a little frustrating, so he continued his search. It took him a solid hour to find anything of use, but luckily he'd only run into non-aggressive animals such as squirrels and rabbits. They were perfectly content to let him leave without a fight.

The break he needed finally arrived when he stumbled upon an old, dead tree. The bark looked dull and gray, and the structure had fallen over and lay on the ground. A splintered stump showed the tree fell due to age, disease, or a storm since it wasn't cleanly cut. When he walked up and swung the hatchet at the tree, it dug in deep with a resounding thud.

With hope finally blossoming in his soul,
Atlas jubilantly swung away, chips of wood
flying with each strike. The limb he targeted
fell to the ground with one final chop and he
picked it up. Not wasting time, he selected
his Create Rough Wood Log ability and
activated it. The hatchet disappeared into his
tool bag as he drew out a large knife. The
blade cleanly swept along the edges of the log
in rapid movements as dead bark and the gray
exterior sliced free, exposing the dried
center of the wood.

With a Rough Log in hand, he contemplated
his choice. At first he considered trying out
a wand, but fell back on the staff. His skill
with spells wasn't that great, and he'd gotten
better at hand to hand combat. He considered
making both, but without armor and a belt he
had nowhere to store the extra weapon yet.

Decision made, he selected Create Basic
Wood Staff and the crafting process began. The
finished product rested in his hands a minute
later, and he breathed a sigh of relief. He
hadn't realized it, but running through the
forest without a weapon had his nerves on
edge. The weight of the wood in his grip
settled some of those nerves and a little of
the tension fell away from his shoulders.

*You received 5 experience in Woodworking
for harvesting Raw Wood Log.*
*You received 15 experience in Woodworking
for Create Rough Wood Log.*
*You received 35 experience in Woodworking
for Create Basic Wood Staff.*

Time to kill stuff!

The first few victims of his rampage faced
a far different Atlas than before. His fight
with the two player-killers showed him the
true strength of playing a defender instead of
aggressively attacking. At his low level, his
Double Slash did minimal damage. With his
basic tier weapon, it wasn't much. The Counter
combo with Blade Chase did far more, even with
a subpar weapon.

Starting the fights with a Charge and a
Double Slash was his go to combo, but after
that he played the turns well. Patiently
waiting on the attacks allowed him to
anticipate them. To his surprise, he finally
noticed patterns to the attacks from different
creatures.

Squirrels, for instance, favored three
different attacks. They rotated through these
three in almost the same pattern in every
fight. A low biting attack, a leaping attack,
and one attack where they would try to confuse
you with a side dash followed by a charge. It
wasn't long before Atlas could almost predict
their attack before they moved. It made
killing them simple.

As soon as he had the furs, the first item
he created was a belt with the built in
pouches. He'd needed to leave behind some meat
he'd earned from the kills because he had
nowhere to put it. Making a new set of pants
or jerkin wasn't as high of a priority since
he was doing great at dodging attacks.

With pouches for storage, he fought his way back to the downed tree. Not wanting to waste the chance for experience and a small amount of money, he set to work. The hatchet cut wood far faster than it would've taken him to complete the task in the actual world, but the size of this tree slowed his work. In the end, after almost an hour of woodcutting, he had a neat stack of twenty Raw Wood Logs. Those logs quickly turned into Rough Wood Logs before he finally used all twenty to make forty Basic Wood Wands.

You received 100 experience in Woodworking for chopping Raw Wood Log x 20.
You received 300 experience in Woodworking for Create Rough Wood Log x 20.
Success! You've reached level 5 in Woodworking.
You received 500 experience in Woodworking for Create Basic Wood Wand x 40.

Most of the wands he left in the woods near the tree. It wasn't feasible for him to carry them. The pouches on his belt were only so large, and while they worked more like bags in games, these were small and had limited slots. He kept five of the small wands. One might be handy for spell casting and the other four he planned to sell for a little money.

The work became monotonous after a while. His grinding continued as he ran in search of different animals that he could skin. It also took him some more time because he kept an eye out for the quest items from his other two quests.

Finding the panther fur was a little depressing since he had to keep it intact and couldn't use it to make armor. The Hippoblooms were a little difficult to harvest. Oddly enough, the plant had a row of outer teeth that looked vaguely like tusks from a hippopotamus. The edges were very sharp, and you needed to reach inside the sharp teeth to pull out the bloom. The plants caused more damage to Atlas than the animals did.

During his hunting he stumbled across another small dead tree. This one still stood upright, but the lack of leaves and graying bark displayed its condition effectively. Atlas chopped 5 logs worth out of it and made them into staves. The staves were worth slightly more experience than the wands and, since he wasn't carrying them back to town, the experience was more important.

By the time he headed back for the village, he replaced all of his armor. He used the advanced patterns for those he'd learned but had to settle with the basic pieces for the others. Hopefully, when he returned to the city, he could buy some new patterns. A glance at his notification showed him how far he'd come during the expedition.

You received 1165 total Leatherworking experience.
Success! You've reached level 8 in Leatherworking.
You received 250 total Woodworking experience.
Success! You've reached level 6 in Woodworking.
You received 920 experience.
Success! You've reached Levels 6 and 7.

Atlas ended the trek with roughly thirty-five animals dead. Eight of those were for the panther hides he needed for his quest. It took him twenty-six hides total to remake his complete armor set, leaving him one spare hide. His belt pouches were stuffed full of meat and the handful of wands he saved. They wouldn't allow him to place anything else in them currently.

His level ups came with another four attribute points. Two of them went into Constitution, bringing his maximum health up to 100, while the other two he placed into Intellect bringing the maximum mana up to 100.

Feeling good about the trip and his achievements, he walked back into town. A crowd gathered in the major thoroughfare near the gate and Atlas peered around to see everyone in excited conversation. Curious about the turn of events, he gently waded through the crowd and closed in on the plaza ahead.

A man in a flamboyant costume that reminded Atlas of the old depictions of court jesters stood on an elevated stage with a scroll unrolled. His gaudy outfit of red and yellow made him easy to spot, but his sonorous voice naturally drew his attention.

"And it's with great pleasure we announce the first event of the season. The Wild Hunt will commence in four days' time. All who wish to enroll in the expedition need to pay the fee and sign up at a registrar's office. If the hunt is successful, those on the team will receive a five gold prize!"

The crowd burst into loud conversation as Atlas digested the news. *Five gold prize? This must be the event that Keenan told me about. I have to sign up for it!*

Chapter 10

The First Event

Excitement buzzed through the crowd as the people in the city struck up random conversations throughout the plaza. Atlas felt a sense of excitement build up at the thought of such a fantastic prize. Five gold wasn't a fortune, but it was a very reputable amount of money if he cashed it in.

It took him time to sift through the crowd and break free on the other side. Atlas didn't know where the registrar's office was, but he saw the direction the announcer walked in and figured to follow them.

Shortly down the road, he spotted a guard and waved.

"Excuse me, sir. Do you know where the registrar's office is?"

"Ah, caught wind of the hunt, huh? Well, the office is down this road. Follow the path until you pass two intersections and it's the first building on the right. Has a sign with an unfurled scroll and quill out front."

"Thanks," Atlas blurted as he continued on his path at a faster pace.

The buildings flew by. He wasn't running, but the speed he walked might as well have been. His heart sank a little as he neared the building. A long line already extended from the door. There must've been forty people in front of him. Resigned to his fate, he walked up and stood in line, waiting his turn.

The crowd shuffled away much faster than he expected. Most people walked into the office to reappear outside less than a minute later. Most of them looked pretty depressed. A name caught his attention as one patron left. The man's tag showed him to be LadyKiller. Knowing it had to be an actual person, Atlas waved to get the man's attention.

When he finally noticed Atlas, he wore an odd look on his face, but he eventually approached.

"What's up?" LadyKiller asked.

"Yep, was hoping you could tell me what's up with the event?"

"What?" was his initial answer before he stopped and looked at Atlas carefully, "You're one of us, aren't you? Hard to tell by your name. Could be a real name or an in-game name. They are signing people up, but the entry fee is high. Twenty silver just to enter the event."

"Twenty silver? With no guarantee of a prize? That's pretty steep."

"I guess it's their way to keep from getting far too many people in the event," LadyKiller said with a shrug, "Either way, good luck to you."

"Thanks for the info. Catch ya later."

Damn. I'm not even close to twenty silver. Guess I won't be able to sign up. I'll just ask how long I have until they close sign ups.

The line moved quickly enough that he was in the building less than fifteen minutes later. The entrance was a wide open lobby space and on the opposite wall were two windows that looked similar to bank teller booths. One counter had a customer there, so Atlas continued to the second.

"Hello. Interested in signing up for the Wild Hunt." Atlas told the man behind the counter.

"Very well. Hand over your twenty silver registration fee and I'll fill out your paperwork," the person answered with a very monotone and bored voice.

"About that. I don't have the twenty silver fee yet. Can you tell me how long I have until sign ups close?"

The teller let out an audible sigh before answering in the same bland tone, "Registration for the wild hunt closes at the end of the business day tomorrow. After that point, no new participants may sign up."

"So I have a little over a day to scrounge up the money? How is the event structured?"

"The event will be a competition between teams. They will split the number of registered people into ten equal groups and will declare the first group to kill all of their targets the winner and receive the five gold prize."

"Are there any other prizes?" Atlas asked.

"I can't answer that question. Are you interested in signing up?"

"I will be, but I have some money-making to do first. I'll be back before the end of the day tomorrow with my fee."

Atlas turned and jogged for the door. *I have some fighting to do. My best bet will be leather armor. I've advanced it far enough to sell the second tier of gear. That stuff fetches a good price here. If I can sell enough of that, I'll easily have what I need to enter the contest.*

Atlas wasted no time and dashed straight for the leatherworker's shop. There should be some good patterns available since he'd gained two levels since his last time here. His pouches were on the verge of bursting with the load of meat and the handful of wands he had to sell.

"Greetings Master Trailia. I have some stuff I'd like to sell."

"Right to the point. Very well, Atlas," she said as she flicked her hand and the menu popped up.

He looked through his inventory and then tapped on the Sell button. It didn't take long for him to select the bundles of food in the bag. Once he acknowledged them, they appeared on the screen in the Sell box. He left the wands in his bag because he was sure he could get a better price for them at the woodworker's place.

Hitting the Sell button, a bag of coins appeared on the counter in front of him. He walked over and picked it up. The coins totaled up to 1 silver and 80 copper. The meat wasn't worth a lot, but it added up quickly.

A quick tap on the menu switched back to the buy screen. Scrolling to the bottom he found three new patterns, each for twenty copper.

Leatherworking - Basic Leather Backpack	
Requirements Leatherworking Level 7 Rarity: Common Requirements: 5 Cured Light Hide, 6 Leather Sinew Thread	Description: Create a backpack made of leather. It allows for far more storage than standard belt pouches.

Leatherworking - Basic Reinforced Leather Jerkin	
Requirements Leatherworking Level 7 Rarity: Common Requirements: 8 Cured Light Hide, 8 Leather Sinew Thread	Description: Create a reinforced leather Jerkin. This has higher defense and durability than the basic jerkin.

Leatherworking - Basic Reinforced Leather Bracers	
Requirements Leatherworking Level 8 Rarity: Common Requirements: 4 Cured Light Hide, 4 Leather Sinew Thread	Description: Create a set of reinforced leather bracer. These have higher defense and durability than the basic bracers.

Atlas bought those and immediately reinvested money into salt. He bought 60 pinches of salt for 1 silver and 20 copper, all the remaining money he had. *I can make that back fast.*

There was no time wasted as he dismissed the menu and quickly waved to Trailia before rushing through the streets to the woodworker's shop. Walking in, he greeted the man behind the counter and immediately asked him to sell stuff. The menu popped up, and he selected four wands and hit Sell.

This only made him 25 copper. Two new skills greeted him on the buy menu.

Woodworking - Create Basic Wood Toggles	
Requirements Woodworking Level 5 Rarity: Common Requirements: 2 Rough Wood Log	Description: Create small wooden toggles used by other professions.

Woodworking - Create Sturdy Wood Rods	
Requirements Woodworking Level 6 Rarity: Common Requirements: 2 Rough Wood Log	Description: Create sturdy rods of wood.

Neither of them seemed very important. The basic skill was only 10 copper, but the sturdy rod ability was 20 copper. Atlas spent his 20 copper buying the sturdy skill. The higher level abilities gave more experience, and the items usually sold for more.

Skills bought and out of the way, he
continued his trek out of the building and
headed for the exterior wall. He considered
running by Master Proth's place, but decided
it would be futile. Barkskin would be
available, but he didn't have the copper to
learn it. Since his technique was so much
better now, he didn't really need it. Once he
had the money he needed and entered the event,
he could use the rest after that to get his
skills.

Crowds of people still gathered around. The
press of bodies was frustrating as he tried to
work his way out of the city. On multiple
occasions he considered physically barreling
over people to get through, but decided
against it. If he got thrown into some kind of
jail by the guards, there would be no way he
could grind the money he needed in time.

A sigh of relief escaped his lips as the
gate came into sight and he dashed through and
out into the open field beyond the city. The
breeze whipped his hair and the crispness to
the air caused him to suck in large gulps.
Being pressed in that crowd for so long meant
he spent that entire time smelling dirty
people and the city. Out here, it was clean
air.

It didn't take long for him to find animals
on his path. His focus was the same as before.
He found animals with fur and focused on
nailing the counter attacks more than he did
the initial two-hit combo. This all changed
when he encountered a small bear.

The fights with the normal creatures were straightforward. The bear wasn't much different. At first, the size of the animal worried him. Going from fighting a squirrel or a fox to a small bear was unnerving. The first round of combat quickly relieved his fears. It started exactly like all the others. Except it wasn't.

Atlas dashed in and activated his two-hit combo. The first image showed up and he followed it. The motion felt smooth and natural. By the time the second hit came, he already knew where it would be. This strike was a quick thrust to the animal's snout. The bear grunted as it fell backward.

You dealt 6 HP damage to Small Bear.

Knowing now was the perfect time, Atlas did something he'd never tried before. He stopped thinking. Instead of focusing so hard on the movement and watching the image, he just attacked and let his body take over. The moves had become commonplace. The swings targeted the same parts of the body when performed. Positional awareness could tell him where and how that strike would happen. His swing on the bear would hit the same place if the bear stood on its hind legs or if it was on all four. The only difference would be how he swung the staff to accomplish it.

Diving forward, he activated the two-hit attack and followed the natural feel of the motion. His staff felt like an extension of his body as it swung out and popped the bear in the side of the head. The vibration from the hit caused a tingling feeling in his fingers, but he immediately moved to the next attack by instinct. The resultant thrust hit perfectly on the snout and Atlas heard a light chime in the air. The notification that popped up startled him.

You dealt 6 HP damage to Small Bear.
Rejoice! You mastered Double Slash.
The new combo ability Triple Threat has been added to your skills.

The cheer that filled him by mastering the ability caused him to forget he was in a fight. The paw of the bear struck a solid blow across his chest and sent him tumbling backward.

Small bear dealt 10 HP damage to you with Swipe.

Kicking himself for getting distracted, he rose to his feet and charged in by activating his new Triple Threat ability. His staff swung in a low arc and caught the animal's foot, causing it to stumble. The second swing reversed from the side and clipped it in the shoulder while the final blow was a two-handed strike directly to the top of the head. An audible crack echoed through the clearing as the bear fell to the ground and stopped moving.

You dealt 12 HP damage to Small Bear with Triple Threat.
Small Bear died.
You gained 25 experience.

The three-hit combo did far more damage than his old one. That extra hit, added with the bonus they seemed to give when completing the entire thing, meant his damage had just increased drastically. *Now if I can get a suitable weapon, I'll be set.*

The day continued on and his grinding stayed the same. More times than not, he found himself just using the Double Slash attack with the assisted movement from his mastery. When using this, it felt like he was just watching a movie through virtual reality as his body adjusted to changes in movement.

Countering the abilities was the only aspect he needed to focus on. When he ran into the larger enemies, he used the three-hit combo instead. A pleasant side effect of the larger animals, such as the bear, was that they had two hides worth of skin on them. This helped speed up his grinding process even more.

The first item he made was the backpack. With this new piece slung over his back, it vastly improved his carrying capacity. Being able to take the skins and meat from the kills and quickly drop them into the bag was nice. It also meant he could fight a lot more before he needed to stop and craft items. Making the new bracers and jerkin were the next items on the list, and he immediately equipped the reinforced versions, dropping the standard versions into his bag.

The hours sped by and he continued his hunting. The farther he ventured from the city, the larger the animals became. With his new combo, this didn't present a problem. Anytime he took too much damage, he just healed himself and continued fighting. Since mana regenerated on its own, he could afford to use it to fix his HP.

During his travel he found five different trees to harvest. They held thirty lengths of wood between all of them. A couple of them were smaller and only yielded four pieces, but two of the others were massive and he gathered much more from them.

Using those logs, he first turned all the lengths of wood into Rough Wood Logs and then used all 30 of the Rough Wood Logs to make 15 sets of the Sturdy Rods.

You gained 1,800 total experience in Woodworking.
Success! You've reached levels 7 and 8 in Woodworking.

The leatherworking was quick and simple. Atlas made what he thought were the two most useful pieces. With only 70 pinches of salt, it limited him in the amount of leather he had. Using that as the guideline, he made six of the backpacks. Those he was absolutely certain would sell well. To round it out with a little more experience, he made five of the Reinforced Leather Jerkins. Chest armor was usually the most sought after. A blade or arrow in the chest was a far more common way to die than an arrow in the knee.

You gained 1,620 total experience in Leatherworking.

Success! You've reached levels 9 and 10 in Leatherworking.

With the pieces made, he didn't immediately return to town. Instead, he spent time with some more grinding. Fully loaded backpacks hung from him, and pieces of armor hung haphazardly all over any free space on his body. He finally returned to the city. A quick check of his messages showed all of his experience and he collapsed them together to see the extent of his gains from killing animals.

You gained 260 total experience.

The trek back was quiet, and everything avoided him with no issues. The guard waved him through, although they gave him appraising looks. Atlas couldn't blame them. It wasn't every day you saw someone walk by with five chest pieces and multiple bags strapped all over them with small scraps of leather. He'd attached so much stuff to him it was difficult to move.

Before he did anything else, he walked directly back to the leatherworking shop. When he entered, the sound of laughter startled him. A deep bellow echoed through the room, and Atlas looked up in surprise to see Master Trailia on the other end. The woman had the laugh of a three hundred pound jovial innkeeper.

"Well, bless be the Lady, I guess that's one way to pack stuff. Guess you don't have a horse or mule to do it. That's some fine leatherwork," she finally said when she stopped laughing, "Those backpacks are fetching a high price right now with all the Reborn in town. I assume you're in the market to sell?"

"Sure am. Trying to make some money for the hunt."

She nodded at that and flicked the menu toward him. When he selected the first backpack, a devilish grin split his face. The first one listed at 3 silver. Each successive one dropped in price by 10 copper, but that was still an incredible amount. It totaled up to 16 silver and 50 copper. Feeling the end in sight, he selected the first of the jerkins. This one wasn't as high, but he couldn't complain when the first one registered at 2 silver. *The price of these must be dropping. Someone else must be making them. I made more money on the gloves in my first city.*

Selling all five netted him an additional 9 silver. With the transactions complete, he switched back to the buying tab. An additional level meant there should be additional items to make. The last two items to complete his reinforced set waited for him.

Leatherworking - Basic Reinforced Leather Belt	
Requirements Leatherworking Level 9 Rarity: Common Requirements: 5 Cured Light Hide, 5 Leather Sinew Thread	Description: Create a reinforced leather belt. This has higher defense and durability than the basic belt with slightly larger storage pouches.

Leatherworking - Basic Reinforced Leather Coif	
Requirements Leatherworking Level 9 Rarity: Common Requirements: 2 Cured Light Hide, 2 Leather Sinew Thread	Description: Create a reinforced leather coif. This has higher defense and durability than the basic coif.

Both patterns cost 20 copper a piece and he bought them without a second thought. With his purchasing complete, he moved to the Woodworking shop. The 15 sets of Sturdy Rods sold for a respectable 7 silver and 50 copper. The amount confused him because the price remained steady when he sold these. Unlike the armor, it didn't drop by 10 copper every piece.

"Just curious. Why does the price of Sturdy Rods not drop like the armor and weapons?" Atlas asked.

"Oh, the city regulates those. They commonly use sturdy rods as building materials within the city. Because of that, they have a price mandated by the governing council and it doesn't change. It ensures building costs don't wildly fluctuate from time to time."

"Good thinking. Hadn't considered that aspect," Atlas told him with a nod.

The Buying screen was far more interesting this time.

Woodworking - Create Sturdy Wood Braces	
Requirements Woodworking Level 6 Rarity: Common Requirements: 2 Rough Wood Log	Description: Create sturdy braces of wood as building materials.

Woodworking - Create Sturdy Wood Staff	
Requirements Woodworking Level 6 Rarity: Common Requirements: 2 Rough Wood Log	Description: Create a sturdy staff of wood.

He bought both skills and added the skill for wood toggles from before that he skipped out on. Fifty copper lighter wouldn't hurt him right now.

With money in tow, he headed for the registrar's office. On his way, he realized he'd been a fool. Last time he entered town, he was so wrapped up in the hunt, he'd forgotten about the tightly bundled rolls of fur and Hippoblooms in his belt pouches. After he registered for the event, he told himself he'd turn those in.

The office wasn't crowded this time, and he walked in without an issue. The same droll man greeted him and he immediately plopped down twenty silver.

"I'm ready to register for the hunt."

The clerk looked at the coins and slowly picked up the bag. With an exaggerated flourish, he tossed the coins behind him onto another desk and pulled out a sheet of parchment.

"Name?"

"Atlas."

"Just Atlas?"

"Sure."

The clerk sighed but continued.

"Here is your contract," he told him as he flipped the page around, "It details the conditions of the event and the prize as agreed upon. Please sign at the bottom to complete your registration."

The man pushed a small bottle of ink with a quill in it toward him, and Atlas snatched it up. He scribbled a quick approximation of his signature and flipped it back around. The clerk grabbed it and let a glob of wax melt on it in the bottom right corner. While it was still liquid like, he pressed a flat metal disk on it and when the disc lifted, the likeness of the registrar's symbol stood out. The unfurled scroll with a quill stood out in the wax.

"All done. Report to this office at 10:00 in the morning in three days' time for the event. Have a good day."

With that out of the way, the man shooed him away and waved the person behind him forward. No sooner had he breathed a sigh of relief than a message popped up.

Warning. You only have 4 hours of game time left this session.

What timing. At least I got that out of the way. With little time to work, he hurried around the city and found the two quest givers for the other quests. Luckily an icon showed up on his minimap showing their general position. After that, he just had to ask around for them. Those two quests gave him 350 experience and another 1 silver and 40 copper.

A quick trip to Master Proth's place allowed him to buy Barkskin for 50 copper. From there, he beat a hasty retreat for the inn. The clock was running down on his time and he wanted to get to the safety of his room before then. With less than a quarter of an hour to spare, he burst into the inn and waved at the innkeeper. Not even bothering to say hi, he ran straight for the stairs and to his room.

Once inside, he locked the door and promptly fell into the bed and closed his eyes.

Do you wish to log out? Yes/No.

He selected *Yes.*

His time back in the actual world mainly consisted of him rearranging his schedule. With the event in three days, he wanted to make sure he was off. His original intent was to log off for a day and then go back in for two before two more days of work. Since he didn't know how long the event itself would take, he opted to delay his return to the game and picked up an extra shift early. He took a coworkers Monday shift and swapped them for their Wednesday off. This would allow him to log back in first thing Tuesday for the event and stay on until Thursday. Since the developers knew of their own restrictions on game time, he was sure the event wouldn't take over two days at most.

The time crawled by as he waited for his chance to return. He attempted to contact Keenan multiple times, but had no luck. Finally, after the boring days at work, he finally returned to Gaia. Jean was there to greet him this time, and she positively glowed when he spotted her.

"Guess you're gearing up for the event?" she asked.

"You know it. Looking forward to this."

"Good luck! I'm rooting for you," She told him as she reached out and gently squeezed his hand. He felt the heat flush to his cheeks at the unexpected touch.

"Thanks. I'll see you later," was all he could manage before he jumped back in the capsule. The whirring started, and the blackness took over.

Chapter 11

The Wild Hunt

The wooden walls of the inn greeted him and he wasted no time snatching up his bags and heading out. Crowds clogged the streets, and Atlas could only assume it was in anticipation of the upcoming event.

The path to the registrar's office took some time to maneuver as he carefully pushed through the crowds. Once the building came into view, he spotted a large gathering outside. Leather and metal armor with a variety of weapons swathed the people in front of the building. *These must be the other participants.*

Atlas calmly walked to the gathering and stood near a small gathering of them.

"This is going to be awesome. I wonder who I'll be partnered with," one guy said. He wore sturdy leather armor and carried two small daggers on his belt.

"As long as I'm not partnered with noobs, I'll be fine. I'm taking that five gold prize," another answered. He stood tall with leather armor on his chest and legs, but he carried a metal short sword and shield and wore metal shod boots, bracers, and gloves.

"Do you think they'll assign teams based on our classes? It'd suck to get stuck on a team of nothing but healers," a female said. She wore a flowing gray robe with white trim on the edges. Her belt had a short wand clipped on it and a backpack was slung over her shoulder.

"Anyone heard how many total people are in the event? Or how many teams there will be?" Atlas asked.

The group of three turned his way before the woman spoke up, "I've heard there were somewhere around eighty people in our region. Not sure how many people they'll put on each team."

"In our region?" Atlas asked, confused.

"They broke the event up into regions. Each region has its own event happening right now. Would be unfair to compete with people in other places simultaneously. Different zones have different animals to hunt. Did you not look into the event at all before signing up?" she asked with a hint of derision in her voice.

"I spent the day of the announcement to grind out the entry fee, then logged off for the last two days due to work. Haven't dug into the details much," Atlas said, sheepishly.

"Humph, sounds like a poor excuse. Can't even bother to check the forums for info either, I guess?" the warrior huffed.

"Another waste of our time. Hopefully he's not on our team," the assassin character said as he nodded toward Atlas.

Instead of trying to argue with them, he ignored them and moved on. He wandered from group to group and listened to snippets of conversation. The big surprise came when he finally saw a few of the other races. A beastkin stood in one group. This one wore leather armor and held a heavy bow. Atlas assumed it was a ranger. The black fur on its body looked soft and gently danced in the breeze. Long rounded ears sat on top of their head and their eyes displayed their slit pupils. Claws stuck out from the hands and Atlas watched them retract and extend as the person talked, almost as if it was a subconscious action.

The second person he noticed was a vulpine character. This person wore robes and looked like a magic wielder. They wielded a staff, and their lithe form exuded a sense of speed. Most casters had difficulty with damage. Their casting usually left them wide open to attacks and most were too slow to dodge. A vulpine character could make an excellent caster if they could perfect casting while moving. If you could dodge and cast at the same time, it would be a deadly combination.

Atlas considered approaching them to talk to them until the door of the registrar's office opened and a man in full plate armor walked out. The only thing not covered in a solid layer of metal was his face. Dark black hair hung to the bottom of his chin in wavy lines, and a black goatee added the appearance of seriousness to his features. A dark red cloak, the color of dried blood, hung from his shoulders and attached to the armor with small metal discs. At his appearance, all conversation in the area ceased and silence descended on the clearing.

"Welcome adventurers! I'm High Marshall
Grant of the Royal Army. It's my pleasure to
be here as you embark on this important event
for the kingdom. Fierce animals have been
encroaching on our settlements, and we can
ignore the issue any longer. It's up to you
brave souls to quell this problem."

The crowd remained silent as the man
continued his speech.

"We have eighty brave volunteers here to
hunt down this menace and bring an end to the
threat. We will divide you into ten groups of
eight people. Each team of eight to hunt down
and exterminate the seven initial creatures we
ask for will receive the last target. The
first team to eradicate all eight of the
enemies will be the winners and each receive a
five gold reward."

The High Marshall scanned the crowd, and
Atlas heard the hushed whispers of excitement.

"Without further ado, let's get this event
started. When we call your name, please step
forward and enter the building to complete the
process before the teams disperse."

The High Marshall spun around with a
flourish as his cape fluttered out to the
side. He marched back into the building and
another man in robes with a symbol of the
registrar's office stepped forward. Names
echoed through the clearing and one by one
people entered the office in orderly fashion.
Every eight names called led to a momentary
delay before they called another set of names.
Atlas finally heard his name called in the
fifth group of people.

The inside of the registrar's office had a small desk set up on the side and two clerks sitting behind it. The two booths in the back were unmanned. Five other adventurers stood around the room as Atlas entered. One of them was the big warrior he'd seen earlier. When the man saw him enter, he rolled his eyes and purposefully looked away. They waited in the room in silence as the last two members of their group entered. The entrance of the vulpine caster from earlier pleased him as he walked in. If this man was truly an agile caster, he would be a treat to watch in action.

One clerk stood up as the last of them entered. He shuffled around a stack of papers on the desk in front of him and then turned his attention to the group.

"Welcome adventurers. Look around at the people in here. They will be your team for the hunt. We tried to balance out the classes for their roles as much as possible. Before we give you your initial quest, sign these contracts to compete. We do not tolerate killing of event members during this hunt. Once you sign these contracts, you're not allowed to attack any member of your party or one of your competitors until you return to the city and dissolve the contract. If you dissolve the contract early, you forfeit the event. Are there questions?"

The clerk looked around, but no one said anything. After a few moments of silence, the two men called out names and people approached to sign their contracts. Atlas stepped forward and quickly inked his signature on the document when called and waited for the rest to finish.

"All done," the first man said as he carefully stood the papers on end and tapped them on the table. They neatly shuffled into a solid stack of even paper, "Your first quest is now granted. Please wait outside until the High Marshal announces the commencement. When he does, you're free to leave the city and begin your hunt."

A message popped up in his vision.

You've been given the Event Mission - The Wild Hunt (Part 1).

The group calmly shuffled back outside and gathered together near the edge of the crowd. Atlas took a few minutes to look over the criteria of the quest. They were told it consisted of seven initial creatures to hunt, and then it revealed their ultimate target when they killed the rest.

Event Quest - The Wild Hunt (Part 1)	
Requirements Registered for Wild Hunt Event Quest Rarity: Rare Quest Reward: 200 experience per target killed, 5 Silver per target killed. 5 Gold to the winning team.	Description: Hunt the following 7 targets: Anaconda - Level 7 Lamia - Level 7 Hellrazer - Level 8 Swiftfoot - Level 8 Black Widow - Level 8 The Yote - Level 9 Umbral Shadow - Level 9

"So, what's our plan? How are we going to make sure we win?" Asked one member of the group. She was a tall and lithe wood elf with a longbow strapped over one shoulder. Her chestnut hair propped up in a ponytail and she wore supple leather.

"We just need to race out and be the first ones out of the gate. Looking at my map, I see vague outlines where each of the creatures should be. They are sizeable areas to cover, though." The large warrior said.

"There must be a better way," Atlas said, "They specifically told us they tried to balance our groups. If that's true, it seems like our best option is to split into two groups and each hunt down specific targets. We can all meet up for the last boss. They never said we had to kill all the targets as a single group. Only that we have to kill them all."

"I like that idea," the vulpine man said, "We can split into two groups of four and each take specific animals. We can coordinate over party chat if we get in any trouble. What's everyone's main role here?"

Everyone answered, and they got a solid count. There was one more healer along with Atlas. Two rangers. Two warriors. An assassin and the vulpine Wizard. After some discussion, they split into two groups of four. Atlas' group was the warrior from earlier and the vulpine caster. The tall wood elf ranger rounded them out as their fourth member.

A quick inspection of everyone brought up their names. The warrior's name was Ragnarok. The tall wood elf was Gemmaline, and the vulpine was Quelin.

They didn't have to wait very long. The last two groups quickly shuffled through the registrar's office before the High Marshall reappeared.

"With that out of the way, let the event commence!"

No one even bothered to see what the marshal did after that because all of them raced for the gate. The targets were all on the southeast side of the city. When they split into groups, they decided the best way to do it was to have his group hunt the group farthest east and head southwest, while the other group would start on the southern side and move northeast until they met in the middle.

This meant their first target was the level 7 Lamia. Atlas wasn't fond of snakes by any means. If this creature was what he suspected, he didn't think he'd like a half snake, half woman, monster any better. They fought through a plethora of animals as they wandered around the highlighted area. The fights were quick and easy. The loot rotated from person to person. Atlas could only take items from every fourth monster.

They finally found where they thought their quarry lived. A tall cave sat on a small cliff side. The dirt around the entrance showed a pattern that looked like scales slithering. With a feeling of dread, they all entered. Ragnarok took the lead with his shield out and ready. Gemmalin, who Atlas quickly discovered preferred to go by Gemma, walked beside him with an arrow nocked on her bow. Quelin walked on his other side. Fire danced around one of his hands as he watched their progress advance.

They crept into the cave until light shone around a corner. A peek around the corner showed their quarry. A beautiful woman lay on a solid wood bed. Her bright red hair shone in the firelight. It flowed along her body in curls until it rested near her waist. That's where the beauty ended and the horror began. Thick scales of dark green lined her lower body. No legs were present. From the waist down, she had the body and tail of an oversized snake. It was hard to tell from their position, but her lower half looked to be around ten feet long.

Before they could formulate any kind of plan, Ragnarok went full Leeroy Jenkins and rushed into the cavern, bellowing a challenge. The lamia rose on her lower half and her hair cascaded down to reveal her totally bare chest. The warrior froze in his charge as he stared at the goods on display, and Atlas watched the creature smile. Her tail lashed forward in a quick strike and smashed into Ragnarok's chest. He flew backward and slammed into the wall. His health took a major hit and almost a quarter of his total HP was now missing.

An arrow whizzed by his face and the woman twisted to the side as her tail half slithered in a tight circle. The arrow grazed her shoulder but didn't strike a solid hit. The movement broke him out of his trance and he focused on Ragnarok. Activating his Nourish spell, he followed the movements. A flash of red lit up the corner of his vision, but he focused on his casting and ignored it. The spell completed, and the magic blanketed the warrior.

The man rose back to his feet with a grumble and picked up his weapons.

"Keep your guard up! Don't let her distract you." Quelin called and Atlas saw another flare of red. He turned in time to see a small arrow of flame dart across the expanse and sizzle into the creature's shoulder. She hissed and turned to focus on the vulpine. Her body slithered toward the caster, but Ragnarok was back in the fight. Charging across the room, he intercepted her advance and rammed her with his shield. He dropped to a knee and thrust the bottom of his shield into the ground. When her tail came around, it reverberated off the shield, and she hissed in pain.

An arrow flew across the room and caught her in the shoulder. With nothing else to do, Atlas fetched his wand from his belt pouch and held it in his off-hand. He didn't want to get into close combat with the monster. They needed him to heal if things went badly. He activated Barkskin and targeted Ragnarok. When the cast finished, a beam of green energy jumped from the small wand and hit the warrior. His armor and skin took on the appearance of tree bark for a few seconds before returning to normal.

Another red streak passed by and Atlas turned to watch the fire arrow, except it wasn't a purely magical arrow, this one was a standard arrow with a glowing red tip. It punched into the left shoulder of the lamia and the skin hissed and sizzled at the impact. A glance to his side showed a grinning Gemma. She already had another arrow on the string. Her muscles bulged as she drew back for another shot and released. The lamia flicked her tail up and deflected the arrow at the same time Ragnarok rose and slashed at her with his sword. The blade bounced off the scales on her lower half and caused no obvious damage.

Atlas activated Nature's Fury. During his spell-casting, Quelin launched another fire arrow while Ragnarok braced himself against another attack. His ball of green energy flew from his wand and hit the creature in the chest. She howled in fury as the power seeped into her.

You dealt 6 HP damage to Lamia.

"How dare you come into my lair and attack me! I'll rip all of you apart!"

The spaces between her scales seemed to glow an eerie green color, and her eyes lit up a furious red. She dashed after Ragnarok again, only this time she was much faster than before. Her tail slammed into the shield and he skidded across the ground as the attack pushed him and his shield backward. Ignoring the warrior, she charged for Quelin.

The vulpine's eyes narrowed as he quickly
built power between his hands. This spell
didn't look the same as his fire arrow, and
the heat emanating from it was noticeable
where Atlas stood. The lamia dashed in and
swung with her claws. Atlas watched with glee
as Quelin ducked under the attack while still
building his fire. The man jumped forward and
pushed the fire directly into the snake
woman's stomach.

For a moment, silence hung in the air, and
nothing happened. That moment shattered when a
resounding boom echoed from the two fighters
and the lamia flew backward to crunch into the
stone wall. A dark black scorch mark adorned
her stomach and thick green blood leaked from
cracks around the wound.

"I think that almost did it," Quelin
breathed out as he tried to catch his breath,
"One more round of attacks should finish her.
Everyone attack together."

No one voiced any objections, so Atlas put
his wand away and gripped his staff in both
hands. They all ran for the monster and he
activated his Triple Threat attack. The staff
swung around in an arc and crunched into the
scales on her hip. The second swing caught her
in the ribs while his final overhanded attack
cracked solidly into her skull. Two arrows
punched into her neck in rapid succession and
a sword blade slid cleanly in to her side. The
lamia shivered and then collapsed to the
ground.

*You dealt 12 HP damage with Triple Threat.
Lamia died.*

Everyone stood back and checked over each
other.

"Everyone alright?" Atlas asked.

They all nodded in agreement.

"Damn Ragnarok, that's straight up disrespectful. Quit staring at those things!" Gemma told him with disgust in her tone.

The warrior quickly looked away from the body and blushed a deep red.

"You have a three-hit combo?" Quelin asked Atlas.

"Yeah, learned it before I logged out last time."

"That must be nice. I figured you were more of a caster."

"I prefer the close up fighting and do more of that while I'm questing and grinding. I save my mana for healing spells. I was trying to stay back to avoid taking too much damage in case someone needed healing."

The group stood near the dead monster and Gemma stepped forward. She reached out and touched it, and her eyes shot wide. A box appeared in front of Atlas and he read it over.

Item - Slither Ring	
Requirements: Level 6 **Rarity**: Uncommon **Quality**: Fine	**Durability**: 45/45 **Weight**: 0.1 lbs. **Slot**: Finger **Traits**: A ring of a green-colored metal, embossed with a snake scale pattern. Grants the following bonus: Increases the wearer's agility by 1.
Roll for item: Need/Greed	

The ring was the first uncommon item he'd seen. At this low of level, increasing a stat by 1 point could be a big deal. Despite that, he didn't want to roll *Need* for it. The ring would be beneficial to Gemma, and even Quelin could put it to better use than he could with his dodging ability. It would work to increase his damage and speed, but he was here as a healer and not for his damage. Atlas selected *Greed*.

Everyone made their selection, and the notification showed up.

Gemmalin won the Need roll for Slither Ring!

The ranger cheered and deftly slipped the ring on a finger. Atlas also noticed another notification.

You gained 200 experience for killing a target in The Wild Hunt.

Atlas checked the experience from the logs as they worked their way here.

You gained 25 total experience.
"On to Hellrazer?" Gemma asked.
"Looks like it." Ragnarok replied.
At that moment, Atlas heard a distinct ping type of sound. It took him a minute to notice the small icon that looked like a chat symbol in the lower right corner of his vision. Mentally, he selected the icon, and a window popped open that said Party Chat on top.

Party Chat

Quelin: Lamia is down. We are moving to Hellrazer now. How are you guys doing on Anaconda?

Nothing showed up for a few moments before a message echoed his earlier sentiment.

Party Chat

JamminGirl: What do you mean 'how are we doin?' It's a big ass damn snake. They should exterminate these things from every world. It's almost dead, though.

Atlas chuckled a little at the message. Apparently JamminGirl hated snakes too. She was the assassin for the other team.

He walked over to the corpse and found another item on it.

You have found Lamia Scales x 20.

Interesting. I can't really use scales now, but I'm sure they'll come in handy in the future. He tucked them into his bag and they exited the cave. Hellrazer's territory was farther southwest, so they headed for the border of its zone. They hadn't made it halfway to their destination when another set of messages popped up.

You gained 200 experience for killing a target in The Wild Hunt.
Success! You've reached Level 8.

Party Chat

PrettyPrincess: The nasty snake is dead. Heading out to look for Swiftfoot.
Ragnarok: Good luck, guys.

    His two points for this level he spent to boost his magic. One went into Intellect and the second into Spirit. His mana regeneration rate wasn't that bad right now, but he knew it could quickly become a problem in the future if he didn't plan for it ahead of time. With a quicker mana regeneration and a larger maximum pool of 110 mana, they continued on their journey.

    The group scoured the area. Briars and thorns covered most of this part of the forest. Stickers snagged on any loose clothing, and Atlas cursed more than once when a stray thorn sunk into his skin. The living conditions here solidified his belief that the animal they hunted was a boar. They were one of the few animals that thrived in these conditions, so they kept their eyes and noses open as they searched.

    A whiff of a pungent smell was the first thing that tipped them off. That caused them all to draw weapons as they continued their search. The group pushed through a thin layer of thorns and emerged into a clear circular area surrounded by briars on all sides. The surrounding thorns shook and the beat of hooves sounded through the area. Leaves shook and figures emerged from them.

    Five pigs arrayed themselves in a line in front of the party. On each end stood animals that showed up as Runner - Level 5. The two pigs next to them were Gorer - Level 6. And the large boar in the center was Hellrazer - Level 8. Hellrazer was a monster of a pig that had to be five feet tall at the shoulder. Tusks the size of his middle finger jutted from the corners of its mouth and it had reddish hair.

"Anyone fancy some bacon for dinner?" Gemma quipped as she loosed an arrow. The shaft headed for one Runner, but it was quicker and dodged the attack. Both of the Runners ran full speed around the clearing while the Gorer's charged for the party. Ragnarok intercepted one of them and bashed it in the face with his shield, but the second charged for Atlas.

Fire sizzled into its side, but it never slowed its charge or changed its direction. He hefted his staff and waited for the charge. Stepping to the side, he brought the weapon down on the hog's back and activated Counter. He swung around to the side and jabbed the staff into the monster's neck. Blade Chase followed, and the three hit combo thumped into the bony skull of the animal.

An arrow sprouted from its throat and a fire arrow sizzled into its side, sending it to the ground.

You dealt 3 HP damage with Counter.
You dealt 12 HP damage with Blade Chase.
Gorer died.

Confusion rocked the clearing as the two runners darted directly into the group. One smashed into Gemma's legs, knocking her to the ground while another one clipped Atlas, causing him to stumble to the side.

Runner dealt 3 HP damage to you. (Glancing)

He steadied himself and watched Gemma vault back to her feet. She pulled up her bow and launched an arrow with incredible speed at the pig that hit her. It was so fast she couldn't hit it, and her arrow skidded across the ground. Atlas heard a muffled cry and turned to see Ragnarok with a puncture wound in his shield arm. Hellrazer attacked him from the side while he held the other Gorer in place.

"We need to get rid of that other Gorer so Rag can focus on Hellrazer. Ignore the Runners for now," Atlas told them all.

The group nodded and everyone turned their attention to the remaining Gorer. Knowing Rag needed all the help he could get, Atlas activated his Barkskin cast. The motions came smoothly, and the energy launched forward to encase the warrior. His skin and armor rippled with the bark texture and then returned to normal. He activated Nourish after that and began the movements. Shortly before the spell finished, a Runner barreled into him and sent him spiraling to the ground.

Runner dealt 5 HP damage to you with Wild Charge.

Runner interrupted your Nurture cast with Knockdown. Spell backlash dealt 4 HP damage to you.

Pain flashed through his head as the backlash of the spell seeped into his body. He looked up and saw Rag was still doing fine on health, so it wasn't a critical problem yet, but he needed to address it now. Trying to chase down healing when the targets were already critically low was a dangerous prospect. One lucky critical strike could end them before the heal went through.

Rag lashed out with his shield and the Gorer stepped back with a squeal. Two arrows thumped into its side within a second of each other. A small burst of fire hit it, and the smell of burned hair filled the clearing and caused him to wrinkle his nose in disgust. Seeing both of the Runners on the side of the clearing near Rag, he activated Nourish again.

This time the spell completed, and the magic settled onto the warrior. Atlas watched him breathe a sigh of relief, and the trickle of blood from the wound on his arm ceased. His health bar jumped back up a little and Atlas focused on the fight again. To his dismay, his healing caused the wrong type of attention.

Hellrazer himself turned his attention to Atlas and charged directly for him. *The healing spell must've pulled aggro.* Ragnarok must not have done much damage to the boar prior to his cast. The enormous pig closed the distance and Atlas braced himself. Instead of seeing the normal moves he needed to block the attack, his vision flashed a tinge of red. *Yikes!*

Figuring it meant nothing good, he dove to the side instead of trying to block the charge. Hellrazer spun and faced him as he slowed. The second attack came head on again and this time Atlas lined up the block as shown. The heavy animal smashed into his staff and he felt the wood creak in his hands. The sheer weight and force of the animal was too much to handle, and it knocked him backward.

The creature swung his head, and one tusk caught Atlas on the leg. A flash of red power announced Quelin's attack as the boar squealed and a patch of hair on its side lit up like a dry cedar tree. Its beady eyes never left Atlas, and he swung his head again toward the druid. This time he was ready and instead of trying to block the attack head on, he deflected the attack to the side. Activating Counter, he smashed the staff into its snout and then followed the attack with Blade Chase. The three hits thumped into the beast and if not for the damage notifications, Atlas would've assumed they did nothing to it. Not wanting to waste his chance, he followed this with his Triple Threat to combo in his attack phase. The final blow of the combo smashed into the animal's head and Atlas looked to the damage.

Hellrazer dealt 6 HP damage to you with Gore.
You dealt 2 HP damage to Hellrazer with Counter.
You dealt 8 HP damage to Hellrazer with Blade Chase.
You dealt 8 HP damage to Hellrazer with Triple Threat.

The boar stumbled backward, obviously dazed from the onslaught. The damage was low, but he was still using the Basic Wood Staff he made after dying. A better weapon was essential to him making a difference. The left side of the beast looked like a pincushion with all the arrows sticking out of the hide. The right side, by comparison, looked like a scorched wasteland. Black burn marks covered it and no hair remained.

A roar of anger assaulted his ears before Ragnarok charged, shield first, into the side of the monster. The exchange was actually pretty comical considering he hit with full force, but the boar didn't budge so much as a step. It made the creature redirect his attention to the warrior. Rag must've included a taunt ability in the attack.

Atlas stepped back with a sigh of relief and activated Nourish, targeting the warrior. He looked a little battered. The spell completed, and he scanned the battlefield. The second Gorer was dead with burn marks and arrows in it. *They must've finished it when Hellrazer attacked me.*

The two runners still darted through the party, and Atlas caught sight of one just in time to step out of its path.

"Quelin, can you repeat your spell from the lamia? We could use some heavy damage on this animal?" Gemma asked.

"It's still on cooldown," Quelin grumbled to the ranger.

"I guess I can do it then," she said as she lifted her bow. Three arrows sat on the string at one time, and the bow glowed for a moment before the three projectiles melded into one large ballista-style bolt. The string pulled taut, and she released. The giant arrow soared forward and punched directly into the boar's side. Blood splattered from the impact and splashed along the ground. The animal teetered on his feet and fell to the ground.

With an obvious struggle, the beast returned to his feet, but he didn't look very steady.

"That time again, boys and girls. One last barrage should finish it," Ragnarok called.

They all rushed forward and activated abilities. Fire and arrows peppered into it, and Ragnarok's sword sunk into its side. Atlas activated his Triple Threat, and the combo ended with the telltale thump into its skull. The barrage was all the beast could handle, and it fell to the ground.

You dealt 8 HP damage to Hellrazer with Triple Threat.
Hellrazer died.

The group let out a collective breath as the monster went still. Smiles dotted their faces for a few moments before Gemma hit the ground. A Runner clipped her feet out from under her. They forgot the two pigs were still on their feet.

The group burst into motion as Ragnarok chased after the closest one. Gemma launched arrows and Quelin flung fire. The pigs moved so fast it was difficult for anyone to land a hit. Rag looked like a kid chasing a chicken around a farmyard. They were much faster than he was, and he couldn't pin one down. They never stopped moving, and it made it difficult to hit them. With a flash of insight, Atlas grinned. He activated Entangle and focused on the space directly in front of the nearest Runner.

The spell completed and vines burst from the ground. The pig entered the area a moment later and one vine snagged a front leg. The pig squealed in surprise and tried to dash free only for additional vines to wrap around it and pull it to a stop. With the creature trapped, Arrows slammed home and a fire arrow took it in the face. It fell to the ground and ceased its movement.

You dealt 1 HP damage to Runner with Entangle.

Atlas repeated his spell with the second pig and drug it to a halt. Ragnarok finally caught up with this one and his sword cleaved into its neck at the same time an arrow caught it where its heart was.

You dealt 1 HP damage to Runner with Entangle.

The group looked around the clearing carefully before relaxing this time. All five animals lay dead in the space. They walked over to Hellrazer and Atlas reached out to touch him.

You received 5 Raw Hog Hide.
You received 2 Thick Hog Hide.
You received 4 Raw Hog Loins.

He collected the items and dumped them into his bag. The thick hide was intriguing but before he could consider what to do with it another box popped up.

<table>
<tr><td colspan="2" align="center">Item – Armored Plating</td></tr>
<tr><td>Requirements: Level 7
Rarity: Uncommon
Quality: Fine</td><td>Defense: 8
Durability: 85/85
Weight: 8.0 lbs.
Slot: Chest

Traits: A chest piece made from the armored plating of a grand boar. This hide is as tough as steel. Grants the following bonus:

Increases the wearer's Strength by 1.</td></tr>
<tr><td colspan="2" align="center">Roll for item: Need/Greed</td></tr>
</table>

"Damn that's nice. That should work great for you, Rag," Atlas said.

He selected Greed and waited. The message didn't take long as everyone made their selections.

Ragnarok won the Need roll for Armored Plating!

Ragnarok immediately equipped his new chest piece. The plating indeed looked almost like steel, albeit with the coloring of leather. He could see the small lines in the material like you usually saw in worn leather, but the piece itself was rigid and strong.

You gained 200 experience for killing a target in The Wild Hunt.
You gained 110 experience for killing the boss' companions.

Party Chat

Atlas: Hellrazer is down. We are headed for Black Widow. How are you guys doing with Swiftfoot?

JonahBrotherWannabe: We are still trying to catch it. It's a damn overgrown rabbit, and it moves way too fast to hit.

Quelin: We had some boars like that to fight. Atlas trapped them with vines for us. Any of you have any type of snaring spell?

JamminGirl: I can slow it with one of my abilities but I have to get close to hit him.

Ragnarok: Have PrettyPrincess get in front of it and force it toward you. That should give you your opening.

JamminGirl: Let's do it.

"Hopefully they can figure it out. We need to go find the ugly spider," Atlas said in a resigned tone.

"Ew, spiders. And I thought snakes were bad enough. You sure it's a spider?" Gemma asked.

"Uh, Black Widow…" Ragnarok said slowly.

"Yeah good point," Gemma whined.

"Let's get going." Quelin called, and they all turned to head farther southwest toward the marked zone.

Chapter 12

Finale

The group looted the nearby creatures, and Atlas took the chance to use some skins he'd collected to make a reinforced jerkin. The added defense would be useful if enemies kept attacking him. The group continued on their way and headed for the area where Black Widow should be.

They were nearly to their hunting zone when Atlas spotted a dead tree on the side of the path.

"Hey, can we stop for a minute?"

The group slowed their pace and looked around.

"Something up Atlas?" Quelin asked.

"Actually, a couple things. I want to make sure I top off all of our health before we get into the zone. That gives me time to regen mana before we get in another fight. Another reason is that tree over there," he said as he pointed at the dead tree.

"I understand the health thing and that's a good idea but what's a dead tree have to do with anything?" Ragnarok asked.

"Need to make me a new staff. The one I have is weak and does minor damage. I can harvest the wood I need from the dead tree to make a new one. Won't take me long," Atlas assured them and began casting his Nourish spell on them all.

"Thought you were a leatherworker?" Gemma asked.

"I am, he answered in between spells. I also took the time to learn woodworking. I wanted to be able to create the key items I needed. It already came in handy once after some asshats ganked me in the forest."

"Damn, I was hoping the plague of player killers wouldn't be that bad here, but I guess your situation proves otherwise. Either way. It's a good idea to have multiple professions." Quelin agreed.

Atlas finished healing everyone and then whipped out his hatchet. The dead tree fell to pieces in no time, and he held eight raw pieces of wood. His knife took the place of his hatchet and eight Rough Wood Logs took the place of the raw pieces. He held two of the lengths of wood and activated his Create Sturdy Wood Staff ability.

The small knife flipped along the length in long motions. Wood smoothed into a solid shaft before his body switched to the second length of wood. This piece divided into three pieces and he carved them down to thin sheathes. These three pieces slipped onto the original staff body and he used small wedges of the carved wood to attach them to the haft. One piece sat in the center of the staff to reinforce his grip and the other two capped both ends, making them larger and heavier.

Item - Sturdy Wood Staff	
Requirements: Level 5 **Rarity:** Common **Quality:** Fair	**Attack:** 4 **Defense:** 3 **Durability:** 75/75 **Weight:** 7.5 lbss **Slot:** 2H Weapon **Traits:** A staff made of basic wood and reinforced in the middle and the ends. It can attack or defend.

Well, four damage is definitely better than two. He took his old staff and tossed it into the woods. It wouldn't be worth enough money to bother carrying it around.

"While we are taking a break, would you mind making me one of those chest pieces?" Gemmalin asked, "I have hides I've collected."

"Sure. You not get a profession?" Atlas asked as she handed over a stack of nine hides. The armor itself only cost eight, but he'd need the ninth to make enough sinew for it.

"I did, but I went with Jewelcrafting. So far it hasn't been very useful. I've been able to make some basic wood pendants and rings, but nothing that is worth much. It was enough to get me the entry fee I needed, but that's about it."

"I'm sure that will pay off in the long run. Professions like that tend to work better toward higher levels." Atlas reassured her as he worked on her armor.

"That's what I was hoping for. I appreciate your help though."

"Not a problem. We all need to be at our best to finish this first."

Atlas handed over the chest piece and she equipped it immediately. She stuffed her old one in her bag and slung her bow back over her shoulder.

"Anyone else need anything while we are here?" Atlas asked.

Ragnarok handed over some hides so Atlas could make him a set of reinforced pants. Quelin asked him what wands he could make but the Basic one was worse than what he already had so he opted out. Atlas finished up the pants and used his other six Rough Wood Logs to make Sturdy Wood Rods. He could be sure their price would hold steady since they were a building material. It also helped they were easy to carry.

You gained 550 total experience in Woodworking.
You gained 1,185 total experience in Leatherworking.

With all the crafting out of the way, the group continued their journey. When they entered the designated area, it confirmed their fears. Enormous spider webs crisscrossed all over the place. Sounds of battle drew their attention. They followed the noise and emerged in a clearing where a party of eight fought the monster herself. Black Widow looked nothing like he expected. Instead of a giant spider, they watched an eight-foot tall woman with four extra legs in her back fight against the party. Eyes covered her forehead and two large fangs protruded from her mouth.

The creature deftly blocked attacks with her extra appendages as she kicked at the party. From time to time she shot bundles of sticky webbing at the combatants from her mouth, either slowing their movement or tying up their weapons. They all stood back and watched the fight with interest.

"Should we help them?" Quelin asked.

"I doubt it. Since they started the fight, I'm sure they'd be the only ones to get credit for the kill. I don't want to have to fight that hideous thing twice. We'll just have to wait for them to finish the fight and for her to respawn." Atlas reassured them.

One of the group fighting the spider monster finally spotted them near the fight. They waved a hand at them and yelled over the noise.

"Hey, can you help us out here?"

"Sorry guys. This is a competition. Not going to help our opponents with a fight." Quelin told them.

The group grumbled, but they were too busy to voice much in the way of an objection. The fight continued and Atlas observed it. The spider moved and attacked in a pattern. Two slashes with her appendages, then a kick from her legs and a special ability completed her combination. The web spitting was one special, but she would occasionally leap high into the air and try to pounce on people and impale them with her spider legs.

She actually succeeded in one of those attacks and speared one of their party members directly through the chest. Atlas watched as the man died and his body dissolved and became nothing more than a gravestone marker.

"Maybe one of his party will be nice enough to get his stuff for him without stealing it," Gemma said.

"Wouldn't hold my breath on that one. He'll respawn in few hours but at the pace we are moving he won't be able to catch back up before the event ends. They'll probably take it and run." Quelin assured her.

"This fight shouldn't be too bad," Atlas said as he watched them.

"Not too bad? They have all eight members and are struggling to beat her. How do you think four of us will have less trouble?" Ragnarok asked.

"You see it too, huh?" Quelin asked.

Atlas turned to the vulpine and smiled, "Sure do. She has a distinct pattern and they either haven't noticed it or don't know how to take advantage of it."

He described the exact pattern he'd noticed, and they all watched the fight to confirm what he said.

"How does that help us, though? We know what she'll do, but the big problem is her ability to block attacks," Gemma said in resignation.

"That's partially true," Quelin quipped, "She has one major weakness. She can't block on both sides at once. It must be a limitation of the limbs. If they would time their attacks and have people attack from each side simultaneously, they could take her down quickly. She looks pretty frail and probably has minimal health. Her strength is in her defensive abilities."

"So, we need to split our attacks. Gemma and Quelin, you think you two can coordinate attacks? Rag can tank her head on and I'll play support with my heals. Each of you pick a side and launch attacks together." Atlas explained.

The group currently fighting eventually won the struggle. They had one fewer member, and a handful of them looked like they were in critical condition. They wouldn't be fighting much for a little while as they recovered.

"Thanks for nothing, assholes," one guy in the group mumbled as they stumbled past them.

They took a seat near the edge of the clearing and waited. It took another ten minutes, but the Spider Queen finally emerged from a burrow on the edge. She walked out toward the center before turning her gaze to the party and waiting.

"Guess we won't have any element of surprise," Ragnarok quipped.

"Nope, let's go get her." Gemma said as the group advanced forward.

"Hello, my lunch," the spider monster hissed at them.

"Not today," Rag said as he charged at her, shield raised.

Gemma and Quelin dashed to the opposite sides and took up position. Atlas cast Barkskin to prepare Rag for the onslaught that was about to start. Her first two strikes rang off his shield before he dropped to a knee and dug the bottom into the ground. The spider woman kicked out and rebounded from the reinforced shield.

Two arrows flew in from one side while an arrow of fire zipped through the air on the other. Off balance from the rebound, she failed to block the attacks and only hit one of the normal arrows with a glancing blow of her spider arm. One arrow sunk in deep in her side and the fire arrow splashed the right side of her chest, scorching the carapace lined breast. The arrow she deflected cut a small glancing blow along her back.

"You insects dare to bother me?"

She turned toward Quelin and spit her sticky webbing. The vulpine grinned, showing his teeth before diving to the side, avoiding the webs. The spider hissed in fury before she turned back to Rag. Ragnarok stepped forward and bashed his shield into her chest where the burn mark now was. She shrieked in fury as the carapace cracked and green fluid leaked from the wound.

Black Widow attacked again, and Rag was ready for her. The two swipes glanced off of the shield and he dropped to block the kick but was too slow. Her sweeping leg caught him in the ankle and knocked him to the ground. With a look of pure malice, she leaped into the air. Knowing what was coming, Atlas charged forward.

There was no way he could grab the warrior and drag him out of the way, so he kneeled as low as he could and held his staff directly upright. The spider came down and Atlas saw her look of maliciousness morph to one of horror. Her body hit the staff with enough force that the blunt object punched into her stomach and fluid leaked from her body. Her outstretched legs twitched as she whimpered in pain.

With a heave, Atlas tipped the staff over, and she rolled to the ground. Before he could move, two more arrows and another fire spell hit her. Her moan of pain slowly gurgled away, and she died, her legs curling into a tight ball around her torso.

You dealt 30 HP damage to Black Widow for countering her special ability.
Black Widow died.

"Awesome work, guys." Atlas said as he reached down and helped Ragnarok back to his feet.

"Holy shit, man. Thanks for saving my ass. I thought I would end up as a shish kebab."

"Don't worry about it. We need the entire team alive to win this thing. It also looks bad on me as a healer if a team member dies," Atlas told him with a smile.

Quelin reached down and grabbed the loot from the boss. It was only a few minutes before the box he expected popped up.

Item – Venomstrike	
Requirements: Level 6 **Rarity:** Uncommon **Quality:** Good	**Attack:** 2 **Magical Attack:** 3 **Durability:** 85/85 **Weight:** 1.5 lbs. **Slot:** 1H Weapon **Traits:** A wooden wand infused with the power of spider venom. Spells cast using this wand can infect the enemy and cause 1 HP damage every 3 seconds.

"That thing is fantastic. The Magical bonus is nice, but the effect is definitely for a damage dealer. Looks like today is your lucky day, Quelin," Atlas said with a hint of jealousy in his voice.

He selected Greed, and in a few moments the game confirmed the outcome.

Quelin won the Need roll for Venomstrike!

The vulpine quickly equipped the wand and a sleek wood object appeared in his hand. The wood was a dark tone, and it looked like dark green spider webs made up its grain. The end of the wand feathered out and looked like a bundle of spider webs.

You gained 200 experience for killing a target in The Wild Hunt.

Atlas checked his experience, and it confused him. He had to look back and figured out why. They'd gained another 200 experience from their fellow group killing Swiftfoot. It happened when he was doing all the crafting and he must've skimmed past it.

Party Chat
Atlas: Black Widow down. Headed to the Umbral Shadow.
PrettyPrincess: Can't talk, fighting the Yote. Will meet you at Umbral.

Atlas healed up the minor damage Ragnarok had, and they headed for the zone with the Umbral Shadow in it. This monster was one that Atlas didn't know what to expect. His fear told him it would be a shadow monster. If that was the case, it would be difficult to defeat the thing. This idea gradually faded as he remembered the teams it placed them in. Some of them didn't have many casters assigned. If the Umbral was a creature that could only be damaged by magic, it would be a drastic disadvantage for many of the groups and make the event unfair.

They continued through the thickly wooded area before Atlas noticed a dark shadow in the trees. He lifted his hand and quietly whispered to the party, "There's something in the trees up ahead."

The group sat still and watched the area that Atlas indicated. They waited in silence until the shadow finally moved. It walked to the side until it passed through a beam of sunlight breaking through the trees. The group saw what they faced in the Umbral Shadow.

A large cat, fur the color of void blackness with swirls of purple, stalked through the trees. It had teeth on the front reminiscent of a saber-tooth tiger.

"Damn," Ragnarok whispered, "Cats are tough to hunt in a forest."

"I'm more worried about fighting him in such a dark space. I have a feeling this thick forest helps hide him in the shadows of the trees exceptionally well," grumbled Gemma.

"Any ideas?" Atlas asked.

"May have to wait for the rest of the group. This one could be far more dangerous than the others." Ragnarok conceded.

You gained 200 experience for killing a target in The Wild Hunt.
Success! You've reached Level 9.

Atlas dumped one point from his level into Constitution and one into Intellect, bringing his health to 110 and his mana to 120.

For getting 10 attribute points in Intellect, you have unlocked a bonus. All your spells base power increase by 2.

Well, that's amazing. Hopefully all the attributes offer bonuses. They hunkered down in the shadows of a tree until a noise caused them to perk up. Clomping of footsteps echoed through the forest and voices joined them. They weren't headed for them but were heading toward the Umbral Shadow.

"We are close to done guys. After we kill this flimsy shadow, we only have the Yote left. I doubt it'll be a problem." One guy bellowed over the group.

"I can already smell that gold. Maybe I'll buy a new set of armor or even a fancy dress?" A female responded.

"Sure, Hathra. You can do whatever you want with your money when we win." The original voice answered.

The group continued and never ceased their loud talking. Atlas and his party peered around the tree they hid behind and watched the Umbral Shadow. He'd caught sight of the approaching group and crouched down to pounce. Atlas' warred with himself on whether to say anything, but in the end he figured it was a contest. Worst case, they'd have a three-hour cooldown for respawn.

A shrill scream pierced their conversation, and the cat leaped from the tree and landed on one adventurer. The young female hadn't expected the attack, and the cat's jaws clamped over her neck in an instant. A crunch echoed through the woods as the shadow lifted his head. The woman's body dangled lifelessly from its jaws as blood dripped down its long fangs.

"That bastard killed Emily. Get him!" yelled the man.

The fighters charged into the opening and engaged the Umbral Shadow. The cat swatted at one, and the poor soul took the full force of three claws across his chest. Ragged tears lined his armor and blood seeped from the wounds. *The idiot should've let the tank lead the fight.*

They watched the fight unfold for a good five minutes. Atlas couldn't figure out how they'd killed five of the seven targets. They looked like an army of toddlers running around and swinging wildly. No tactics of any kind were visible, and they didn't work as a team.

"This is painful to watch," Quelin said.

"You're telling me. If nothing else, that means there will be one less team to worry about in this contest. I can't see how they might come out on top."

"I'd say that's mean, Rag, but I think you're right," Gemma winced.

The cat continued to pounce around the clearing, eliminating the fighters one by one. Atlas and Quelin used their observation skills to see its pattern as they had with Black Widow. This creature's pattern wasn't quite set in stone, though. It had three different three-move attacks. It didn't always use them in the same order, though. If you could remember the initial attack of each of the combos, it would be easy to counter.

Only two people remained as they watched the slaughter. The woman named Hathra stood in the back with a bow while another man stood toe to toe with the cat, daggers in his hands. The animal lunged forward, and the assassin dodged to the side and sunk in both blades. Blood dripped down the shadow's side, but it only glared at the fighter. He gulped before the animal turned and bit into his chest.

The woman screamed and flung down her bow, "I can't die here. I'm too young to die on a stupid quest."

She sprinted away from the fight as the cat watched her leave. It lowered itself into a pounce and launched toward her again. The wound on his neck now perfectly healed.

"Doesn't want to die? I understand losing your stuff sucks, but we are reborn in a matter of hours." Ragnarok said confused.

"She's not a reborn…" Atlas started, "We have to help her. She doesn't get to respawn."

Atlas rose to his feet and dashed to help the woman when an arm grabbed him.

"Atlas, it's just a game. There's no reason to interfere until we're ready," Rag said calmly.

"I know but we can't just let her die. Who knows, she may be someone important, or related to someone important in the game. It could be a big deal," he pleaded with them.

"I'm in," Gemma said as she stood and readied her bow.

Quelin stood to join him as well. Rag looked like he wanted to object but just grumbled they were all fools and they dashed after the shadow. They found the woman and the cat not far away. She was steadily trying to keep a tree between herself and the animal, knowing she couldn't possibly outrun it.

Rag charged in and Atlas started with his Barkskin again. Arrows and fire sizzled through the air, and the cat howled in pain. It turned its attention to them right as Rag met him with a shield to the face.

"Get out of here, Hathra. Get back to the city. We'll take care of this."

"Thank you so much. I owe you all my life," she said as she turned and ran.

"Rag watch the combos. He only has three different attack sequences." Atlas told him.

"He does? I couldn't find any pattern to his attacks while we watched."

"It doesn't use the attacks in the same pattern. The first attack tells you what follows."

The warrior just grunted and continued the fight. Arrows continued to fly, but Gemma had trouble targeting the creature. The shadows of the trees made it difficult to get an arrow in it. Quelin had a little more luck since his fire spells lit up the area when he launched them. Atlas watched the fight unfold, ready to cast spells. The Barkskin spell was paying dividends in this fight.

Rag was taking far more hits than usual. For whatever reason, he wasn't able to anticipate the attacks. Atlas cast two Nourish spells back to back to top the warrior off in health.

"Quelin, watch my back. I'm going in to help," Atlas called to the mage.

He charged into the fight and immediately triggered Triple Threat. His staff thudded into the animal's side and then spun to catch it in the leg before bashing down on its skull. He ensured he stood on the shield side of Ragnarok so the warrior could still swing his sword without the chance of hitting him.

You dealt 16 HP damage to Umbral Shadow with Triple Threat.

A wide swipe came in front of them, trying to catch both, but Atlas took that time to deflect the swing upward with a timed twist of the staff. Activating Counter, he dashed in for a smack to the skull and followed with a Blade Chase. The three-hit combo rocked the cat backward, and it cowered and tried to go on the defensive. Without giving it a chance to recover, he followed with Triple Threat. All the attacks landed solid hits, and he was astonished to see his damage output.

You dealt 4 HP damage to Umbral Shadow with Counter.
You dealt 16 HP damage to Umbral Shadow with Blade Chase.
You dealt 16 HP damage to Umbral Shadow with Triple Threat.

The feline remained cowed as the rest of
the party launched attacks. The giant arrow
that Gemma used before punched into its side.
*She must be really mad about missing all those
shots.* Not long after that, a small ball of
fire hit the animal in the shoulder and it
whimpered in pain. A strike combo from Rag
finished the round of attacks.

Atlas thought the creature dead, until it
lifted its head and growled, fiery anger
dancing in its eyes. It pounced forward in a
move they hadn't seen yet and landed on top of
Rag. The weight of the monster pinned him to
the ground as it began clawing at him. Luckily
for the warrior, it pinned his shield between
the cat and himself, so it took the brunt of
the damage.

They all activated another round of
attacks. Two quick arrows thumped into its
ribs while a ball of fire sizzled into its
right eye. Atlas launched forward with his
Triple Threat and the final blow smashed into
its now burned eye. The animal hissed in pain
and leaped backward.

*You dealt 16 HP damage to Umbral Shadow
with Triple Threat.*

Atlas helped Rag to his feet and then
immediately cast Nourish on him while the
others distracted the creature. The warrior
nodded in relief as the spell settled over him
and charged back at the cat. Atlas ran beside
him and they both attacked with their combos.

His Triple Threat connected solidly and on
the last hit a loud crunch echoed through
their surroundings as he felt a spot on the
cat's head collapse slightly. The feline
wavered as if drunk before Ragnarok's sword
caught it in the neck and it sunk to the
ground.

*You dealt 20 HP damage to Umbral Shadow
with Triple Threat. (Critical)*
Umbral Shadow died.

Ragnarok backed up until he ran into a tree
and sunk to the ground. He'd taken quite a
beating during the fight and although Atlas
had healed most of it already, it would take
time for his Stamina to recover. Gemma leaned
heavily on her bow while Quelin looked mainly
unfazed.

The vulpine walked to the corpse and
accessed the loot. An item popped up for all
to see.

Item – Umbral Cloak	
Requirements: Level 7 **Rarity:** Uncommon **Quality:** Good	**Defense:** 2 **Durability:** 75/75 **Weight:** 2.0 lbs. **Slot:** Back **Traits:** A cloak made of an umbral cat's fur. This dark black and purple fur helps reduce your threat: Threat from all abilities reduced by 10%.

"That could be useful. Never fun having something try to attack you while you're healing," Atlas commented.

"Go for it," Quelin told him.

Atlas selected *Need* on this roll instead. Not long after, a beautiful message showed up.

Atlas won the Need roll for Umbral Cloak!

Before he'd got the cloak clasped on, the next set of messages appeared.

You gained 200 experience for killing a target in The Wild Hunt.

Congratulations, your team has completed The Wild Hunt (Part 1). You are now granted The Wild Hunt (Part 2).

Event Quest – The Wild Hunt (Part 2)	

Requirements
   Finished The Wild Hunt (Part 1)
 	
Quest Rarity: Rare
 	
Quest Reward: 500 experience, 5 silver. 5 Gold to the winning team.
	Description: Hunt the last boss of The Wild Hunt:
	
	   Goreclaw – Level 10

Atlas considered sitting and waiting for them, but remembered something.

"We have some more loot to collect first."

"What do you mean? There weren't any other monsters." Quelin said.

"There are seven dead Reborn gravestones at the original site of combat. If we don't loot it, one of the later parties will. We can call it our rescue fee for saving the girl."

The group was giddy at the prospect of the loot, and all walked to the stones. They bounced from one to another as they looked to see what each person had. They found two rings that looked like loot from the event targets they killed. One of them Ragnarok kept because it increased Constitution by 1. The other one was an Intellect ring that Atlas and Quelin played a game of ro-sham-bo for. Atlas lost when Quelin's scissors cut his paper. The group had a total of 2 gold on them. Atlas couldn't believe it until he remembered the quest. They all received 5 silver per kill. If they killed five monsters already, each of them had 25 silver in event kills alone. They split it evenly among the four of them and each received 50 silver.

Two more items popped up in addition to the rings. Since they weren't spoils from the boss, they were free game. One was a staff that Atlas greedily snatched up.

Item - IronHide Staff	
Requirements: Level 7 **Rarity**: Uncommon **Quality**: Good	**Attack**: 5 **Defense**: 5 **Durability**: 105/105 **Weight**: 8.5 lbs. **Slot**: 2H Weapon **Traits**: A staff made of basic wood and reinforced with the hide of Hellrazer. It can be used to attack or defend. • Damage inflicted to the wielder has 15% less chance to break spell casting.

The other item was a new robe that boosted Quelin's health and added some armor to the magic user.

"That's one hell of a payday. Didn't realize looting gravestones could be so lucrative," Rag quipped.

"It wouldn't be if not for the quest rewards. That's the only reason they were toting around so much money," Gemma reminded him.

Atlas couldn't argue. Between the money they looted from the gravestones, the money he had left from his crafting sales, and the money from the quest rewards, he almost had 1 gold.

Less than ten minutes later, the remaining four members of the team burst through the trees and nearly barreled over Gemma. They came to a quick halt as everyone took a quick breather.

"No time to waste. We don't know if we are the first to this stage or not. Let's get going," the other healer, a man named PiousOne, said.

They all agreed and left at full speed for the final quest location. The zone to search was much smaller for the last creature, so it didn't take long to locate him. It also made it easier when they heard the sound of battle. As with Black Widow, they peered through the trees to see another group in combat with an enormous bear. Goreclaw stood a good eight feet tall at the shoulder. When he reared up on his hind legs, that length almost doubled.

"How the hell do we fight something so large?" CalvinBoy asked. He was the final member of the other team and played the role of ranged attack.

"Carefully. Rag, do you and Pretty think you can hold its attention while we attack?" Atlas asked.

"Not sure," Rag answered, "that thing looks awfully powerful."

Pretty only gulped and nodded in agreement.

"We may not get the chance. This group only has five members left, but they are holding their own right now. If they kill him first, it's game over for us," Gemma said.

"Do we want to stop them?" Jammin asked.

"We can't attack other groups. It's against the rules," CalvinBoy reminded the assassin.

"I know, but I don't remember them saying anything about a little sabotage…" Jammin said with a grin.

Atlas perked up at that. They couldn't afford to lose this fight, but if they could keep this other party from winning first, all the better. At least, as long as they stayed within the rules.

"What do you have in mind, Jammin?" Atlas asked.

"I can redirect threat to one of their healers. If he gets mauled and taken out of the fight, their party will crumble."

"It's a solid plan," Quelin agreed, "but let's observe the fight to figure out our strategy before we do that. If it looks like they may win the fight, we can intervene sooner. Redirecting the threat shouldn't count as us fighting them, since it wouldn't do direct damage to anyone. Would be like one of us casting a buff on one of them to help."

The group all agreed, and they watched the fight unfold. Goreclaw could use four hit combos, as they quickly discovered. This meant that blocking and countering his attacks was vital to keep him from adding up damage. The current party fighting him didn't grasp this concept.

"Don't think we'll need to intervene," Atlas finally told them, "Their warrior is taking far too much damage and the healers will run out of mana soon. This party is going to die."

"Rag, do you have any counterattacks?" Atlas asked.

"I have Counter that I learned from the Weaponmaster. I haven't been able to learn any of the combo attacks that work with it. Spent the money I was saving on them to enter this contest."

"Anyone else?" Atlas asked.

"I have two counterattacks," Quelin said.

"Great. The healer and mage are the only ones right now. PiousOne, you think you can hold the fort on healing if I charge in with Rag? I need to hold some threat of my own to counter the attacks. Jammin, if I get in trouble or we need the extra healing, you can redirect my threat to Pretty."

"I don't like our druid healer tanking a fight, but it seems the best option. I watched how well you deployed those counters in our last couple attacks. With your new weapon, you should do even more damage," Gemma grumbled.

A triumphant roar echoed through the trees and the group turned to see the bear standing victorious over the broken bodies of the party. Their conversation caused them to miss the end of the fight. Small gravestones lifted from the bodies, waiting for someone to loot them.

The group reluctantly agreed to the plan, and Atlas nodded to Rag. The two charged for the now healed bear and began the attack. Atlas used his Triple Threat while Rag swung with his own combo. Arrows and spells entered the battlefield from all angles, and Atlas had trouble keeping track of the action. Blades flashed as their melee fighters attacked from the animal's flanks, and Atlas had to tune out the distractions.

The first heavy attack came in and Atlas had no choice but to drop to the ground and let the swipe go over his head. The flashing red told him he couldn't possibly block it so he wouldn't take that chance on a monster this big. Dodging the attack allowed him to activate Counter, and his staff popped the bear in the nose. Activating Blade Chase allowed him to go on the offensive. Flesh rippled from the attacks as his heavy blows hit the thick layers of hide and fat on the monstrous animal. Triple Threat followed until the last hit struck the beast's head.

You dealt 5 damage to Goreclaw with Counter.
You dealt 20 damage to Goreclaw with Blade Chase.
You dealt 20 damage to Goreclaw with Triple Threat.

Another attack came for him, but this one didn't flash red. Figuring he'd be okay, he blocked the attack with his staff. The force of the blow sent him stumbling sideways and before he could recover, a claw swiped across his body. He fell backward in time to avoid the worst of the attack, but rents in his armor and the burn of some bleeding cuts marked his failure.

Goreclaw dealt 10 damage to you with Swipe. (Glancing Blow)

Holy crap! Ten damage on a glancing hit. I better watch myself.
Atlas saw a blanket of white power settle on him and Rag, and he felt instantly better.

PiousOne healed you for 10 health.

    With a nod of thanks, he returned to the fight. They continued hammering the boss with attacks, but the fight was one of endurance. Its health pool was enormous as they watched their attacks slowly chip away at Goreclaw.
    Rag took a solid hit to the chest, and the bear turned his full attention to Atlas.
    Mommy, he thought before a giant paw came crashing down. Rolling to the side, he activated his combos again. Another 45 damage rolled out for his three attacks as the bear tried to get out of the way. When the creature finally neared the 25% health mark, something strange happened.
    Its eyes glazed over a purple color and its claws and muscles bulged and grew bigger. Atlas met his gaze and stared into its alien looking eyes.
    You challenge me, little druid? I'll devour you.
    Probably, but I've always been a sucker for loot and I hate to fail quests. Let's finish this.
    Their battle of minds went unnoticed to the others in the group, but the physical changes didn't.
    "Atlas, get away from it. That thing is liable to kill you in one hit!" Quelin yelled over the noise of the battle.

    While Atlas wanted to disagree, he knew the
mage was right and disengaged. He felt
something peculiar for a moment, and then
Pretty charged in with a large two-handed
sword. She worked as a tank, but she didn't
use the shield method. Her two-handed sword
served as both her shield and her weapon.
Jammin appeared nearby and grabbed him by the
arm.

    "Get back. I redirected your threat. Keep
them alive until we can drop the last of its
health," she told him with a rough shove.

    Atlas focused on the fight and cast his
Barkskin spell on both Pretty and Rag. The
bear continued its relentless assault, but
they both did a fine job of blocking and
dodging while returning them with Counters.
They were only the standard one-hit counter,
but it was better than nothing.

    Gemma decided it was time to bring out the
big guns and had her large ballista bolt ready
to fire. Atlas also spotted Quelin running
toward it, hands glowing like molten lava. *He
must be repeating his spell from earlier.*

    The rest of the damage dealers in the group
all appeared to be activating special
abilities. Jammin's weapons took on the sheen
of poison. One dripped a purple liquid while
the other a green. CalvinBoy launched a
special ability as well, but instead of the
large ballista that Gemmalin used, his looked
to be a rapid fire ability. Moving with
unnatural speed, the archer loosed eight
arrows in a tight swirling pattern in less
than two seconds. These ultimate attacks hit
home and buried into the bear.

Its health bar plummeted until only a sliver was visible. The creature stumbled for a moment before its eyes flashed red. A gigantic roar issued from its maw. Waves of force radiated through the clearing and pummeled the party with its power. Atlas braced himself as the energy and sound battered at him. Pretty dropped her sword and covered her ears in pain. Her proximity causing her to take the worst of the onslaught. Seeing its opening, Goreclaw slammed into the small warrior. The creature pinned her to the ground with a massive paw and then descended on the lithe woman with his mouth open. Her shriek filled the clearing as Atlas tried to cast a Nourish her way. The spell completed and immediately fizzled. As he looked toward the bear, he saw the broken remains of her body. Blood leaked from large punctures on her chest and neck. Her metal armor looked like Swiss cheese.

Furious at the turn of events, the entire group roared in rage and all charged the bear for one final showdown. Atlas triggered Triple Threat and swung his staff with all of his might. The heavy thumps echoing through the clearing as he connected with each blow.

Multiple arrows sprouted from Goreclaw's side and blood trickled down from the wounds. A ball of fire hit its hind leg and flames erupted from the impact, charring flesh and cooking hair.

Atlas' attacks felt inconsequential until his last hit smashed into the skull directly between its eyes. The purple light faded from the animal and for a moment, clarity returned to its mind.

Thank you for setting my spirit free, young druid.

It sunk to the ground and finally heaved
one last breath before its body stilled.
    The group looked around in stunned silence.
"We won!" They all hollered in joy.

Chapter 13

Nature's Transformation

The group cheered in exultation as they surveyed the scene. They beamed at their accomplishment and all walked to each other. Some members hugged each other while others high-fived. Atlas watched the celebration with an enormous grin of his own. They won the contest and now were going to loot the boss.

His grin quickly turned to a frown as his vision caught the gravestone. The others saw his expression and looked around as though preparing for an attack.

"What's wrong, Atlas?" Quelin asked.

He nodded toward the stone, "We won, but we lost Pretty during that last attack."

The group went silent as everyone turned to look at the gravestone.

"Does anyone know her personally?" Atlas asked.

They all shook their heads no.

"How about in game friends?"

The same shake answered his question.

"One of us needs to save her gear for her. She should respawn in the city. She'll be able to turn in the quest since we won, but it would suck if she had to waste her winnings on new gear immediately," Atlas said.

"I agree. Without her help, this group wouldn't have been successful. We all played our parts and worked well as a team. I think you should take it Atlas," Gemma said with a soft smile.

"You've been honorable this entire time and even made us some stuff asking nothing extra. I agree with Gemma. You should take her stuff to return to her," Quelin echoed.

The rest all nodded in agreement.

With a heavy sigh, he bent down and gathered the items. The armor went into his bag while he stashed her money into his belt pouch. He counted the amount to be sure he gave her exactly what he owed.

"Rag, care to do the honors?" Atlas asked and motioned toward the corpse of the bear.

The big warrior stood up straight and thrust his shoulders back in a stance of pride. When his hand touched the bear, two things popped up.

Item - Goreclaw	
Requirements: Level 7 **Rarity:** Uncommon **Quality:** Good	**Attack:** 6 **Defense:** 2 **Durability:** 85/85 **Weight:** 4.0 lbs. **Slot:** 1H Weapon **Traits:** A claw of the bear Goreclaw. Increases Agility by 1.
Roll for item: Need/Greed	

<table>
<tr><td colspan="2" align="center">Item – Ring of Burgeoning</td></tr>
<tr>
<td valign="top">
Requirements: Level 7
Rarity: Uncommon
Quality: Good
</td>
<td valign="top">
Durability: 110/110
Weight: 0.1 lbs.
Slot: Finger
Cooldown: 15 minutes

Traits: A ring of polished wood with the likeness of a bear on its face. Infuses the body of the wielder with power for a short time.

Trigger the ring to increase Strength by 3 for 2 minutes.
</td>
</tr>
<tr><td colspan="2" align="center">Roll for item: Need/Greed</td></tr>
</table>

The items were cool, but neither really fit his play style. The claw was tempting for its raw damage and Agility boost, but he'd grown accustomed to the staff and enjoyed its versatility. Strength wasn't a big stat for him, so the ring was much better for someone else. Selecting Greed on both, he waited for the results.

JamminGirl won the Need roll for Goreclaw!
Ragnarok won the Need roll for Ring of Burgeoning!

"Congrats, guys. We about ready to go claim our reward?" Atlas asked.

The group nodded in agreement before Ragnarok spoke up.

"Uh, Atlas, there's an item on the bear that I can't loot. It says it's your loot."

"What? It's not my turn for loot."

"It looks like a special item. I think it's class specific."

The thought of it intrigued him and he walked to the bear. Reaching out, the loot window appeared. He selected the item to see what it was.

Item - Soul of the Dire Bear	
Requirements: Level 8 **Rarity:** Epic **Quality:** Good	**Durability:** 50/50 **Weight:** 0.1 lbs. **Slot:** Druid **Traits:** This crystal contains the soul of a dire bear. Absorbing this energy unlocks the Dire Bear special transformation for a druid.

He took the item gently in his hand. The small crystal glimmered with a faint purple light as the jagged edges dug into his palm. Peering into the light gave him the same sense he felt when he communicated with Goreclaw, mind to mind.

"What's that, Atlas?" Quelin asked.

"It's the Soul of the Dire Bear. I can use it to unlock the Dire Bear transformation for my class."

"That's bad ass!" Jammin said as she ran over to look at the crystal.

The assassin oohed and ahhed over the little gem.

"You going to keep that thing or you going to cash in on it?" Ragnarok asked.

"It's class specific so I don't think I can sell it," Atlas told him.

"Does it say it's bound to you?" Quelin asked.

Atlas looked at the description again, "No, it doesn't."

"Then I bet you could sell it. Would you really want to, though? It seems like a special item. Is it something all druids can get?"

"I don't think so," Atlas responded with a shake of his head, "it says it's a special transformation. I assume you could find it by killing any dire bear, but I don't know how common they are. This one was the last boss of an event. I'd bet this is something I could sell for a fortune. Also helps that it's an Epic item."

"That thing is probably worth more than the reward for this event by far. So, what're you gonna do with it?" CalvinBoy asked.

Atlas struggled with the decision. On one hand, he was sure he could sell this thing for tons of gold. Early items like this in new games attracted vast amounts of gold. Those serious collectors and streaming stars loved to have the best items in the game from the start.

The benefits it could offer were too hard to pass up. He focused little on his spell casting unless he was healing. This form would give him something to fight with and could save him in a pinch. If it worked like most games, this form would transform him to something more akin to a tank with higher health and defense.

"I'm going to keep it and use it," he said with confidence as he stared at the gem. With a force of will, he pushed the thought of absorbing it toward the crystal.

*Do you wish to absorb the Soul of the Dire
Bear to learn Dire Bear Transformation? It
will destroy the item in the process. Yes/No.*

Yes. Power swirled from the gem and hit him
in the center of the chest. Spiraling ropes of
purple energy spun as they poured into his
body. The process only lasted about five
seconds, and then the light faded. The gem
lost its shine and then a sharp crack rung
through the clearing. The crystal faded to
dust in his hand.

Druid Spell - Dire Bear Transformation	

Requirements
   Druid Class
   Absorbed the Soul
   of the Dire Bear
	Description: Your body undergoes a physical transformation and turns into a Dire Bear. The form has its own attacks and additions to learn. This effect lasts until canceled.
	
	Mana Cost: 50 MP
	Cast Time: 20 seconds

"It's done. I now have the transformation
spell," Atlas told them with a grin.

"Well, what the hell you waiting for? Show
us!" Quelin said.

Atlas nodded and activated the spell. No
images showed up, but he felt power surge in
his core. His vision shifted perspective as he
grew taller and watched the wide eyes of those
below him. Bones audibly snapped, but no pain
came through. Picking up his hands, he watched
them shift and grow. Claws sprouted from his
nails and hair covered the appendages.

His newfound height finally knocked him off balance, and he fell to land on his hands, now claws. The strange feeling of the bones in his face shifting and growing sent chills down his spine. Five seconds later, he felt his body stop changing and looked to his party members. Wide eyes greeted him on all faces. Jammin's mouth even hung open.

Atlas shifted his weight as he felt the new bulk of his body. The feeling was akin to bear walking back during athletics. It was definitely odd, but he thought he could get the hang of it.

"Whoa, you must be six foot tall at the shoulders in that form. Did it change your stats any?" PiousOne asked.

That's a good question. Atlas looked to his stat sheet.

Name: Atlas	**Agility:** 6
Class: Druid (Transformed)	**Constitution:** 7
	Intellect: 2
Level: 9	**Strength:** 8
HP: 220/220	**Spirit:** 3
Mana: 70/120	
Experience: 106/1300	
Combat Skills: Charge Brutal Swipe Maul	**Magic Skills:** N/A

"It looks like it cancels out my spell casting ability, but it also took the extra stat points from my casting skills and moved them to physical traits. Double my health as well," Atlas grumbled.

"It's good you can still talk, but now it sounds like a menacing growl. You trying to become a villain?" Jammin said with obvious glee.

"Bow down to your new bear overlord," Atlas told her with a rumbling laugh.

"You should stick to that form while we return. You may get a chance to fight in it. Should be cool to see," Quelin suggested.

"I think I will. Let's head for town."

"We not going to finish looting?" Quelin asked.

The group turned to look at him in confusion, and he motioned to the gravestones. They forgot about the party that wiped.

Checking the gravestones, they found a handful of other items. None were anything Atlas could use. They were all Agility and Strength items. The money was a different matter. They had a combined 4 gold and 40 silver on them. Each of them ended up with 55 silver from that haul.

The group gathered up their belongings, and all turned toward the city. They continued their trip in the most direct path they could. As luck would have it, not far away they ran into two wolves.

"Let me have the one on the left. You guys knock down the other. I wanna test this form," he told the group.

Atlas activated Charge, and his body lurched into motion. The sheer power of his muscles astonished him as the distance closed to nothing. The image showed him head-butting the wolf as he charged. He was weary of the idea of charging head first into a creature with a mouth full of teeth, but he wanted the hit so he could continue his attack.

His head thumped into the shoulder of the wolf, and it howled. He barely felt the impact as he activated Maul. Following the images, he raised up on his hind legs with front paws extended. Both paws came down in a crushing blow as his claws dug into the sides of the animal. The second attack was a little harder to stomach as it forced him to come forward and bite directly into the wolf. Thankfully, he tasted nothing from the bite itself, although he felt the squish of flesh and the crunch of bones as his teeth dug into the skull.

You dealt 8 HP damage to Wolf with Charge.
You dealt 22 HP damage to Wolf with Maul.
(Critical) (Crushing)

Holy crap. That was incredible. This form packs a punch.
The wolf snarled as it took its turn. To Atlas' astonishment, no images showed up for him to block. The wolf dove for him and a claw raked across his snout. The sting of the injury took him by surprise, and then the wolf lunged forward and sunk his own teeth into his shoulder.

Wolf dealt 8 damage to you with Tenacious Bite.

What was that about? Can this form not block or dodge? Before the wolf could start another attack, he triggered Swipe. He followed the image, and he swung one paw in a wide arc, scratching across the face of the wolf before turning and swinging the opposite way with the other paw. *They obviously designed this attack to hit multiple targets and piss them off.*

You dealt 14 damage to Wolf with Swipe.

The animal whimpered in pain but returned to attack again. Atlas was helpless again as he took the two-hit combo without being able to respond.

Wolf dealt 8 damage to you with Tenacious Bite.

Roaring in frustration at not being able to block, Atlas activated Maul. The tremendous blows hit the wolf, and it crumpled to the ground as a limp sack of meat.

You dealt 18 damage to Wolf with Maul. (Crushing)
Wolf died.
You gained 10 total experience.

Atlas swung his head and saw the rest of the party watching the fight. The other wolf had already disappeared, showing they'd killed it quickly and looted it. He looted the one he killed and was at least happy that the items automatically stored in a pack for him, even though it wasn't visible on his body.

"That was pretty fun to watch. Why'd you let him keep hitting you, though? You've been great at dodging and countering," PiousOne said.

"This form has one big downside I've found. It doesn't seem capable of blocking or countering, at least not yet. I can't do anything but take the hits."

"That explains the extra health it gives. It seems to pack on some damage if nothing else," Jammin said with admiration in her voice.

The group continued on their way and when they were close to the edge of the forest Atlas activated his transformation spell. His body distorted as it shrunk. His form reverted fully, and he was back in his normal body on hands and knees.

"That's still cool as hell to watch," Quelin whistled.

"It's a very odd feeling for sure. Let's go get our rewards," Atlas told the mage.

The group walked into town, heads held high. They strutted through the streets toward the registrar's office. Almost no one looked their way as they walked through the city, but they didn't care. These people didn't know they were the champions of the event. They came to a stop in front of the building.

"It's been an honor, ladies and gentlemen. We made a hell of a team. If you guys need anything in the future, hit me up," Atlas told them.

All agreed and offered their help to the others if ever needed as well. They looked back toward the building and walked for the door. It burst open and the High Marshall himself marched from the building. He took in the sight of the party and smiled.

"Looks like the champions have arrived. Congratulations adventurers."

"Thank you, High Marshall," the group all responded.

"Because of all of you, this area will be much safer. As a token of my appreciation, I'd like to present you with this special writ. This world needs more brave souls like you to help govern and lead. Present this writ at Nirithan to the registrar's office there for your choice of governance position," The High Marshal told them as he walked to each and handed a rolled scroll.

The Marshal shook each of their hands and told each of them good work before he turned and walked from the plaza toward the city center. The group looked at each other in shock and then entered the building.

"Greetings, adventurers. Do we have our champions in front of us?" One clerk asked.

They each stepped forward and accepted their rewards. The clank of small sacks of gold filled the room, and Atlas stepped forward to a clerk when Jammin finished turning in her own quest.

"I'm here to turn in the quest," he told the man, and the quest box popped up.

Event Quest – The Wild Hunt (Part 2)	

Requirements
   Finished The Wild
   Hunt (Part 1)
 	
Quest Rarity: Rare
 	
Quest Reward: 500 experience, 5 silver. 5 Gold to the winning team.
	Description: You successfully killed Goreclaw. Turn in the quest to the registrar's office.

Do you wish to complete the quest? Yes/No.

He hit *Yes* to complete the quest. The coins felt great in his hands and he stashed them in his pack. A glance at his finances showed him sitting around six and a half gold from all the quest rewards. He turned to leave the office when a thought hit him.

"Excuse me," he said as he waved at the clerk.

"Is there something else I can help you with?"

"Maybe," Atlas started, "If I leave some equipment with you, can you ensure it gets to the owner?"

"We rarely do stuff like that. There's no guarantee they'll ever visit here again."

"It's for the other champion. One of our members died, but they were a Reborn. She'll respawn and come turn in her quest. I wanted to leave her gear with you so you could give it back."

"Well, since it's for a champion, we can make an exception. We'll store her gear here and give it back. What's her name, just so we can verify?"

"She is PrettyPrincess. A warrior," he told the clerk as he handed over the equipment. Her bag of coins was the last item he placed in his hand. The clerk nodded, and Atlas thanked him for his help.

Emerging from the building, he took a deep breath and sighed in contentment. The air was a little foul in the city, but he just completed the first event of the game as the winner and it felt good. He spun, not sure what to do at first. After thinking through his options, he decided he needed to visit Master Proth. With his levels gained, he could learn Harmony.

He stepped foot on the tree-lined porch and walked through the door. Master Proth sat in a chair with a book in his hand. A steaming cup of what looked like tea sat in front of him. Sweat beaded off the side of the metal cup.

"Hey, Master Proth," Atlas said with a wave.

"Ah, Atlas. How goes the leveling?"

"Not bad. Up to level nine. Working on ten. Had to finish the event first. Wanted to pick up Harmony from you before I continued with my leveling."

"Excellent work. Here you go," he said.

The menu popped up in front of him and Atlas chose the Harmony spell. It cost him 30 copper, but that was a trifle to him now. He selected the *Learn* button, and the skill was now his.

Druid Spell - Harmony	

Requirements
   Druid Class
   Level 8
	Description: Draw on the power of nature to heal your target. This ability restores health over time.
	
	• Restores 3 HP every 5 seconds for 50 seconds.
	
	Mana Cost: 10 MP

"So, how'd the hunt go?" the master druid asked.

"Went great. I was actually on the winning team. That reminds me. Are transformation spells rare?"

Master Proth perked up at that and closed his book.

"Transformation spells? That depends. Some are very rare, while others not so much. You will actually have a quest when you are higher level that lets you chose one out of three transformations you wish to learn. Acquiring others can be tricky. Why do you ask?"

"Well, Goreclaw was the last boss of the event and when I killed him he dropped Soul of the Dire Bear. I used it and can now transform into a dire bear myself."

"That's amazing!" Proth said as he stood, "You're extremely lucky. Dire Bear souls have such a low drop rate that most people stopped farming for them. There aren't a lot of dire bears around, so finding them can be difficult. With Goreclaw being a boss, he probably had a better drop rate than others. You have something very special there. The transformation into a dire bear is a coveted thing and can be super beneficial."

"It was pretty neat to fight as a bear. There is one large drawback. While fighting in the transformation, I received no prompting on how to block or counter. It would only let me stand there and take the damage."

"That transformation has that downfall early on. You can learn new abilities and fix some of those gaps, but it takes time. I only personally know one person with that transformation and have only heard of one other. The only hint I can give you is they said they had success fighting other bears to learn from how they moved."

"I appreciate the help. I'll have to give that a shot. That also reminds me. Is there a bank or anything here that can secure my belongings or coins? That way if I die, I don't lose everything."

"There is a bank. We rarely look at it as anything other than a way to control the markets, but it should be able to serve the purpose you describe. I don't think they'll let you store items, but I imagine they'd store money," Master Proth said.

"Can you point me in its direction?"

"Sure. Head toward downtown and it's the large stone building with the columns in front. There's a symbol of scales on the sign."

"Was a pleasure, as always. I'll come find you when I get to level ten for that quest."

"See you then," he said with a wave before sitting back down and opening his book.

Atlas walked outside and headed for the leatherworking shop. Master Trailia greeted him as he arrived with her normal sour scowl before he opened up a trade menu to see what she had. There was one ability available at level ten. It was a reinforced version of the backpack. It was slightly larger but far more durable than the first. The cost was cheap as well. It only added one hide and two sinew to make the better version. He paid the 30 copper for the pattern.

It stunned him when he switched to the buy page. She had 118 raw hides in stock. Unable to comprehend why, he had to ask.

"Why do you have such a sizeable amount of hides? Are people advancing too far past the low level stuff?"

"Oh that? Nope. Everyone wasted all the money they had on the hunt and when they lost they came straight here to sell all the hides they couldn't use. The ones who weren't in the hunt didn't have the money to buy them. So now I'm left with a ton of hides that are almost worthless. It would take me half a year to process that much leather by myself."

An idea hit him, "What is it you need the most here in the city? I know you are limited by how fast you can produce items, but I can make stuff much quicker. I could make everything you need, I'll even agree to do it for nothing more than the salt needed to cure them and a 20% take on the profits after you sell it. I'll also have all the inventory ready for you in a couple of hours."

Her eyes lit up with greed at that point as she wrung her hands, "How about 10% of proceeds, same deal?"

"Come now. You know 20% is a steal. I can make you reinforced items almost instantly. I know you charge a premium for that."

"Fine," she grumbled, "20%. But I want all the work done here in the shop if I'm going to hand over that much merchandise."

"Planned on it anyway. Same room as before?"

She nodded, and they walked to the room. Instead of bothering trying to load him up with the items, she merely dumped the massive pile of hides on the counter in the workroom. She then dropped a large bag of salt nearby to cure them.

"Cure them all and make me four reinforced bags, belts, and jerkins. I also want five reinforced pants," the leatherworker listed off.

"I'll get right on it."

She left the room, and he turned to look at the mountain in front of him. He methodically selected each of the abilities. The skins he cleaned and tanned while stacking them in the corner. Although it was a quick process, it still took a long time to complete one hundred and eighteen of the things. He truly wished for a *Craft All* button with the ability to go AFK.

The process for creating the pieces wasn't much better. His senses were almost numb with the seemingly endless job of his body going on autopilot to do these tasks at such a high speed. His true motivation for this had nothing to do with the money. It was a pleasant bonus, but his purpose was a little more in depth than that.

First off was the experience. The amount of
experience gained from this would be
remarkable by the time he finished. It'd give
him a head start in the market when he reached
the next city. The second motivation was a
little deeper. In his starting city, it became
apparent that the city guards needed the armor
they made. The more stuff he made, the quicker
he saw the guards get outfitted. These types
of interactions had to add up to something.
The feature wouldn't have such a living and
breathing interaction with their surroundings
if it might not come in handy. Atlas banked on
the hope that helping the cities as he went
would pay off in the end.

*You gained 5,880 total experience in
Leatherworking.*
*Success! You've reached levels 11, 12, and
13 in Leatherworking.*

The workspace was a complete mess by the
time he finished. An immense pile of hair
littered the corner and spilled under the
workbench. Scraps of leather littered the
floor and table. He picked up each piece of
equipment and dusted them off before tossing
them out the door and into the large open
space. After sorting them all, he turned to
picking up the trash. The scraps piled up in
the bucket, causing it to overflow. The stack
almost toppled over, but he got it balanced
and tried to avoid it from there.
It forced him to go out into the larger
space to find more buckets to stuff the hair
in. Finally cleaned up, he walked to the front
to find the leatherworker. A customer just
stepped out of the door when he walked up
front.

"All done. Everything is stacked in the main room back there. I put all the scrap leather in the bucket from before and found other buckets to stash the hair. Anywhere specific you want it?"

"No, no. Don't worry about it. I'll take care of that. It's the least I can do for the profit we are about to turn. Come find me in a day's time and I should have all of this sold. Sadly, I can't teach anything past level ten for skills so you'll have to wait until you get to Ixala."

They shook hands, and he waved to the woman as he left. His second trip took him to the woodworker's shop. After seeing the inventory from the leatherworker's place, he wanted to see if the woodworker had a good stock. He was still the same level as before so couldn't learn anything new, but that wouldn't stop him from power leveling a little.

The menu of the woodworker showed 40 Rough Wood Logs in stock. Instead of haggling for a deal here, he instead bought them outright. The demand must've been low because he only paid 5 silver for the entire stack.

Using the same logic as before, he turned all forty logs into twenty Sturdy Wood Braces. It would help with construction in the city, and they also held a steady price. Oddly enough, each of those braces sold for 80 copper, giving him 16 silver for the sale. In that short amount of crafting, he made 11 silver and a hefty amount of experience.

You gained 2000 total experience in Woodworking.
Success! You've reached levels 9 and 10 in Woodworking.

Looking at the menu again, he found the pattern for a Sturdy Wand and paid 30 copper to learn the ability. The pattern for a Standard Short Bow Frame appeared at level 10 and he paid the 30 copper for too.

With his trade skills settled, he bid farewell to the woodworker and headed in the direction of the bank. The building was exactly as Master Proth described. Grayish stone towered high with large columns in front that reminded Atlas of fancy courthouses. A small set of stone stairs led into the building. The inside looked similar to bank lobbies in the physical world. Small cubbies held people behind a solid wall. Bars covered these openings where transactions took place. He approached the nearest window and saw a young woman standing behind the bars.

"Can I help you, sir?"

"Yes, you can. I would like to store my money here under an account in my name."

"That's not a problem. Your funds will be available at any branch of our bank. You'll be issued a writ that declares the amount you have stored. This writ is bound to you and won't disappear. How much would you like to store?"

Atlas took stock of his money before answering, "Five gold."

"Not a problem. What's your name?"

"Atlas."

She scratched away at a small piece of paper and turned it to face him.

"Sign this and give me the five gold and you're set."

He looked at the paper, and it registered as a Writ of Credit. It stated in bold letters: 5 Gold. He dropped the gold on the counter and scribbled his name on the paper. She scooped the money through the opening and he left on his way, much happier about the security of his money.

Pondering what to do next, a message interrupted him.

You have 8 hours of game time left before you must log off.

Damn. That hunt sucked up more time than I thought. It was a lot of running and searching.

Instead of doing anything fancy, he just went out in the wood and spent six hours farming for hides. He did the fighting in bear form so he could get more practice with it. Unfortunately, he didn't run into any bears he could fight. When he took more damage than he cared for, he would shift back to his normal form to heal and then shift back.

When done hunting, he walked back to the inn and nodded to the innkeeper. Opening his door, he walked in and locked it behind him. His messages showed the results of his latest trip.

You gained 145 total experience.

I need to find a couple quests when I log back in to finish my trip to level ten. He lay on the bed and closed his eyes.

Do you wish to log out? Yes/No.

Yes.

Chapter 14

Catching Up

Atlas heaved himself from the capsule as Jean finished disconnecting everything.

"How'd the event go? I heard they have completed it in every region," Jean asked.

"It went great. The team I was on won our region."

"Congrats. That must've been a hard fought victory."

"It sure was. Eight creatures, some of which looked pretty nasty. I mean one was part woman, part spider for god's sake," Atlas said with a chuckle.

"Gross. I think I would've just given up and walked away. I've seen how real the world is in the game and am not about to fight something like that."

"How's work been?"

"Busy as usual. Luckily, my shift is up in a few hours."

"Hopefully, the rest of your day is calm. I've got to head out. Take care of yourself."

She looked to the control panel and Atlas turned to go before he stopped in his tracks. *She really is pretty. Seems like a great girl. It's worth a shot.*

He turned back to her.

"You have any plans this evening?" Atlas asked.

She looked up from the panel and flashed a
brilliant smile.

Such a beautiful smile.

"Well," she said with a slight blush, "I
don't have any plans. You have something in
mind?"

"Actually. I hoped you might join me for
dinner?"

"I don't know if that's a good idea. We
know nothing about each other."

"It's just a date. I'd like to get to know
you. At least, the you that exists outside of
work."

A pang hit him in his lower stomach. The
unfortunate aftereffects of two days in the
game were catching up fast. She merely grinned
and lifted her clipboard. A quick bit of
scribbling and she ripped off a small piece of
paper.

"Call me this afternoon and let me know
what you have planned."

"Thanks," he said as he took the paper,
"Talk to you later."

Wasting no more time, he dashed for the
stairs and to the restroom. It wasn't as bad
as the first time, but a few more minutes and
there could've been an accident.

His trip home was uneventful, and he
cleaned up as soon as he walked in. The
excitement of his upcoming date made the rest
of the day crawl by. Shortly after lunchtime,
he called Jean. They agreed to meet at a small
pizza place close to his house. He considered
offering to pick her up at her house, but
thought she might find it a little too much
for a first date. They didn't know each other
after all.

The tiny shop was well known for its hand tossed pizza. Everything was made from scratch and as authentic as it could get. He waited at one table in a pair of blue jeans and a button-up shirt. She walked through the door in a stunning little black dress. Her hair twisted upward and pinned into a bun. Atlas stood up and pulled her chair out for her before sliding it back in.

"Thanks for coming. You look fantastic."

"You don't look too bad yourself. It's nice to see you when you don't smell like two days' worth of chemicals," she said with a chuckle.

Atlas grimaced, "It's not the best smell, I know. The first thing I do is race for the shower to rinse it off."

The server approached, and they both ordered drinks and a pizza to split.

"So, tell me about yourself. How did you end up working at Gaia?"

"I went to school for neurological interfacing. When I completed my degree, I worked for a couple small companies in their virtual reality departments. That was during the early days of VR, back when everyone was just trying to develop a full interface. Needless to say, they all fell through. Eventually, Gaia hired me to work on their new prototype. Most of my initial days focused on testing their new system. When it entered the functional phases, they moved me to monitoring of the pods. Now I get to check on you guys and gals when you log out. How about you?"

"About the same. I went to school and became a nurse. Now I work at a clinic. I started off in a hospital but didn't like how they managed the work load. The hectic schedules and understaffing annoyed me. I like the clinic more because it's more of a steady work schedule and I have a little more freedom."

Their evening continued with small talk and their food. Atlas discovered she had no siblings and her family lived far away. She was truly alone here and moved here just to work for Gaia. This left her pretty lonely since she didn't have many local friends yet.

They rose from their chairs after Atlas paid for dinner and decided on a casual stroll. As they walked around the streets, Jean reached over and grabbed his hand. Atlas smiled at her and they continued their trek. When they finally came back around to her car, they stopped.

"Looks like I need to get going. I had a great time. Will I get to see you again?" she asked.

"Of course you will. I had a great time as well. We have to do this again sometime. It's going to depend on our odd schedules though," Atlas assured her.

She leaned in and kissed him on the cheek before sliding into her car.

"Take care, Atlas."

The engine rumbled to life, and she drove away. *This is one of the best nights I've had in a long time.*

****

Work moved slowly until his phone rang. A glance at it showed Keenan calling. A quick swipe and he put it to his ear.

"What's up, Keenan?"

"Nothin much. You stuck at work?"

"Yep. Kinda boring today. Not many patients."

"You get back on your feet in game?"

"Oh yeah. Completely swung everything around in my favor. Got all my gear back and got to level 9. As soon as I log back in, I plan on hitting 10 and traveling to Ixala."

"I just got to my third city when I last logged out. I'm almost to level 11. I've been able to make some decent money with my Alchemy so far. I entered The Wild Hunt, and we ended up killing six of the targets before we were beat to the last boss. Ended there with our winnings and went back to questing. An extra thirty silver wasn't bad though. I also got a cool dagger from one of them."

"Sweet. I was also in The Wild Hunt. It was crazy."

"Oh, you recovered your gear and made enough money to enter the event? You must've been hustlin' hard. How'd you fare?"

"We won," Atlas blurted into the phone.

"Won? You're group killed all eight first?"

"Sure did. Our final boss was a giant bear. It was so cool. I got an epic drop from him. I received an item that lets me transform into a dire bear. It's hella cool."

"For real? That sounds wild. You kept that item instead of selling it? It sounds like something that would fetch a fortune this early."

"Yeah, I considered selling it, but in the end I'm glad I didn't. My druid trainer said the form is exceptionally rare, and he only knows of two people who have it."

"Damn, you could've scored a fortune. I saw on one forum earlier that someone sold an item that granted a special skill to warriors for over 500 gold. Your skill actually sounds rarer than that."

Atlas leaned back in his chair and let out a heavy breath, "Yeah, it was a tough decision, but I wanted the spell more than the money. Honestly, I make enough money right now with my professions. Oh, I almost forgot, I mastered my first addition and gained another. It's a three-hit attack. I'm slowly getting better with countering attacks and responding with chained combos."

"I've got that down pretty good and do a lot of damage. My new dagger also helps bump my damage a lot. I also got my three-hit combo. I did as you suggested and just let my body take over."

Atlas waved at his fellow nurse, Cassandra, as she brought a patient back.

"Hey Atlas, can you enter their information while I get them checked in?" she asked.

Atlas covered the mouthpiece on his cell phone, "Will do."

He removed his hand and resumed his conversation.

"Hey man. Sorry to interrupt you, but I've got to get back to work. I'll catch you later."

"See ya bud." Keenan confirmed.

The afternoon passed far more slowly than he cared for, so he delved into his phone to help speed up time. Keenan mentioned one of the forum sites, and they had also scolded him for not researching any on them prior to coming into the event. He maneuvered back to the site he'd looked into earlier. Divine Genesis Fanatics displayed on the banner, and he noticed a bunch of notifications on his account. When he checked them, he was astonished to see over 100 upvotes for his post. A few even responded directly to thank him because they'd mastered their current addition because of his help.

The site had more guides posted on it now. He saw one major post pinned for each of the professions. The leatherworking one was just a basic description of the patterns up to level 15 in the skill. No real information on the skill in general. The Woodworking one was the same, so he didn't bother checking any of the others.

A post caught his attention with its strange headline. The Corruption of Gaia. Intrigued by it, he tapped the link.

The Corruption of Gaia

Fellow gamers. Please be wary when you log into Divine Genesis. We've spoken with some devs who built the game and they acknowledged to us that they were forced to inject code into the game that didn't appear to have anything to do with the game and it seemed malicious. They had to override certain safety protocols to do it. They couldn't tell us what it was supposed to do, but they weren't happy with it.

Humanity United

Humanity United? Never heard of them. A scroll through of the replies showed many people calling them conspiracy theorists. A few asked for proof of these claims, but they provided nothing. The thought baffled Atlas. Why would they mess with the game? With the real world market tie in, Gaia Corporation was bound to make a fortune on it. There would be no reason to do something so reckless.

Chalking it up to crazy people, he backed out of the post. Not seeing anything druid specific, he debated with himself. *Do I share the information about transformations? Not sure if it's a good idea.* His feelings warred with himself before he finally posted. He wouldn't give exact details of his character or name.

He started a new post named Druid Transformations. In this he detailed druids could choose one of three forms as they reached a higher level. In addition, he told them they could find rare crystals that granted them a transformation as well. He mentioned the Dire Bear transformation being one of them. His explanation also listed that there was a tiny chance for this item to drop from dire bears in the game, and any that were named had an even higher chance to drop the loot.

After a quick read through to check for spelling errors, he hit submit. He closed the browser on his phone and returned his attention to work.

***

His trip back to Gaia and into the game was very uneventful. Disappointment filled him when Jean wasn't working as he came in. Instead of the normal small talk, he just hopped right in and they fired up the machine. His vision faded and blackness filled him before shifting back into his room at the inn.

Scooping up his belongs, he walked downstairs. A handful of people dotted the room, but no one he recognized, so he continued outside. His number one priority was to get to level 10 as fast as possible. He needed almost 500 experience to get there. Instead of grinding for countless hours on monsters, he scoured the city looking for quests.

It took him more than an hour, but he eventually found three quests to go on.

Quest - Exterminator	
Requirements Level 7 Quest Rarity: Common Quest Reward: 140 experience, 80 copper coins.	Description: Kill 6 wolves in the surrounding forest.

Quest - Jumboroots	
Requirements Level 8 Quest Rarity: Common Quest Reward: 150 experience, 90 copper coins.	Description: Collect 10 Jumboroots from the surrounding area.

Quest - A Strange Occurrence	
Requirements Level 9 Quest Rarity: Common Quest Reward: 160 experience, 1 silver coin.	Description: Reports of an odd location of rot northeast of the city warrant investigation. Determine why the rot has infected the area and stop it if possible.

    Most were pretty straightforward. *The quest with the rot could be interesting.* If video games taught him anything, it was that rot usually meant an undead somewhere nearby.

    The wolves and the herbs were just time-consuming. Those he grabbed as he found them. His trip started by heading for the reported location of the rot. During his trek, he spotted three of the Jumboroots and successfully harvested them. The large bulbs reminded him of the roots for elephant ear plants. As long as he dug around them far enough, they were easy to extract without harm. It also came with one other benefit during his gathering.

Success! You reach level 4 in Herbalism.

Two wolves crossed his path, and he dispatched them without trouble. When he neared the location of the rot, he slowed his pace. The change in the forest was negligible at first. A speck of mold here, a piece of discolored bark there. Before long, the patches of rot grew larger and larger until everything looked dead. The center of the phenomenon was a clearing in the trees. No grass grew and only dark dirt covered the space. The trees around the edge looked old and about to collapse. A slight push on one caused the trunk to crack and the thing to fall. It broke into countless pieces of dried material as it smashed into the ground.

Atlas lifted his staff to a ready position and walked into the clearing. Nothing stood out in any direction he looked. The barren expanse shocked his senses. Not a single blade of grass brushed against his boots as he walked. A slight tinge of death filled the air, but he didn't see a carcass anywhere.

When he reached the center of the space, his boot thudded against something hard. Unsure what it was, he took a step back and looked down. A small piece of metal stuck from the ground. Bending over and grabbing it, he pulled. Dirt cascaded away from it as he withdrew a fragment of a gauntlet. Half of it was rusted, but the other half was intact enough for him to make out the general shape. The piece confused him until he felt the ground rumble.

He dropped the glove and looked around. The surrounding dirt seemed to crawl and undulate. A hand of pure white bone burst from the ground near him and scrabbled to pull itself free. Three more of these popped up around the clearing and, before long, he stood in the center of four skeletons. He inspected one. *Haunted One - Level 7.*

Wanting to get a head start on this fight, he ran at the nearest one and activated Triple Threat. His staff reverberated against the bones as each swing connected. Its dried ligaments flexed as he struck at the joints, but none of them snapped or gave way. The monstrosity remained standing and glared at him with glowing green eye sockets.

You dealt 20 HP damage to Haunted One with Triple Threat.

Its health bar didn't shift as much as he hoped, but it was better than nothing. The monster lurched toward him and slashed with a skeletal hand. He followed the images and ducked under the swing and activated Counter. After the initial smack, he followed with Blade Chase and then another Triple Threat. The damage added up quickly, and the skeleton rocked backward.

You dealt 5 damage to Haunted One with Counter.
You dealt 20 HP damage to Haunted One with Blade Chase.
You dealt 20 HP damage to Haunted One with Triple Threat.

The health of the monster neared the end, but his turn was up. The next attack came for him and he began to block the swing when his vision flashed red. With a yelp, he tumbled backward just as another of the skeleton's hand clawed through the space he'd been.

Too many to isolate them for very long. So much for my surprise attacks. Taking a few running steps to the side, he turned and cast Entangle on the closest enemy. The monsters were slow and clumsy, so when he entangled the lead one, it made the ones behind it stumble trying to get past. With the time he needed, he activated his Dire Bear Transformation.

His body flexed and grew as he fell to all fours. The transformation finished right as a skeleton finally came within reach of him. There was nothing he could do to stop the attack and braced for the impact. The hand swiped at him but bounced off his thick fur, doing almost no damage.

Haunted One dealt 1 damage to you with Bash.

A low grumble of pleasure escaped his throat as he activated Charge and head-butted his original target. As soon as his head hit the skeleton, Maul followed. His thrill climbed higher as he struck. When he clamped his jaws over the monster's skull, the force of his bite shattered the skeleton and it fell apart.

You dealt 8 damage to Haunted One with Charge.
You dealt 28 damage to Haunted One with Maul. (Critical)
Haunted One died.

The rest of the fight that followed was simple. The creatures could barely damage his thick hide, so he literally laughed at their attacks. He alternated swiping at the group and mauling them. One by one, their bones crunched under his assault until he was the only one left standing. As the space quieted, he checked the area again. Something caught his eye in the dirt near one skeleton. A small stone that seemed to drink the light rested on a small mound. When he approached it, he saw the name of the item. Corruption Crystal.

The crystal went into his bag. As soon as it did, the quest changed and asked him to deliver the crystal back to the magistrate in town.

With that quest done, he returned to his wood elf form. While it was fun fighting as a bear, he was much quicker as an elf. It also made woodcutting and herbalism difficult in his bear form.

The next few hours consisted of him roaming the area near the city in search of his objectives. Eventually, he found all the Jumboroots and killed the last of the wolves. Not wasting an opportunity, he also killed most of the other animals he crossed paths with. Their skins were still useful to him. *I also need to go see Master Trailia about my cut of our deal.*

He turned in the two quests for the herbs and wolves near the gate as he entered. The final one he had to travel to the center of the city to turn in. The magistrate thanked him profusely for ending the undead threat before it spread too far to control. The man promised to have the Corruption Crystal destroyed or purified.

With that business out of the way, he
looked at how things fared.

You gained 165 experience total.
*You gained 140 experience and 80 copper for
completing Extermination.*
*You gained 150 experience and 90 copper for
completing Jumboroots.*
*You gained 160 experience and 1 silver for
completing A Strange Occurrence.*
Success! You've reached Level 10.

*Finally, level 10! Now to go check with
Master Trailia before I go get my druid quest.*
He dropped one point into Constitution
bringing it to 10 and the other into Intellect
putting it at 11. This brought his HP to a
maximum of 120 and his mana to 130.

*For getting 10 attribute points in
Constitution, you have unlocked a bonus. You
now regenerate health at 1 HP every 20 seconds
when out of combat.*

*Even better. Now I don't have to keep
healing myself in between the grinding.*
The spoils of his battle also included more
meat from the animals and an additional 23
hides. Master Trailia greeted him with an
uncharacteristic smile as he entered. When he
approached the desk, she dropped a small pouch
of coins for him.

"Twenty percent, as we agreed. The total
sale came out to eighty-five silver, so your
cut was seventeen silver."

"That's glorious news. I guess the influx
of items didn't damage prices too much?" Atlas
asked with concern.

"Oddly enough, it actually increased many of the prices. Armor around here has been selling faster than we can make it. The influx of new people and Reborn has caused shortages in weaponry and armor. Building materials have plenty of supply."

"Do you have any more hides you'd want to do a similar deal on?"

She shook her head, "I only wish I did. With the hunt over, the influx of hides has gone down. I only have a handful to work with now. Nothing that would be worth your time. I also suggest you save whatever you have for the next city. I see you hit level ten so I know it won't be long before you move on."

"Good idea. Thanks for the advice and your business."

They shook hands and Atlas sold off his excess meat to her. It only raked in three more silver, but it was money in his pocket. She handed him a rolled letter with a seal before he left.

"Give this to Master Grant in Ixala. He can continue your skill training."

"Thank you," Atlas told her as he walked out the door. From there, he walked through town and into Master Proth's house. The druid didn't look like he moved an inch since he saw him two days ago. The same sweating cup of tea sat on the table and a book rested in his hands. The cover of the book didn't look the same as before, so if nothing else he moved to a new one.

"Master Proth. I'm at level ten and have come to get my quest for Resurgence."

"Knew it wouldn't take you long," he beamed, "come over here for a moment and have a seat."

Atlas joined him at the table and took up a position in the chair across from him.

"The quest for Resurgence requires you to enter the realm that sits between life and death. A place called the Remembrance. Souls linger her for a short time until they are called to the next realm. This is the same place that necromancers use for their foul magic to twist and capture souls. Enough about that nasty business, though. Your task will be to heal a soul in this realm and re-affix it to the body. This requires the use of a Focus Crystal," the druid told him as he reached into a pouch and produced a glimmering green gem.

Atlas took the crystal and held it in his hands. He wasn't sure if it was a trick of his mind or not, but he smelled the faint breeze blowing through trees, the comforting feeling of resting on a bed of thick grass, and the calm warmth he got when he used his Nourish spell. With a careful hand, he placed the crystal back on the table.

"Go ahead and keep that one. It requires one of those every time you use the spell. Those need to be stockpiled ahead of time before you go into danger. Any of the druid trainers you find can sell you empty ones. You can't use them until they have been filled with souls of nature. The average one takes eight animal kills to fill with enough soul energy. Always remember, to bring back life, requires life in exchange."

Atlas only nodded at the explanation.

"Now, join me in the back," he said as he snapped his book closed and laid it on the table. Atlas grabbed the gem from the table and followed. They walked to the space behind the house where he initially demonstrated his skills. The druid stopped in the center and turned to face him.

"Do not fear. This task is pretty simple. I warn you, it's a painful process. After this quest, it won't be an issue anymore though."

Proth whistled and a small squirrel ran from the wall near the garden and directly toward the mage.

"I'll kill this little creature and it will be your duty to bring him back. Fair warning. You won't like this. Whatever happens don't freak out and trust that I won't let you die."

I really don't like how he said that.

Proth shared the quest, and he accepted it.

Quest - Resurgence	

Requirements
  Druid
  Level 10
 	
Quest Rarity: Common
 	
Quest Reward: 175 experience, Resurgence Spell.
	Description: You must walk the Remembrance and help restore the life of a dead creature. You will learn the Resurgence spell upon completion.

The druid stood directly in front of him and pulled out a dagger. The poor creature in his hands wriggled as it realized what would happen, but it couldn't escape the iron grip of the druid.

"Be one with nature," the druid whispered before plunging the blade into the animal. It squeaked before going limp in his hands.

Atlas stared at the squirrel in shock. Unsure what to do, he tried to hold the crystal to the creature, but nothing happened. At a loss, he looked to the druid master.

"What do I do?"

"Well, here's the crappy part. Your first trip into the Remembrance requires you to be on the cusp of death," the druid said solemnly before his dagger flipped around and lodged directly into Atlas' heart under his armpit.

He staggered at the pain as he felt blood gush down his side. His vision grew fuzzy until the druid's hands glowed green and power suffused him. The master didn't remove the weapon from the wound but kept a steady flow of power.

"Now, while I hold this, look near the squirrel for its soul. When you see it, use nature magic and aim that power at the soul. Once the rope of energy tethers itself to the spirit, drag it back to the body. A final surge of nature magic will heal the body and spirit enough for the soul to reattach and restore life."

Atlas struggled to think straight with the pain. He remembered the man's words about this sucking and had to agree with the assessment. Instead of trying to fight it, he grit his teeth and looked toward the dead animal. A small ghostly figure of the squirrel lay curled in a ball above the corpse. It looked lost and frightened, as it huddled and shivered in place.

He lifted his hands and pushed magic toward the creature. With his focus directed at the animal, the beam of green magical power shot forth and connected. He followed the instructions as he pulled the soul to the corpse and sent one last burst of power. Master Proth withdrew the blade and pushed a vast sum of energy into him. His body tingled from the experience and all the pain faded. His health returned to max, and he breathed a calming breath.

"Sorry about that. I told you it wasn't fun," Proth said with sorrow in his voice.

"Yeah, I'm not sure whether I should be mad you didn't tell me what you would do or relived you didn't. I'm not sure I could've made myself do that if I knew exactly what it required."

"It can be a tough concept to understand. That's why only a master druid can teach this spell. The balance between life and death is precarious, and we must strive to hold you there. Now that you finished the ritual, I could alter your soul. When you are near a corpse, you can push power into a Focus Crystal to shift into the Remembrance so you can revive them."

"At least I don't have to be on the edge of death every time to resurrect. That would suck."

"It would indeed. I assume you plan on moving on to Ixala now?"

"Sure do. I think I've done most everything I can here. Before I go, can I buy more of those crystals from you?"

"Of course. I warn you, they're not cheap. On the plus side, they are soulbound to you so they can't be stolen or looted."

"That's fine, I have plenty of money right now."

The menu appeared, and Atlas saw the new listing for Focus Crystal. The listed price on them was 10 silver a piece. He wasn't lying when he said they weren't cheap, but they had to be pricey. For a Reborn, that price meant a quick return to a dungeon or fight. For an NPC, it was literally life or death permanently.

Deciding to invest up front, he bought five of them for 50 silver. The druid handed him a letter of introduction and told him to find Master Greenfoot in Ixala. With a final handshake, Atlas bid him farewell and left the building.

Chapter 15

Ixala

The trip to Ixala took him northeast of
Lairthyn. The path was a well-worn road and
clear the entire way. People cluttered the
road in a few places. The steady thump of his
staff on the dirt kept him moving at a
leisurely pace.

The city eventually came into view, and it
was even larger than Lairthyn. A full-sized
wall of solid stone surrounded the entire
city. Towers dotted the outer ring, and tiny
figures stood along the battlements. From this
distance, he couldn't get an exact size on the
wall.

As he drew nearer, the sheer scope of the
structure finally became apparent. The wall
itself stood twenty feet tall. The towers
attached to it stretched another ten feet
higher than that. A large wooden gate framed
in iron with riveted bands of metal
crisscrossed along the front.

People lined up near the gate as guards
checked those that entered and ushered them
through. Atlas stepped forward and one guard
waved to him.

"State your business in Ixala."

"Here to continue my druid training."

The guard nodded at the explanation, "New
to the city then? What's your name?"

"Atlas, sir."

The man quirked an eyebrow at the title but scribbled on his paper and handed it to him.

"Take this to your druid master and then, when he signs it, take it to the magistrate to register for the city. They'll give you a token that lets you freely pass without the questions and delays."

"Thanks," Atlas told him as the guard shooed him on his way and turned to the next in line.

Unsure of where to go, he looked around the streets. The outer part of the city held most of the stables to protect the animals while also keeping their stench farthest away. Inns were popular because of travelers. A patrol of three guards walked through the streets near him and he flagged them down.

"Hey guys, sorry to bother you. Do you know where I can find the druid, Master Greenfoot?"

The three looked at each other for a moment before shaking their heads. The eldest of the group spoke up.

"Don't know him personally. Most of the magical class masters keep residence in the Ring of Mages," he said as he turned and pointed farther into the city, "This city is divided into rings. This outer ring is the Ring of Trades. The next ring is the Merchant Ring. Following that is the Ring of Mages. A small stone wall denotes each ring, separating them."

"Thank you for the help!" Atlas said as he took off in the direction the man indicated.

The principal thoroughfare he walked stretched all the way into the city, and it looked like it went to the city center itself. Instead of testing out his theory, he followed the guard's directions until he entered the breakpoint for the Ring of Magic.

The buildings in that section of town all had signs depicting magical things. Book shops lined many of the roads that crossed the main street. A shop with the picture of a staff on the sign sat nearby. With curiosity derailing his search for Master Greenfoot, he stepped into the place.

The smell of sawdust filled his air as he looked around the room. Small racks lined the walls, and piles of staves lined each one. Little signs marked each one with prices listed on them. It reminded Atlas of price tags back in the real world. As he moved farther into the shop, the amount of staves on the racks diminished, but the prices rose.

One of them near the desk even stood in a glass case. A price tag on the box listed it at two gold. *This thing must be super high level!* An examination of it proved him wrong.

Item – Wizard's Meditation	
Requirements: Level 15 **Rarity:** Epic **Quality:** Exquisite	**Attack:** 8 **Defense:** 5 **Magical Attack:** 14 **Durability:** 205/205 **Weight:** 3.0 lbs. **Slot:** 2H Weapon **Traits:** A staff made of the sturdiest, yet lightest wood and imbued with magical power. It grants the wielder the following traits: • Increases Intellect by 3. • Increases Spirit

	by 4. • Increases experience gained from kills and quests by 15%.

Holy crap. That thing screams overpowered. No wonder it commands such a high price.

The greedy part of his soul wanted to buy it. The experience gain would be invaluable once he hit level 15. The practical part of him told him he was stupid. The problem with low-level items like this was obvious. You'd out level its usefulness eventually, and when you did, you wouldn't get nearly enough money trying to sell it. The price rarely paid off as a solid investment. The stats on it were higher than anything he'd seen so far, so he guessed this would be a formidable weapon until at least level 20, maybe 25. After that, something better would come along. He also focused more on physical attack than magic, so there was that to consider.

"Admiring that beauty are ye?" A small man said as he walked into the room and took his place behind the counter. He couldn't be over four and a half feet tall. A bushy beard covered his face. It could be described as a Santa Claus beard by how thick it was, except his was a dark black and not white. A bulbous nose sat in the center of his face and thick furry eyebrows cast shadows over his eyes.

"Sure was. That thing is sure nice. Don't think it's worth the investment, though. Too much money for something I can outpace with leveling in a short time."

"Aye, there is that. It's for the people who value their time far more than their money. The added experience boost helps them climb higher, faster. It'll be here for a while. Items like that usually sit and wait for one specific person. But that's neither here nor there. I'm Kilkanic, purveyor of this shop. What can I help you with…," he let the sentence hang as if waiting for Atlas, so he slipped in his response.

"Name's Atlas. I was just browsing your goods. I am a druid myself and a woodworker. I'm sure I'll eventually come by to sell merchandise to you."

"Druid you say? I guess your training with Master Greenfoot?"

"I actually just arrived but, yes, he'll be my druid master. I was looking for his place when the sign drew me in here."

"You're not far away. Go back to the main road and head toward the center of town. The next road up, take a left and follow it. It's a little of a hike, but his house is about a quarter of the way around the circle. If you came from Lairthyn, you'll spot it immediately. It has a similar design to Master Proth's house. Proth apprenticed under Master Greenfoot for a while and picked up some of his style."

"Thanks for the info. I'll stop by and visit when I have something to sell."

"You do that. Don't be afraid to come looking for something to buy. Your staff looks like it'll serve well for at least a few more levels, but you'll eventually need an upgrade," the man called as Atlas walked away.

"I'll keep that in mind," he chuckled as he walked outside.

The directions were straightforward, and he followed them through town. The merchant, who Atlas assumed was a dwarf but didn't want to seem rude if he was wrong, wasn't lying about how far the trip was. By the time he reached the building, his legs hurt. Part of that was the trip here in the first place, but he'd been on his feet for a long span of time with no rest.

The house was indeed almost identical to Master Proth's, if his house was twice its current size. The same style of trees lined the front porch, and similar wood patterns marked the outside of the building. Even the smell of the wood remained identical as he walked through the door.

An older man looked up from the desk he sat at. Patches of gray stood out in his hair and beard. He puffed on an old pipe of carved wood and his midsection looked like he enjoyed eating. His jovial smile made Atlas immediately forget those details. He emitted a warmth, almost like a comforting blanket with that simple expression.

"Welcome, young druid. What brings you to me?"

"Master Greenfoot?" Atlas asked.

The older man only nodded in response.

"I'm Atlas. I'm here to continue my druid training with you," he said as he walked forward and presented the letter from Master Proth.

"Ah, little Proth. How is he faring anyway?"

"Last time I saw him he was sitting at a table, drinking tea, and reading a book," Atlas answered honestly.

"Sounds like he's living his dream. He's always been a fan of reading. Looks like taking that quiet post out there truly paid off for him after all.

"By the looks of things here, you showed your knowledge of all previous spells and you picked up all three of the newer ones, including Resurgence. Sure glad I don't have to teach you that one. Nasty business it is."

Atlas only gulped and nodded his head at the memory. The druid continued to scan the letter until his eyebrows rose at something.

"Did you truly obtain the Dire Bear Transformation?"

"Yep. I earned the soul from Goreclaw. He was the last boss of the recent Wild Hunt event, and our team won."

"Truly marvelous. A rare transformation and completely caught up on your skills. It's nice to have a well-rounded student for once. Most that I've seen lately are missing a skill or completely inept at anything not physical combat. You even had the common sense to go with the staff," he said with an approving nod toward the weapon.

"I'll admit I picked up the staff on a whim, but Master Longstride suggested I stick with it since it fit so well with the class."

"Good to see some of our younger masters remember their lessons. Looks like you're fresh at level 10 and haven't made it very far since. I only have one spell you can pick up now. Even then, it's not really new. I have Rank 2 of Nature's Fury for you."

"I'll take whatever you can teach."

The druid smiled, and a menu popped up in his view. The spell and more Focus Crystals were the only items on the list. The spell cost 60 copper, so he purchased it.

Druid Spell – Nature's Wrath (Rank 2)	

Requirements
   Druid Class
   Level 10
	Description: Summons two balls of raw nature energy to launch at your target.
	
	Damage: 7-9 HP
	Mana Cost: 20 MP

So, extra damage per hit and now it hit twice instead of once? That's a pretty fantastic bonus for 5 extra mana. If I had the magical bonus of that staff from earlier, I could do a ton of damage. The two added base damage from my Intelligence makes this useful.

"Do all the spells have extra ranks like this?"

"Most do. A few of them, like Resurgence, don't. You can find special items that increase the benefits, such as resurrect people with more HP and stuff like that, but that is a spell that doesn't have additional ranks. Most of your offensive spells do, and you'll get them as you level."

"That's good news. I was beginning to think magic spells would be useless other than healing. Now I can see how well they may scale, especially with a suitable weapon that has a decent boost to magical attack."

"I'm afraid that's all I can do for you right now. Oh, before I forget, let me see your entry paperwork so I can sign it. Don't want you getting grief at the gate while trying to quest."

"Oh, forgot all about that already," Atlas said with a grimace before handing the paper over to Master Greenfoot. He scribbled on the slip before handing it back.

"Now run off to the magistrate's office. If you came in the gate directly from Lairthyn, head back to that same main road and continue toward the center of the city. In the innermost quarter, The Sanctum, lies the magistrate office. It's on the main road as you enter."

"Thanks, Master," Atlas said with a bow. He turned and walked back out of the building without another word.

On his return trip to the main road, an odd thought distracted him. He only just noticed he'd been uncommonly polite to the masters since entering the game. Bowing and always addressing them as master didn't seem normal now that he thought about it. He couldn't figure out if it was something to do with his southern upbringing or if there was something inherent in the game causing it as an instinct.

His mind didn't wander far down that rabbit hole before he met back up with the main road he'd traveled earlier. Turning toward the city center, he continued his trip. He dodged out of the way of the occasional mounted guardsman and merchant cart, but eventually found the magistrate's office.

The magistrate wasn't in office but his assistant was and quickly took care of the matter. A quick signature on the slip and he handed a small token of an unknown metal to Atlas. Stamped on it was the name Ixala, and the back showed the scales he'd seen on the sign for the registrar's office.

The assistant ushered him back out of the building and told him to stay out of trouble before promptly closing the door behind him. With the necessary work out of the way, he focused on next steps. It was time to find some quests, and he needed to check in with the profession trainers for Leatherworking and Woodworking.

He backtracked his steps and searched out for quests. A bulletin board in one of the fancier districts gave him a quest, while he also found three others from random people.

<table>
<tr><td colspan="2" align="center">Quest -The Finest of Fur</td></tr>
<tr><td>Requirements
   Level 9

Quest Rarity: Common

Quest Reward: 180 experience, 1 silver and 10 copper coins.</td><td>Description: Collect 6 hides of Elegant Fur from nearby animals.</td></tr>
</table>

<table>
<tr><td colspan="2" align="center">Quest - A Hunting We Will Go</td></tr>
<tr><td>Requirements
   Level 10

Quest Rarity: Common

Quest Reward: 200 experience, 1 silver coin.</td><td>Description: Kill 8 Jackalopes in the nearby forest.</td></tr>
</table>

Quest - Wide Open Spaces	
Requirements Level 10 Quest Rarity: Common Quest Reward: 200 experience, 1 silver and 20 copper coins.	Description: Hunt and kill 8 WildRunners in the nearby grasslands.

Quest - Sunshine Blossoms	
Requirements Level 10 Quest Rarity: Common Quest Reward: 210 experience, 1 silver and 30 copper coins.	Description: Collect 12 Sunshine Blossoms from the nearby grasslands.

With a load of quests lined up, he walked into the Leatherworking shop. He'd reached level 13 while back in Lairthyn because of his deal with Trailia. He should have some patterns to learn immediately. A middle-aged woman sat behind a small table. Sheets of leather covered the top as she meticulously cut pieces from them.

"Hello," Atlas said with a wave, "I'm Atlas. Are you Master Grant?"

The woman peered up from her work. She clutched a needle tightly in her lips as she held on to her knife in one hand and the leather in the other. Getting the hint from her glare, he quickly amended his question.

"My apologies. Please finish what you're doing and we can talk."

The woman's frown turned into a small grin, and she returned to her task. Atlas took the time to inch closer to see what she was doing. Her stitch work on the leather was impeccable as she deftly wove thread through the holes.

The section of work finally complete, she pinned the needle into a small cushion and stood up.

"I appreciate your patience. What can I do for you, Atlas?"

"I'm here to continue my leatherworking training. Master Trailia sent me," he told her as he produced the rolled letter.

"Ah, Master Trailia, she still sour and grumpy?" Master Grant asked with a chuckle.

"She was when I first arrived. She was a little more cheerful when I left. Must've been in a good mood that day," Atlas reflected.

"I doubt it. She's always perpetually grumbling about something. The paperwork looks in order. It also appears you did quite the work for her. That's probably why she was happy. Name's Natalie Grant. Just call me Master Grant. I didn't work all those years for the master title for people to ignore it," she lectured while waving her finger at him.

"Yes, ma'am." Atlas said with a nod.

"Good. First thing's first. You need to learn how to soft cure hides before you can continue your training."

"Soft cure, Master?"

"Well, of course. You've been working with stiff leather from the basic curing techniques you normally use. When you reach level 10. We teach you how to cure the leather in a better fashion that leaves the skin durable and more flexible. You'll need this," she told him as she handed him a small vial filled with a yellowish liquid.

"Don't sniff it. It smells like piss," she told him with a wink and a smile.

She led him to a back room with a basin in it. Polished wood lined the basin with a drain in the bottom. A small tube extended from the bottom and drained back into a closed bucket. A wooden slab sat nearby and slid into the pipe to block the flow until you wanted to drain it.

"Now listen up. This process usually takes forever, but you pesky Reborn have it easy. The process is like your previous work. You're going to take a raw hide and clean it and coat it in salt. You don't get to use your shortcut this time, though. Do it at normal speed and by hand. Once the skin is properly salted, I need you to roll and stretch it three times. No more, no less. From there, you're going to place the hide in that basin and fill it with the liquid in that vial. It's dirty work, but you need to knead the leather with the liquid in there for a short time to make sure it soaks into every bit. When you finish that, remove it and unfurl the leather. You should learn your skill. Questions?"

Atlas shook his head no, and she left the small room. He set to his task without complaint. The process was familiar to him. He'd done it far more times than he could count, and even though he'd done it automatically and at super speed, his body still knew the movements. The hair sliced free of one of his hides and he covered it in salt. He got on his hands and knees and used all of his strength to wrap the bundle tight to roll it before rolling each end over a wood dowel and stretching it using his hands and feet.

The final step had him place the leather in
the basin and dump the pungent liquid in. She
hadn't been lying when she said it smelled
like piss, but she neglected to mention it
smelling like week old rotten piss at that. He
finished rubbing all the liquid into the hide
and picked it up. The sheet dried on its own
and the outside became soft and smooth. A
notification popped up.

*You learned the Leatherworking ability:
Cure Soft Hide.*
You gained 35 experience in Leatherworking.

Remembering his initial lesson on shop
cleanliness, he took the time to drain the
liquid and gather the hair into a small bucket
in the corner. With those tasks complete, he
left the room to find Master Grant. She was
back to work on her project at the small table
when Atlas approached.
"Already done, are we? That's quick work.
Now that the hard part's out of the way. You
can learn the rest of your skills the easy
way," she said as a menu popped up in his
vision.
Four new abilities popped up. Each of them
cost 40 copper, but he bought all four and
gave each an appraising glance.

Leatherworking - Soft Thread	
Requirements Leatherworking Level 10 Rarity: Common Requirements: 1 Cured Soft Hide	Description: Creates 14 soft thread

Leatherworking - Create Soft Leather Gloves	
Requirements Leatherworking Level 11 Rarity: Common Requirements: 2 Cured Soft Hide, 2 Soft Thread	Description: Creates a set of soft and flexible gloves that offer a moderate amount of protection.

Leatherworking - Create Soft Leather Boots	
Requirements Leatherworking Level 12 Rarity: Common Requirements: 3 Cured Soft Hide, 2 Soft Thread	Description: Creates a set of soft and flexible boots that offer a moderate amount of protection.

Leatherworking - Create Soft Leather Jerkin	
Requirements Leatherworking Level 13 Rarity: Common Requirements: 5 Cured Soft Hide, 6 Soft Thread	Description: Creates a soft and flexible leather chestpiece that offers moderate protection.

He also spotted Vial of Curing Liquid for sale. Each of them cost 20 copper. A quick check confirmed that was the new ingredient he needed besides the salt for these patterns. A check of his bags showed he had twenty-two hides left plus the one he just turned into a soft hide.

To play it safe, he bought forty of the Vial of Curing Liquid. It set him back 8 silver, but it was nothing that concerned him. He knew he'd use them all in the end, plus many more. He also stocked up and bought another two-hundred pinches of salt. That was only 4 silver, so not as bad.

"Mind if I use your room again to work?"

"Go ahead. Make sure you clean up before you leave."

Atlas moved back to the room and pulled all his hides out of his bags. One by one he activated his Cure Soft Hide ability. Now that he'd properly learned the technique, his super speed kicked in and his body did it on autopilot again.

With a nice stack of soft hide, he looked over his options. After a few struggles with himself, he made one of each of the new items for himself. With the leftover leather, he crafted three sets of boots to sell. It was the most efficient way he could see to do it and would leave him with no leftover leather and twelve leftover thread.

The process worked identical to his original patterns, only this leather stitched together in a much smoother fashion. Its flexibility allowed the seams to meld together perfectly as it folded, and the work looked much cleaner than it did with his rougher leather. All the work finally done, he looked at his gains.

You gained 2,220 total experience in Leatherworking.

Success! You've reached level 14 in Leatherworking.

The new armor pieces all had higher defense than his previous pieces, so he took a chance to look them over.

<table>
<tr><td colspan="2" align="center">Item – Soft Leather Jerkin</td></tr>
<tr><td>
Requirements: Level 10
Rarity: Common
Quality: Good
</td><td>
Defense: 8
Durability: 125/125
Weight: 3.0 lbs.
Slot: Chest

Traits: A jerkin made from soft leather. Provides moderate protection for the upper body.
</td></tr>
</table>

<table>
<tr><td colspan="2" align="center">Item – Soft Leather Boots</td></tr>
<tr><td>
Requirements: Level 10
Rarity: Common
Quality: Good
</td><td>
Defense: 6
Durability: 105/105
Weight: 2.0 lbs.
Slot: Feet

Traits: A pair of boots made from soft leather. Provides moderate protection for the feet.
</td></tr>
</table>

Item - Soft Leather Gloves	
Requirements: Level 10 **Rarity**: Common **Quality**: Good	**Defense**: 5 **Durability**: 95/95 **Weight**: 1.5 lbs. **Slot**: Hands **Traits**: A pair of gloves made from soft leather. Provides moderate protection for the hands.

A quick trip around the room allowed him to get it back in order and cleaned up. Master Grant sat at her table working at a quick pace. She didn't have the speed of a Reborn, but the efficiency with which she sewed could almost make you think she did. She reached the end of her line and made a few quick loops to tack the end down before turning to Atlas.

"Something else I can help with?"

"I'd like to see your level 14 patterns and sell a few items."

"Very well," was her response as the menu popped back up and she went back to her work. There were two patterns available for level 14.

Leatherworking - Create Soft Leather Pants	
Requirements Leatherworking Level 14 Rarity: Common Requirements: 5 Cured Soft Hide, 6 Soft Thread	Description: Creates a set of soft and flexible boots that offer a moderate amount of protection.

Leatherworking - Create Soft Leather Belt	
Requirements Leatherworking Level 14 Rarity: Common Requirements: 2 Cured soft Hide, 2 Soft Thread	Description: Creates a soft and flexible belt that offers a moderate amount of protection and contains built in storage pouches.

After he bought both, he looked at the Sell window. His old jerkin went for 2 silver, while his old boots and gloves each sold for 1 silver. Bummed at the low market price, he selected the Soft Leather Boots. A price popped up on them and he had to look at it a few times.

"Master Grant? Surely this price is wrong for these boots?"

"What price?" she asked before she looked ahead and swiped through the air, "Oh for Soft Leather Boots? I assure you the price is correct. The stock on them is dangerously low. It takes us so long to make them that they fetch a high price during normal times, anyway. The nobles find them much more comfortable than normal shoes and wear them around daily."

Wow, 20 silver for a single pair of boots seems insane but who am I to argue. He selected all three sets and hit sell. The demand must hold pretty steady because there weren't any diminishing prices. All three sets sold for exactly 20 silver a piece bringing him a hefty 60 silver in his pocket.

"Are there few other Leatherworkers around here doing this work?" Atlas asked.

"Hmm, of the Reborn variety? Not many. Most I've seen are lower level in the craft and can barely make reinforced equipment. I guess they are more focused on hitting things than making things."

"Thanks for the info, Master Grant. I'll come back and see you when I can collect more hides."

"You do that, young man," she said with a wave, although her eyes never left the work on her table.

From her shop he wandered around the area until he found the woodworking trainer. It took some time popping in and out of random shops, but the man behind the desk answered his question upon entering.

"Is this the Woodworking trainer's shop?"

"This is indeed. I'm Master Grannith. Can I help you with something?"

"Yes, sir. I'm Atlas and came here to further my studies in woodworking. I'm recently arrived from Lairthyn."

"Very well. Do you have a letter of introduction?"

Atlas thought about it and realized he'd never grabbed one from the Woodworking shop there. For that matter, he couldn't even remember ever learning the master's name there.

"No, sir. I left and forgot to get one."

"Humph. Well, try to pay attention next time. What level are you in woodworking?"

"Level 10, sir."

The man smiled at that, "About time I get someone of the proper level before they get here. I'm dreadfully tired of teaching old abilities they should've learned before they arrived. Well, young man, are you ready to learn the next version of wood you need to work with?"

"Of course," Atlas said eagerly.

"Then follow me," the master said as they moved to the back.

They walked past many pieces of partially finished wood. Intricately carved staves with a section of blank wood in them hung on racks. Others were everyday items such as bowls but carved with reliefs and pictures. A small room in the back ended up being their eventual destination.

In the corner stood a rack with multiple pieces of Raw Wood Logs. The middle held a workbench with a device that looked like a lathe. The master walked over to the bench and motioned for him to join.

"Alright, let's do this step by step. First off, walk to the rack and select a piece of wood," Atlas did as commanded and selected a piece that was relatively straight.

Master Grannith showed him how he needed to attach it to the device. Small wooden rods adjusted the length of the grip and allowed it to clamp firmly. *This is definitely a lathe, just a more old school one made of wood.*

The master pointed out the floor pedal that would make the device spin using a leather belt. With an effort of will, Atlas started spinning the wooden piece while he showed him his next steps.

    His tool bag contained a small gouge that
he hadn't noticed before. Probably because he
didn't expect something like a lathe to exist.
The half circle shaped piece of metal stood
out now that he realized what it was.

    The master made him pedal the device while
using the gouge to clean the edges and rough
it down to a uniform shape. None of the jagged
blade lines marred its surface.

    When that task was complete, he had him
take a leather strap covered in a thick gritty
substance. He brought it to his face and
looked closely. *It's sandpaper!* Small specks
of sand dotted the surface, held on by a resin
glue.

    The master showed him how to use the
sandpaper to smooth the surface even farther.
Holding it against the wood while it spun cut
the time to clean the wood. Once finished, he
pulled it from the device and ran his hand
across it.

    Not a single bump or blemish was visible.
The wood itself held the perfect shape from
one end to the other. No bulging sections that
were carved slightly larger than another. A
notification popped up in his view.

You learned Create Smooth Wood Log.
You gained 35 experience in Woodworking.

    "Fantastic. This is so much nicer than the
rough wood I've had to work with so far."

    "The craft gets even more detailed as you
stick with it. Before you know it, you'll be
carving intricate scenes and inlaying gems to
give it boosts. Until then, work on leveling
up."

Atlas agreed with the assessment and looked at the available skills. There were two he could learn.

Woodworking - Create Smooth Wood Rods	
Requirements Woodworking Level 10 Rarity: Common Requirements: 1 Smooth Wood Log	Description: Creates eight small rods from a single piece of smooth wood. Used for construction.

Woodworking - Create Smooth Wood Wand	
Requirements Woodworking Level 10 Rarity: Common Requirements: 1 Smooth Wood Log	Description: Creates two magic wands from a single piece of smooth wood.

The abilities should prove interesting. He was really interested in seeing what the stats looked like for the Smooth Wood Wand, but needed to wait until he could make one. With a farewell, he left the shop.

One last check of all of his belongings and he turned and headed for the city gate. He needed to get back to questing.

Chapter 16

Grinding

The monotony of the questing was grueling. Atlas ran out to the surrounding area, fought a bunch of monsters for the quests, and went back to town. The first set of four quests didn't take him long. After a few hours of walking through the grasslands and the trees, he successfully eliminated the targets.

Oddly enough, the Jackalopes were exactly what he thought they would be. The comical creatures with their deer antlers and rabbit bodies were almost difficult to kill because of their awkward cuteness. He had no problem killing the Wildrunners. They looked like a goat and a deer had a baby. Their long and slender body made them really fast, but their curved horns and thick skull gave them real knockdown power if they hit you.

More than once, Atlas took a solid thump to the chest. The attacks hurt, but when he grew frustrated, he would shift to his dire bear form and the animals would all but wet themselves as he ripped them apart. The Elegant Fur took the longest to find. It dropped from pretty much anything that contained fur. A couple came from the Jackalopes while some also came from the Wildrunners. Luckily, they dropped in addition to the actual animal hide, so he still got his hide to turn into leather in addition to the quest item. The first set of quests yielded a nice reward.

You gained 700 total experience.
You gained 790 quest experience, 4 silver, and 60 copper for turning in The Finest Fur, A Hunting we Will Go, Wide Open Space, and Sunshine Blossoms.
Success! You've reached level 11.
Success! You've reached levels 5 and 6 in Herbalism.

Not only did he rack in enough experience for another level, he also grabbed thirty-three more hides to add to his pack. His luck even held, and he grabbed a few additional Sunshine Blossoms to sell over what the quest required.

He switched it up with his 2 skill points, choosing to drop them both in Agility. His slow pace caused him to take a few hits in this area. Even with the images showing him how to counter, he struggled to keep up with the speed they required and a lot more attacks landed before he could deflect or block.

   While looking for his next set of quests, he realized a few errors he made. One major problem was he didn't ask Master Greenfoot what abilities the druid could teach. That didn't bother him too much since he doubted there would be anything new before level 12. The class skills commonly skipped at least one level.

   The even more glaring problem was he never checked the prices of basic hides or wood in town to see if it would be worth it for him to buy them out like he had before.

   Scouring the city, he found five quests this time. Each with a similar style. All find me x amount of herbs or kill x amount of animals. Nothing special, but they all added up to quick experience. As soon as he was certain he'd gathered all currently available quests, he went back to Master Grannith's place. A quick inquiry showed him the stock the woodworker had available. Unsurprisingly, there were forty-three pieces of Raw Wood Logs. The master had more important projects to work on than sanding down bare wood and didn't bother messing with them. The price on them was a measly 20 copper a piece. *Even if I don't make any money, the experience alone is worth that price.*

   Atlas purchased all forty-three for 8 silver and 60 copper. He also spent another 12 silver and bought 60 sheets of sandpaper. The ability required one per use. With the master's permission, he used the workroom in the back. It took him a solid two hours, but he smoothed out all the raw logs.

   You gained 1,505 total experience in Woodworking.

Success! You've reached level 11 in Woodworking.

Before he decided what else to make, Atlas returned to see what new patterns he had for level 11. The first pattern he expected. It was the Smooth Wood Staff. The second was a bit of a surprise. It was a Smooth Wood Ring. He bought both, but confusion about the purpose of a wood ring caused him to ask the master about it.

"Master Grannith, why would we have a pattern for a wood ring?"

"That seems pretty obvious. It's for making rings, of course."

"But, the rings don't have any stats or abilities on them, do they?"

"Well, no. That's what Jewelers are for!" The woodworker said in exasperation.

"That's what I don't understand. I thought the Jewelers actually made the rings and necklaces. Why would we make them?"

"Ah, I see the confusion. Let me ask you this. Do you think you should have to learn the patterns to sew cloth if you're a leatherworker?"

"I don't see how it would help, so no."

"Then there's the problem. Jewelers don't want to dedicate much of their time to being Woodworkers or Blacksmiths just to make the base form of the items. They take the pieces we create and carve the glyphs and inlay the gems needed to create works of art."

Atlas never considered it in that light, but it made sense. Each profession needed to rely on each other, and it would be unfair for one to need to specialize in another just to operate. Atlas shook his head and went back to work.

The first item he made was a Smooth Wood Staff. He doubted it would beat out his IronHide Staff, but he wanted to see how good it was. When the finished piece fell in his hands, he examined it.

<table>
<tr><td colspan="2">Item – Smooth Wood Staff</td></tr>
<tr><td>Requirements: Level 10
Rarity: Common
Quality: Good</td><td>Attack: 5
Defense: 3
Magical Attack: 2
Durability: 75/75
Weight: 4.7 lbs.
Slot: 2H Weapon

Traits: A staff of smooth wood.</td></tr>
</table>

You gained 250 experience in Woodworking.

So I'd lose the Agility bonus, but gain magical damage with this new staff. I guess that makes sense. Staves are usually magical weapons.

The piece itself wasn't good enough to swap out what he currently had, but it gave him hope that the next staff he could make would definitely be an upgrade.

The experience on the piece was impressive for something that only used two pieces of wood. The thought of turning all the wood into staves crossed his mind, but he wanted to check the experience of the rings first.

Selecting Create Smooth Wood Ring, his body sped into motion. The rod of wood quickly separated into twelve equal tubes. His hands clamped each of these sections on the lathe in turns and spun them as he used the gouge and sandpaper to smooth them down. When the exterior resembled a ring, he removed the pieces from the lathe and carved the center hole.

The pattern used 1 Sandpaper and 1 Smooth Wood Log but created twelve small rings that slipped easily onto his finger. Not only did it give him twelve rings to sell, but the experience was even better than the staff.

You gained 190 experience in Woodworking.

He used one log instead of two and had to use an item that cost a small amount of money but ended up with far more than half of the experience. The ultimate test was the price. He got Master Grannith's attention and opened the menu. The staff sold for an impressive 22 silver. When his attention moved to the rings, his hopes deflated. They each listed at 75 copper. All 12 would only bring 9 silver to him. If he doubled it to match the materials in the staff, that was 18 silver to the 22. It would be more efficient to make money using the staff while the rings would be better experience.

He looked to the master's inventory, and it listed the Smooth Wood Staff at a selling price of 21 silver and 50 copper now. To his surprise, when he checked the rings, their price was unchanged.

"Master, do the rings not drop in price with each sold?"

"The Smooth Wood Rings? No. They are a controlled item, like building materials. They have a set price and stay at that price."

That news brought joy to his soul. The staff would eventually devalue while the rings stayed constant. This fresh development solidified his decision to make nothing but rings. They were worth far more experience and the influx of rings would help Jewelers level their craft.

His body went into motion as he churned out a tiny factory of rings, one by one. The process quickly became monotonous. It also took more than twice the time to make the rings, as it did to make the staff. This was due to all the small pieces he had to work on. With the last of the items complete, he looked on in amazement at the veritable pile of rings in the corner. The process bogged him down so much he'd begun tossing the finished items in the corner without regard for how they stacked.

You gained 7,790 total experience in Woodworking.
Success! You've reached levels 12, 13, and 14 in Woodworking.

The enormous boost in his experience was fantastic. All told, he had 492 rings to sell. The pure profit from the deal was insane and made him wonder why others hadn't done it yet. If his estimates were correct. He'd get 3 gold and 69 silver from them all.

"Master Grannith, can I ask a question that may seem odd?"

"Wouldn't be the first time," he said with a smile.

"Does no one else consider buying these materials like I have and getting fast experience?"

"Not a terrible question. I'm not sure if they've done it in other places, but I know I've seen no one doing it yet. Typically, it's because of one of two reasons. The first is the most common. They are usually broke. Their skill training and food sets their pockets back in addition to their class spells. They save every bit of money they have to buy new armor or save up for combat skills at the Weaponmaster."

Damn, I forgot all about the Weaponmaster. I need to find one here and see what he may have available.

"The second reason is impatience. The locals can't craft anything nearly as fast as you Reborn so they don't try it and the reborn are in a hurry to continue running off to fight and hunt items for quests. Few dedicate the time to pursue a craft seriously."

"That sounds about like us," Atlas grumbled, "Always in a rush to the end and never stopping to enjoy the moment."

"That's an excellent summary, and I can't disagree with the assessment."

"Well, I have four-hundred and ninety-two of the Smooth Wood Rings I'd like to sell you in the back room. It's a large stack and didn't want to carry them all up here."

"You made that many in a few hours of work? Truly marvelous. Are you sure you want to sell them?" he asked.

"Why wouldn't I? I can get a decent amount of money for them."

"If your goal is to make a good profit, I'd suggest an alternate route. Have you considered taking up the Jewelcrafting skill? I know the early stages of the skill require some carving of pieces and little trinkets, but once you hit level 5, you can use these rings. Almost five hundred of them would launch you pretty far in terms of skill, and since the items you need to change these are mostly from a vendor, it would greatly increase your profit."

Hmm, do I really want to invest in another skill? It's a lot of work to invest time in these, but they have paid off handsomely so far.

"What would you suggest? I'm tempted to do just that, but I worry it will take up too much time juggling so many skills?"

"It's an investment of your time to be sure, but at early stages, Woodworking and Jewelcrafting go hand in hand. When you reach a higher level in Jewelcrafting much of the work shifts focus to blacksmithing but, done properly, you can have enough money to buy the items you need without trouble."

The woodworker made an excellent point. If these rings sold for a silver a piece now, there's no telling what each would go for if boosted by a jeweler.

"I think I need to talk to the Jewelcrafter. Can I store these rings here with you for a short time?"

"I suppose so. I have some buckets in the back storage room. Fill them up and put them back in there. No one will disturb them. Just make sure they don't stay there long or I'll sell them and keep the money for myself."

Atlas nodded and did as told. He ran around the room, scraping wooden rings off the floor and tossing them in the buckets. Three buckets later and he had them all stashed in the room Master Grannith showed. With a wave, he dashed from the building and headed in the direction the master told him to go.

The sign of the Jewelcrafting shop was easy to spot. The image of a ring with a large gem attached decorated the sign. It reminded Atlas of the old school wedding rings with their gaudy diamonds sticking way away from the main body.

Inside, he found a large room filled with carved wooden items of varying styles. Most looked to be purely decorative, while others had symbols etched into them. As he moved closer to the desk, the little knick-knacks disappeared and wooden rings and necklaces filled the shelves. At the desk, a beautiful necklace of some type of silver metal sat in a display case, much like the one he'd seen the staff in earlier. This piece held a large sapphire in the center of a teardrop shaped piece of metal and hung from a chain around a wooden prop.

"You in the market?" the old man at the counter asked.

"Actually," Atlas said slowly, still marveling at the item, "I'm here to learn Jewelcrafting."

"Starting a little late, aren't ya?"

"Better late than never."

"Fine, fine. No use trying to talk you foolish kids out of anything. Here ya go," he said with a flick as the menu popped up for Atlas. He selected Learn Jewelcrafting and hit Buy. Ten silver drained from him as the messages flooded his senses.

  *You have learned the trade skill:
Jewelcrafting.
  You have learned the Jewelcrafting ability:
Create Wooden Slabs.
  You have learned the Jewelcrafting ability:
Create Wooden Idol.
  You have learned the Jewelcrafting ability:
Create Wooden Figurine.
  You have learned the Jewelcrafting ability:
Create Wooden Buttons.
  You have received Jewelcrafter's Tool Bag.*

  *Huh, Wooden Buttons? Looks like some items
can be made by more than one profession.*

  This profession was pretty straightforward.
The Create Wooden Slabs ability used 1 Rough
Wood Log and turned it into 6 Wooden Slabs.
These slabs were the base building material
for the other skills he'd learned.

  A scan through his other wares showed he
also had Rough Wood Logs for sale. Twenty of
them were currently available, and it listed
them at 30 copper each. Not as good as the
Woodcrafter's shop listed them for, but close.
Selecting all twenty, he hit *Buy* and 6 silver
disappeared from his bag.

  The twenty lengths of wood appeared in
front of him and he asked the older man about
a workroom. The Jeweler led him to a room in
the back and left him to his work. Since none
of the patterns used anything but Wooden
Slabs, he turned all twenty of the logs into
slabs.

  *You gained 500 total experience in
Jewelcrafting.
  Success! You've reached levels 2 and 3 in
Jewelcrafting.*

I guess they make it easier to get the experience since you need to buy the materials. I didn't see Wood Chopping in the list of skills as a Jewelcrafter.

Armed with 120 Wood Slabs, he surveyed his options. They all seemed similar, so he took the approach he recently did with woodworking. He made one of each to gauge their experience.

You gained 40 experience for crafting Wooden Idol.
You gained 40 experience for crafting Wooden Figurine.
Success! You've reached level 4 in Jewelcrafting.
You gained 50 experience for crafting Wooden Buttons.

The idol and figurine were identical in experience, but the buttons offered a little more on top. They all used only 1 Wood Slab. Not worrying about their sell value but knowing the buttons would probably stay steady since they were a crafting item, he used his Create Wooden Buttons ability 100 times. His body sped into motion and his small knife from the Jewelcrafter's Tool Bag whittled the pieces down to size. It took a couple hours to complete, but he finally finished.

You gained 5,000 total experience in Jewelcrafting.
Success! You've reached levels 5, 6, 7, 8, 9, and 10 in Jewelcrafting.

Damn, it's nice having spare money to power level some crafting.

Collecting the plethora of buttons in buckets, he walked back to the master jewelcrafter.

"I'd like to sell some items."

The old man looked up at him before his eyes bulged.

"That's an enormous amount of buttons. How many do you have?"

"I'd guess one thousand and ten. I also have one figurine and one idol."

"That should make the tailors exceptionally happy. Some of their stock has been running low lately with the influx of new people."

The menu popped open and Atlas checked the prices. The idol and figurine each sold for 35 copper, making him 5 copper on each sale. The buttons were a different story. He made 1 copper on each button. At face value, it sounded horrible. Then he realized he'd made 10 silver and 10 copper on an initial investment of 6 silver. He also still had 17 Wooden Slabs left.

Excited about his gains, he checked for new patterns. Multiple greeted him and he bought them all without a care.

You have learned the Jewelcrafting ability: Create Wooden Wards.

You have learned the Jewelcrafting ability: Create Wooden Earrings.

You have learned the Jewelcrafting ability: Create Wooden Necklace Beads.

You have learned the Jewelcrafting ability: Create Wooden Clasps.

You have learned the Jewelcrafting ability: Create Wooden Necklace Charms.

You have learned the Jewelcrafting ability: Create Wooden Ring of Spirit.

You have learned the Jewelcrafting ability: Create Wooden Ring of Intellect.
You have learned the Jewelcrafting ability: Create Wooden Ring of Constitution.
You have learned the Jewelcrafting ability: Create Wooden Ring of Strength.
You have learned the Jewelcrafting ability: Create Wooden Ring of Agility.
You have learned the Jewelcrafting ability: Create Wooden Necklace Charm of Spirit.
You have learned the Jewelcrafting ability: Create Wooden Necklace Charm of Intellect.
You have learned the Jewelcrafting ability: Create Wooden Necklace Charm of Constitution.
You have learned the Jewelcrafting ability: Create Wooden Necklace Charm of Strength.
You have learned the Jewelcrafting ability: Create Wooden Necklace Charm of Agility.

Holy crap! I'm about to make a fortune!

The advice he received from Master Grannith was fantastic. The sheer amount of rings he had to use meant he was about to skyrocket in levels, and there was a superb chance that these would sell for much more than he was going to get otherwise.

"I need to go check on something, but I'll be back," Atlas said as he dashed out of the building.

His path led him straight back to the woodworking shop. The buckets of rings called to his need to craft. He barged through the door and Master Grannith smiled at him.

"Took my advice, huh?"

"Sure did. I owe you one for that. He had enough logs in stock for me to get high enough to make rings, so I'm about to get to work."

The woodworking master nodded at that, "Just make sure you don't make them all into the same ring otherwise the price will be next to nothing by the end."

Atlas dashed to the back and grabbed the buckets out of the storage room and carried them to the workroom. With mindless abandon, he sat in the room and crafted ring after ring. The process was simple and most of it was him using a fine tool to carve symbols into the ring. When he finished the last of the lines, the rings sucked in a small surge of magic from their surroundings and turned into uncommon items. Each were for their specific attribute and each granted +1 to the attribute.

Originally he planned to create 98 of each of the rings. This idea stopped when he realized few people were bound to search for Spirit rings. Instead, he made 52 of the Spirit rings and 110 of each of the others.

You gained 1,300 experience in Jewelcrafting for making Wooden Ring of Spirit x 52.

You gained 2,750 experience in Jewelcrafting for making Wooden Ring of Intellect x 110.

You gained 2,750 experience in Jewelcrafting for making Wooden Ring of Strength x 110.

You gained 2,750 experience in Jewelcrafting for making Wooden Ring of Constitution x 110.

You gained 2,750 experience in Jewelcrafting for making Wooden Ring of Agility x 110.

Success! You've reached levels 11, 12, 13, 14, and 15 in Jewelcrafting.

The amount of experience stunned him. The items themselves hadn't taken long to make. The amount of experience was slightly depressing when he first saw it. It only gave him 25 experience per ring made. When he realized it was less than a minute worth of carving, he understood why it was so low.

"Master Grannith. I'm finished in here. Can I sell some of these to you before taking the rest to the Jeweler?"

"Of course. That's always a good business idea. The overall price is going to drop as you sell them, but it drops slower if you spread it among different vendors."

Atlas only nodded as the menu popped up. A devilish grin split his face when he saw the price of the first ring. It listed for 3 silver. Three times the amount of a normal ring for less than a minute of work on his part. He sold half of each ring he had on him to Grannith. Out of the 246 total rings he got rid of, he made 5 gold 41 silver and 20 copper. The price dropped as he sold them, but his average sell price by the time he finished was around 2 silver and 20 copper each.

The rest of the rings he dumped into his backpack and stuffed into the pouches on his belt. With an abundance of money and bags full of more rings, he strutted over to the jewelcrafting shop.

Without bothering to talk to the master, he asked to see his inventory, and the menu popped up. He sold the rest of his 246 rings. This time he averaged only 1 silver and 60 copper but that still brought him 3 gold 93 silver and 60 copper.

His last act, after giggling at the astounded face of the jewelcrafting master, was to train his new skills.

You have learned the Jewelcrafting ability: Create Wire Wrapped Wooden Ring of Spirit.
You have learned the Jewelcrafting ability: Create Wire Wrapped Wooden Ring of Intellect.
You have learned the Jewelcrafting ability: Create Wire Wrapped Wooden Ring of Constitution.
You have learned the Jewelcrafting ability: Create Wire Wrapped Wooden Ring of Strength.
You have learned the Jewelcrafting ability: Create Wire Wrapped Wooden Ring of Agility.
You have learned the Jewelcrafting ability: Create Wire Wrapped Wooden Necklace Charm of Spirit.
You have learned the Jewelcrafting ability: Create Wire Wrapped Wooden Necklace Charm of Intellect.
You have learned the Jewelcrafting ability: Create Wire Wrapped Wooden Necklace Charm of Constitution.
You have learned the Jewelcrafting ability: Create Wire Wrapped Wooden Necklace Charm of Strength.
You have learned the Jewelcrafting ability: Create Wire Wrapped Wooden Necklace Charm of Agility.

Four silver was enough to train all the skills. They were identical to the original patterns, but they had slightly more durability and added 1 Defense to the pieces. *I guess every minor point of defense reduces damage taken.*

The ability worked the same, but it also required a Spool of Copper Wire per pattern. The jewelcrafting master had some for sale and each spool cost 30 copper. Out of materials to use, he closed the menu and thanked the master.

It's time to get back to questing.

Chapter 17

An Animalistic Quest

Time slowly blended together. He stayed active and continued questing, but you could only run so many of the same style of quests before boredom sank in. His first action was to run to the local branch of the bank and deposit 9 more gold. He was supremely uncomfortable carrying around over 10 gold. If he died, it would all be for nothing. He spent the rest of his time doing nothing but questing and gathering any materials he found while out.

When he returned to the city, he got a room in an inn on the road to the woodworking shop and dumped a lot of his materials there. He figured out his items stayed safe in the room if he locked it when he left in the same way that his body stayed safe. With that discovery, he didn't feel as hard pressed to craft every time he returned to reduce the load on his bags.

Piles of wood lay stacked in the corner while a random bushel of herbs were in another. He was immensely thankful that the hides didn't smell. A large bundle of them sat on one side of the room. He put in a lot of work and made excellent progress on quests.

You gained 950 total experience.

You gained 2,400 quest experience, 12 silver, and 40 copper for turning in Cherry Blossoms, A Flying Menace, For the Love of Spuds, Once a Sandbag - Always a Sandbag, The Grim Task, Search and Rescue, and The Milk Vine.

Success! You've reached level 12.

Success! You've reached levels 7 and 8 in Herbalism.

With a room full of random items and a comfortable stopping point, Atlas logged out of the game and wandered back to the real world.

** * **

Two days later found him back in game. The entire time he was at work, all he could do was picture what he needed to accomplish when he logged back in. His room demonstrated the extensive amount of crafting he needed to do. The collection of materials greeted him upon his return to the game.

His leveling grind continued shortly after he returned. He had to restrain himself from spending a ton of time crafting. Instead, he focused solely on grinding through more quests. Naturally, he couldn't stop himself from gathering more wood, hides, and some herbs, but he didn't spend more time than necessary looking for them. It took him an entire day of game time, but he reached a significant turning point for his progress. Level 15. The increased experience from quests as he leveled helped him move forward quicker.

You gained 1,900 total experience.

You gained 4,100 quest experience, 21 silver, and 20 copper for turning in Once Upon a Lyrican, Root Out the Culprit, A Simple Request, Save Him Please, Looney Lumkins, Thieves!, Jewelry Heist, Hidden Agenda, and Bandits?.

Success! You've reached levels 13, 14, and 15.

Success! You've reached level 9 in Herbalism.

With his questing done for this location, he realized he had a lot of catching up to do. Multiple trips in and out for quests meant he now had a verifiable mountain of crafting materials in his room at the inn. His druid training was far behind. He'd largely neglected it and hadn't trained a single skill past the Rank 2 Nature's Fury. The problem required a planned approach.

The first thing that needed to be done was to take care of the crafting. As soon as he finished his skill training for his class, he'd be moving to the next city. The herbs were a simple solution. Those were sold off quickly. He'd already been selling the meat to the inn as he came in from questing. Briefly, he considered taking up Alchemy but then finally talked some sense into himself. He didn't have the time to keep up with the skills he had now, much less invest in yet another. *Maybe when I get closer to max level I can branch out some more?*

From there he wanted to visit Master Grants, then Grannith's place to work on his Woodworking, and he'd finish with Jewelcrafting. One last pit stop at the Weaponmaster would be his last step before his class trainer.

Loading his backpack and all of his pouches
was a delicate process. He needed to fit
everything he could without damaging the
herbs. In the end, it took him three trips,
but he found an alchemy shop nearby and sold
all of his herbs, giving him 31 silver and 40
copper.

His bundle of hides wasn't much better. It
took two trips to lug all of them to the
leatherworking shop, which left Master Grant
nearly speechless. He explained he'd just
saved all of his hide since he saw him last as
he leveled and the leatherworker merely shook
his head. A quick count told him he had 148
Raw Leather Hides. The process took a while,
but he eventually ended up with a neat stack
of Soft Hides for his effort.

*You gained 5,180 total experience in
Leatherworking.*
*Success! You've reached levels 15 and 16 in
Leatherworking.*

Before he began crafting, he checked with
Master Grant and bought his new abilities from
leveling. There were two of them.

*You have learned the Leatherworking
ability: Create Soft Leather Backpack.*
*You have learned the Leatherworking
ability: Create Soft Leather Belt.*

With his full complement of craftable
leather armor now at the soft level, it was
time for him to upgrade his remaining gear. A
new coif, pair of pants, a belt, and the soft
backpack all joined his ensemble. He sold the
older pieces as he replaced them for 3 silver.

You gained 985 total experience in Leatherworking.

While selling off the old pieces, he confirmed Master Grant didn't have any new patterns after level 15. That would have to wait for the next city. With 129 hides left, he went back to work. Instead of wasting a lot of time and trying to gauge what would be the best in terms of experience and money, he just said screw it and made twenty sets of soft boots and twelve backpacks. He knew the boots would sell well until they depreciated and backpacks always brought a decent price. It used all of his hides up with only some Soft Thread to spare.

You gained 7,700 total experience in Leatherworking.
Success! You've reached levels 17 and 18 in Leatherworking.

His idea proved even more fruitful when he sold the items. The price of the boots had risen to almost 22 silver. By the time he sold all twenty pairs, he averaged out to the original twenty silver each and made 4 gold. The backpacks averaged out at 15 silver and brought him another 1 gold and 80 silver.

Done with his leatherworking, he bid the master goodbye. Master Grant gave him a letter of introduction to his next trainer. From there he moved on to the Woodworking trainer and turned all of his Raw Wood Logs into Smooth Wood Logs. This gave him 54 to work with. Checking the trainer, he found three new abilities.

You have learned the Woodworking ability: Create Smooth Wood Necklace Charm.
You have learned the Woodworking ability: Create Smooth Shortbow Frame.
You have learned the Woodworking ability: Create Smooth Longbow Frame.

Since he made so many of the rings before, Atlas was certain the prices were still low. To his immense shame, he realized he'd neglected to keep any to equip on himself. He used one of the Smooth Wood Logs to make a single batch of twelve Smooth Wood Rings. The other 53, he turned into Smooth Wood Necklace Charms. That left him with 424 necklace charms and a load of experience.

You gained 10,070 total experience in Woodworking.
Success! You've reached levels 15, 16, and 17 in Woodworking.

There were two more abilities available at level 15 and he bought both.

You have learned the Woodworking ability: Create Smooth Axe Handle.
You have learned the Woodworking ability: Create Smooth Spear Handle.

Master Grannith also sent him on his way with an introduction letter. All the charms took multiple buckets to haul over to the Jewelcrafting shop. The original thought was to just craft them in the woodworking shop, but he didn't have any Spool of Copper Wire.

His work was quick in the Jewelcrafting shop as he loaded up on Spool of Copper Wire. It cost him 42 silver and 40 copper to get the wire he needed. He turned 50 Wood Necklace Charms into Wire Wrapped Necklace Charm of Spirit. Same as before, he wanted a smaller amount of spirit charms since they probably wouldn't be as useful. From there, he made 92 of the Agility, Intellect, and Strength necklaces while turning his last 92 charms into Constitution.

You gained 12,960 total experience in Jewelcrafting.
Success! You've reached levels 16, 17, and 18 in Jewelcrafting.

A glance at one showed him their stats. It was identical to the rings.

Item – Wire Wrapped Smooth Wood Necklace Charm of Intellect	
Requirements: Level 10 **Rarity**: Common **Quality**: Good	**Defense**: 1 **Durability**: 85/85 **Weight**: 0.6 lbs. **Slot**: Crafting Item **Traits**: Combine with necklace beads and string to create a Wire Wrapped Wooden Necklace of Intellect • Grants the wearer 1 Intellect.

This was when he realized he was a complete bonehead. He'd used all of his wood making the charms and forgot to save some for the necklace beads. He checked the master's inventory and there was only one set of beads. He bought the set for 30 copper and a string and clasp for another 2 copper each. He strung the necklace together and completed one of the Intellect necklaces. He immediately equipped the completed version.

All the remaining pieces, he sold. Someone else could invest in the beads and string to finish them. He feared the price would be low because it was unfinished, but they still averaged out to 1 silver each. The result was another 4 gold and 91 silver in his bag.

For the rings he made four Intellect and four Constitution. They had the exact stats of the necklaces. That said, he equipped all eight of those and they fit without a problem. The last four he turned into Spirit ones and kept them in his bag.

You gained 300 total experience in Jewelcrafting.

The master bid him farewell and gave him a letter of introduction for the next master before he headed for the Weaponmaster.

Atlas had to ask a guard but eventually found the Weaponmaster. A man stood in a training ring as multiple opponents ran at him. He spun to the side and knocked a wooden staff out of the way. A quick side-step allowed him to counter with a punch, and then he followed with a leap over his opponent. An elbow to the back sent the attacker flying in the opposite direction before he fell to the ground.

The Weaponmaster didn't even get a chance for a breath before another person charged him with a wooden sword. He spun and deflected the weapon with his small wooden dagger and thrust both hands into his attacker's chest. The solid thump of the blow propelled the man backward as he struggled to keep his feet. The Weaponmaster stood, and the challengers saluted him as the gathered spectators clapped.

"That was fantastic work," Atlas commented as he approached.

"Thank you, Reborn. Can I help you with something?"

"Actually, I wanted to train skills."

A brief nod was all he gave before a menu popped up.

Weaponmaster Jordan Cooper	
Ability	Description
Fallback Requirements: Level 3 Cost: 8 Silver	A retreating jump. Only useable following a Dodge. Increases the chance you can Flee from a battle.
Disrupt Requirements: Level 8 Cost: 15 Silver	An ability that lets you counter low-level spells. Uses your innate mana to disrupt the magic. Counts as a standard combat Counter.

Pursuit Requirements: Level 13 Cost: 20 Silver	A combo attack that follows a normal attack addition. It allows you to chain two attack additions together. The second addition must have fewer hits than the first.

All three abilities joined his set of skills. The Fallback ability was one he neglected from the very beginning. It would be a good way to get away in an emergency. Disrupt could be a lifesaver in the future if it could stop a spell from hitting him. Pursuit was an ability he truly wished for. Being able to chain additions together during attacks allowed him more freedom. If he could start off with a three-hit attack and then immediately go to a two-hit, it would increase his damage between forced stops.

A trip to the bank let him drop another 10 gold for safekeeping. With 24 gold in the bank, he felt pretty secure. He still had a little over 2 gold on him. His last task left him standing on the master druid's porch and entering his house.

"Master Greenfoot?"

The older druid entered the main room from a door on the side of the house.

"Atlas, what can I do for you?"

"I'd like to train my new skills," He said with a reassuring smile.

The master stopped the questioning and just gestured, bringing up the menu.

Two skill rank upgrades were available and one new skill. He bought all three for 6 silver.

Druid Spell - Nurture (Rank 2)	

Requirements
   Druid Class
   Level 12
	Description: Infuses the target with the healing magic of nature.
	
	HP Restored: 25 HP
	Mana Cost: 15 MP

Druid Spell - Entangle (Rank 2)	

Requirements
   Druid Class
   Level 14
	Description: Thorns erupt from the ground and encircle the target's legs. Temporarily immobilizes target.
	
	Damage: 2 HP/ 3 seconds
	Mana Cost: 15 MP

Druid Spell - Sunfire	

Requirements
   Druid Class
   Level 14
	Description: Calls down the cleansing power of fire to sear your target.
	
	Damage: 10 HP
	Mana Cost: 20 MP

One other skill remained, but it had a yellow icon next to it that listed it as a quest reward. His attention shifted back to the master.

"I've made it to level fifteen. Is there a druid quest I can get at that level?"

The druid smiled as he responded, "Ah, the progress of youth. It's finally time to commune with the animal spirits. Your level fifteen quest allows you to choose your first animal form… well, normally. For you, it'll actually be your second form, but not the point."

"Choose the form? So I just have to run around hunting for what I want?"

"No. Choose between three options and I'll grant you the quest for your choice."

"So what are the options?"

"Eager I see. Good, you'll need that passion. You're first choice is that of a giant ape. The second choice is for a nightstalker cat. While the final is a cheetah."

"So, I can either have a super strong climbing form, a sneaky form, or one that moves very fast?"

"That's the gist of it. Each has their own unique abilities, like your dire bear form, but you guessed their primary function."

Atlas immediately ruled out the ape. While being very strong and able to climb might prove useful, he already had the dire bear, and it was also very tough and strong. The other two options proved a little tougher. His decision bounced back and forth as he mulled it over. On one hand, being able to travel quickly and possibly escape dangerous situations would be great. As a healer, though, he needed to remain nearby to help people.

In the end, he went for the nightstalker cat. Stealth would be his friend if he got in trouble.

"I choose the nightstalker."

"Wonderful choice," Master Greenfoot said with a thoughtful nod, "Being able to hide from sight is invaluable."

A message popped up in his vision.

Quest - Animalistic Ritual	

Requirements
  Druid
  Level 15
 	
Quest Rarity: Common
 	
Quest Reward: 1500 experience, Nightstalker Cat Form.
	Description: You must hunt down and kill the nightstalker Shadefire. When it dies, use the provided Soul Crystal to extract its essence.

The Soul Crystal in the quest description confused him for a moment until he spotted Master Greenfoot with an outstretched hand. A clear gem sat in his palm. The surface looked like the Soul of the Dire Bear he'd found before, but there was no light coming from it. It looked like any other piece of oddly shaped stone.

"So, is this how all the forms work? I just need a Soul Crystal to capture their spirit? Can I buy more Soul Crystals?" Atlas asked.

"No. Soul Crystals are only given for quests and only work in conjunction with that quest. They are not sold and even if you had one, it wouldn't capture the soul unless you had a quest specifically telling you to do so. As you know, though, you can find complete soul crystals as rare drops for other forms."

That sucks, but I guess it would make it far too easy otherwise.

"Any advice for this hunt?" Atlas asked.

"Yeah, don't die," the druid said with a blank expression.

Atlas chuckled, and the old man grinned.

"Noted. I'll come find you when I'm done."

Atlas exited the building and checked his map. A small section showed a green outline notating the location of his hunt, so he left the city and headed directly for it.

The clear grasslands outside of the city gave way to a small forest. His feet brushed along the leaves as he traversed under the tall canopy. The location of the quest drew closer, and the forest darkened.

Shadows encroached farther into the undergrowth and Atlas grew nervous. Knowing his target was a stealthy cat made the shadows far more ominous than he cared for. It was hard enough hunting a predator as it was, especially one that could probably use stealth. He felt like a dangling piece of meat just waiting to be devoured.

His attention snapped to the surrounding path. Knowing his quarry caused him to attempt to hunt the hunter. He scanned every inch of the surrounding dirt, praying for any sign of a large cat. The hard pack soil told him nothing. A scan of his surroundings yielded nothing more.

As much as he might like to pretend, he didn't know the first thing about tracking animals. *It's not like a giant footprint will be perfectly preserved in hard dirt and lead me all the way to the animal.*

Instead of focusing on tracking it down, he brought his staff to the ready and stayed alert, hoping he could react fast enough to counter a surprise attack.

It wasn't much farther when the hairs on his neck stood on end. A chill ran through him, as though his life just ended. Not knowing what else to do, he dropped to a knee and hunched forward in a crouch. His move definitely paid off as a sleek figure of black and purple soared over his head, its tail brushing his own hair, and landed ten feet in front of him.

The long black tail swished in what Atlas assumed was annoyance before the lithe body turned and the creature's silver eyes stared into his soul.

Welcome to your death, druid.

That the best you can do, Shadefire?

The animal pulled back its lips and exposed a row of razor-sharp teeth, glistening in the light as it drifted through gaps in the canopy. Atlas stood back to his feet and launched forward, triggering Triple Threat.

The cat lurched to the side as he swung forward. The attack met nothing but air, and Atlas stumbled.

Shadefire dodged your attack!

He regained his balance and turned toward the animal just in time to see a paw with claws extended slashing toward him. The nails dug into his shoulder and ripped free with the power of the swing. He spun slightly as he cried out in pain.

Shadefire dealt 12 damage to you with Heavy Counter.

This bastard can counter? That's not good.

The thought didn't last long because he knew what came after a counter. Atlas whipped his staff around and barely caught up to the image for the block. His staff thumped against the paw of the cat and it roared in pain as it stepped backward.

He activated Counter and swung forward. The nightstalker tried to dodge to the side, but the pain in its paw caused it to stumble as it tried to put weight on it. His attack hit the side of its shoulder. Before it could recover, he activated Triple Threat, and the staff became a blur as it spun and struck. Two rapid hits followed by one solid strike on its head smashed into the creature before he tried his new combo piece, Pursuit.

He dashed forward again and came in with another strike at its side. Activating Triple Threat, he tried to launch forward, building on the Pursuit, but he stopped in place.

You dealt 5 damage to Shadefire with Counter.
You dealt 18 damage to Shadefire with Triple Threat.
You dealt 5 damage to Shadefire with Pursuit.

What the hell? Why did I stop?
A low growl interrupted his thoughts, and the cat leaped toward him. In a panic, he struggled to get his staff in place. The creature's claw connected with his staff as his mind registered a small feeling of relief. That feeling lasted only a moment before the attack continued and the claws pushed through to rake him on the shoulder.

*So they can push damage past my weapon.
That explains the defense rating on my staff.*
Another attack followed that one, but Atlas
snapped back into focus, angling his staff and
deflecting the swing. He activated Counter and
smacked the beast on the side of the face
before using Blade Flurry. After the second
hit of his Blade Flurry, his vision flashed
red, and he leaned out of the attack.

He spotted the counterattack coming in and
tried to bring his weapon around to catch it.
His precarious balance caused him to stumble
and fail in his block. Razor-sharp claws dug
into his cheek as burning pain radiated
through his face and neck.

*You dealt 5 damage to Shadefire with
Counter.*
*You dealt 10 damage to Shadefire with Blade
Flurry. (Interrupted)*
*Shadefire dealt 7 damage to you with
Counter.*

Cursing and clutching his burning face, he
missed the next attack as the animal reared up
on both hind legs and came down. Its paws each
snagged a shoulder and ripped lines straight
down his torso. Large rents cleaved through
his leather armor and his body felt as though
it were dipped in molten lava.

*Shadefire dealt 35 damage to you with Rake
and Tear. (Bleeding) (Critical)*

Atlas fell to a knee and feebly lashed out with his staff. It hit nothing, but the cat did back away, giving him a few moments to compose himself.

Holy crap, that hurts. Wonder what triggers an actual bleed effect?

His focus snapped back to the cat as he saw it crouch down again. Instead of trying to get his staff ready and get to his feet, he got to a knee and dove to his right. The move worked, and the cat sailed by.

He rolled to his feet and immediately charged for the nightstalker triggering Counter. The weapon smashed into its spine and he used Blade Chase. The flurry of blows rang through the trees as his staff spun and connected. Triple Threat followed and after the first attack the red flash showed back up.

This time, Atlas was ready for it and brought his staff across to intercept the attack. The plan worked for a moment as the paw connected with the smooth wood, but it didn't stop. Instead, it pushed through his defense again and slashed him across the chest.

You dealt 5 damage to Shadefire with Counter.

You dealt 18 damage to Shadefire with Blade Flurry.

You dealt 5 damage to Shadefire with Triple Threat. (Interrupted)

Shadefire dealt 7 damage to you with Counter.

Bleed dealt 3 damage to you.

Son of a bitch! Atlas screamed into his mind. The constant slashing and tearing of the animal's claws finally threatening to break his pain tolerance.

My mother was not a dog, human. How dare you insult me so!

What? Oh… Atlas realized as he chuckled to himself.

I'm going to turn you into a really nice chest piece before we're done.

Try it, puny man.

Atlas bared his own teeth at the animal as he charged in, adrenaline pumping in his veins. He reared back his staff to swing, activating Triple Threat, when he saw the cat tense and crouch. Knowing it was going to dodge, he waited until he saw the direction it moved and then swung that way instead, ignoring the phantom image.

The weapon smacked hard into the cat's skull and it mewled in pain.

You learned the ability Anticipate!

The following two attacks thumped into the animal, and he activated Pursuit. His dash took him to the side of the creature, and the staff stabbed into a soft spot on its neck. He almost activated Triple Threat again until he remembered it failed last time. Scrambling for an option, he realized his folly.

You can't chain two of the same abilities. The second attack needs to be a lower hit combo than the first. He activated Double Slash instead and was relieved as his combo continued and both attacks landed.

You dealt 18 damage to Shadefire with Triple Threat.

*You dealt 5 damage to Shadefire with
Pursuit.*
*You dealt 12 damage to Shadefire with
Double Slash.*

The cat wobbled on its feet but remained
standing, glaring at him. *This thing can't
have a lot more health left. I've already done
around 70 damage to it, and its health bar
looked like it had a little less than a third
remaining.*
The nightstalker stumbled toward him as if
to attack, but he easily swept his staff to
the side and countered it. He activated his
full combo with Counter, followed by Blade
Chase, Triple Threat, Pursuit, and Double
Slash.

*You dealt 5 damage to Shadefire with
Counter.*
*You dealt 18 damage to Shadefire with Blade
Chase.*
*You dealt 18 damage to Shadefire with
Triple Threat.*
*You dealt 5 damage to Shadefire with
Pursuit.*
*You dealt 12 damage to Shadefire with
Double Slash.*

The final thump of the staff cracked into
the skull. The cat fell to the ground, and no
longer moved.
Well done, druid. Take your reward.

The voice sounded lethargic in his mind and faded to nothing. He approached the creature and dug through his pouch for the crystal. The clear gem vibrated as he held it close to the animal. When it touched the fur, a flash of light lit the area and a swirl of purple energy traveled from its eyes and swirled in the air before darting into the gem.

You received Nightstalker Cat Transformation Crystal.

The crystal registered as a quest item and he couldn't absorb it like he did the Dire Bear version. *Time to get back to the city.*

Chapter 18

Climbing the Ladder

Atlas pushed open the door to the druid master's home. The old man stood near the back of the house, watering a small plant in a wooden bucket. He glanced over to Atlas and nodded for him to approach.

"Finished the task. Shadefire is dead and I have the filled crystal."

"Well done. Didn't think it would be that bad for you, but you never know. Let me see the crystal," he said as he sat down the small clay cup he'd been pouring water out of and extended his hand.

Atlas plucked the crystal from his bag and placed the gem of swirling purple light in Master Greenfoot's hand. The druid turned it in his palm a few times and smiled.

"Such a wondrous thing. You ready?"

"I guess so?"

He motioned for him to follow and led him to a small stone gazebo behind the house. The building was worn and weather-beaten but still looked solid. Inside was a small pedestal. Master Greenfoot placed the crystal on the pedestal and told Atlas to put his hand on the gem but to leave it there.

Atlas did as he was told and watched as Master Greenfoot touched the other side of the small column. A surge of power rippled through the pedestal and radiated outward. The air hummed and vibrated as the crystal in his hands cracked. The purple light slowly escaped the crystal confines and bled from the gem.

It coalesced over his hands into a small vortex of power directly even with his eyes. The energy lurched and sped to hit him in the face. The blackness scared him and he stumbled backward, clutching at his eyes. The smoky power seemed to crawl around his hands and sink into his eyes. The building darkened, and it blinded him for a few moments before his vision finally cleared and a new message greeted him.

You completed the quest Animalistic Ritual. You gained 1,500 experience. You learned Nightstalker Transformation.

Druid Spell - Nightstalker Transformation	

Requirements
  Druid Class
  Complete Quest
  Animalistic Ritual
	Description: Your body undergoes a physical transformation and turns into a Nightstalker. The form has its own attacks and additions to learn. This effect lasts until canceled.
	
	Mana Cost: 50 MP
	Cast Time: 20 seconds

"That was scary," Atlas commented.

"We learned a while back to not warn people about things like that. Makes them stress out even more with the anxiety beforehand and they still always freak out during the event."

"I guess it's bound to be crappy either way. Thanks for the help. I'm about to head to the next city. Finished up everything here."

"Oh really? I guess at level 15 you would be pretty much done here. Finally off to Nirithan? At least you should finally meet some new people and more diverse races. It's one of the major hub cities in this part of the world and a common meeting place for guilds and parties."

"Nirithan, huh? Sounds fun, except it means more people I'll have to avoid. Had some bad luck with other Reborn early on and prefer to work alone."

"If that's what you want, then go for it. In the meantime, take this," Master Greenfoot said as he handed him a letter, "It will let your next trainer know where you are in your progress. Master Harrama can be a trying woman, but she is fair. Do your best and you'll have no problems."

"What's the best way to get to Nirithan?"

"Follow the road to the east. It veers slightly north as it goes, but leads directly for Nirithan."

"Thanks again, Master Greenfoot. Until we meet again," Atlas said and shook the old man's hand firmly.

He left the building and headed directly for the eastern gate. Before he walked through the enormous gates, a young woman ran up to him, breathing heavy.

"Are you Atlas?"

"Sure am. Can I help you with something?"

The woman nodded and reached into a small
bag on her side and withdrew a piece of paper.
She handed it over and smiled.

"Delivery complete. We appreciate you using
the Kingdom Courier," she said before she
turned and ran away, off to another task.

The Kingdom Courier? Odd.

He looked at the paper and noticed it had
his name on the front. In the top left corner
was the name PrettyPrincess. With a smile,
Atlas opened the paper and looked at the
contents.

Hey Atlas,

*I can't thank you guys enough for getting
my stuff back to me after the hunt. I found
out from the registrar that you handed it
over, but I knew it was a group decision since
it was all there. If you ever need anything,
please let me know. I'll see you again,
eventually.*

Pretty

Atlas fidgeted on the side of the road as
he read the letter. By the time he reached the
bottom, a smile plastered his face. *Glad she
got her stuff back.*

With his spirits a little higher, he
continued his trip out of the city and along
the road.

* * *

"State your purpose," A guard called to him
as he approached the city of Nirithan.

"Here to continue my training as a druid."

"Very well. Proceed to the Magistrate's office for your Seal of Passage before you go about your business," the man said as he waved him through.

"How do I get there?"

"Just follow this street until you come across the central square. Turn to the left and it's the third building down the road. Look for the sign," The guard said as he almost forcibly shoved him through the gate and out of the way.

Atlas followed his directions and found himself on the steps, the sign of the magistrate swinging in a light breeze. When he pushed through the door, he found two clerks seated at desks. One had a small placard stating Local while the other's read Regional. He walked over to the Local desk and the man behind the desk peered at him.

"Can I help you?"

"I need to get a Seal of Passage. The guard at the gate directed me here."

"Of course, sir. Name and reason for arrival?"

"Atlas. I'm here to continue my druid training."

The clerk nodded along as Atlas spoke, and he scribbled furiously at the paper. He placed the document in a small wicker basket by the side of the desk and then opened a drawer and rifled through the contents. The clerk extended his hand and Atlas saw a small metal disc. He plucked it from the outstretched hand and examined it.

The metal object was slightly larger than an old half-dollar coin. The center of the coin appeared to be some kind of iron, while a brighter metal circled the outside. He couldn't tell for sure what it was, but it reminded him of aluminum foil. A stamp of a tree was on one side and a crown on the other. Nirithan was embossed below the crown.

"Have a good day," the clerk told him as he stared at him, obviously expecting him to leave.

Atlas took the hint and exited the building. As soon as he touched the road, he looked around.

Where to go now?

Turning to his right, he spotted the sign for the Registrar's office. He fumbled around in his belt pouch and grasped the letter he received from the High Marshall. He'd totally forgot about it. Decision made, he walked into the office.

A young woman approached with a slab of wood in her hand, "Welcome, sir. Can I help you with something?"

"Yea. I'm here to turn this in," Atlas said as he lifted the writ and presented it to her.

She grabbed the letter and examined the front. Her eyes grew wide.

"The High Marshall gave you this? Were you a winner of The Great Hunt?"

"Yep, I was in one of the winning parties."

"Well, this writ allows you a position in the city if you choose," she began as she flipped through papers on the slab of wood, "Currently, we have four positions open. Constable, Overseer of Commerce, Master of the Trade Guild, and Master of the Wood. Do any of these sound to your liking?"

Atlas considered the options. *There isn't enough information to begin to decide on this.*

"What do these positions entail? Do they require me to become a permanent resident?"

"No, sir. We understand that a Reborn commonly travels and moves from place to place. When you end your time here, you merely request a transfer to the next city. We send you with a new writ to allow you a new set of options in the next place.

"Regarding what they entail, the constable is exactly that. You are the head of law and order in the city. It's your job to deal with disputes and justice. Overseer of Commerce organizes the manufacturing and the imports and exports of the city to keep trade flowing and the city earning money. Master of the Trade Guild is a similar position, but the primary purpose is to look out for the best interest of the trade guild members and not necessarily the city. Finally, Master of the Wood has the priority of protecting the forest and surrounding area similar to the constable. It's their job to respond to threats and monsters along the trade routes, and to keep the roads clear and safe. Each position comes with different perks."

So, they have responsibilities, but the perks could be worth it.

"What perks are there for the Master of the Wood?"

She flipped through a few more pages on her board before scanning the contents.

"The Master of Wood is given a stipend of 5 silver a day. In addition, they also have access to a work order system that allows them to send out assistants to complete tasks for rewards. These vary depending on the task."

Easy silver per day and all I have to do is answer the occasional call for help? That's not too bad. The tasks she mentioned sound like they could benefit me as well.

"I'll take the Master of the Wood position." Atlas confirmed.

"Wonderful choice," she told him as she shuffled the papers around again. She motioned for him to follow her to a desk as she pulled out a sheet of paper with writing on it. The paper looked like a standard form the city used and she quickly filled in the position of Master of the Wood and then his name before she handed him the quill and pointed at the line near the bottom.

Atlas scratched his name on the paper and she took the quill and nodded. She dug through a pocket and produced a metal emblem. Another clerk walked over with a lit candle and allowed some wax to drip on the bottom before she quickly pressed the emblem in. A notification popped up.

You have been named Master of the Wood for Nirithan.

Do you wish to access the control panel for the position? Yes/No.

Atlas ignored the message for a moment while he turned his attention back to the woman.

"All done. Anything else you need?"

"Where's the closest inn? I need to find a place to stay since I just arrived."

"Oh, I'm sorry. I forgot about that. The
position actually includes lodging. The home
for the Master of the Wood is near the
southwestern gate. If you came in from Ixala,
that's the gate you probably entered. The
house actually borders the outermost wall.
It's only a few spots away from the gate
itself for easy access," she said as she
turned and waved another clerk over, "Jimmy,
can you get this man the key for the Master of
the Wood's house?"

"Yes, ma'am," he said as he scurried to the
back of the building. He dashed through a door
and they waited for less than a minute before
he emerged again.

"Here you go," he said as he handed the key
to Atlas.

"Thanks."

"You're welcome to stay in that residence
as long as you remain the current Master of
the Wood. If you have any more questions now
or in the future, come find me and ask."

"Will do," he told her and left the
building. An alert popped up on his interface.

You only have 4 hours of game time left!

*Knew it had to be getting close. Guess I
can log out as soon as I get settled in the
house.*

He traveled back down the streets, and through the crowds toward the gate he'd entered. A tall sign on the edge of the main square showed a map of the city. They depicted it like an airport map and the zones were color coded. He was in the administration portion of the city. Near to him was the Trade District. All the profession masters would be there. He considered stopping by now but didn't want to get caught up in a project and run out of time, so he kept walking.

The house in question wasn't too hard to find. It was three houses from the gate off of a side road. The building had a door with a stylized tree on it and said Master of the Wood. The key glided in silently and the door popped open. The inside looked like a log cabin. Wooden plank walls covered every surface. The furniture was all made of wood, much of it solid logs and not just lumber. The smell of leather and wood permeated the space and soothed him. He turned and locked the door behind him.

Surely this place works like an inn if I lock it.

It took him a few minutes of wandering around to see the whole place, but he eventually settled himself in the bedroom and dropped his bags. The bed welcomed him in its soft folds and he closed his eyes.

Do you wish to log off? Yes/No.

He selected *Yes* and drifted back to reality.

★★★

The clink of nails on glass stirred him from his slumber. Atlas opened his eyes to see the Jean's beautiful face staring at him through the clear top of the pod. She waved and smiled before returning to work on the screen on the side. The tubes and helmet retracting as he waited.

The top popped open, and he slowly climbed from the device.

"How're you doing?" Atlas asked.

"Been good. How was your time in the game?"

"Productive. Finally gaining some ground. You busy today?"

"It's been really steady all day. Not too fast-paced, but also no real downtime. I was disappointed I haven't got to talk to you since our date," she told him with a frown.

Atlas raked his hand through his hair as he tried to hide his embarrassment, "Yeah. Sorry. Work drug on and I had trouble thinking about anything other than the laundry list of stuff I needed to do. I'm available for the next two evenings. I'd like to see you for one of them if possible."

She stared at him with a ferocious look as she tapped her foot. Her expression made him think he'd royally screwed up somehow. After a few seconds of rhythmic tapping, she finally sighed.

"Fine. I'll give you this one pass. If you want to have an actual relationship, you'll have to like me enough to remember me," she said in a huff.

Atlas sputtered apologies to her before she smiled and giggled.

"Ah, gamers sure lose track of time. How about tomorrow night? I won't be working then."

"Tomorrow night it is," Atlas agreed.

"Be careful when you head out. The lobby area is absolutely packed with people."

"Odd. There almost seems to be no one here every time I log out. Why would it be crowded?"

"The first player in the game has earned the right to become the next executive for the company. They are upstairs confirming it."

"Wow, really? Someone already discovered the secret? That's amazing. Think I'll run by and check it out."

He almost continued the conversation before a rumble in his stomach changed his mind.

"Yikes, got to go. I'll message you later and see if we can come up with a place."

He rushed down the steps without so much as a goodbye and dashed for the hallway.

His business taken care of, he took the elevator to the stairs and entered a crowd of people. Making any progress in the room was difficult, but he maneuvered far enough to be within view of the announcement podium on the far end.

He didn't have to wait long before a group of three walked out. The one in the lead was none other than Leonard Hale, founder and CEO of Gaia Corporation. The room fell silent as the legend himself walked to the microphone.

"Ladies and gentlemen, welcome. I have the extreme pleasure of announcing the first person in Divine Genesis to earn their place as an executive in the company. I considered many speeches for this and contemplated reciting the vaunted history of this company and how it strives to make this place a better world, but decided against all of that. Instead, we'll make this easy," he said as he gestured to his right, "I present to you the newest executive of Gaia Corporation, Keenan Hall."

The crowd cheered and hollered, but Atlas heard none of it. The room felt like it came to a halt as he watched Keenan, his best friend in the world, walk to the center of the small stage and shake hands with the CEO.

Keenan? How did you find the secret?

Sound and motion snapped back into place as the room continued to cheer. Keenan walked to the microphone with hands raised, trying to calm the crowd.

"Thanks for that," he began as he got the crowd to quiet down, "I am extremely grateful to be given this chance within the company. A stroke of luck led me to this position, but I plan to use my experience in gaming to help this company and the game grow. I believe I officially start in a few days?" he asked as he turned to look at the CEO.

"That's correct, Mr. Hall. You start in two days."

"Then I look forward to this new adventure." Keenan finished to another round of applause. The crowd dispersed as Keenan and the other executives shuffled from the room. Everyone around muttered in disbelief that they actually made someone an executive.

Atlas reflected on his friend. Something didn't sit right. Keenan would've never been that cool and collected. He would've been yelling and partying away. He also didn't speak very formal on most occasions.

I wonder if they gave him a speech to follow. That would make sense. I've also never seen him stand without slouching as long as I can remember. They must've trained him well for this event.

He immediately pulled out his phone and messaged Keenan.

What the hell, man? They made you an executive and you couldn't send me a message?

It took a few minutes, but he messaged back. *Sorry man, couldn't tell ya. I'm under an NDA, and I couldn't tell anyone until the company announced it. It just happened yesterday.*

Either way, congrats man. Bet it was an interesting experience. Want to meet up and chat?

I'd love to, but they have me booked pretty solid for the next few days. They want me doing some press announcements and interviews since I'm the first. I'll try to call you if I can, but I doubt I'll be available much in the near future.

Well, hit me up when you can.

Will do, man. Catch ya later.

Atlas just sighed and headed back to his apartment. His boring life crashing back into him after the vividness of his time in game.

★★★

"You seem a little distracted?" Jean commented.

"Huh? Oh, sorry. Still hung up on the fact that my best friend is now an executive of the largest video game company. Kinda difficult to wrap my head around."

She giggled, "Kinda surreal, isn't it? To think we could get a high-paying job like that just by playing a game."

"It's tempting for sure. My job doesn't pay the greatest, but it's steady. With the game tied into the real world economy, it is certainly tempting to play it as a job." Atlas told her before he picked up a fork full of noodles and slurped them down.

"I couldn't do it. I've never been good at games myself. I played a little of Divine Genesis early during development and thought it was amazing from a neurological aspect, but I wasn't very good at it."

She plucked a meatball from her plate of spaghetti and bit into it. A splash of sauce spilled over onto her lip and Atlas smiled as she chewed. When she saw his face he continued his grin but lightly mimicked wiping the corner of his mouth and she blushed. Her unoccupied hand flew to her face with a napkin and quickly cleaned the spot.

"You're still pretty, even with sauce on your face," Atlas teased her.

"Oh shut up. How long did you let me sit here with that on my face?"

Atlas laughed, "You just got it on there with your last bite."

Jean stared at him for a few moments before returning to her food. Atlas chuckled to himself as she spooned food in and immediately covered her lower face with her hand.

"Come on now. That's ridiculous."

"Quiet, you. If I want to cover my mouth while I eat, I will."

"But how am I supposed to see your beautiful smile behind your hand?"

She rolled her eyes at him, "Laying it on a little thick tonight?"

He blushed and lowered his head, "Sorry. Still a little nervous about whatever this is. That combined with the weird day has me all kinds of confused."

"Well, how about you just focus on me for the rest of the night? This dinner is delicious, but what are we doing next?"

Atlas froze for a moment, trying to figure out what to do before he remembered they were close to a public park.

"How about we walk through the park down the road? I hear the flowers are lovely this time of year."

"That's more like it," she told him with a soft smile.

✦✦✦

The alarm blared and startled him awake. He jumped to his feet and swiped it off. His trip through the house was a breeze as he threw on his clothes and dashed straight for his car. It had been a grueling two days of work and he hadn't been able to meet up with Jean again.

Atlas flew down the highway, headed directly for Gaia Corporation. He was itching to hop back in game and try out his new cat form in combat. A laundry list of crafting things waited on him too.

He fired off a quick text message to Keenan on his way.

Hope the new job is working out. I'm sure you'll do great!

No response, but it didn't surprise him. Keenan told him they had him booked solid for a few days at least.

His car screeched to a halt in the multi-story parking garage and Atlas winced.

Seriously need to get those brake pads replaced.

He didn't talk to anyone until the check in point. The elevator actually had two other people on it this time, but he didn't bother to speak to them either. They all remained silent until it came to a halt and each walked directly for their assigned pod.

"Atlas! Good to see you again," the bubbly voice of Jean told him as he approached.

"Good to see you too. How's work been?"

"You know. I think I'm going to institute a new rule. You can no longer ask me that question. You better come up with something new. My answer is always the same."

Atlas grinned at her antics but finally came up with a different question, "So, are you always a messy eater or was that just the other night?"

She slapped him lightly on the arm with a laugh, "Get in that capsule before I strangle you. Call me when you get out. If you stay in the entire time, I'll be off work when you get done."

"Will do," he said as he lightly squeezed her hand and hopped in. He wanted to try a quick kiss but knew this place had to be loaded with cameras.

He adjusted himself in the seat as the helmet slid on and the pod closed.

'Have fun' Jean mouthed to him through the glass and everything went black.

Chapter 19

A Daring Rescue

Atlas woke up to the smell of fresh cut lumber. The Master of the Wood's cottage looked exactly as it did when he left. He grabbed his bags and left without a second thought. The house was nice, but it served no real purpose other than a safe place to log out and store his stuff.

The street bustled with activity as people went about their business. He spotted more of the Reborn walking around. The names usually tipped him off, but the occasional person stood out by a gaudy collection of armor. Most of the natives wore matching garments. Even the guards commonly wore matching styles in all of their armor. The players wore anything they could find.

Heading to his trainers for his skills was his priority. He turned toward the trade district and started walking.

"Help me! Help me!" someone screamed as they ran through the gate.

The guards stopped the frantic looking woman as she ran in. Atlas joined them to find out what was happening.

"But you have to help me. You can't sit around and do nothing." The woman pleaded with the guard.

"Ma'am, please calm down. We can't send out people to rescue others without the proper authority." One guard told her.

"What's going on?" Atlas asked the group.

The guard who spoke before looked at him for a few moments before something seemed to click, "Ah, Master of the Wood. I'm glad you're here. This woman has a dilemma that seems to rest in your area of influence."

Atlas turned to the woman and finally inspected her. She wore a tattered dress that looked more like an undergarment than a true outfit. Minor cuts covered the garment and the bottom edge was frayed from brushing on the ground. Mud stains and spots of what appeared to be blood marred the white surface.

"What's wrong?" Atlas finally asked.

"They stole my sister! We were out in the woods hunting for herbs and a group of bandits ambushed us. She told me to run for it while she confronted them and bought me time to escape. You have to save her!" she wailed.

Quest – Damsel in Distress	

Requirements
   Master of the Wood
   Level 15
 	
Quest Rarity: Uncommon
 	
Quest Reward: 1200 experience, 40 silver, unknown rewards.
	Description: Find the woman's sister and rescue her from the bandits.

Unknown rewards? Interesting premise. That and an Uncommon level quest. Maybe it means I can find some decent gear during this trip.

"I'll go find her," Atlas told the woman in a soft and reassuring tone and turned to the nearest guard, "Go with her back to her home and allow her to get cleaned up."

When the young guard escorted her away, Atlas turned to the original man at the gate, "Have one of your men monitor her. I don't want her roaming around causing panic in the town. If you have to, keep her confined to her home until I come back."

"Yes, sir," the guard said with a salute across his chest.

Atlas watched the man scurry over to another guard at the post and relay the instructions. The woman saluted with her arm across her chest and followed the initial guard and the woman.

With the issue currently in hand, Atlas turned toward the gate. *I guess this is my job after all. You got this.*

He lifted his head high and strode from the city with a confident gait. The duty of his position offset all thoughts of delaying to work on his crafting.

The path into the forest was clear, and he headed for the quest outline it showed on the map. It wasn't far from one of the main paths through the forest, so he kept to the trail until he neared the border.

Once in the quest area, he skirted the edges of the quest zone and tried to find clues. The forest floor was relatively clear, and the lack of recent rain made it impossible to find any tracks in the hard-packed dirt. He strained his minimal skills in tracking to find any hint that someone traveled through here. Recalling every TV show or random video he'd ever seen, he tried to look for broken twigs, rustled leaves, foreign objects scattered anywhere, but found nothing.

I'm not cut out for this type of work. Why did I even accept this position without skills to use out here?

The sound of a low growl cut his self-pity short. He froze in place and slowly turned toward the sound. The bushes rustled and slowly parted as a sleek feline emerged.

Red fur covered its face and the hair gradually faded to black as it traveled farther down the cat. It stood four feet tall at the shoulders and large ivory teeth glistened from its mouth. A glance showed what he was up against. *Blood Hunter - Level 15.*

Atlas gulped and scrambled to get his staff out and ready. The cat sensed his panic and dashed in for the kill. His weapon came around just in time to knock the animal to the side and deflect its attack. He breathed a quick sigh of relief, but it was premature as the agile creature had already turned with the attack and dashed back in. His reflexes weren't fast enough, and it raked claws down his side. It didn't stop there and continued to maul and swipe at him with four attacks.

The pain from the claws staggered him as the cat watched with a wicked gleam in its eyes. The pain faded quickly, but his health had taken a significant hit.

Blood Hunter dealt 32 damage to you with Savage Strikes.

With a roar of fury, Atlas retaliated. The speed the cat showed made him all too aware he'd need to Anticipate its action. His staff came around in a wide swing and he focused on the cat. He saw the animal tense as it readied itself to move and smiled. The position it took clued him in, and he adjusted his swing. The animal leaped from its place and soared high over the staff as it whizzed by through empty air. The feline immediately dashed forward and clawed Atlas in a three-strike combo before backing off and watching him again.

Blood Hunter dealt 24 damage to you with Rend and Tear.

How the hell am I supposed to match that kind of speed? His jumped launched him so much farther than I expected that I wasn't even close to hitting him. I guess I can Entangle him but with his speed I might not catch him that way either.
Then it hit him. He had a spell he could use. One he'd recently learned and hadn't yet used in combat. With a grin, he activated Nightstalker Transformation.
Power surged through his body, and it shifted. Hair sprouted along his hands and arms as his body fell forward to land on all fours. Luckily, the Blood Hunter seemed so astonished by the ordeal that it merely retreated a little way and arched its back, causing the hairs to stand on end down the ridge of its spine.

The transformation halted and Atlas felt reinvigorated. Smells from the surrounding area assaulted him and almost overwhelmed him. The hint of pine, a few small animals, even the lingering stench of blood drew his attention. The most astonishing smell, though, was one he was sure was the smell of people. It even hinted at a general direction to follow.

All thoughts of this ground to a halt as his eyes caught the movement of his opponent. The cat dashed forward with a yowl and its mouth open to attack. It didn't seem nearly as fast to him now, and Atlas inwardly rejoiced when the familiar images showed up. Instead of showing him how to block, they showed him how to dodge, so he followed the projected path and jumped to the side.

The Blood Hunter soared past him and he turned to follow. His muscles pumped, and he dashed forward, faster than he'd ever moved until he closed in on the enemy. Only one skill appeared in his interface, so he activated it. A two-hit combo of claws dug furrows into the animal and it howled as it backed up.

You dealt 14 damage to Blood Hunter with Furious Claws.

The Blood Hunter attacked again, and Atlas dove to the side to clear it. The move mostly worked, but a small line of blood trickled down his side where it glanced off of his hide.

Blood Hunter dealt 3 damage to you with Rend and Tear. (Glancing)

Atlas selected Furious Claws and dove forward with the attack. His first swing sliced across its left shoulder. As he began his second attack, his vision flashed red, and he slowed his movements to look for the danger.

The Blood Hunter's paw raced for the side of his head, forcing him to jump backward to avoid the strike. The swing met empty air, and the cat hissed in fury. It propelled itself forward in a leap and extended both paws forward, claws gleaming.

Atlas let out a low growl and focused on the attack. Now was the perfect time to counter. With the creature in the air, it couldn't dodge out of the way of any attack and left itself open. Since he didn't have a Counter ability, he recalled the attack the animal just used on him. A pretty simple strike to the side of the head should knock him off balance and stop his leap.

He stretched forward and used every bit of reach he had to swing his paw in a wide arc. The farther away he could make contact, the better chance he could push the animal off course. A brief flash of surprise lit up the animal's eyes before Atlas' paw connected with the side of its head, tearing rents across its face with his claws.

You learned Counter. (Cat Form)
You dealt 6 damage to Blood Hunter with Counter.

Whew, that'll be helpful. I've grown to rely on that move way too much to be without it.

Feeling a little better about the situation, Atlas activated Furious Claws. He pounced forward and carved furrows into the poor cat, causing it to hiss in alarm.

You dealt 14 damage to Blood Hunter with Furious Claws.

His mouth stretched into a wicked grin, fangs bared. The creature shied away with a look of trepidation in its eyes. It slowly circled to his right for a few steps before gaining its courage back and charging forward.

Atlas studied its movements and saw it using the same pattern it did when it hit him with Rend and Tear. Knowing what was coming allowed him to dodge to the side and activate Counter, followed by Furious Claws again.

You dealt 6 damage to Blood Hunter with Counter.
You dealt 14 damage to Blood Hunter with Furious Claws.

The cat fell to the ground and writhed for a few moments before pulling itself to its feet. Atlas knew its time was up and it did too. The Blood Hunter made one last attempt to attack, but it was halfhearted and slow. It took minimal effort to dodge the attack, and a quick Counter and Furious Claws finished it.

Blood Hunter died.
You gained 75 experience.

Atlas looked around the clearing. His ears twitched as he turned and picked up even the tiniest of sounds. Some of them he couldn't quite tell what they were, but he could swear one of them was the sound of an ant walking along the dirt.

Nothing near him sounded dangerous, so the cat must've come alone. A sniff told him to head west. It was the direction of the blood he detected earlier. His body glowed and changed form again until he returned to his elf body. He considered staying in cat form but desperately needed to heal himself. The fight took a little over a third of his health from him and, while not immediately threatening, another surprise fight like that could end him.

A couple casts of Nurture and a cast of Harmony were more than enough to top him back off. His hike led him farther into the forest. Nothing looked out of the ordinary as he continued his walk. No obvious signs of a struggle or even disturbed ground. His hike continued this way for over an hour before he resigned himself to shift back to cat form.

There was no reason not to, anyway. His mana was mostly recovered, and he'd still regenerate more while in cat form. The familiar glow returned as his body fell forward and slowly morphed into the sleek feline form. With a flash of insight, he mimicked the most common move he'd seen cats do. He rocked back and stuck his butt up high in the air while his front legs stretched forward.

Man, that really feels good. Now I see why they do it all the time.

With a quick shake of his body, he walked forward. The smells drifted to him again. The forest was alive with movement. Something his elven body just didn't comprehend. It took a few minutes of travel, but he finally detected a hint of something odd. He couldn't pinpoint what it was, only that it smelled out of place.

Crouching down, he followed the scent. It wove through the trees and followed what looked to be a game trail. He sniffed on plants and tree branches as they passed and couldn't detect anything on them. Whatever he tracked, it had an incredible sense of forestry.

A clatter of metal brought him to a halt. His ears perked up and twitched as they searched for the source. Looking through the trees, he spotted a clearing at the edge of his vision. His senses told him the noise came from there. He stalked to the edge of the trees and peered past.

An unexpected site greeted him. The building looked like an old abandoned wilderness fort. A short stone wall surrounded the place and a three-story stone tower sat in the middle. Vines wove along the surface of both, but the grass on the inside of the wall was cut short and maintained.

The inhabitants also disturbed him. When the woman told him bandits attacked, he expected to find a group of thugs roaming the place. Instead, a group of study looking dwarves walked along the border inside the walls. Another stood on the roof of the tower. His short stature made him difficult to pick out at first.

Six of these fighters circled the outside perimeter. Those numbers wouldn't trouble him too much, but one minor detail scared him. They carried muskets, not swords. He was well aware that this was a game, and he'd taken a lot of damage during his time playing. That damage had been easy to spot and was all in close combat. All he could picture was the devastating effects of a firearm in the real world and how bad that would hurt if hit.

I need to play this smart. I don't know if they will worry about crossfire or not, so I can't just rush them. Each of them is wearing sturdy leather armor. The hostage must be inside the tower.

Deciding on caution, he crept around the edge of the clearing so he could survey the entire area. The guards did a good job of protecting the entire wall, and he couldn't spot any noticeable gaps anywhere. His cat form had one advantage he could use. It could stealth.

During his excursion around the place, he identified one spot near the back corner of the building that was well shaded. It also was right where two of the guards met on their patrol. The tall grass around the exterior wall was a fatal flaw in their defense. It made it easier for someone to sneak up.

A low crouch allowed him to creep through the space toward the wall. He was careful to watch how his body displaced the grass as he moved. Large clumps of grass randomly swaying and heading directly for the wall would be a dead giveaway.

When he finally butted up to the wall, he could smell the dwarves. They smelled like leather and freshly turned dirt. No other explanation came to him as his nose picked up those scents. Body odor didn't seem to trouble them overly much. His ears perked up as he heard the footfalls headed his way, slowly plodding through the grass.

A guard approached from each direction, and when they met, they would both turn and head directly away from each other. Atlas planned on using that moment to leap over the wall and slink toward the shaded area to blend in. The footsteps pounded in his head as he listened. The heavy thumping in his cat senses pounded through his head.

He heard the brief stop and waited. The feet shuffled as they both turned and he gave them a handful of seconds to march away before he crouched and leaped for the short wall. At only about four feet tall, the height wasn't a problem, and he lightly bounced off the ledge and landed quietly in the inner yard. He heard no shouting so he hurried to the shaded area and didn't waste time to look around.

Once inside the dark recess of the building, he crouched low and swept his gaze around. The patrols didn't cease their pattern and hadn't even faltered. Luckily, the guard on the roof wasn't paying attention to anything on this side of the building.

Well, I didn't think this through very well. What am I going to do once I do rescue this person? I can't sneak her out the same way I came in…

The solution to his problem evaded him so, instead of dwelling on it, he moved forward. Two small windows sat on this side of the building. He watched the guards' helmets approach each other again over the short wall and waited for them to turn. Using the opening, he dashed for the nearest window and heaved himself inside.

He landed in a stone room that was the base of a stairwell. A long spiral of stone steps curved ahead of him and a bare hallway stretched behind him. Both were clear, so he stalked up the stairs.

A door swung open above him and he froze. Muffled voices echoed through the stone stairs. He tried to make out what they said, but his enhanced hearing worked against him in this space. The constant echoes and vibrations distorted all the sounds as his delicate ears tried to pick up all of it.

The door closed and the sound of boots heading his way took its place. Whoever it was wasn't thrilled based on the grumbling noises they made as they practically stomped down the stairs. Tired of doing nothing but hiding, Atlas found a shadowed alcove on the side of the stairs and waited. It wasn't a very big dip in the wall, but just enough for his stealth properties to activate.

A figure emerged around the bend and he spotted another dwarf. This one was wearing chain armor that hung to his mid thighs. His legs were mostly bare, short of his metal shod boots he clomped around in. Two small hatchets hung on his hips. Atlas crouched down and waited for his chance.

His leap carried him through the air, and his claws immediately reached for the dwarf's face. The man never saw him coming, and they tore through his face as his prey squealed in surprise.

You learned Pounce. (Stealth)
You dealt 18 damage to Tower Dwarf with Pounce.

The short man stumbled backward as he clutched at his face. Atlas activated Furious Claws and his body continued the attack. The speed of the fight didn't allow him to check the details on Pounce, but he figured it must be an opening combo move, similar to his Charge ability.

His claws tore furrows through the metal armor and small rings popped free. Faint tinkling sounds of metal on stone filled the small passageway. A muffled grunt of anger escaped the dwarf's mouth as it stepped backward and fetched his hatchets from his belt.

"A dinnae whit gowk let a wild animal intae th' tower bit a'm aff tae crush someone's skull."

The baritone voice rumbled through the passageway as he dashed forward and swung his axes. Atlas grinned and flashed his long teeth before nimbly hopping to the side. The man appeared to move in slow motion with his heightened senses. As soon as the axes cleared his body, he activated Counter and dashed forward, claws raking down the dwarf's leg. He followed with Furious Claws and the warrior dropped to a knee, clutching at his shoulder.

You dealt 6 damage to Tower Dwarf with Counter.
You dealt 14 damage to Tower Dwarf with Furious Claws.

"Ye sure ur a feisty beasty. Think ah will mak' a cloak oot o' ye."

The slow man dashed for him again, and Atlas nonchalantly slid to the side. The dwarf redirected his axes, and one of them clipped him on the side. He hopped backward and a soft growl escaped him.

Tower Dwarf dealt 6 damage to you with Cutting Chop. (Glancing)

"Ye'r sure an odd yin. Even hae yersel' a name…," he began as recognition dawned on his face. Rolling his shoulders back, he belted out a quick statement, "Intruder in th' keep!"

"You'll regret that, slow man," Atlas responded.

The dwarf's face went pale as he stared at Atlas. Surely a talking cat would alarm almost any sane person.

Atlas went in and hit him with another Furious Claws. The attack was infuriating because it's all he had. It limited his options in this form.

You dealt 14 damage to Tower Dwarf with Furious Claws.

Knowing his cover was already blown, he activated his shapeshift ability. The light flared in the stairway as his body shifted back to size. Now he looked down on a significantly shorter person, holding axes and shaking.

"Shouldn't have kidnapped people," Atlas said as he rushed forward and used Triple Threat. His staff spun and blurred as it deftly thumped into the meaty dwarf. Grunts and yells punctuated each hit as the short man attempted to deflect them with his axes. He wasn't successful. An application of Pursuit followed and then he rounded it out with a Double Slash.

You dealt 18 damage to Tower Dwarf with Triple Threat.
You dealt 5 damage to Tower Dwarf with Pursuit.
You dealt 12 damage to Tower Dwarf with Double Slash.

"Nae mah fault thay didnae wantae pay th' toll fur passage. We figured her ransom wid pay us back fur oor lost coin."

"That's exactly your fault! Because you don't own that road and, unfortunately for you, it's my responsibility to keep it safe."

Atlas taunted as he flashed a grin.

The dwarf roared and charged forward. Following the counter images was child's play, and he quickly batted the attack away.

"Pathetic," was the only response he gave before he ran his entire combo. Counter hit, followed by Blade Chase, Triple Threat, Pursuit, and Double Slash.

You dealt 5 damage to Tower Dwarf with Counter.
You dealt 18 damage to Tower Dwarf with Blade Chase.
You dealt 18 damage to Tower Dwarf with Triple Threat.

You dealt 5 damage to Tower Dwarf with Pursuit.

You dealt 12 damage to Tower Dwarf with Double Slash.

Tower Dwarf died.

You gained 75 experience.

The onslaught was too much to handle and the dwarf finally collapsed to the ground. He walked forward and didn't get a loot box prompt. It seemed strange at first until he reached forward and grabbed the body. He could physically move everything the guy wore.

I guess we can literally loot the playable races as though they were real people?

Shuffling through the dwarf's pockets, he found a handful of coins and tossed them in his belt pouch. The two hatchets fell into his bag and he left the rest where it lay.

Time to find myself a damsel!

Chapter 20

A Desperate Escape

Atlas ran up the stairs. With the dwarf calling out the alarm, he abandoned all pretenses of stealth. Now he just needed to find the girl and get out. He passed two doors and ran straight for the end of the stairs.

A door waited for him at the end of the stairs. As he closed the distance, the door cracked open and Atlas pulled himself to a halt.

"Whit's tha noise out 'ere. Who's yelling in mah tower?"

A surly-looking dwarf grumbled as he exited the doorway. Their eyes met, and they both froze.

"Where's the prisoner?" Atlas asked.

"How'd ye git in 'ere?"

"Hopped in a window. Now your turn, where's your prisoner?"

The dwarf spluttered in confusion before he growled and reached over his shoulder. When the hand emerged, a double-bladed axe came with it.

"Just one o' ye fur a rescue party? This shud be easy."

The little man dashed forward with a wide swing of the axe. Atlas started to intercept the attack before he thought better of it and jumped backward. The blow swooshed past and a gust of air buffeted him from the blow.

That would've surely broke through my defense.

He activated Triple Threat and charged in. The first hit landed on the dwarf's side. As he spun the staff for the second hit, his vision flashed a red tint. Pivoting his feet, he redirected the staff to block the new incoming attack. His swing knocked the downward slash of the axe off course and it sparked against the stone floor. Activating Counter, he thrust the staff forward and punched directly into the guard's sternum.

A rush of air burst from his mouth and Atlas felt a small crunch against the bone. The dwarf's axe hung by his side as he brought a hand toward the impact site. Atlas never slowed down and continued with Blade Chase and another Triple Threat attack. This time, the small man couldn't do anything to stop him. All three attacks landed with solid blows before he finished the attack with Pursuit and Double Slash.

You dealt 5 damage to Tower Dwarf with Triple Threat. (Interrupted)
You dealt 5 damage to Tower Dwarf with Counter.
You dealt 18 damage to Tower Dwarf with Blade Chase.
You dealt 18 damage to Tower Dwarf with Triple Threat.
You dealt 5 damage to Tower Dwarf with Pursuit.
You dealt 12 damage to Tower Dwarf with Double Slash.

The poor dwarf fell to a knee and held himself upright with his axe handle as the bladed end rested on the stone. He heaved for breath, trying to regain some strength to continue the fight.

"Tell me where the prisoner is!" Atlas demanded.

"She's two floors doon. Lest room oan th' right. Wilnae dae ye any gud. Ye cannae beat a' o' us."

"I don't plan on fighting all of you, but I will if I have to."

The dwarf grunted and hoisted himself to his feet.

"Ye have tae git thro' me first," the dwarf roared as he charged.

The speed of the attack surprised Atlas, and he couldn't dodge in time. The blade sliced through his side and a line of burning fire flared to life along his ribs.

Tower Dwarf dealt 6 damage to you with Wild Swing. (Glancing)

Instead of rushing in for a volley of attacks, Atlas changed his strategy. He activated Entangle and followed the careful movement patterns. The dwarf looked confused at first before his eyes widened in recognition. His next charge didn't make it very far before Atlas completed the spell and vines punched through the stone and grabbed the man.

Atlas grinned and activated Nature's Wrath. He weaved through the motions and the two balls of glowing energy burst forth, hitting the dwarf in the chest.

You dealt 3 damage to Tower Dwarf with Entangle.
You dealt 16 damage to Tower Dwarf with Nature's Wrath.

The dwarf was so weak from the attacks that it sagged in the grip of the vines. Atlas put him out of his misery and used Triple Threat. The first two hits connected, but an unexpected flash of red lit his vision and he spun. Another small axe blade dug into his shoulder before he could react.

You dealt 10 damage to Tower Dwarf with Triple Threat. (Interrupted)
Tower Dwarf died.
You gained 70 experience.
Tower Dwarf dealt 12 damage to you with Chop.

Two more dwarves stood in the stairwell behind him. One held the axe, now wedged into his shoulder. The other stood with a long musket raised to his eye. Atlas panicked and shuffled backward, pulling the axe out of his shoulder. He grit his teeth at the pain and growled to distract himself. The sight of the gun barrel pointed at him commanded his focus, and he couldn't take his eyes from it.

The dwarf with the axe stepped to the side and fear blossomed in his heart as he heard the loud crack of the gun and watched a small ball of fire belch from the barrel. A pressure in his right shoulder caused him to rock sideways and stumble backward. Looking down, the edges of his clothes smoked around a small hole, now leaking a tiny trickle of blood.

Tower Marksman dealt 20 damage to you with Crack Shot. (Critical)

His mind caught up to what he saw as the pain burst to the forefront of his thoughts. *Damn, that hurt!*

The dwarf with the gun stood in the same place, desperately pouring powder into the gun to reload it. Angry at the turn of events, Atlas roared and charged for the man. His trip lasted two steps before the red flashed again and he spun toward the axe man. With a flash of rage, he didn't even look at the incoming attack. Instead, he swung hard for the second dwarf's head.

His attack was faster and a loud thump punctuated the strike. The axe pulled down and swung short. Atlas pushed harder and strung out the combo. He couldn't afford to let the marksman reload.

You dealt 5 damage to Tower Dwarf with Counter.

You dealt 18 damage to Tower Dwarf with Blade Chase.

You dealt 18 damage to Tower Dwarf with Triple Threat.

You dealt 5 damage to Tower Dwarf with Pursuit.

You dealt 12 damage to Tower Dwarf with Double Slash.

The last hit knocked the fighter back and
Atlas used Entangle again. The vines sprouted
as the dwarf regained his senses. As soon as
he saw the first vines grip the man, he turned
and ran for the marksman. The dwarf was using
a metal rod to pack down the contents of the
rifle at a frantic pace. When he saw Atlas
approaching, he tossed the rod to the ground
and quickly pulled up the musket.

The weapon belched fire again, but the rush
of the attack pushed off his aim and the
projectile hit Atlas in the left bicep as he
continued forward with his staff. A tiny
blossom of pain registered in his mind, but
the adrenaline of the fight helped him ignore
the sensation.

The staff came around and began his
devastating combo. The marksman was obviously
lacking in hand to hand skills and couldn't
even attempt to put up a fight. The best he
managed was trying to use his musket like a
staff to block attacks, but he was so clumsy
that the ploy never worked.

*Tower Marksman dealt 12 damage to you with
Crack Shot.*

*You dealt 18 damage to Tower Marksman with
Triple Threat.*

*You dealt 5 damage to Tower Marksman with
Pursuit.*

*You dealt 12 damage to Tower Marksman with
Double Slash.*

The dwarf sagged backward with the last
hit, but quickly straightened.

"Ye wilnae git out o' 'ere alive, Elven scum," he said with defiance as he reached into his pouch and pulled something free that looked like a small metal horn. Placing it against his lips, he blew a long hard note as Atlas tried to charge and stop him.

A deep rumbling noise reverberated through his very soul, and the sheer force of it surprised him with how small the instrument looked. His staff connected with the dwarf's head and stopped the note, but Atlas was sure the damage was done. He used the same combo as before and punished the marksman with another 35 damage.

The short man made one last attempt at resistance as he fished out a small dagger and charged for an attack. Atlas almost felt bad for the little guy as he stepped to the side and batted it away. He triggered Counter, Blade Chase, Triple Threat, Pursuit, and then Double Slash for the full fury of his combo. The last smack of his staff rang hollow and the dwarf's eyes turned vacant as he collapsed to the ground.

You dealt 58 total damage to Tower Marksman.
Tower Marksman died.
You gained 70 experience.

As he turned to the remaining combatant, he spotted the telltale look of fear in the short man's eyes. He still struggled frantically to escape the vines, but had minimal luck. Atlas charged in and finished him with his attack combo.

You dealt 35 total damage to Tower Dwarf.
Tower Dwarf died.

You gained 70 experience.

Knowing he had limited time, he dashed to each of the three dwarves. A quick search of them revealed 5 silver coins. He considered packing away their weapons, but the axes didn't look like anything special. The guard he'd killed from the top of the tower had one item of note that he desperately needed.

Item – Prison Key	
Requirements: Damsel in Distress Quest **Rarity:** Common **Quality:** Fair	**Durability:** 35/35 **Weight:** 0.2 lbs. **Slot:** Quest Item **Traits:** Used to access the prison in the forest tower.

His feet carried him down the stairs at a sprint. He took the steps two at a time as he raced toward the door with his target. The first door flew by in no time and he slowed as he approached his target. This door wasn't locked, and he opened it to peer through.

Before it opened more than an inch, a loud crack echoed behind it and a crunch of wood punctuated the noise. His hand vibrated on the door from the impact.

Damn. Another marksman.

Letting the man reload would be a mistake, so he readied himself and kicked the door wide as he rushed through. Another burst of gunfire echoed in the passage and he cried out in pain as the bullet hit him in the side. Now that he was charging in, he saw two marksman standing near the only door.

*Tower Marksman dealt 20 damage to you with
Crack Shot.*

*Luckily there aren't any real melee people
here. I should be able to handle these
quickly.*
The distance shrunk quickly as he ran down
the hall. He activated Triple Threat and aimed
for the shooter that fired first. A musket
intercepted his attack. This dwarf didn't
fumble with his blocking like the last did.
The marksman dropped his hands toward the end
of the barrel and swung hard with the wooden
stock leading the way.
Atlas dropped to a crouch as the weapon
passed overhead. His hair rustled from the
breeze as it passed and he activated Counter.
Thrusting forward, his staff slammed into the
dwarf's chest and Blade Chase followed. On the
last hit, his vision flashed red, and he spun
just in time to see a thick wooden stock slam
into the side of his face.
He stumbled backward and his hand shot to
his face as he mumbled, "Son of a bitch, that
hurt."

*You dealt 5 damage to Tower Dwarf with
Counter.*
*You dealt 10 damage to Tower Dwarf with
Blade Chase. (Interrupted)*
*Tower Marksman dealt 15 damage to you with
Stock Smash.*

Shaking off the attack, he removed his hand from his face just in time to see another attack heading for him. Diving to the side, he avoided the attack and continued attacking his original target. If he could take out one of them, the other would be easy for him to deal with.

Activating Triple Threat, he rushed for the dwarf. This time, the man wasn't fast enough to intercept the attack, and the combo pummeled him. Pursuit and Double Slash followed to round out the attack.

You dealt 35 total damage to Tower Dwarf.

The dwarf's moves were sluggish as he tried to attack. A quick flick of his staff knocked the man off balance and he stumbled past. Atlas turned in pursuit when he caught the glint of metal out of the corner of his eye. His gaze swung toward the object just in time to see the other marksman with the gun up to his shoulder and one eye squinted as he aimed down the barrel.

Atlas panicked and dropped to the ground. His timing worked out perfectly as fire exploded from the barrel and he heard something zip over his heard. A loud shout accompanied the shot, and he turned his head to see the dwarf he pushed past him sink to the ground, a hole leaking blood punched into his back.

"Daggart!" the other dwarf exclaimed in shock as he lowered his weapon in disbelief.

Atlas took advantage of the situation, pushed himself back to his feet, and charged the stunned marksman. The man didn't even attempt to block as his combo rattled off. When the last hit of his Double Slash landed, the dwarf only slumped to a knee, dropping his musket, and stayed there with his head bowed. He never even attempted to protect himself or fight back.

You dealt 35 total damage to Tower Dwarf.

His staff came overhead as he readied for a powerful attack. The weapon came down, but he pulled it to a quick halt.

He's not even attempting to fight. He just killed someone he knew. I can't do this to him.

Atlas lowered the staff and backed away from him. The dwarf remained in his place and stared at the dead body of the other marksman. Atlas decided he couldn't be completely careless, so he addressed a few issues. First off was his health. While not critically dangerous, 75 health remaining wasn't something he was comfortable with.

Two casts of Nurture boosted him back up to 129, while a cast of Harmony allowed his health to trickle back to full. This set him back 50 mana, putting him at 105 mana with the small amount he'd regenerated since the fighting started.

He considered looting the dead marksman but thought it might rile up the still living dwarf. Instead, he calmly walked over and picked up their muskets. He dropped them into his bag and walked toward the door. Knowing he couldn't just rely on chance, he spent a little more mana and cast Entangle on the living marksman. The vines wrapped around the kneeling man and cradled him in place.

Confident the situation wouldn't backfire, he focused on the door. It refused to open as he tugged on it, so he pulled out the key he'd found and inserted it into the door. A soft click sounded as he turned the key and pushed the door open with ease.

Inside was a large room, divided into four sections by metal bars. The front looked like a spot for the guards, and a table with two chairs sat in the space. Behind that sat three areas that appeared to be the actual cells.

Two of them were empty, but the one in the middle contained a scrawny looking young woman. Dirty clothes with spots of dried blood covered her lithe frame. Disheveled brown hair cascaded down and framed her face.

Must be from the struggle when they captured her.

When he was a couple of steps from the cell, the woman looked up at him. Lines streaked through the dirt caked on her face from the tears she'd shed. At the sight of him, she froze. Her eyes narrowed as she looked him over.

"You're not one of them, are you?"

Atlas smiled, trying to help keep her calm, "No, I'm Atlas, the Master of the Wood of Nirithan. Your sister reported bandits had abducted you and I've come to save you."

She looked around the room and even stood
up and stepped to the side to peer past him.

"You came by yourself? You didn't bring a
party to help?"

"I'm here by myself," Atlas affirmed with a
nod, "I'm going to get you out of here and
back to your sister. Although, your sister was
so frantic I don't recall her giving me your
name."

She stood in silence for a few moments, her
mind trying to process that he'd truly
infiltrated this place alone, before she
finally answered.

"I'm Penny."

"Good to meet you Penny, although I wish it
was under better circumstances. I need you to
come with me and do as I tell you so we can
get out of here. Think you can do that?"

The woman's face changed into a look of
resolve, and Atlas finally noticed how young
she was. She couldn't be much older than
eighteen.

"So, what's the plan?"

"I'm going to unlock this door," he said as
he walked over and inserted the key into the
cell door, "and we are going to leave this
place and get you home."

"That's not a plan! Have you ever done this
before? Seems like a poor rescue attempt." She
said with a frown.

"Not saying I disagree with you, but time
was of the essence. Our exit depends on how
many dwarves are blocking the way. Just do as
I say and I'll get you out."

She still looked skeptical about his
complete lack of an actual plan. Truth be
told, Atlas wasn't very confident either, but
he couldn't let her know that. Eventually, she
sighed and relented, "Okay, let's go then."

Atlas led the way out of the room and spotted the dwarf from earlier still on his knees. His expression was vacant, and he hadn't moved since their fight. They continued past and hurried to the stairs.

Metal clattered on stone below them and the thump of heavy boots filled the stairwell.

"So, Master of the Wood, now what?" Penny asked with sarcasm lacing her voice.

"Can it! I told you I'll get us out," Atlas huffed at her. He almost felt bad about the response. She'd been a captive for a while, but her attitude was already grating on his nerves.

The noise grew closer as he struggled with the situation.

What am I going to do? I can't possibly fight them all. I also have to protect Penny. It'd be nice if we could just plow through them and make a break for it outside…

A smile spread over his face as an idea came to mind, and he turned to Penny, "I'm going to charge down these stairs and I need you to stay as close to me as you can. We are going to trample right through the dwarves and get out of the building. Once outside, we're going to make a break for the city."

"How are you going to charge through a bunch of dwarves? I know they're short of stature, but let's not kid ourselves. You're not exactly a mountain of muscle."

"Oh, that's easy. I'll just get a lot bigger," Atlas told her.

Her confused expression was comical, and Atlas turned to face down the stairs. He activated his Dire Bear transformation spell and the familiar glow of power erupted from his body. Fur sprouted down his back and spread to his limbs. His face elongated bones popped as they shifted to his new size. He fell to all fours, and he heard Penny squeal in surprise. With the transformation complete, he turned to look at Penny.

Her eyes looked on the verge of popping out of her head and she screamed at the sight of him. As she turned to run, Atlas called out to her.

"Told you I'd just get a lot bigger, remember?" He grumbled. The tone of his voice was noticeably deeper, but still easy to understand. Being able to frighten her after her display of attitude made him feel a little better.

She froze mid-turn and looked back at him, "Atlas?"

"Yep, still me. Call me your personal mobile shield. I'll charge them and you stay right behind me. No matter what happens, don't fall too far behind. We can't stop to fight them or they'll trap us."

A large gulp was her only response before she finally nodded in agreement. Atlas turned and faced down the stairs.

Smells of the tower drifted to him with his newly heightened senses. Wood and smoke drifted from downstairs, mingled with oiled metal and leather. Penny was a little ripe herself after being trapped in this tower.

He heard Penny shuffle up right behind him
and he charged down the stone steps. The
smaller width of the stairs made the trip a
little precarious, but he got the hang of it
quickly. The clanking footsteps below halted
as he thundered down the passage.

The first guard to see him round the bend
yelled in alarm and turned to run the other
direction. Atlas could only imagine the terror
of a massive animal charging at you down a set
of stairs.

Crunching noises filled the space as he
charged. Every chance he could, he swiped at
nearby enemies and launched them toward the
walls while metal scraped against stone and
bones snapped under his enormous claws. Two of
the dwarves had the fortitude to swing at him
and caused a small amount of damage before he
trampled them.

*Tower Guard dealt 5 damage to you with
Chop. (x2)*

One last dwarf with a musket waited at the
bottom of the stairs. His gun was up and aimed
for him. He couldn't get close enough to
attack before the dwarf fired, so he lifted a
paw to cover his face and continued in a
three-legged run. The sound of the shot rang
through the confined space and a small sting
burned in his leg.

*Tower Marksman dealt 15 damage to you with
Crack Shot.*

Roaring in anger, he returned to all fours and charged for the last target. The dwarf whimpered and dropped his gun just as Atlas crashed into him and bit into his shoulder. He carried him for a couple of feet before he thrashed his head to the side and flung the man like a rag doll.

The main floor was empty as they continued their charge, and he headed for the front door. A quick glance behind him showed Penny keeping pace, but she looked terrified at the current ordeal. He slammed into the front door and it splintered as the shearing sound of metal marked the hinges breaking free. The door clattered to the ground in a battered heap and he rushed outside.

His momentum froze a few steps out the door as four dwarves stood with guns all drawn and aimed at him. Penny squealed, and he turned to see she'd come around his side and was staring at the weapons. He dove to the side and covered her with his body as the shots rang out across the field. Pain stabbed into multiple parts of him along his side, but luckily nothing hit him critically.

Tower Marksman dealt 15 damage to you with Crack Shot. (x4)

Thank God for this big body and thick hide.
The extra health from his bear transformation allowed him to take a beating, but a quick glance at his health showed he couldn't take much more of this 195/280 HP.

Atlas couldn't decide. On one hand, he wanted to just run and try to get away. He wasn't sure they could do that without being taken out. At the same time, he didn't think he could kill all four guys before dying. His bear form was tough, but it lacked enough combat abilities to do much damage in an open fight. The cat form was too squishy and didn't do enough damage yet.

I can charge the marksmen and try to fight them as Penny runs away, but if one shoots at her my entire plan fails and this quest is a bust.

"Penny, we are going to make a run for it. The city is directly southwest of here. I want you to run as quick as you can in that direction and no matter what happens, you don't stop. I'm going to run behind you and make sure they don't shoot you. Can you do that?"

"I suppose I can do that, but doesn't that mean they'll shoot you instead?"

"Yes, it does. Just remember, no matter what happens, you don't stop until you get to the town wall. I will find you when I can," Atlas told her.

She looked down and sighed, but she nodded.

"Now, go!"

The two took off at a run and Atlas had to slow his pace. Penny couldn't move anywhere near as fast as he could, and he stayed between her and the marksmen at all times. Their conversation had given a couple of them a chance to reload and he heard them yell and curse, followed by blasts of gunfire.

One bullet seared into his back leg while another bounced off the dirt to his right. Instead of focusing on the gunshots themselves, he looked straight ahead to the tree line. If he could get Penny there, they'd be okay. First, they had to get over the short wall.

Tower Marksman dealt 15 damage to you with Crack Shot.

Penny stopped at the solid wall and looked around frantically.
"How do we get through?"
"You don't, you go over," Atlas told her.
"I can't climb that. I don't have the strength," she huffed.
"Climb onto my head and hold on," he told her.
She looked skeptical as she eyed him, "I have nothing on under this slip…"
"For the love of God woman, I'm not here to peek at you naked, I'm here to rescue you. Get on!"
She scrambled to do as he said and wrapped her legs around his neck and over his shoulders. Atlas' mind immediately flashed back to some epic chicken fights in the pool before his attention snapped back to the present.
With a heave, he rose to his back legs and braced himself against the wall with his front paws. He leaned forward and rested his nose on the stone.
"Now hurry and stand on my shoulders and get over the wall. I'll cover you."

Atlas lifted one of his paws to shield Penny's back as she fought to stand and get on and over the wall. Gunfire continued to snarl through the clearing and three more bullets tore into his flesh, one of which struck the paw covering Penny's escape.

Tower Marksman dealt 15 damage to you with Crack Shot. (x3)

Penny finally crested the wall and looked back, "Are you coming over?"

"Hurry and go. Hop down and get to the city. I'll keep them distracted long enough for you to get away."

Her eyes hardened as she looked at him, "I guess you weren't the worst option for a rescuer after all."

Without another word, she hopped over the wall and he listened to the rustle of the tall grass as she sprinted away. Another bullet tore into his side and he roared in anger.

Tower Marksman dealt 15 damage to you with Crack Shot.

Now that Penny was safe, and he was tired of running, Atlas turned to face the four marksmen. With another roar, he charged the four in a frenzy. The sight of the large animal running toward them and no longer away spooked the dwarves, and they scattered to put distance between themselves. Atlas veered toward the one farthest to the right and triggered his Charge ability.

The distance melted, and he plowed into the
stunned dwarf at full speed. The compact
figure fell to the ground and Atlas
immediately activated Maul. Both claws came
down with crushing force and tore into the
flesh of the marksman.

*You dealt 13 damage to Tower Marksman with
Charge.*
*You dealt 33 damage to Tower Marksman with
Maul. (Critical) (Crushing)*

The dwarf remained on the ground clutching
a deep gash in his side, so Atlas turned and
activated Charge for the next opponent. Two
more gunshots rang and smacked into his side,
but he remained on course and slammed into the
dwarf. This one remained standing when Atlas
crashed into him. Activating Maul, the claws
came down with incredible force and the dwarf
tried to lift his musket to block it. His
enormous paw met the firearm and broke it
clean in half. The claw continued down and
slashed ugly furrows down the dwarf's face.

*Tower Marksman dealt 15 damage to you with
Crack Shot. (x2)*
*You dealt 13 damage to Tower Marksman with
Charge.*
*You dealt 25 damage to Tower Marksman with
Maul. (Critical)*

*Damn, only 105 health left. I can't
possibly beat these guys. Worse yet, if I die
inside these walls, it's going to be a pain in
the ass to come get my stuff back. Penny
should be far enough away that I can safely
flee.*

Running out of options, Atlas decided he'd have to change to cat form and leap back over the wall. If he could escape into the forest, they might leave him alone. The bad part was it would cut his health in half when he transformed.

Two more shots tore into his side, forcing him to decide.

Tower Marksman dealt 15 damage to you with Crack Shot. (x2)

Using the last of the mana he had left, he activated his Night Stalker Transformation spell. He'd never transformed straight from one animal form to another, but the process was easy. His body just shrunk and changed appearance. Since the bear and cat had similar forms, other than size, the transformation barely interrupted his stride.

He turned and raced for the wall at full speed.

"He's trying tae escape. Load up th' special shot." Atlas heard one dwarf call out. He looked over his shoulder and saw the remaining three dwarves packing jagged pieces of metal in the barrel and tried to move faster.

Leaping high, his feet touched the wall right when the sounds of gunfire blasted out again. He tried to leap to the other side, but multiple pieces of metal hit him in the back and sent him flying over the wall. Landing on the hard ground in the most uncat-like way possible, he fought to get back to his feet and ran for the city.

Tower Marksman dealt 8 damage to you with Shrapnel Shot. (x3)

Shrapnel shot has inflicted Bleed. You will lose 3 health every 10 seconds until healed.

Damn. I have less than a minute until I die. My 14 remaining health won't last long and I have no mana to heal myself. Resigned to his death, he got as far as possible before it happened so he'd have less of a trek back to pick up his stuff. The health ticked away as he ran and dread settled into his stomach.

When his health dropped to 2, he found a secluded spot near the base of a tree to obscure him from easy view. He didn't want someone to stumble upon his stuff and take it before he respawned. Laying down, he closed his eyes and waited for his fate. The last of the damage ticked away, and he felt a sharp pain in his chest before blackness gripped him.

You have died.

Chapter 21

Specialized Weaponry

You will respawn at your designated bind spot.

He sighed and replayed the fight as he sat in the comfy recliner. *I've got to figure out more combat skills with my animal forms. They have such incredible potential and are next to useless half the time.*

This time around, he fired up one of his favorite games to pass time. Arguably, the JRPG sucked a lot of time with its early cut-scenes, but he patiently waited through them. After fighting as Dart and seeing Rose make her brief appearances, he idly wondered if this game was partially responsible for the combat system in this game. In almost no time, his respawn timer ticked to zero, and he returned to the game world.

The Death Penalty has removed 721 experience from your current level. (40%)
Your stats and damage are decreased by 40% for the next hour.

Atlas opened his eyes to a log style cabin. The smell of freshly cut wood filling the air. He jerked upright and looked around. The interior of the Master of the Wood house greeted him.

I bet this gets set as my spawn since it is my house.

The hit to his experience sucked. On the bright side, he knew turning in the rescue quest would get him all of it back, plus more. Although he was itching to complete the quest, he knew he needed to go get his gear first. The longer it sat in the forest, the higher chance someone would find it and steal all of his stuff.

With nothing but his starter clothes on, he walked to the gate and continued past. The two guards sent skeptical looks his way as he casually sauntered out with no weapons or armor, but none said anything to stop him. When he reached the trees, he shifted into cat form. With his stats diminished, he wanted the more nimble form for stealth.

His trip through the woods was quick and uneventful. All of his gear was still exactly where he'd died. Reequipping everything was a breeze, and he was quickly on his way back to the city.

"Welcome back, Master of the Wood," one guard greeted as he entered.

"Good to be back. Have either of you seen the woman named Penny? I freed her from her captivity and wanted to make sure they escorted her to her sister."

"She told us you saved her, sir. We took her to her house to reunite with her sister. We left a guard on the place as you ordered."

"Thank you, soldier. Can you lead me to the house?"

"Of course," he said with a quick salute. He told the other guard to watch the gate and that he'd send someone to fill his spot for now.

They trudged through the city and eventually came to a large two-story house. Carefully trimmed shrubs lined the knee high stone wall around the perimeter. The stone pathway to the front door was clean and well maintained. He approached the door and carefully knocked.

It swung open to reveal a young woman with golden brown hair, cascading down in wavy lines. Her lips sported a slight shade of red while a faint sprinkling of blush lit up her cheeks. The gown she wore was slim fitting and accentuated her curves while still looking fancy.

"Atlas!" she exclaimed as she practically leaped into his arms. His confusion changed as his mind processed her face.

"Penny?"

She backed up and smoothed the fabric on her dress, "Penelope Voi' Deer, at your service."

She dipped into a short curtsy before her face returned to his with a beaming smile.

"Who is it, Penny," the voice of her sister said.

"It's Atlas, Raina. He's finally returned after his daring mission."

"Oh, Atlas! I can never thank you enough for saving my sister. We are both forever in your debt," Raina said as tears welled in her eyes.

"It's my job, ma'am," he told them with a slight nod.

Quest - Damsel in Distress	

Requirements
   Master of the Wood
   Level 15
 	
Quest Rarity: Rare
 	
Quest Reward: 1200 experience, 40 silver, unknown rewards.
	Description: You have successfully returned Penny home.

Do you wish to complete the quest? Yes/No.	

Atlas selected *Yes*. The experience flowed in and the coins appeared in his bag.

"Atlas, can you come in for a few minutes? I'd like to discuss something with you," Raina told him.

"Sure," he said and turned to the guard with him, "you can return to your post. Also, take the guard stationed here. I think everything is fine now."

The young man saluted and waved to the man on the edge of the small yard to follow. Atlas turned and entered the house. The two ladies walked ahead of him and took him through the building. No one crossed their path as they continued through the monstrous house. Atlas at least expected to see a maid or something in a place this large.

They led him to a small study and motioned for him to take a seat on a plush looking chair. Bookshelves lined the walls and a formidable collection decorated the shelves. The two ladies took a seat opposite of him on a small loveseat.

"I wasn't joking when I said we are both forever in your debt," Raina began, "this house has fallen on hard times. We are all that's left of a once illustrious house. My sister is literally my whole world."

"At least you have someone. Plenty have suffered worse."

"Oh, don't mistake me. Or lives aren't terribly difficult, but the lifestyle has changed. Our mother died when we were young but our father, Sam, did a good job raising us. As luck would have it, he passed on as well last year. Now we just have a struggling business."

"What business is your family in? If you don't mind me asking," Atlas inquired.

"Daddy was a Woodworker. A pretty good one at that," Penny told him.

Raina smiled at her enthusiasm, "He was indeed. When he passed away, he only had one young apprentice and his training was far from complete. Now we have a business that can't keep up with demand, and we are bleeding customers because of quality issues."

"Sorry to hear that. Can you not find another artisan?"

"We've tried. Master Onon, the Woodworking trainer here, has essentially blacklisted our business with the craftsmen. He doesn't like competition," Raina explained.

"That seems petty. There should be plenty of work for you both in a city of this size."

"There was, until the Reborn arrived," she grumbled.

Her eyes shot open as she remembered who she was speaking to and she immediately put up her hands, "Not that I have a problem with Reborn. I am just frustrated with the situation."

Atlas chuckled, "It's okay. Have you considered trying to hire a Reborn?"

The two ladies looked at each other for a moment before Raina responded, "Reborn seem to be fickle. They don't stay in one place very long and are constantly running off. It'd be impossible for them to keep up with production. We also don't know if we can trust them. We know we could trust you though after all you've done."

"That's true. We move around a lot and don't stay in one place very long. Are you aware of our crafting advantage though?" he asked.

"What advantage?" Raina asked as she perked up.

Atlas looked through his bag and found a Wooden Slab and a Spool of Copper Wire.

"Do you mind if I get your floor a little dirty?" Atlas asked with a smile.

"Uh, okay," Raina answered hesitantly.

Atlas picked up the slab and activated Create Wooden Necklace Charm. His body went into overdrive as the small knife came out and he carved it to shape. The moment the blade stopped moving, he used Create Wooden Necklace Charm of Intellect.

The pace picked up, and he quickly carved the symbols into the piece to imbue it. Finally, he used Create Wire Wrapped Wooden Necklace Charm of Intellect. His fingers deftly wove the wire around the charm until it was complete. With the piece finally finished, he handed it over to a shocked-looking Raina.

The woman stared at the charm with wide eyes and a slightly open mouth, "But, how? That was so fast it was hard to keep up with," she said as she turned the charm over in her hands.

"This would've taken my father most of the day and you completed it in minutes. Can you do this all the time?" she asked in disbelief.

"Pretty much. I can make anything I have the required crafting level for at incredibly fast speeds. I have Woodworking, Jewelcrafting, and Leatherworking currently."

"You can do all three skills in this same way? That's incredible!" Penny chimed in.

Raina's eyes changed from a look of shock to one of determination.

"Atlas, I think we may be able to help each other. Would you consider mass producing items for us when needed?" Raina asked.

"I probably could but, as we've already established, I'll be leaving this city, eventually. I also don't know how it would benefit me. I'm sure I can get more money selling directly to the market itself."

"That's true. You probably could get a little better profit," Raina began, "How do you feel about experience, though?"

Atlas perked up at that, "What do you mean?"

"Well, we can create quests. That's how I made the one for you to rescue my sister. If you work in a business, or own a business, you can also make quests related to the business. For instance, I can create quests for you to supply us with certain amounts of items. It will reward you with a sum of money slightly lower than normal market price, but they will also grant you additional crafting and normal level experience."

"Wait, you can do that? You can help me gain normal experience with crafting quests?"

"Sure can," Penny said in a bubbly tone.

"Why have I not seen crafting quests yet? Other than to learn special recipes, anyway."

"Competition. The crafters are required to teach you the skills. They don't have to do anything else to help you if they choose."

That makes sense. We could run them completely out of business. If people knew you could gain experience through crafting as well, far more would do that all the time instead of gathering materials and fighting stuff outside of the cities.

"So, how do we want to do this?" Atlas asked.

"I think it's best if we keep you and the business separate. We can just use you like work for hire. If we have to put you on the payroll, it may draw attention you don't want. Instead, you let us know your level and patterns. We search the market for items that are selling high, place an order with you for anything you can make, and you deliver in bulk. We can make the work order for 70% of the market price for the goods? To sweeten the deal, we'll even supply the raw goods and subtract them from the cost," Raina said.

"That seems a little low. What is the experience gain?"

"We can't control that. The world mechanics calculates experience itself. It automatically assigns it based on item difficulty and quantity. I'm told you can get bonuses for producing higher-quality items than the order requests as well."

"How about 80% market price and we call it a deal? In exchange, I'll agree to make items from any crafting skills I have available, not just Woodworking," he countered.

The ladies looked at one another before both nodded and said, "Done."

"Well, I'm currently level eighteen in Jewelcrafting, eighteen in Leatherworking, and seventeen in Woodworking," Atlas summarized.

"That should do well in the current market. It seems many of the Reborn are still working on items from the tier below your skill level. It should help us jump ahead of the market. Right now we should have enough supplies for two major orders I need filled in Woodworking. Once we get the business rolling again, we can expand into the other two. Anything you make with your own materials you will need to sell to us to prevent flooding the market in the wrong way, but we'll pay the agreed market price."

"Sounds good. What do you have for me?"

"You can have these two orders to fill. Our shop is The Lacquer Stop. You can find it in the merchant quarter of the city near the main street. A man named Joe attends as the apprentice. He can let you know where the supplies you need will be. Here are the orders," she said with a wave.

Tradeskill Quest - Supplying the Blacksmith	
Requirements Woodworking Level 14 Quest Rarity: Uncommon Quest Reward: 700 experience, 5 gold 80 silver.	Description: The Lacquer Stop needs to fill an order for the following pieces: Smooth Spear Handle x 30 Smooth Axe Handle x 30 Smooth Wood Staff x 20

Tradeskill Quest - Custom Armaments	

Requirements
   Woodworking Level 14
 	
Quest Rarity: Uncommon
 	
Quest Reward: 700 experience, 4 gold 90 silver.
	Description: The Lacquer Stop needs to fill an order for the following pieces:
	
	   Smooth Longbow Frame x 30
	   Smooth Shortbow Frame x 30
	   Smooth Wood Wand x 20

The two quests excited him. Not only would they mean a good amount of money, it also meant he'd gain some much needed experience without as much grinding.

"Sister, I think we should give it to him," Penny said, "it's only right after he's helped us so much. I have to admit I was a bit of a jerk to him during the rescue. Daddy never had the time to do anything with it, and I think it could prove useful."

Raina snapped her head to her sister, "You think so? It's essentially father's legacy."

"I think he'd want Atlas to have it," Penny said with finality.

"I guess so," Raina sighed, "It looks like we have one more gift for you."

She walked over to the bookcase on the side of the room and grabbed a book on the shelf. Instead of pulling it free, she tilted it forward, and he heard a distinct click. Raina grabbed the wooden case and the front of it swung away from the wall, revealing a wooden case with a glass front embedded into the stone wall. A quick turn of the small handle on the front caused the case to slide open on quiet hinges. The young woman reached in and gently withdrew a long piece of wood.

Atlas couldn't identify the type of wood. A few bands of metal crossed it in different places and a gem sat on one end of the staff, encased in another metal bracket. The piece had cracks along its length and the metal looked worse for wear and tarnished.

"This was our father's prize possession. He had hopes of restoring it one day but never got the chance. Hopefully it will serve you well if you can find the time to fix it," Raina said as she handed over the item.

Atlas looked skeptical as he accepted the battered-looking weapon. A quick inspection of it changed his mind.

<table>
<tr><td colspan="2" align="center">Quest Item - Damaged Staff</td></tr>
<tr>
<td>

Requirements: Level 15
Rarity: Unique
Quality: Exquisite

</td>
<td>

Attack: ?
Defense: ?
Magic Attack: ?
Magic Defense: ?
Durability: ?/?
Weight: 6.0 lbs.
Slot: 2H Weapon

Traits: A mysterious staff of unknown properties. Grants the quest, Return to the Living.

</td>
</tr>
</table>

Atlas triggered the item, and the quest popped into view.

<table>
<tr><td colspan="2" align="center">Quest - Return to the Living</td></tr>
<tr>
<td>

Requirements
   Level 15

Quest Rarity: Epic

Quest Reward: 800 experience, 600 Woodworking experience, 600 Jewelcrafting experience.

</td>
<td>

Description: A unique staff, damaged from age. Find a way to repair it and return it to its former glory.

</td>
</tr>
</table>

His eyes almost bulged out of his head when he finally noticed the item and the quest were listed as Unique rarity. He'd seen nothing better than Rare yet. The vagueness of the quest bothered him, though.

"Thank you for entrusting me with this. I'll do what I can to restore it. Do you know of anywhere I can start?" Atlas asked.

"Well, I'm guessing you'll need to talk to the Master Woodworker, the Master Jewelcrafter, and possibly the Master Smith to find out how to fix it. Our father never made much progress because they didn't like competition," Raina told him.

"I'll see what I can do. I'll run over to the shop and fill your orders for you. Can I turn them in to Joe or do I need to come back here?"

"He can accept delivery of the items and complete the quest for you," Penny confirmed.

"Great. Send me a message when you have more orders for me. The courier service seems to work fine."

They bid each other farewell, and he left the house. Living up to his word, he headed straight for The Lacquer Stop. It took him a little searching, and he had to ask passing people twice for directions, but he finally found it.

Smooth wood logs created a banister around the front of the building. All of them were layered with lacquer to make them shine as though encased in epoxy. The sign on the polished door clearly stated The Lacquer Stop.

Inside was much of the same. The counters were all polished to a smooth sheer. Even the floor held some luster, although not as reflective. A younger man with dirty blonde hair sat in a chair whittling away at a piece of wood. When he finally noticed Atlas, he sat up straighter and fumbled with his project.

"Can I help you, sir?" The young man asked.

"I'm here to complete some work. Can you show me where the supplies you have for work orders are located?" Atlas asked.

"Um, I mean, I don't know what you're talking about. I'm the crafter in this place," the man stammered.

"Your owners have contracted me to complete some projects for them. I was told to use the supplies on hand. So help me out here, Joe."

"How do you know my name?"

"Raina and Penny told me, now I don't enjoy repeating myself," Atlas huffed. He had far too many things to do than to keep up this useless string of conversation.

"I'll need to verify you're supposed to be working here before I can do that."

Atlas only sighed. It would take forever to wait on this guy to check on this. A flash of inspiration hit him, "Do you know about the last master's pet project?"

"Yes…," the man answered slowly.

Atlas reached into his bag and carefully withdrew the battered staff.

"This should serve as proof then. The owners gave me this as a gift and sign of our contract."

Joe's eyes nearly bulged out of his head as he saw the old staff.

"Sam only brought that here once for me to see. He harped on about how he'd restore it one day but never did," Joe reflected, "I guess if you have that, your story must be true."

Joe stood from his seat and placed his partially finished piece on the table, "Follow me."

He led him to the back room where piles of materials lay stacked along the floor and on racks on the walls. Each section had a label that identified the order it belonged to.

"Which orders did they task you with working on?" Joe asked.

Atlas looked back at the quests and figured they must be the quest names for the orders.

"Supplying the Blacksmith and Custom Armaments."

Joe whistled at that, "You'll be here for a long time trying to fill those. How many days do you plan on working here?"

"Oh, I'll finish today," Atlas said with a casual wave.

"Today? How will you finish it all?"

"Don't worry about me. You can return to your work. I'll take care of this."

Joe didn't look like he wanted to leave, but Atlas also got the feeling that he was slightly allergic to work. The slow speed of his production alluded to this already. After a few minutes of staring at him, Joe returned to the front, presumably to his desk.

This back room held the lathe he needed to make the Smooth Wood, and a large stack of Sandpaper sat near the device. Atlas cracked his knuckles and got to work on both of the orders. It took hours to finish up the laundry list of pieces, but he finally stepped back and surveyed his work.

You gained 51,400 total experience in Woodworking.

Success! You've reached levels 18, 19, 20, 21, 22, 23, and 24 in Woodworking.

Holy crap, that's a lot more experience than I expected. I was a little disappointed when the quests didn't specifically give me Woodworking experience, but since the materials are free, I can see why.

Atlas stacked all the weapons on their respective pallets with the order's name tag and walked back to the front of the shop.

"Order's all done. I never discussed clean up duty with the ladies, but I'll just assume you've got that covered. I'll see you next time they have work for me," Atlas told him as he walked out the front.

"Oh," Atlas said as he stopped, "I need you to accept the quests as completed."

The look on Joe's face was comical. If he wasn't careful, his jaw would hit the ground. The man leaped to his feet and ran to the back. He came back with a look of bewilderment plastered on his face. With an awkward nod from Joe, both quests marked as completed.

You gained 1,400 experience.
You gained 5g 80s for turning in Supplying the Blacksmith and 4g 90s for turning in Custom Armaments.
Success! You've reached level 16.

Not wanting to waste any more time, Atlas decided it was time to visit the Master Woodworker. He needed some insight on the damaged staff and some new skills. It felt like he'd been in this city forever, but he'd truly just recently arrived. The trainer here should have plenty of new abilities for him, especially with his recent windfall of levels.

He took the chance to drop one of his points into Intellect, bringing it to 17, and the other into Spirit, making it 7.

A few questions to nearby people led him directly to the Woodworker's place. He noticed more players wandering around the city and guessed he was finally catching up with some of his leveling. His long breaks from work didn't let him grind the game as hard as others.

An old man with a sour expression sat behind an ornately carved desk. His wrinkled hands looked far too fragile to still do much in the profession, but a simmering fire lit his eyes.

"Can I help you, young man?"

"I'm here to see if you know how to repair this staff," Atlas said as he withdrew the Damaged Staff.

The old man reached out with trembling hands and took the piece from him. He ran his gnarled hands along the rough wood.

"How did you come by this?"

Atlas didn't want to tell the truth, so instead, he merely told him he bought it.

The guy's eyebrows shot up with skepticism, but he didn't press farther.

"This piece is possible to restore, but it'll require work. I can repair the wood if you can gather a couple items. A quest box greeted him after the announcement.

Quest - Repair the Staff (Woodworking)	

Requirements
   Level 15
 	
Quest Rarity: Unique
 	
Quest Reward: 800 experience, Wood pieces of Staff repaired.
	Description: The Master Woodworker has informed you he can repair the wooden section of the staff but he needs the following two items:
	
	  • Mahogany Dust
	  • Sap of an Ent

"Seems pretty straight forward. Do you know where I can find the items?"

"Mahogany dust is easy. You can collect it when you use sandpaper on Mahogany while crafting. The Sap of an Ent is a little trickier. I've heard there is a small grove to the west of the city where they have spotted Ents in the past, but don't know if anything lives there still."

"Thanks for the help," Atlas told him as he fetched the staff back and placed it in his bag.

"Is there anything else I can help you with?"

"I'd also like to train my new Woodworking abilities," Atlas added.

The man smiled and waved his hand, making the menu pop up in his vision. The options were the same he'd grown accustomed to. The difference was his tier of wood rose. Now, instead of smooth wood, all the abilities shown were Mahogany. Create Smooth Mahogany Log, Create Smooth Mahogany Rods, Create Smooth Mahogany Wand, Create Smooth Mahogany Ring, Create Smooth Mahogany Longbow Frame, Create Smooth Mahogany Shortbow Frame, Create Smooth Mahogany Necklace Charm, all added to the list of items he could now create.

Atlas bid the crafter farewell and went in search of the Blacksmith shop. This was a little easier to find. The smell of burning coal was simple to pinpoint, and the sound of hammers ringing on steel led him directly to the building.

A dirty man who looked like he could've won a Strongman competition stood near the central anvil as he swung a hammer with incredible force. The glowing red metal seemed to mold like butter as strike after strike landed with pounding force.

The sight fascinated him, and he stood there and watched the man ply his craft. Sooner than he expected, the smith laid the piece near one forge and looked up at Atlas.

"Something I can do for you?"

"Actually, I was hoping you could help me repair the metal pieces on this staff," Atlas said as he fished the piece out again.

The smith grabbed the damage weapon and winced as he examined the pieces.

"This metal isn't easy to work with. The binding agent on it is difficult to come by. I can fix it, but I need you to bring me two things."

Quest - Repair the Staff (Blacksmithing)	
Requirements Level 15 Quest Rarity: Unique Quest Reward: 800 experience, Metal pieces of Staff repaired.	Description: The Master Blacksmith has informed you he can repair the metal sections of the staff, but he needs the following two items: • Elemental Core • Ironwood Root x 3

"Any idea where I can find them?" Atlas asked with a sigh.

"Elementals commonly roam the land to the east of here. They don't appear very often though, so it may take some searching. You can find the Ironwood to the west. They used to be a common drop from Ents."

Atlas perked up at that. He worried the quest would send him all over the place for each of these items, but it looked like some would share a central location.

"Thanks for the help. I'll come back when I find them," Atlas said as he collected the staff and left.

His last stop was at the Jewelcrafter. He repeated the same process and got another quest to find two more items.

Quest - Repair the Staff (Jewelcrafting)	

Requirements
   Level 15
 	
Quest Rarity: Unique
 	
Quest Reward: 800 experience, Jeweled socket of Staff repaired.
	Description: The Master Jewelcrafter has informed you he can repair the socket of the staff but he needs the following two items:
	
	    • Elemental Flame
	    • Measure of Silver Shavings x 5

"Where are these located?"

"The Elemental Flame should be on random elementals to the east of here. Silver Shavings are byproducts of Jewelcrafting at the appropriate level."

"That reminds me, I need to train my Jewelcrafting," Atlas said, and the Master Jewelcrafter obliged with a wave.

Most of the skills mirrored what he'd seen in Woodworking. He got the ability to enchant the new Mahogany pieces he could make. He also received an ability called Shave Silver. Spells like Create Smooth Mahogany Ring of Strength now required a Measure of Silver Shavings to complete. So far, rings were all he could do. He needed to level higher to get the necklace enchantments.

A trip out of town was in order to get this staff repaired. Before he did that, he made a pit stop at the local bank. Even with the money he'd spent on learning new skills, he currently held slightly over 13 gold. Playing it safe, he dumped 10 of it in the bank, giving him a stockpile of 34 gold securely stored.

On the way out the gate, he spotted an interesting sign. Ability Trainer marked a building on the main street. Unable to fight his curiosity, he ducked inside.

"Can I help you?" A woman at the desk asked.

"What is this place?" Atlas asked.

"I offer training in basic magical skills."

"Oh, the ones that don't require specific classes?"

"Yep. Need anything?"

"Let me see what you have." Atlas told her.

She waved a hand and a menu appeared. Almost every option was grayed out. There was only one skill he was offered, Basic Firestarter. The price was 1 gold but being able to light a fire anywhere he was could literally save his life. He spent the gold and thanked the woman as he left.

Feeling better about his day, he trudged out the gate and headed west. It was time to hunt some elementals.

Chapter 22

Rebirth

His trip east gave him time to practice more combat. The fight with the dwarves had shown him the importance of working on his spells. Instead of trying to overpower the normal mobs in the area using his large counter combo, Atlas focusing on snaring them and dealing magic damage.

Mana was the limiting factor. Since his mana pool wasn't as high as many others, he resorted to physical combat often, but that didn't stop him from employing spells.

Most of his targets were standard creatures. The terrain to the east was mainly flat grasslands. Flowing green stalks brushed against his knees as he traveled.

The animals he encountered were ones that commonly held to grasslands. The herd animals were the most interesting. More than once Atlas ended up in a fight with multiple creatures because he attacked one on the edge of a herd and others came to help it.

The most common animal he fought was a zheevra. It looked like a cross between a bulky cow in the front with long horns and the backside of a striped zebra. If you just walked around near them, they were relatively docile and would usually ignore you. Attacking one of them would draw the attention of at least two others to the scene.

Occasionally he had to deal with a
predator. When he squared off with a cheetah,
he was able to counter its attacks and almost
kill it, only to have it try to race away. He
wasn't nearly fast enough to catch it in his
human form, so he ended up having to catch it
in his cat form. On the plus side, he'd gained
a new ability in his cat form from the chase.

You learned Sprint. (Nightstalker Form)

Without a solid path or destination to go
by, he gradually worked toward the extensive
area on his map highlighted by the quest. It
took him a couple of hours, but he finally
found his target. The difficulty came when he
discovered it was a cave.
*Small enclosed areas are disconcerting when
you have to fight monsters.*
The entrance appeared as a jagged tear
across the face of a small cliff. The rise of
the cliff wasn't very high, but if the cave
went further underground, it could be any
size. He'd actually passed it once, not
thinking anything of it on his trek. The
second time he'd come near it, he noticed a
flash of blue barely visible inside the
entrance. When he stalked closer to inspect
the sight, he caught his first glimpse of his
prey.
Blue crystals formed a somewhat humanoid
body that was almost seven feet tall. The face
was a blank slate of the colored gemstone with
two glowing orbs for eyes. The entire creature
looked like an old polygon model from classic
video games with its blocky appearance. *Water
Elemental - Level 16.*

Fighting these creatures was a different story. His cat form was nimble and great at dodging, but it still badly lacked combat skills. He needed to make it a priority to attack similar creatures in the form to pick up new skills. It worked great with the cheetah and the blood hunter.

His bear form suffered from a similar problem. While great at soaking up damage, it lacked much in the way of powerful combo attacks. This left him standing in front of the cave entrance in his normal form, staff at the ready. Not wanting to fight more than one elemental at a time, he targeted the creature just inside the entrance and cast *Nature's Wrath*. The green balls of energy rocketed forward and slammed into the crystal body of the monster.

You dealt 26 damage to Water Elemental with Nature's Fury. (Elemental Weakness)

Ooh, perfect. They are weak to nature style spells.

With a smile, he followed that spell with *Sunfire*. The cast time on the spell was almost nonexistent as a beam of golden light appeared over the elemental's head and seared into the creature. The downfall was it did less base damage at the same casting cost.

You dealt 20 damage to Water Elemental with Sunfire. (Elemental Weakness)

The crystalline monster plodded toward Atlas as though nothing happened. It walked in a slow and steady rhythm, causing slight tremors in the ground as it moved. Atlas could make out a few small cracks from his spells, but they were barely hairline fractures.

Lifting his staff, he activated *Charge* and closed the distance. The staff thudded into the torso of the monster and he followed with *Triple Threat*, *Pursuit*, and *Double Slash*. The monster never even attempted to dodge or counter as the wooden staff thwacked against its head, arms, and chest. The final blow of *Double Slash* landed, and Atlas grimaced at the notification.

You dealt 2 damage to Water Elemental with Charge. (Elemental Armor)

You dealt 6 damage to Water Elemental with Triple Threat. (Elemental Armor)

You dealt 2 damage to Water Elemental with Pursuit. (Elemental Armor)

You dealt 4 damage to Water Elemental with Double Slash. (Elemental Armor)

Atlas looked down at his staff. *I need something that has more power behind it.*

His mind turned toward his nightstalker form but quickly dismissed it. The creature was fast but lacking in raw strength.

I could keep blasting it with magic.

That thought swirled in his head, but he realized if that was his only option, he was woefully unprepared and would probably have to go back to town. He'd need a real caster weapon if he intended to go that route. Without the damage amplification and some bonuses to his mana pool, he'd be almost useless for more than one fight.

With only one genuine option left, he transformed. His body shifted and changed as the power coursed through him, and after a couple of seconds, the fearsome form of a Dire Bear confronted the elemental. The blue creature swung its arm in a powerful strike, and Atlas hopped backward.

The arm flew past his nose. Air buffeted his face from the powerful attack. Without hesitation, Atlas rushed back into the fight and activated *Charge*. He burst forward in a rush of speed before slamming into the creature's chest with the top of his head. Crystal crunched as the elemental stumbled backward. *Maul* followed and his giant bear claws slammed down onto the creature, expanding the previous cracks while the claws dug furrows through the body, flakes of gemstone flying away from the impact.

You dealt 20 damage to Water Elemental with Charge. (Crushing) (Critical)
You dealt 32 damage to Water Elemental with Maul. (Crushing) (Critical)

Perfect, the strength of this form lets me punch through its armor. It must be really weak without the armor since it's giving me a lot of critical and crushing damage.

The elemental froze in its movements and raised both of its arms over its head. Blue energy swirled and grew larger as it gathered between the limbs. After watching the display for a few seconds, Atlas kicked himself for being an idiot and attempted to dash forward. His rush was too late as the elemental lowered his arms and rested the power in one hand. The ball solidified into a solid orb of ice and the creature punched forward with his other hand, shattering it and sending shards of ice catapulting toward Atlas.

Standing mere feet from the elemental, he had no time to dodge, so he lowered his head and took the blast. Shard of ice cut into his thick hide and pelted his head and shoulders. An icy chill filled him as the small spears melted and the cold seemed to seep into his very bones.

Water Elemental dealt 40 damage to you with Ice Shards.
Your movement speed is slowed by 15% for 2 minutes due to Chill.

Atlas growled in response and activated Charge again. His rush forward wasn't as quick as before because of the Chill effect, but the creature didn't seem interested in attempting to dodge, anyway. The attack shattered more crystal from its chest and he used Maul. The impact of the claws was the final straw as the creature broke into multiple pieces and collapsed to the ground.

You dealt 20 damage to Water Elemental with Charge. (Crushing) (Critical)
You dealt 32 damage to Water Elemental with Maul. (Crushing) (Critical)

Water Elemental died.
You gained 80 experience.

Atlas breathed a sigh of relief and shifted back to his Wood Elf form. Crystal flakes covered the area from the battle. An inspection of the corpse allowed him to pick up the loot.

Shards of Elemental Water x 5
Essence of Water x 2

No quest item waited for him, but he couldn't be lucky enough for the first one to drop what he needed. Feeling better about his chances with his bear form, he observed the inside of the cave.

The inside of the main cavern surprised him. He expected a dark and dreary cave where he would have to suffer with minimal light and possibly keep a torch nearby. Instead, a brightly lit scene greeted him. Sunlight filtered in through small spaces in the ceiling, and an extensive collection of random gemstones reflected the light throughout the room. A veritable kaleidoscope of colors shimmered through the air, and Atlas froze to take in the sight.

"It's beautiful," he breathed to himself as he watched the colors dance around the cave.

In the back left corner of the cavern, another tunnel branched off and continued further back. An identical passage marked the same space on the right. In front of the tunnel on the left, stood another of the water elementals he'd just faced off against. A different creature stood in front of the one on the right. This one looked almost identical in every way, but instead of being a blue color stone, it was red with streaks of orange. He was too far away to identify it, but he was confident it was a Fire Elemental.

Atlas contemplated which way to go. He knew how to fight the water version, and if the fire worked the same way, it would be an easy fight. Unsure of where to go, he consulted his quests. Two items he needed in this place were Elemental Flame and Elemental Core. The flame was sure to drop off of the Fire Elementals. The core he couldn't be sure. It might drop off of any elemental, or may even require a special one he hadn't seen yet.

Since he knew for a fact he needed to kill the Fire Elementals for his quest, he started with the passage to the right. It relieved him when they fought the same way as the Water Elemental. When he'd done a little over 100 damage to the monster, it cast a fireball spell that splashed into him before he could finish it.

Fire Elemental dealt 40 damage to you with Fireball.

Expecting the ability, he tried to rush and counter it as before but never could manage.

This must be one that can only be stopped with a stun or a true silence type of spell. I can't physically interrupt it.

    This elemental dropped almost identical
loot to the first, except they were Shards of
Elemental Fire and Essence of Fire. His saving
grace was the elementals were clunky and slow
because of their high armor and defense. The
downside was he took 40 damage during the
fight because he couldn't stop the spell. This
added time to his grinding since he had to
shift back to elf form and heal before
shifting back to bear.
    It took him three more fights and another
120 damage from fire spells before he
accidentally stumbled upon a solution. On the
fourth fight, he anticipated the spell and did
something he'd never tried before. He
activated Charge and dashed the short
distance. These creatures were resilient, and
he knew he couldn't interrupt the spell by
just hitting it in the chest or face.
    His momentum allowed him to duck down low
as he closed the distance and swing a heavy
paw out to the side, essentially clothes-
lining the legs out from under the elemental.
Aside from being pretty humorous, it actually
worked, and the spell fizzled as Atlas
activated Maul and smashed down on the
creature to finish it.

    You learned Sweep. (Bear Form)

    *That's interesting. I wonder what triggers
to allow me to learn abilities without copying
them from other animals?*

The revelation sent his mind spinning with implications of things he could do. His use of the animal forms so far had been limited because of their lack of combat skills. If he could somehow learn more, the forms would become much more useful. More than anything, he needed better combo attacks.

Satisfied with his new ability, he rampaged through the cavern. It took him twenty-three kills to find one of his items. He also netted a fair amount of other materials.

You gained 1,840 experience.
You found the following items:
Shards of Elemental Fire x 62
Essence of Fire x 28
Elemental Flame

He sighed in relief as the Elemental Flame finally appeared on one of the dead creatures. Grinding monsters was rarely a fun prospect, but sometimes necessary. The passage he'd traveled was a linear pathway. He'd emerged into two different open caverns before ducking back into another tunnel to continue. So far, this direction only revealed the fire elementals.

Banking on the fact that the core was probably on a water elemental, he returned to the original room. With a deep breath, he continued his rampage against the water. Fighting them was another exercise in grinding and thoroughly reminded him of older games as he spent long hours grinding away for experience, reputation, or gold. Even with the realism of this game, the task still sucked. His work finally paid off after he'd taken out eighteen elementals.

With those two items found, he rushed to the other side of the city. His time was running short, and he wanted to complete this quest before he had to log off again. Dying on the rescue mission and waiting for the respawn timer took away a chunk of his time.

During the trip across the open plains and to his next destination, he took out some more animals. The creatures provided him with some much needed furs to help him level his Leatherworking some more.

The level up notification was a welcome sight but brought up more problems. So far, he'd focused primarily on his forms and physical damage. He'd dropped most of his points into attributes that helped his spell casting. It was almost inevitable he'd end up as a healer by the time end game came around.

His saving grace was how his forms worked. Luckily, they redistributed his stats for him when he shifted to better support that particular form. Although he was good with his staff in melee combat, he couldn't try to make that his default style. With resignation, he put one point into Intellect, bringing it up to 18 and the other into Spirit making it 8. This gave him an effective mana pool of 200 counting the stat boosts on his items.

When he neared the outlined quest area on his map for the other items, he slowed and shifted to cat form again. The heightened senses of the form allowed him to better stalk the landscape. This time he found himself back in a forest. He expected no less considering he was hunting what were essentially sentient trees.

He stalked through a set of trees and entered a small clearing. A rustle near him caused the hair on the back of his neck to stand up. Out of instinct, he leaped forward and spun. The ground shook slightly as the roots of the tree he was near smashed into the dirt where he previously stood.

Atlas looked at the tree in question and made out the faint outline of a face in the bark. The old gnarled branches hung at odd angles before they slowly creaked and moved. Dirt flew up in large clumps as the creature ripped its remaining roots out of the ground and focused all of its attention on him. *Elder Ent – Level 19.*

A cluster of branches blurred toward Atlas, and he jumped out of the way. The bundle smashed into the ground, creaking and cracking as they hit, dust flying into the air. Atlas activated Counter and dashed forward. His claws dug a furrow through its back and he followed the attack with Furious Claws. His two-hit combo raked across the Ent as the monster grumbled in pain.

You dealt 7 damage to Elder Ent with Counter.
You dealt 15 damage to Elder Ent with Furious Claws.

A root swung around and Atlas jumped to dodge it. The end of it clipped him as he moved and knocked him off balance, causing him to land in an awkward heap on the ground.

Elder Ent dealt 22 damage to you with Root Slap. (Glancing)

Holy crap! That's a lot of damage for a glancing blow.
The creature dealt heavy amounts of damage. Atlas considered changing to his bear form, but decided against it. The bear was too slow and had trouble dodging attacks. While able to take more damage, the trick here was to avoid it. His Wood Elf form wasn't as nimble as the nightstalker, so he needed to whittle down its health using the few attacks he had available as a cat. All while avoiding getting hit, of course.

Getting back to his feet, he rushed at the creature and used Furious Claws. The monster had no chance to block with how slow it was. His claws easily dug into bark and tiny rivulets of dark yellow liquid oozed out like syrup. *Must be sap.*

You dealt 15 damage to Elder Ent with Furious Claws.

A large section of branches crashed toward him again, but he deftly jumped out of the way. Using Counter, he rushed back in, claws extended. More sap oozed from the claw marks as he passed, so he activated Furious Claws. Leaping onto the back of the creature, he used both swipes to dig long grooves down its back. Lines of the sticky yellow fluid quickly filled the claw marks.

You dealt 7 damage to Elder Ent with Counter.
You dealt 15 damage to Elder Ent with Furious Claws.

"This is going to take forever with only two abilities," Atlas huffed.

His eyes focused on the sap leaking from the tree, and an idea struck him. *I know pine sap is extremely flammable and the sap from this tree looks very similar to it. I wonder if it's flammable as well?*

His mind shot back to his recent spell he learned for Basic Firestarter. If he could cut a few more long grooves down the body, he should be able to light the entire tree on fire and kill it much quicker.

With this new plan, he leaped for the tree
and bounced off of its roots. When he neared
the top of the canopy, he activated Furious
Claws again and ripped large furrows down the
side. With a toothy grin, he tried to use
Basic Firestarter.

*Unable to use that ability in shapeshift
form.*

Crap. This would be difficult if he needed
to light the fire in his Wood Elf form.

A look around the tree showed a relatively
flat spot near the base of the trunk. A
section of the roots there flattened out and
looked sturdy. It also didn't seem to move as
the monster did. He leaped down and landed on
the spot before quickly shapeshifting back to
his Wood Elf form. The transformation only
took a couple seconds, and he quickly
activated Basic Firestarter.

Flames burst from his hand in a small
stream and he directed it toward a groove on
the trunk that was full of the sap. As soon as
the fire touched the amber liquid, it ignited
and flames crawled up the tree at an
incredible pace. Atlas stumbled as he backed
away from the intense heat. His foot caught on
a raised root and he tripped backward, landing
heavily on his back after falling a few feet
to the ground.

The tree groaned and creaked as the flames
quickly engulfed all of it. Its limbs and root
flailed wildly, and a stray root smacked Atlas
hard across the ribs. His breath exploded from
him as the pain seared across his side. A
flaming bundle of roots descended toward his
face, and he mustered the effort to roll clear
from the creature.

You dealt 80 damage to Elder Ent with Basic Firestarter. (Critical Weakness)
Elder Ent dealt 48 damage to you with Death Flail.
Elder Ent lost 15 health from Ignition.
Elder Ent lost 15 health from Ignition.
Elder Ent died.
You gained 95 experience.

The large tree crashed to the ground, its body still smoldering from the flame. He approached a small section that wasn't on fire and gathered the loot from the monster. It was disappointing to see there wasn't any Sap of an Ent, but not unexpected. They dropped something else of interest.

You found the following items:
Tea Leaves of the Tranquil x 8.
Nurturing Bark x 12.

Both registered as crafting items. He was sure the leaves would be useful to someone with the cooking skill while he'd probably get the chance to use the bark himself with Woodworking. The area around the clearing was quiet. Trees swayed in the light breeze and birds chattered. It was an odd feeling after the fight that just took place.

Guess I need to go find some more living trees. Have to grind out this Sap of an Ent. Hopefully I can improve my dismount next time.

Atlas looked around, trying to figure out his destination, and consulted his map. The best choice was to circle the current area and gradually push farther outward. Shifting to cat form, he ran to the edge of the clearing and stopped.

A large vine wound around one tree nearby and drew his attention. The vine looked normal at first glance. What caught his attention was the shine. Light seemed to shimmer off of the surface like it was made of metal. Small grooves that looked like a short coating of bark covered the surface. Remembering his other quest item, he approached it. A quick inspection identified the item. *Living Ironwood Root.*

This is the root? It looks like a vine? Atlas noticed the root extended up into the tree canopy. The bottom part of it certainly went into the ground as he would expect from a root, but usually they didn't climb that high. Tracing the path of the root with his eyes, he discovered it wove through the entire canopy.

This thing must make this tree impossible to move!

Atlas shifted back to his Wood Elf form and walked to the root. He pulled his woodcutting hatchet from his bag and swung. The axe reverberated in his hang as the vibrations crawled up his arm. When the feeling returned, he looked to the spot he struck. A tiny piece was missing, but it barley did any damage.

Not knowing what else to do, Atlas started swinging as fast as he could. The axe rebounded with every strike, and he kept adjusting his grip to stop as much of the vibration as possible. After what felt like an eternity, the axe sunk in deep on one of his swings. An inspection of the area showed the inner core of the root was soft like normal wood. It had taken him almost an hour to chop through the external layer of the vine.

With some light at the end of the tunnel, he continued his assault on the root. It only took a handful more strikes until the axe bit through the entire core. As the final soft portion of the root died, the entire thing shriveled and shrunk into itself. It unwound from the canopy and constricted until only a compact bundle of the roots remained. The item registered as *Ironwood Root*.

He placed the root in his bag and continued with his original plan. Now that he knew what the Ironwood Roots looked like, he could hunt for those in his trek for the Ent sap.

A grueling three hours later and another seven dead Ents and he finally found the Sap of an Ent. At that point he'd only found one additional root, so it took him another hour and a half to find and cut down the last root.

You gained 665 experience.
You found the following items:
Tea Leaves of the Tranquil x 48.
Nurturing Bark x 65.
Sap of an Ent.
Ironwood Root x 2.

Finally done with the endless grinding, he dashed back to the city. The quests were all ready to turn in, and he was itching to see what the staff turned out to be. His game clock was running short and he wouldn't have enough time to test out the new weapon, but he should be able to get it repaired.

He barely took the time to shift back to Wood Elf form as he rushed back into the city. The streets were packed with players and NPCs alike, but he ignored all of them as he made a beeline directly for the Jewelcrafting shop. When he entered, the master waved at him.

"Welcome back, Atlas. You here to do some crafting?"

"Not really. I'm here to complete the quest to repair the staff. Do you have any Measure of Silver Shavings for sale?"

"I think I do. Here, take a look," he said as the shop menu popped up in Atlas' view.

The menu popped up and Atlas confirmed he did in fact have the shavings. The price of them wasn't very attractive, but he also didn't plan on taking up Mining any time soon. Figuring it'd be worth the investment, he bought all 28 the Jewelcrafting master had for 3 silver each.

Giddy with excitement, he handed over the staff. The Jewelcrafter looked at it with reverence as he carried it to a nearby workbench and laid it down. Without prompting, Atlas laid down the Elemental Flame and five Measure of Silver Shavings.

The master jeweler brought out a small bowl made of an unfamiliar metal and dropped the Elemental Flame into it. He took a small hammer and smashed the red gem, causing a puddle of liquid flame to form in the bottom. The silver shavings joined the flame and immediately melted into the mixture.

With careful precision, the jeweler poured small amounts of the liquid into the cracks in the socket where the gemstone rested. The mixture flowed into the cracks and tiny flashes of light flared to life as the cracks in the metal seamlessly flowed back together. The process only took a handful of minutes, and Atlas would've sworn he held his breath through the entire thing.

Quest - Repair the Staff (Jewelcrafting)	
Requirements Level 15 Quest Rarity: Unique Quest Reward: 800 experience, Jeweled socket of Staff repaired.	Description: You've returned the necessary ingredients and the socket on the staff has been repaired.
You have completed the quest!	

 With a quick word of thanks, Atlas scooped up the staff and ran for the Blacksmith shop. The smith was hard at work when he entered, and Atlas wasn't about to interrupt him. The bulk of his muscles and size of his hammer wasn't something he would tempt fate with. The smith finally noticed him and waved him over.

 "Something I can do for you?"

 "Yes, sir. I have the items you requested to complete the quest to repair that staff."

 "Fine, fine. I guess I can take care of that real quick. Hand over the items," the smith said with a gesture.

 Atlas did as requested and gave him the staff along with the Elemental Core and 3 Ironwood Root. The smith looked at the items and whistled.

 "That Ironwood Root sure is tough as nails until you learn how to harvest it."

 "There's a trick to it?" Atlas asked.

 "Yep, how did you get these without knowing the trick to it?"

 "I spent forever whacking on it with a hatchet," Atlas grumbled.

A booming laughter rang through the smithy at his statement. The few people milling around stopped and stared at the smith in surprise. After a few moments, they just shook their heads and resumed their work.

"That must've taken forever. Since you suffered through that and have that kind of dedication, I'll let you in on a little secret. Ironwood Root softens if you hit it with heat for a short time. Then it gets much easier to chop through."

Atlas slapped himself on the forehead. *Of course it would. Heat it up in the forge and it gets pretty soft too. Figures I'd waste time doing it the hardest way possible.*

The smith walked over to his anvil and propped the staff up against the nearby wall. He tossed all three of the Ironwood Roots in his coal pit, and the inner cores quickly burned out as the exterior metal glowed a dark red.

The smith pulled the roots out and hammered them into thin, flat sheets of metal. He put the Elemental Core on the anvil next and shattered the small crystal. Tiny fragments littered the air as the smith continued to pound on the item until only a small pile of dust remained. Sweeping the powdered crystal into his hand, he walked over and grabbed the staff.

The smith's sweat mingled with the wood of the staff as he laid it onto his anvil. He threw the sheets of metal from the roots back into the fire and waited for them to turn a bright red. His tongs grabbed the first sheet and laid it on the first metal fitting. Some taps of his hammer allowed the metal to form perfectly around the exterior. As a final step, he sprinkled some Powdered Elemental Core on to the metal. A flash of light, followed by a slight popping sound, echoed through the space before the metal melded into place.

He repeated the process for the rest of the metal pieces before handing Atlas the staff back.

Quest - Repair the Staff (Blacksmithing)	
Requirements Level 15 Quest Rarity: Unique Quest Reward: 800 experience, Metal pieces of Staff repaired.	Description: You gathered the necessary items, and the smith repaired the metal pieces of the staff as promised.
You have completed the quest!	

"Take care of that weapon. I have a feeling it's something special."

"Sure will. Thanks for your help," Atlas told the smith as he gathered up the staff and left the building.

Entering the woodworking shop, he found the same old man sitting behind the desk as before. Upon seeing Atlas, his eyes lit up with excitement.

"Did you complete my quest?" he asked with a tinge of hope in his voice.

"Sure did. I just need to buy a few Mahogany Dust from you if you have them in stock."

"Sure do," the old man said with a wave.

Atlas browsed through the items until he located Mahogany Dust and purchased 10 of them for 1 silver each. He dug the staff back out of his bag and laid it on the counter with a pouch of the Mahogany Dust and the Sap of an Ent.

The master woodworker took the small pouch filled with the sticky sap and scraped the contents into a small wooden bowl. He sprinkled the Mahogany Dust into the sap as he continually mixed. Atlas couldn't be certain, but he didn't think dumping the whole thing in at once would work correctly. When the mixture was a smooth red color, the old man turned his attention to the staff.

Fetching a small brush from his desk, the master dipped it in the mixture and slowly painted all the wooden surfaces with the thick goo. Everywhere the sap mixture touched, the wood seemed to shine with a new luster. Cracks slowly mended, and the wood looked more vibrant and alive.

When the last of the sap covered the tip, a soft chime rang out in the room. Atlas and the master both looked at each other as if to ask if they both heard the noise. They nodded and Atlas took the staff from the old man.

Quest - Repair the Staff (Woodworking)	
Requirements Level 15 Quest Rarity: Epic Quest Reward: 800 experience, Wood pieces of Staff repaired.	Description: You gathered the necessary ingredients, and the master repaired the wooden sections of the staff.
You have completed the quest!	

Success! You've reached level 18.

Atlas ran his hands over the now smooth staff. The gemstone shone brightly while the polished metal glimmered. His examination was interrupted by someone clearing their throat. He looked down to see the old Woodworking master staring at him.

"Yes?"

"You going to complete that thing or what? I'd like to see what it really is."

"Oh yeah, sorry."

He turned his attention to the original quest.

Quest - Return to the Living	
Requirements Level 15 Rarity: Unique Quest Reward: 800 experience, 600 Woodworking experience, 600 Jewelcrafting experience.	Description: You repaired the staff back to its former glory, but it is far weaker than before. Take the staff and work to strengthen it.
Do you wish to turn in this quest? Yes/No.	

Atlas mentally selected *Yes*. The staff in his hands burst with a brilliant green glow and pulled out of his hand. It floated to the middle of the room and hovered a couple feet off the ground. Large slashing arcs of green energy coalesced around the staff and circled it in a vortex of power before the power shrunk down and absorbed into the staff.

The staff floated back to Atlas and hovered in the air until he grabbed it. The piece looked like a genuine work of art. Intricate runes appeared scrawled over all the surfaces. With nervous anticipation, he examined the item to see its actual identity.

Item – Breath of Life	
Requirements: Level 15 **Rarity:** Unique **Quality:** Masterwork **Class:** Living Weapon **Special Properties:** Soulbound	**Attack:** 4 **Magical Attack:** 4 **Defense:** 3 **Magical Defense:** 3 **Durability:** 225/225 **Weight:** 6.5 lbs. **Slot:** 2H Weapon **Level:** 1 **Experience:** 0/100 **Traits:** A rare and elusive Living Weapon. This staff feels as though it has a mind of its own.

This staff is sweet! I'm a little disappointed in the stats on it for a Unique level weapon. I mean, no attributes? Seriously?

The key benefit Atlas saw was it contained boosts for both his physical and magical attacks. It was the first weapon he'd seen in the game that did both. Two other factors made this weapon more attractive than he could reasonably explain. A soulbound property meant it would stick with him through death and it couldn't be looted from him. It was the first item he'd seen with that property.

The second, and possibly most intriguing of all, was the level and experience portion of the weapon. He wasn't sure what a living weapon was, but if it could level up and grow in power, it would be a game changer for him. His clock showed he only had an hour until he needed to log out, but his curiosity was too much to fight.

Dashing for the door, he finally noticed the Woodworking master's face. A look of childish joy framed the man's expression.

"In a bit of a rush, thanks for your help. I'll come by and see you later if you want to get a closer look at the finished item," he told the master as he ran past and out of the door.

Ignoring everyone around him, he ran for the gate near his house. He realized he'd leveled up turning in the woodworking quest, so he put a point in Constitution and the other in Intellect. The guards blurred by his vision as he passed in frantic motion. The closest area for monsters near the city wasn't far from this gate, and he made a path directly for it.

An antelope was his intended prey, and he rushed toward the animal in the grassland around the city. It didn't take him long to work his magic and finish the creature, but he was disappointed in the notifications.

Grassland Antelope died.
You gained 80 experience.

    His heart fell as he looked at the staff. The experience counter on the weapon hadn't moved. With his hope deflated, he slunk back to his house near the gate, locked the door, and immediately crashed on the bed. The prompt to log out soon greeted him and he hit *Yes*.

Chapter 23

Crashing Down

Atlas opened his eyes to the familiar hum of the electronics in the pod. He searched the glass dome for the technician outside. A burly man with black hair and a goatee stood at the control panel as he tapped away on the screen. The top popped open and Atlas slid out of the machine.

"Welcome back," the tech said as he scanned the control panel and looked back up, "Atlas."

"Thanks. Where's Jean? She working today?"

"No, sir. She's off work today."

Atlas sighed and thanked the man before he walked off and took his direct path for the restroom. Taking care of his business, he continued his normal dull trek back home. Only a handful of people littered the hallways and the lobby as he exited.

His old car fired up, and the belt squealed under the hood as he shifted it into gear. The sound continued until he cleared the parking garage and gave it some gas. The partially burned out neon from a small burger place caught his attention and he went through the drive through to grab a bite to eat on his way home.

Entering his apartment, he looked around in despair. The bland place was the same boring spot he was used to. He immediately missed his adventure, the smell of sawdust, the thrill of fighting, and the fresh scent of the forest. His time outside of the game was slowly dragging down his spirit.

His afternoon and evening consisted of him cleaning up the apartment, including himself, and making sure his clothes were clean and ready for work the next day. He rewarded himself by sitting on the couch and watching anime. When he began to nod off, he stood up, brushed his teeth, and walked to his room to collapse on the bed. Soft snoring soon filled the place as his head hit the pillow.

***

"What do you mean, let go?" Atlas fumed.

He arrived at work as usual to see people swarming the place. Unfortunately, they weren't patients. Trucks were loading up some of their testing and diagnostic equipment to haul them off. All of them had the company name on the side.

"Just what I said," Kathryn told him, "My worst fears came true. Our clinic was one they ditched. They said we didn't bring in enough money."

"That makes little sense! Where are these people going to go? There isn't much around here."

"I guess the company doesn't care. We get plenty of customers. Apparently, they aren't the kind the company is interested in. They want people who will actually pay the bills. I guess this place is 'too poor,'" she emphasized with air quotes.

"What am I going to do now?" he mumbled to himself.

"Well, the company has decided to be ever so generous and offer to pay you for an additional two weeks while you look for another job. They did this for all of us here. Personally, I think they are just trying to avoid a media disaster because of the decision."

The two lapsed into silence as Atlas surveyed the work. The job itself wasn't anything special, but he enjoyed it. Best yet, he was good at it. He should be able to find a decent job with his education. It was just going to suck to go on the hunt again.

Unless… I decide to shift career paths.

The thought struck him fast. Liking the job and wanting to do it forever were two very different things. Now that Divine Genesis was a big part of his life, maybe he should decide to do that as a full-time job? He'd done well for himself so far in the market, and he was still low level. If he could dedicate a solid schedule of playtime and not have to worry about only playing on days off, he should be able to make good money. He already had 34 gold stashed in the bank which meant he had somewhere in the neighborhood of $3,400. That was coming up close to one month's worth of pay already.

"Anyone in there," Kathryn asked as a hand waved in front of his face.

"What? Did I miss something?" Atlas asked as he shook himself back to reality.

"I asked if you wanted me to write you a letter of recommendation. You've done an outstanding job here, and it's the least I could do."

"Thanks, Kat. I'm going to explore my options first, I think. I may take you up on that offer, though. I'll let you know."

"Well, you have my personal cell number. Call me if I can help," she told him with a soft smile.

"I appreciate it. I guess I'll head back home and start looking around. I'll talk to you later," he told her with a wave.

Atlas turned and walked back to his car. His drive home was a struggle with himself. The lights and signs swam by in a blur as his mind drifted over his current problem. No job, no places nearby that he could think of that would be a good fit, and to top it off, his mind kept drifting back to the possibility of playing the game full time to make a living.

It was a colossal risk to consider but at the same time, felt right. He'd done very well for himself in the game so far and now would be the perfect chance. When his car came to a halt in the parking lot of his apartment, he settled on a plan.

He would give himself a month to make it work. The gold he had in the game could float him that long if things got serious. Unemployment could make up for it for a little while. If the plan was a bust and he couldn't make the money he needed, he'd give up and start hunting for a regular job again.

Walking inside, he went directly for the kitchen and poured himself a bowl of his favorite sugary corn flake cereal with a little milk. There was time to kill if he wanted to get back into Divine Genesis. It was still a few more hours until he hit the 24 hour logout mark so he could log back in.

Atlas picked up his phone and tried to call Keenan. To his surprise, his friend actually picked up.

"What's up Atlas?"

"A lot actually. I'm a little surprised you actually answered."

"Sorry, man. I spend most of my day in meetings. I never realized how boring earnings and marketing reports are. What's new with you?" Keenan asked.

"Well, lost my job today. They closed my clinic. Think I might go full time gamer in Divine Genesis."

"That sucks. I didn't think they'd close that place down. I've heard of plenty of people making the switch to full time gamer though. The market tie in has made professional gamer a truly viable option."

"I've been doing good in the gold department so going to try it for a month and see how it works. Also been kind of dating a woman."

"Oh, she hot?"

Atlas chuckled, "Still more important things than that but yep, she is."

"Hey, I'm just a sucker for the curvy women, especially if they have long sleek black hair."

That's odd. Usually Keenan goes for the bouncy curls of brunettes.

"Guess your tastes are finally changing as you grow up," Atlas said with a chuckle.

"Maybe," his friend stated until the line went quiet for a few seconds.

"Hey man, gotta go. Another meeting is starting. I'll catch ya later."

"See ya la…," Atlas started before the phone hung up.

When has he ever hung up on me like that?
This new position has him turning into a snob.

He stared at his phone in disbelief before he opened the browser. A few quick taps brought him back to the Divine Genesis Fanatics forum page, and he browsed through the entries. He was both shocked and amused to see they stickied the post about additions he responded to toward the top under a subforum for beginner tutorials. Over a thousand people viewed it, so he stopped by and check the comments.

Most of them were basic things with people thanking the author for sharing the info, while others were people replied to his comment asking if he'd discovered anything else.

Going to the class specific forums, it also showed his post about druid transformations stickied as well. More likes and upvotes for it showed on the screen and some of the same responses as the other posts.

He didn't feel like adding anything to the forum right now and wanted to keep the information he knew about crafting and the game market to himself, especially now that his livelihood might depend on it.

One title caught his eye, and he clicked on it.

Log Out and Stay Out.

More has come to our attention, and the nefarious ways of Gaia Corporation have hit a new low. They are using your bodies without permission while you're logged into the game. A time of reckoning is coming soon and everything will come to light. Stay out of Divine Genesis or risk losing yourself!

Humanity United.

The crazies were still at it. I'm sure the tinfoil mafia were truly interested in following these posts. Atlas noticed it was a different username than last time, so they must keep getting banned and posting on new accounts.

On a whim, he checked the forum for dungeons. Few posts showed up in the subforum, but one caught his eye and he tapped it.

Need a Healer for Rare Dungeon,

We are a full party LF healer for a rare dungeon we found. Must be below lvl 20 and have good healing skills. Prefer people who are versatile and can do more than blindly heal, though. Message FaceStomper55 in game if you'd like to apply. We will meet in Nirithan, so be somewhere close.

Sounds interesting. Didn't know they had such a thing as rare dungeons, much less one that had a level cap.

Atlas noted the name so he could follow up.

Hopefully, my credentials as a winner of The Great Hunt will help me get this spot. I didn't do a ton of healing, but it was enough and I'm definitely versatile.

With nothing else of interest on the site, he finally put his phone away with a sigh. Instead of staring at the ceiling for no reason, he turned on the TV and switched to a music streaming app to blare through the room. Electric guitar blared through the room as he rocked an air guitar.

After a few songs, he ceased his playing and worked to clean up the apartment. Sweeping and mopping the place was tedious, but he didn't like things to get too dirty. He also hoped he'd get to bring Jean over before too long and wanted the place to be presentable.

With all the chores finished, he turned off the TV, grabbed his keys, and left the apartment. He had little time left to kill before he could log back in, so he spent the time finding something to eat. Now was the best time for him to get a good meal since he didn't know what his financial situation would look like later.

Butter dripped over the caramelized edge of the steak as he shoved it into his mouth. A scoop of mashed potatoes soon followed, and he washed it down with a gulp of sweet iced tea. An excellent medium rare steak was almost impossible to beat. He finished the meal by practically licking the plate clean and scraped the last of the juice off with the complimentary bread served with the meal.

With his belly full and him feeling better about his current situation, he went back to Gaia Corporation. A small crowd of people milled around the entrance. Most looked to be his age or younger, so he assumed it was a fresh batch of gamers that just logged out for their break.

The lobby was fairly busy with people chatting. The few snippets of conversation he overheard were decidedly about the game and mainly just them bragging about their gear or level.

When he made it to his designated pod, his favorite beauty greeted him. Jean's smile lit up his day as he approached.

"Good afternoon, Atlas," she told him with a nod.

"Good afternoon to you as well. How've you been? I missed you when I logged out."

"Just juggling work and the little time I have free. Was actually in a cooking class with a friend for some fun," she said with a giggle.

"Cook anything interesting?" Alas asked as she prepped the pod and the lid lifted.

"Not really. A bunch of crap that's far too healthy for me to eat very often, but it was fun. How've you been?"

"Been better. My job closed down today, so going to have to find a new one. May even consider playing this game full time for the real world market prices. Right now I just want to log in and take my mind off all the nonsense. Any chance you'll be available in a couple of days?"

She looked up in thought before tapping a few times on her small tablet.

"Actually, if you end up playing your full amount of time, I should be ending my shift shortly after you log back out. You have something in mind?" She asked with a wry smile as he hoisted himself into the capsule and shifted his body to get comfortable.

"Dinner?"

"Sounds great… after you shower, of course."

He smiled at the comment, "Naturally."

"Then it's a date. I'll see you when you finish up in game," One final big smile and a quick wave was all he saw before the blackness took him.

* * *

The house for the Master of the Wood greeted him and, as usual, nothing appeared out of place. Hefting his bag of goods, he walked out of the place and took in a breath of air. Being inside the city meant it wasn't nearly as clean and fragrant free as he hoped, but it was still much cleaner than a lot of the air in the major cities outside of the game.

He examined his staff and sighed in disappointment that it still showed no experience on it. His first trip was to find the Kingdom Courier. Sending a message to FaceStomper55 was his primary concern.

One of the nearby guards directed him down the street to a building with a sign outside showing a rolled up scroll over a generic-looking crown. Inside was nothing more than a few desks scattered around and a large map on the back wall.

Atlas walked over and studied the map. *The detail on this is rather well done.* It clearly marked the forests and highlands. Each city was meticulously labeled, and Atlas could trace the path he'd come since entering the game. On the grand scale of things, he'd seen little of this world.

He walked over to the nearest desk and waited for the clerk to look up.

"Can I help you?" The man asked as he stared down his long nose.

"I'd like to send a message."

"Standard mail, or Reborn mail?"

"Uh, Reborn mail I guess."

"Reborn mail costs 1 silver per letter. Who is it going to?" The clerk asked as he pulled out a sheet of paper and dipped a quill pen into a bottle of ink.

"It needs to go to FaceStomper55."

The clerk nodded before looking back up, "Please compose your message and I'll have it sent."

A window popped up in front of him and a floating keyboard came with it. Atlas was happy he didn't have to write this message out, especially since he was sure he'd mess it up with a quill pen. He was lucky if he could read his own handwriting half the time, much less someone else.

He typed a quick message and reviewed what he wrote.

FaceStomper55,

I'm Atlas, a level 18 druid, responding to your request for a healer on the Divine Genesis Fanatics forum. I've got a pretty firm grip on the mechanics in this world so far, including counters, and am good with my spell casting under pressure. I was on the winning team for The Great Hunt in my region. Let me know if you want to meet up so we can discuss the mission.

After looking it over for a few seconds to ensure it was good, he hit a green Submit button in the lower right corner. The message box closed, and he looked down to see words rapidly fill the paper in front of the clerk. The man nodded in satisfactions and looked up.

"If you'll give me the silver, I'll have this sent immediately."

Atlas fished through his bag and grabbed a silver and placed it on the desk, "How long does it usually take these messages to be delivered?"

"That depends on where the recipient is. If you're in the same city, it's typically there in a matter of a couple of hours. If not, it could take days."

Atlas sulked at that news but figured it was to be expected. Instead, he left the building and walked back into the street. There were plenty of things he needed to take care of and leveling was always on that list, but his focus drifted to his crafting. He'd come here and hadn't checked in with his druid trainer or his profession masters. It was time to do some exploring.

Figuring the druid training should take precedence, he found another guard and got directions to Master Harrama's place. The building stood out just like every other one of his trainers as he neared it. This one was even more austere than the others and looked like someone hollowed out a giant tree and lived in it. A door was carved into the front in a gentle arch, and if not for the decorative vines around the border, he'd have missed it with how well it blended in.

Inside he found a short woman with dark brown hair and a bit of a scowl. Lines furrowed her brow as she watched him enter the building.

"Can I help you?"

"I'm here for druid training. Are you Master Harrama?"

"I am. What's your name, young one?"

"Atlas."

"Well, come here with you and let me see the extent of your training," she told him as she waved him forward.

Atlas moved to walk past her toward the back of the house, and she held out a hand and stopped him.

"That's far enough," and shed placed her palm on his chest.

A warmth blossomed through him and radiated all the way to his toes.

"So, you're completely trained up to level 15 and even got your animal form. I also notice it shows you unlocked another form but it won't tell me what it is so it must be a rare one. Haven't seen one of those in a long while."

"I have the Dire Bear Transformation," Atlas confirmed with a nod.

"Ooh, the Dire Bear is a formidable form. I guess I can let you move forward with your training without restrictions," she told him with a sniff.

"Excuse me, but can all the trainers do that where you can sense my skills?" Atlas asked.

"All of them should be able to, why?"

"They had me demonstrate my abilities for them instead of just seeing them." Atlas grumbled.

Master Harrama let out a throaty chuckle, "Doesn't surprise me. Some of them probably wanted to see how you handled spells."

Atlas could only nod at her explanation.

"Speaking of spells, can you show me what I can learn?"

The druid master waved her hand toward him and the menu appeared. He checked the Buy tab to see what was available to him. Two upgraded ranks to existing spells and a new spell greeted him. Each cost him 15 silver.

Druid Spell - Barkskin (Rank 2)	

Requirements
   Druid Class
   Level 16
	Description: The target's skin takes on the toughness of bark.
	
	• Increases target's Defense rating by 17.
	
	Mana Cost: 15 MP

Druid Spell - Harmony (Rank 2)	

Requirements
   Druid Class
   Level 17
	Description: Draw on the power of nature to heal your target. This ability restores health over time.
	
	• Restores 8 HP every 5 seconds for 55 seconds.
	
	Mana Cost: 10 MP

Druid Spell - Tranquil Fountain	

Requirements
   Druid Class
   Level 18
	Description: Channel the power of nature to heal your target. This ability lasts up to 20 seconds, but distractions while channeling can break it early.
	
	• Restores 32 HP every second while channeling.

	Mana Cost: 30 MP
	Cooldown: 2 hours

He thanked Master Harrama and left her to her business.

Back on the road, he turned and headed for the crafting sector of town. His first order of business was to find the Leatherworking trainer. He had his letter of introduction from the last trainer, but he hadn't gotten the name. A glance at the letter showed him he needed to find Master Kinkaid.

When he reached the industrial part of town, he asked around until he found the shop in question. Walking through the door, a burly man with a long beard and mustache greeted him. His long brown hair hung down in scraggly, loose curls. Deep brown eyes glimmered as he watched Atlas enter.

"Can I help you?"

"Yep. Are you Master Kinkaid?"

"Sure am. Do I know you?"

"No. I'm Atlas. I'm new to town and was sent here to continue my Leatherworking training," Atlas explained as he handed over his introduction letter.

The big man opened the letter and breezed over it before setting it down on the small desk near him.

"Good to know they can send me fully trained leatherworkers from time to time. I guess you need your latest skills then?" Master Kinkaid asked.

"Yes, sir," Atlas confirmed.

The trainer waved a hand, and the menu
popped up in Atlas' view. Like his
woodworking, he now had a new tier of armor to
work with. Thick leather was the new set of
gear, and he trained everything he could until
his current level of 18. The five abilities
cost him 2 silver and 50 copper.

Leatherworking - Cure Thick Hide	
Requirements Leatherworking Level 15 Rarity: Common Requirements: 1 Raw Animal Hide, 1 Pinch of Salt, 1 Vial of Viscous Curing Liquid	Description: Turn animal hides into a Cured Thick Hide. Cured Thick Hides are used for Leatherworking patterns.

Leatherworking - Create Thick Leather Gloves	
Requirements Leatherworking Level 15 Rarity: Common Requirements: 2 Cured Thick Hide, 2 Soft Thread	Description: Creates a set of rigid and flexible gloves that offers a moderate amount of protection.

Leatherworking - Create Thick Leather Boots	
Requirements Leatherworking Level 16 Rarity: Common Requirements: 3 Cured Thick Hide, 2 Soft Thread	Description: Creates a set of rigid and flexible boots that offers a moderate amount of protection.

Leatherworking - Create Thick Leather Jerkin	
Requirements Leatherworking Level 17 Rarity: Common Requirements: 5 Cured Thick Hide, 6 Soft Thread	Description: Creates a rigid and flexible leather chestpiece that offers moderate protection.

Leatherworking - Create Thick Leather Pants	
Requirements Leatherworking Level 18 Rarity: Common Requirements: 6 Cured Thick Hide, 7 Soft Thread	Description: Create a set of rigid and flexible gloves that offers a moderate amount of protection.

Seeing the Vial of Viscous Curing Liquid, Atlas checked the Buy tab for the ingredient. The trainer had plenty on hand and each sold for 50 copper. A check of his inventory showed he had 34 hides on him from his hunting trips. Most of those were from fighting the animals while heading to and from his quests for his staff. He bought the 34 vials he needed to cure his current hides and handed over the 17 silver.

"The process for curing the same on thick hide as it is on soft hide?" Atlas asked.

"Yep, just use the other curing liquid instead."

Atlas walked away before he realized his mistake. The new patterns still needed Soft Thread, so he needed a few of the older curing liquids to make more thread. He bought 4 Vial of Curing Liquid and then walked to the back of the shop until he found the room with the basin.

Four hides became Cured Soft Leather that he turned into 56 Soft Thread. The other 30 hides became Cured Thick Leather. A quick count showed he needed 16 hides to make the four new pieces of armor he learned. Since he would need them for his possible dungeon run, he made those four pieces first and then swapped out his armor.

You gained 2,795 total experience in Leatherworking.

Item - Thick Leather Jerkin

Requirements: Level 15	**Defense:** 13
Rarity: Common	**Durability:** 155/155
Quality: Good	**Weight:** 5.0 lbs.
	Slot: Chest
	Traits: A jerkin made from thick leather. Provides moderate protection for the upper body.
	Thick Leather Set Bonus:
	2 Pieces - + 10 Defense
	4 Pieces - + 10 Maximum Mana/HP
	6 Pieces - + 5% chance to Parry

Item - Thick Leather Boots

Requirements: Level 15	**Defense:** 9
Rarity: Common	**Durability:** 125/125
Quality: Good	**Weight:** 3.0 lbs.
	Slot: Feet
	Traits: A pair of boots made from thick leather. Provides moderate protection for the feet.
	Thick Leather Set Bonus:
	2 Pieces - + 10 Defense

<table>
<tr><td></td><td>4 Pieces - + 10 Maximum Mana/HP
6 Pieces - + 5% chance to Parry</td></tr>
</table>

Item - Thick Leather Gloves	
Requirements: Level 15 **Rarity:** Common **Quality:** Good	**Defense:** 7 **Durability:** 105/105 **Weight:** 1.8 lbs. **Slot:** Hands **Traits:** A pair of gloves made from thick leather. Provides moderate protection for the hands. **Thick Leather Set Bonus:** 2 Pieces - + 10 Defense 4 Pieces - + 10 Maximum Mana/HP 6 Pieces - + 5% chance to Parry

<table>
<tr><td colspan="2" align="center">Leatherworking - Thick Leather Pants</td></tr>
<tr><td>

Requirements: Level 15
Rarity: Common
Quality: Good

</td><td>

Defense: 11
Durability: 145/145
Weight: 3.4 lbs.
Slot: Legs

Traits: A pair of pants made from thick leather. Provides moderate protection for the legs.

Thick Leather Set Bonus:

2 Pieces - + 10 Defense
4 Pieces - + 10 Maximum Mana/HP
6 Pieces - + 5% chance to Parry

</td></tr>
</table>

The stats on defense were pretty standard and about what he expected, but the surprise was the set bonus boost his new armor provided. He really needed to find a good enchanter to work on getting some added boosts to the gear he made. Ideally, it'd be better if he could do it himself to maximize profits, but it would take a lot of time he didn't have this early in the game.

Using the rest of his leather, he made four more sets of boots and a set of gloves.

You gained 1,370 total experience in Leatherworking.
Success! You've reached level 19 in Leatherworking.

The Thick Leather Boots commanded an impressive 35 silver each while he sold the gloves for 18 silver. His older armor only sold for 5 silver combined. With a wave, he left the shop and went to the Jewelcrafter next.

This one he'd already visited for the staff quest but hadn't bothered with introductions yet. The master greeted him as he entered, and Atlas showed him the completed staff. He oohed and awed over it for an appropriate amount of time before he said something that caught Atlas off guard.

"Already done some fighting with the new staff, I see."

"Huh? I think I fought one animal. That's about it."

"Surely the staff didn't gain that much experience in one fight?" The master asked him in confusion.

"Experience? It didn't give me any when I killed the creature."

"Then how did you level this?"

Atlas stared at the man as though he'd gone crazy for a moment before looking at the stats on the staff.

<table>
<tr><td colspan="2" align="center">Item - Breath of Life</td></tr>
<tr><td>

Requirements: Level 15
Rarity: Unique
Quality: Masterwork
Class: Living Weapon
Special Properties:
Soulbound

</td><td>

Attack: 4
Magical Power: 5
Defense: 3
Magical Defense: 4
Durability: 225/225
Weight: 6.5 lbs.
Slot: 2H Weapon

Level: 3
Experience: 166/300

Traits: A rare and elusive Living Weapon. This staff feels as though it has a mind of its own.

</td></tr>
</table>

What in the world? How did it gain experience?

The thoughts swirled in his head as he contemplated the situation.

His mind reflected over his time in game. *I didn't complete any quests since I logged on. The only thing I've done was craft…*

A thought struck him, and he looked at the logs to see what experience he'd gained since logging in for his crafting. The total showed 4,165. Hidden amongst his experience gains in crafting were the gains for the staff. It got 10% of his total crafting experience toward weapon experience. He'd glazed over it with the onslaught of experience notifications.

It was also nice that the Magical Power and Magical Defense both rose by 1 point. If he could continue to upgrade the weapon, it could prove invaluable in the long run.

"It appears the staff gains a percentage of my crafting experience," he told the Jewelcrafter.

"Really? I've only heard of a few of those and all of them are usually tools of the trades, not combat weapons."

"That's what it tells me in the logs. It is a living weapon, so it would seem right that it feeds on creation and not destruction. I'll have to monitor it. Can I see what new skills I can train?" Atlas asked as he handed him the introduction letter.

"Oh, you're a Jewelcrafter as well? You could've given this to me last time."

"Yeah but I was in a hurry and excited about the staff. Sorry."

The master only nodded and waved toward him. The menu showed up and he looked at the Buy tab. Since he was currently at 18 Jewelcrafting, he had a decent number of options. He already knew the next tier was the mahogany items, so there wasn't much surprise when all the ring and necklace enchantments were there.

He gave 5 silver for all ten of the patterns and then checked the rest of the man's wares. He had no Mahogany Logs or wood available and Atlas had found none while out questing, so he just bid the man farewell and headed for The Lacquer Stop. He'd already trained everything up to level 20 in Woodworking here, so he wanted to check in and see if any new work orders came in.

An exhausted looking Joe greeted him as he walked into the shop.

"Man, am I glad you're here. The work orders came in pretty heavy after you completed those last ones so quickly and I've been struggling to keep up but still can't work at a fraction of your pace."

"No worries. What can I help with?" Atlas asked as he walked in and surveyed the room.

Joe didn't answer. Instead, he stood and waved Atlas to follow. The two walked to the back room and Atlas froze as he walked through the door. Multiple stacks of raw materials covered the entire warehouse in the back of the shop. Only the barest of space was open to navigate through the stacks.

As before, each of the sections was divided up by their specific materials and had a sign on them that labeled their order. A count of the stacks showed what he thought was five orders.

"This is a lot of work. I can see why you're stressed out," Atlas mused.

"Yeah. After that last set of orders you completed, we were hammered with this set of orders because of how fast we turned around the delivery. Everyone else takes up to a month to deliver on the smaller orders and we turned around multiple larger orders in a few days' time."

"Well, to be fair, that was the plan when I agreed to this arrangement with Raina and Penny. Why don't you take a break while I get to work on these? Can you assign me these work orders?"

"I sure can. The ladies came by and gave me permission to assign them to you when needed. How many do you want?" he asked hesitantly.

"Just give me them all and I'll get to work."

Joe smiled and looked relieved. With a quick wave and a few taps in the air, boxes appeared in front of Atlas and he accepted them all.

<table>
<tr><td colspan="2" align="center">Tradeskill Quest - Supplying the Blacksmith II</td></tr>
<tr>
<td>Requirements
   Woodworking Level 14

Quest Rarity: Uncommon

Quest Reward: 800 experience, 7 gold 40 silver.</td>
<td>Description: The Lacquer Stop needs to fill an order for the following pieces:

• Smooth Spear Handle x 35
• Smooth Axe Handle x 35
• Smooth Wood Staff x 25</td>
</tr>
</table>

<table>
<tr><td colspan="2" align="center">Tradeskill Quest - Detailed Mahogany</td></tr>
<tr>
<td>Requirements
   Woodworking Level 17

Quest Rarity: Uncommon

Quest Reward: 900 experience, 8 gold 95 silver.</td>
<td>Description: The Lacquer Stop needs to fill an order for the following pieces:

• Smooth Mahogany Staff x 20
• Smooth Mahogany Wand x 20</td>
</tr>
</table>

Tradeskill Quest - Supplying the Jewelcrafter	
Requirements Woodworking Level 19 Quest Rarity: Uncommon Quest Reward: 1200 experience, 9 gold 90 silver.	Description: The Lacquer Stop needs to fill an order for the following pieces: • Smooth Mahogany Ring x 120 • Smooth Mahogany Necklace Charm x 80

Tradeskill Quest - A Matter of Infrastructure	
Requirements Woodworking Level 15 Quest Rarity: Uncommon Quest Reward: 400 experience, 3 gold 10 silver.	Description: The Lacquer Stop needs to fill an order for the following pieces: • Smooth Mahogany Rod x 80

Tradeskill Quest - Defending the Walls	
Requirements Woodworking Level 20 Quest Rarity: Uncommon Quest Reward: 1300 experience, 12 gold 20 silver.	Description: The Lacquer Stop needs to fill an order for the following pieces: • Smooth Mahogany Shortbow Frame x 20 • Smooth Mahogany Longbow Frame x 20

Atlas twisted his neck from side to side, feeling the small crunch of bones popping before he walked to the first pile and got to work. All the supplies were in the room and the lathe was nearby, so his work was a steady flow.

He fell into a rhythm with each work order. Sawdust flew everywhere and scraps of wood collected in piles as he created all the items. From time to time, he glimpsed Joe as he walked through and cleaned up some of the mess to get it out of Atlas' way. It took roughly the entire day, but he finally finished and stepped back to admire the neat stacks of finished items on each of the pallets.

His attention shifted to notification since he'd drowned them out during his work.

You gained 55,650 total experience in Woodworking.

Success! You reached levels 25, 26, and 27 in Woodworking.

You've advanced to Journeyman in Woodworking! Proceed to your trainer to learn more.

Better yet, his staff jumped significantly from the experience and even gained a trait when it hit level 10.

Item - Breath of Life	
Requirements: Level 15 **Rarity:** Unique **Quality:** Masterwork **Class:** Living Weapon **Special Properties:** Soulbound	**Attack:** 5 **Magical Power:** 7 **Defense:** 5 **Magical Defense:** 5 **Durability:** 225/225 **Weight:** 6.5 lbs. **Slot:** 2H Weapon **Level:** 10 **Experience:** 31/1600 **Traits:** A rare and elusive Living Weapon. This staff feels as though it has a mind of its own. ● Grants a 10% bonus to healing spells

Giddy with excitement, he had Joe accept all five work orders after he verified they were complete.

You gained 4,600 experience.
Success! You reached level 19.

Not only did he get a level and gain a ton of experience for both his crafting and his weapon, he also netted a hefty profit of 41 gold and 55 silver. That payday alone was enough to cover an entire month for him in the real world and he accomplished it in a day in game.

    With the stress of finances falling off his
shoulders, he bid Joe farewell and walked from
the shop. A quick detour to the bank was his
first priority, and he dropped 40 of his
almost 44 gold into the bank for safekeeping,
increasing his stockpile to 74 gold in the
bank.
    When his foot hit the cobblestone path
outside the bank, a young man approached him
with sandy blonde hair and a dust covered
face. A leather satchel rested on his hip and
he dug out a rolled piece of paper.
    "Atlas?" the young man asked.
    "Yes. Can I help you?"
    The messenger handed him the letter with a
slight bow of his head.
    "Courtesy of The Kingdom Courier, sir."
    Atlas accepted the letter with a grin and
dug through his bag. He placed a silver piece
in the boy's hand with his thanks and the
messenger scurried away. Atlas unfurled the
letter.

    Atlas,

    *We've decided to evaluate you for the
mission. Meet us at The Dusky Lady at 7PM.*

    FaceStomper55

    He read it over again to verify the message
and glanced to his game clock. It showed
6:30PM. He dashed to the closest guard and
asked for directions. The inn wasn't far away,
so he ran through the streets, dodging around
people as he made a beeline for the location.

His foot landed on the small porch in front of the building as his clock ticked to 6:58. He took a few seconds to catch his breath and take in big gulps of air before striding into the building.

A busy crowd filled the place and the smell of something that looked like stew mingled with the smell of slightly sour beer. He scanned the room until he spotted a group of five people mingling near the back corner. They looked out of place and didn't blend in to the natural atmosphere, so Atlas approached.

"Looks like the druid made it in the nick of time," a burly man said. A bushy beard and patches of chain mail rounded out his appearance.

Atlas nodded in agreement before extending a hand, "Atlas."

The man took his hand in a firm grip and shook, "FaceStomper."

He motioned for Atlas to sit in an empty chair nearby and then continued talking, "Alright people. The three of us," he began while waving at himself and his two closest companions, "have a dungeon to clear. It's an unknown place and a bit of a secret. Honestly, we don't know what to expect but because of the secrecy of it we plan to approach it cautiously. We decided bringing in a healer would be the best option. You three," he said as he waved at Atlas and the two robed figures near him, "are here to try out for the job."

"As much as I enjoy exploring unknown places. What are the loot rules and is there a guaranteed payout for this?" One of the robed figures asked, his face obscured by a hood.

"Loot Master rules. We control all loot and have first pick from our core group. Anything we don't want, you are given if you plan to use it. If you only plan to sell it, we keep it instead."

The other two figures shuffled in place while Atlas frowned.

Doesn't seem worth it to take this kind of risk for a chance at nothing more than cast-offs.

"Don't worry though," FaceStomper began with his hands raised in placation, "there is a mercenary fee for you and it will be in the party contract. We are offering 20 gold if we take you on the trip and an additional 80 gold for completing the dungeon."

What? 100 gold for running a dungeon? That can't be right. We are still low level.

"You're serious?" The other robed figure asked.

"Absolutely. It's a guaranteed pay day no matter what loot we do or don't find."

The group's energy picked up at the news.

"You three still want to try out or anyone going to leave?"

Atlas shook his head while the other two mimicked the movement.

"Sweet. Call me Stomper to make it easier. I'm the tank in the group."

Stomper turned toward the man on his right. A shorter guy that looked like a stiff breeze could topple him. Atlas caught the glimmer of small knives around his waist.

"This is Shade. Our resident Rogue."

    With another quick movement, he motioned to the other party member. Curly brown hair framed a square-jawed man with a medium build standing somewhere close to six feet tall. This leather armor with splotches of chain mail rounded out his ensemble.

    "This is Carhein. He's a melee warrior."

    "Good evening fair adventures. Tis a fine day to go adventuring with Carhein, is it not?" The man called in a baritone voice.

    "Uh… something wrong with him?" One of the robed figures asked?

    "He fancies himself a role-player. Just go along with it, it's much easier that way," Shade said with an exasperated sigh.

    Well, this should be interesting.

Chapter 24

The Trial

Stomper led them from the room and onto the street outside. They walked to the registrar's office, and he ducked inside. When he emerged, he held a rolled scroll in his hand and made his formal offer.

"You three will accompany us out of town so we can gauge your skills and will remain safe from us until we return to these city walls."

A message appeared in Atlas' view.

Stomper has invited you to join a Safe Party Agreement. Do you accept? Yes/No.

Atlas selected *Yes* and waited as the different people all appeared on his party screen. When Stomper was satisfied, he put the scroll away and motioned for them to follow. As they walked, Stomper waved one of the robed figures over. Atlas knew one of them was named Francis and the other was Kangaroo since they appeared on the party menu, but he didn't know who was who.

The two spoke for some time as they traveled before the figure returned to them and Stomper waved Atlas up to him. He trudged forward as the dusty city road passed by. Most of the inhabitants ignored them.

"So Atlas, I was intrigued by the fact you were on a winning team for The Great Hunt. Are you very close to level 20?"

"I just recently hit 19 so have close to four-thousand experience to go."

"Good. No danger of you leveling up while we do this tryout. Do you fight much or mainly heal?"

"I usually only heal when necessary. I typically fight on the front line either in this form or an animal form."

"Which form did you choose when you reached level 15?"

"I chose the nightstalker, but I also have a Dire Bear Transformation."

"Wow, two forms? I'm guessing the dire bear version is rare since I haven't heard of anyone with it yet?"

"Yep, got it from the last boss in The Wild Hunt. My trainer said it was exceptionally rare."

"And you didn't sell it? You kept it?" Stomper asked in surprise as he led them through the city gate.

"Figured it'd do me more good in the long run to keep it. I make money other ways."

"I imagine so. Your staff also looks unique," Stomper said with a gesture at the weapon.

"It's funny you mention that because it is classified as Unique and happens to be Soulbound."

Stomper whistled, "Impressive. I hold out hope for you so I'll tell you what I am looking for. While fighting, we are going to be working our normal group dynamic. I'll tank while the other two deal damage. I plan on pulling larger amounts of enemies to test you three's skills. I want to see how you keep us alive with both healing and your other abilities. I don't want a spam healbot that stands in the back and does nothing. I could find those anywhere. I'm looking for someone who is a bit of a jack of all trades."

"I'll keep that in mind." Atlas said with a grin.

"Head on back and we'll see how you do," Stomper said while gesturing behind them.

Atlas only nodded and walked back to his place. They closed in on the trees and Carhein walked over to him.

"Tis time for us to embark upon our quest and slay the wicked. What manner of foul beast shall Carhein find to best this time? None shall survive my fury," the man rattled off as he shook his fist at an imaginary enemy in front of them.

"Yeah, not a big role-player myself. How about we just go out and kill some stuff?"

"Dost thou not hunger for glory and fame?"

"Loot works. Glory and fame bring more trouble than they're worth."

Carhein only shook his head and moved to another of the candidates to bother them. Atlas breathed out a sigh when he finally left and trudged forward.

"He can be a little too much sometimes," a voice whispered near his ear.

Atlas nearly jumped out of his own skin and spun to see the form of Shade appear beside him.

"Damn. Care to warn people first?"

Shade merely chuckled and walked in step with Atlas as they continued following the group.

"Love the guy and all, but he goes overboard with that stuff sometimes," Shade mused.

"Well, not everyone can get their excitement from frightening people while stealthed," Atlas quipped.

"Meh," the rogue said with a shrug, "we all have our uses."

"Something occurred to me and I haven't had a chance to ask so far," Atlas began, "Why only three of you? Aren't parties usually five people?"

"Oddly enough, you're the first of the group to ask that so bonus points to you. The simple answer is we can't have five."

"Care to elaborate?"

"Nope. If you make the cut and are selected, we will tell you why. Until then, just know it's not an option."

"Fair enough, I guess. Have any other neat skills besides scaring people?" Atlas asked.

"A few. You'll get to see some of them soon enough," he said as shadows swirled up his body and he disappeared.

"Fucking rogues," Atlas muttered.

The trip continued farther from town than he'd ventured on his own. They passed a few items he could harvest, most notably a Mahogany Tree, but he didn't think now was the time to ask to take detours.

Their trek through the forest ended at a large cave mouth in the face of a jagged rock wall. The wall rose for over one-hundred feet while the rocks stuck out like barbed wire on the cliff face.

"All right. This is our testing ground. We're going to head into the cave and square off with monsters. This will be a test in how you handle the stress of the situation. We won't be playing this safe. I'm not carefully pulling mobs or worrying about crowd control. Do that yourself if you see fit, but your job is to keep us alive while we do foolish things. Everyone understand?" Stomper asked the assembled candidates.

Atlas mind snapped to the stupidity of that statement. *Are they planning on abandoning all reason for this test? Do they want to die?*

He found himself nodding in agreement, anyway. Stomper pulled a large square shield from his bag and drew the sword on his belt. Carhein stepped up behind him and to his right while Shade was nowhere to be found. The two fighters walked at a fast clip as they entered the cave. Atlas and the other two healers followed along in hurried steps.

They rounded the first corner, and chaos greeted them. Odd looking monsters the size of Great Danes with black sandy hide and red eyes raced around the wide open cave. They bunched up in groups of three and four as they ran from one side to the other. Black fins protruded from their front shoulders and hind legs. Atlas stared at one until the name came to him. *Demon Landshark – Level 16.*

"What the hell?" Atlas breathed before the party truly started. Instead of doing the logical thing and trying to pull them in small groups, Stomper did exactly as he promised and ran to the center of the room, attracting the attention of all the creatures at once.

Panic gripped Atlas as he saw at least two dozen creatures racing for the two fighters. His attention snapped into place and he instinctively cast Barkskin on Stomper. The spell was quick and an aura of slightly brown power settled over the fighter.

Stomper did an amazing job of interposing his shield as the claws and teeth closed in on his body. A column of white light smashed into one beast and it sizzled in place. Atlas looked to his side to see Kangaroo standing there with his arms outstretched and power radiating from him.

Carhein swung with wild abandon at any landshark that came near.

"You'll rue the day you crossed Carhein the Mighty! Taste my righteous axe foul demon!" His blade sunk into the skull of one monster.

Atlas could only shake his head and return his attention to Stomper. Two of the monsters got through his defense, and he now sported bleeding cuts on his leg and side. A look at the party menu showed he was still at almost 90% HP. No reason to use mana to fix him yet.

Carhein took a hit and stumbled. The creatures used this chance to jump on him, and three of them took him to the ground. Atlas took three running steps toward the man before an explosion of shadow rocked the area around Carhein.

Shade appeared from the power and dashed around so quickly Atlas had difficulty keeping track. It looked like a straight up Killing Spree in action. The area around the downed fighter cleared and Shade jerked him to his feet before the rogue disappeared in a flash.

"Fear the shadows, demons. They work with Carhein now."

Atlas watched Stomper's health slowly tick down and cast Harmony on the warrior. The magical power settled over him, and Atlas watched the few trickles of blood dry up. A flash of white light bathed Carhein and his health jumped up as well.

You healed Stomper for 17 HP with Harmony.

What? 17? That's crazy. He scrambled to figure out what happened. That was more than half of his Nourish spell in one tick. His attention snapped to his staff, and he remembered he now had a large bonus to his magical power and it also had a special ability to increase his healing by 10%. Those bonuses were truly putting in the work now. It healed for more than double its normal tick.

Kangaroo unleashed another dazzling blast of power near the edge of the landsharks. His foolishness pulled the attention of the nearby monsters and a group of five broke off from Stomper and Carhein, charging for the healers.

Atlas lifted his staff and braced for the attack. Two of the creatures headed for him while another two went for Francis and the final one headed toward Roo. The first attack came fast, and he struggled to keep up with the counter. He knocked the blow off course and was about to trigger Counter when he spotted the second landshark jump to attack.

Instead of going for the damage, he dropped to a knee and crouched forward, letting the monster soar over his head. Hopping back to his feet, he squared off again.

A scream to his right drew his attention, and he watched one creature maul Francis as the man frantically swung a small mace with wild abandon. The attacks rarely connected with anything and did pretty much nothing when they did.

One landshark had a firm grip on Francis' leg while the other clamped onto his shoulder. Knowing he couldn't delay, Atlas took a few large strides and swung his staff at the creature latched onto the healer's shoulder.

The landshark's skull cracked as the metal cap on the staff smashed into its head. It released its grip and leaped backward. Atlas spun just in time to see one of his original targets charging for another bite. He swept his staff to the side to push it off course, but the distraction of helping Francis didn't give him enough time to protect himself. While his slight push saved him from the monster's teeth, it didn't prevent the claw from digging furrows through his pants and into his legs.

Demon Landshark dealt 15 damage to you with Rend.

You are bleeding for 2 damage every 5 seconds from Rend.

The feeling of blood flowing down the inside of his pants leg sent chills up his spine. The warmth sent an involuntary shiver down his spine, as though he needed to shake, but he ignored the sensation and shifted focus to the fight.

Another landshark was right behind the
first, and Atlas didn't bother trying to dodge
or parry. Instead, he grit his teeth in anger
and slid his grip to the end of the staff. A
quick wind up was followed by his favorite
home-run swing, and the heavy metal on the end
of the staff caved in the side of the
creature's skull.

*You dealt 110 damage to Demon Landshark
with Breath of Life. (Critical) (Fatal)*
*Breath of Life loses 20 experience for
taking a life.*

*Whoa, what? It loses experience when I kill
something with it? This is a truly odd weapon.*
His surprise at the notification caused him
to miss the next attack, and his remaining
enemy slashed across his back. The claws
caught in the leather of his jerkin and the
force of the blow drug him to the ground.
Rolling to the side, the claws slid free,
and he got his staff in between him and the
landshark right as it launched for his face,
mouth spread wide open.
The teeth crunched against the hard wood of
his staff but didn't do any visible damage to
the weapon. Drool leaked from its mouth and a
few drops landed on his face. He shoved with
all his strength and the monster stumbled
backward, off balance. A quick roll and twist
that a gymnastics coach would be proud of
brought him back to his feet in a flash, and
he waited for the next attack.

It never came. Instead, Shade appeared near the landshark and dispatched it with a few quick blows to vital points. Atlas took that time to look around. Francis was kneeling nearby, clutching his injured arm, but the landshark that had been on his leg was now dead. Puncture wounds riddled its body, obviously Shade's work.

On his other side stood Roo. The guy looked like he would fall over with a stiff breeze. Francis was a little below half health and Roo was at a quarter health. Roo bled from scratches all over his body. His attacker was also dead from an onslaught of dagger blades.

"Get them patched up if you can," Shade told Atlas as he nodded at both of the others and disappeared.

Atlas activated Harmony and cast it on the other two healers and then himself. The spell was enough to seal up his own bleeding debuff. Without waiting, he also cast Nurture on Roo since he was so low on health.

You healed Kangaroo for 17 HP with Harmony.
You healed Francis for 17 HP with Harmony.
You healed Yourself for 17 HP with Harmony.
You healed Kangaroo for 38 HP with Nurture.

The man stood up straighter and heaved in a deep breath. Unconcerned with their status now, Atlas scanned his party menu and saw Stomper was nearing half health. The Harmony spell on the warrior had lapsed, so he refreshed it. For good measure, he tossed in a Nurture on the warrior as well.

You healed FaceStomper55 for 17 HP with Harmony.

You healed FaceStomper55 for 38 HP with Nurture.

The number of landsharks in the room dwindled quickly as Stomper bashed them, Carhein chopped through them like trees, and Shade carefully diced them apart. Atlas and the other two healers just watched the slaughter for a short time.

As the last of the mobs died, the cave floor rumbled. Stomper spun around until he spotted an entryway on the side of the cave and watched the dark tunnel carefully. Seven monsters emerged from the darkness and dashed toward Stomper.

Their appearance closely mirrored the landsharks they were previously fighting only on a larger scale. A quick check showed their status. *Alpha Demon Landshark – Level 19.*

The lead one hit Stomper's shield, and a shriek of metal echoed through the cave. The warrior held his ground until the second target pummeled into him. His footing slipped, and he stumbled backward. Atlas watched the rest of the monsters approach and decided to lessen the blow. He activated Entangle and began the casting sequence. As soon as the spell finished, he targeted the area in the path of the farthest landshark. Large thorny vines erupted from the ground and quickly snagged hold of the creature's powerful legs as it tried to continue its charge against Stomper.

A soft glow caressed Stomper, and a cascade of glitter dusted over him. His body flashed with a golden light and then returned to normal. Atlas didn't know what that spell was, so he checked the party screen and saw a new buff called Fountain of Light on Stomper.

The description on the menu said it healed him for 8 HP every 2 seconds for a minute. Atlas assumed the spell belonged to Roo since the light from it appeared similar to the attack spells he'd cast earlier.

With those pieces in place, Atlas checked the status of the other two fighters. Carhein was holding on but down to half health. Shade was still near full health since he kept popping in and out of stealth.

Carhein was the next to receive his healing. Harmony was the better option for his mana and was more efficient, so he used it on the fighter.

You healed Carhein for 17 HP with Harmony.

Worried about the status of his mana, he willed the bar to appear.

Mana:	95

It wasn't as bad as he feared. He'd done a decent job of conserving mana so far. It helped that the three fighters with them were fantastic at their jobs. They had Counters and Additions down to an art. They really only took damage when the creatures surrounded them, and they couldn't block that many attacks at once.

Power leaped from Francis' hands and hit Carhein, quickly refilling a chunk of his missing health. Naturally, this also drew the attention of one of the Alpha Landsharks. It ignored its fight with Stomper and Carhein and charged for Francis. The healer stood frozen in place, unsure of what to do.

Atlas dashed forward and interposed himself
between the charging beast and Francis.
Knowing he couldn't stand up to this monster
in his normal form, he cast Dire Bear
Transformation. His body morphed while green
pulsing energy emanated from his skin. Hair
sprouted down his arms and legs as his armor
and clothes vanished from his body. Falling
forward, he rested on all fours as the
transformation finished.

His shapeshift finished right as the Alpha
Landshark arrived and it lunged for him, jaws
open and saliva dripping from its teeth. Pain
blossomed in his shoulder from the pressure of
the attack. Atlas growled in frustration and
the creature reared back and bit into him
again.

*Alpha Landshark dealt 35 damage to you with
Double Bite.*

He took the chance to strike back and used
Maul. Rising onto his hind legs, he brought
his front claws down with tremendous force.
The power of the attack caused his claws to
slide through the sandy hide of the beast
without resistance. Blood spilled from the
monster and splattered on his paws and the
ground.

*You dealt 33 damage to Alpha Landshark with
Maul. (Critical)*

The lack of additions in his bear form was
frustrating. It also didn't help he had no
counters either. After transforming into a
bear, he only had 45 mana left so he couldn't
shift into his nightstalker form for the added
speed and agility.

Limping because of the damage in its side, the landshark circled him, observing him. Instead of charging back in again, it leaped into the air and angled directly for him, claws forward and jaw open.

Frustrated at this form, he decided to at least try something instead of standing there and taking another attack. Judging the speed of the approach, Atlas twisted his body and brought his claw across in a fast backhand. The meaty paw smashed into the side of the landshark's face and knocked it off course, causing it to face-plant into the ground near Atlas' feet. As a follow-up, and admittedly a bit of payback, Atlas lunged forward and sunk his teeth into the front shoulder of the creature.

He'd eaten shark a few times outside of the game and had to admit this creature tasted how he imagined a raw one would at home. Even though it was above ground, it still had a fishy taste to it. The texture of the meat was also a little thicker, like a shark from the real world. Whipping his head to the side, he flung the creature away.

You dealt 15 damage to Alpha Landshark with Bitch Slap.
You learned Backhand Counter. (Bear Form)
You dealt 26 damage to Alpha Landshark with Biting Throw.
You learned Biting Throw. (Bear Form)

Man, who names these abilities? They could use some help in the creativity department.

It also thrilled him to learn two new abilities, one of which was a counter. This game system didn't seem to work how he ever expected. He'd done a few attacks from time to time on his own and rarely ever had it given him new abilities. It would be beneficial if he could find someone who could tell him how these mechanics actually work.

Atlas braced himself for the next attack as the monster stared him down again. It never came. Instead, it let out a roar and then collapsed to the ground. A figured slid down its back with two long daggers in his hands, dripping blood. Shade had finally arrived to deal with the problem. With a sigh of relief, Atlas returned to his elf form.

"What the hell was that?" Francis yelled behind him.

Atlas spun, staff at the ready to attack only to find no one there but a bewildered looking healer. Francis' eyes were glued on him and it appeared he hadn't moved since Atlas jumped in front of him.

"What was what?" Atlas asked.

"He saved your worthless ass, that's what that was," Shade commented as he walked to the group and glared at Francis, "Looks like our assumption about you was true. You are nothing more than a paper warrior. Your application you sent in for this quest looked great, but you have next to no combat experience in this game based on your performance here today."

"On the bright side, it sure makes our choice here easy," Stomper said as he walked to the group.

Atlas turned to look at him and noticed the pile of carnage behind the man. Bodies of the landsharks lay scattered across the cave floor. They hacked some into pieces. Atlas was sure that was Carhein's work. Others looked beaten and broken, with odd lumps under their skin from the trauma. Those he placed money on Stomper. The rest were bleeding from well-placed strikes in vital areas, showing just how deadly Shade was.

"We have a healer who spent their time only trying to deal damage instead of his job and another who is a coward and I doubt has fought anything larger than a fox. Our final healer not only handled most of the healing, but he also stepped in to save their asses. Twice." Stomper summarized.

Shade and Carhein both nodded in agreement, and Carhein walked over to Atlas and threw an arm over his shoulder.

"Only the druid is worthy of his place with the mighty Carhein. We shall bathe in the blood of our foes!"

"Yep, hard pass for me, but thanks for the offer. Sounds sticky."

The group chuckled.

"Songs will be told of our glorious victory today. All shall hear the tale of Carhein the Shark Chopper," the man continued in his baritone voice.

Shade sighed, "I wouldn't put it past him to hire a bard to create some stupid song to sing."

"Regardless of the musical outcome, it's time for you two to leave," Stomper said and pointed at Francis and Roo, "The rest of us have business to attend to."

The two healers grumbled and looked mad, but walked away saying nothing. Everyone else waited until they left the cave.

"Now that they are gone, we can truly talk about the mission, but first, let's finish up this mess," Shade said and walked over to one of the landsharks. It was struggling to get up and Atlas hadn't noticed it. In one quick motion, Shade pulled out a dagger and thrust it down through the top of its head and it crumpled to the ground. A message appeared in front of Atlas.

You have successfully completed the Cave of Fins Mini-Dungeon. You are granted 1,000 bonus experience and 1 attribute point for your first completion.

"Well, that's nice," Atlas commented.

"Yep, we didn't want those two getting the bonus since they were so bad. Now that they have left, they can't get it."

Atlas could only smile. It's good to play with others who properly understand how to use game mechanics.

Stomper walked over to one corpse and reached out. A few items popped up over its head and he snagged them. He did this to three others before he spoke up.

"More damn leather hide, as usual. Told you that you should have taken Leatherworking, Shade."

"Didn't seem as useful to me. Especially not at low level."

"I'm a Leatherworker," Atlas said.

The two turned to look at him.

"What level?" Shade asked.

Atlas glanced at his stat sheet, "Nineteen."

"Looks like he can probably use them. The Alpha hides are even Uncommon rarity," Stomper told Shade.

The rogue only shrugged and Stomper walked over and handed Atlas the hides he'd collected. The items were interesting for sure, but he'd need to find some way to use them.

Item - Landshark Hide	
Requirements: Level 15 **Rarity:** Common **Quality:** Good	**Durability:** 45/45 **Weight:** 5.5 lbs. **Slot:** Crafting **Traits:** The hide from a landshark. The flexible sandy textured skin can be used for crafting.

Item - Alpha Landshark Hide	
Requirements: Level 15 **Rarity:** Uncommon **Quality:** Good	**Durability:** 55/55 **Weight:** 5.5 lbs. **Slot:** Crafting **Traits:** The hide from an alpha landshark. The flexible sandy textured skin can be used for crafting. • 20% chance for special traits to appear on items created using this hide.

That could definitely prove useful.

Stomper handed him 14 of the alpha hides and 40 of the normal landshark hide. Each of them dropped 2 hides.

"Thanks."

"Consider it payment for having to carry those noobs through that fight. Let me gather the rest for you," Stomper told him.

Atlas watched the two walk around and loot all the bodies. He didn't bother asking about the loot because he doubted he'd get anywhere with it. They were giving him all the hides anyway so he wouldn't complain.

Atlas waited at the entrance for the two guys to come back. As they arrived, he gestured toward the opening the alphas charged out of earlier.

"We going to check that out?"

Stomper looked over his shoulder at the entrance, "Nah, we have a dungeon to get to. I don't want to delay any longer in case someone else finds it. Besides, it said we completed the place. Don't feel like searching for some obscure loot back there."

"Care to fill me in on this dungeon?"

Stomper led the way, and they all left the dungeon.

"You have everything you need for a dungeon run?"

"I could use a few potions, but otherwise I'm fine."

Stomper nodded, "I have some extras I'll sell. I can give them to you at cost since you're helping us out and it's short notice. What kinds you want? Mana and health?"

"That should be good. A couple of each, maybe? What do I owe you?"

The man fished through his bag, and his hand came out holding four vials in between his fingers. Each looked like a standard glass tube from a high school science class. Two looked the color or a strawberry syrup while the others reminded him of blue raspberry.

"One gold for them all."

Atlas grimaced a little at the price.

Stomper saw the look and continued, "That's half the market price. They usually run fifty silver each."

Atlas just nodded and grabbed a gold coin from his bag and handed it over. Stomper gave him the potions, and he tucked them into his bag.

"How much time you have left for this login?"

Atlas did some quick math in his head as he looked at the game clock.

"Close to a day."

"Should be enough. Let's get to the dungeon as fast as we can."

They picked up their speed, racing through the trees and headed for an unknown destination. Atlas used the time to dump his free point from the mini-dungeon into Spirit, bringing it to 9 and then focused on the trip.

Chapter 25

Secret Dungeon

The forest blurred by as the party raced toward the city. They made the trip back in half the time it took them to get there. Francis and Roo were already off on their own somewhere. Atlas kept pace with the fighters, although he was cheating using the nightstalker form.

When the gate came into view, he shifted back into an elf and they hurried through the gate and back to the registrar. They dropped their old party, formed a new one, and then hustled toward the gate on the other side of the city.

People gave them odd looks as their group rushed through town. A few guards reached down to their swords as they passed. Their suspicion obvious from the incredulous looks on their faces. The party just ignored them and continued past, and no one called for them to stop.

They avoided roads with heavy traffic and instead skirted by on the side roads. A good half hour of weaving through people and carts brought them to the other side of the city and past the wall.

Stomper changed course, and they headed in a northern direction. Returning to his cat form, he kept a good pace and didn't tire. Three hours of near full speed running brought them to a massive wall of stone. The cliff top was over a hundred feet high and loomed over them, casting its shadow across the landscape. Most of the terrain was grassland with the occasional scattered tree.

Standing in the shadow of the monstrosity, Stomper slowed to a walk and looked around the area. Atlas couldn't figure out what he was looking for. Originally he thought the man was trying to figure out where we were so we could find this dungeon, but then he remembered the minimap and knew that was foolish. Surely the guy had the location marked on his map.

"Something wrong?" Atlas asked.

Stomper swung his head toward Atlas, "Stay as quiet as you can. Someone else is out here looking for the location."

Atlas nodded and walked over to the warrior. He gestured toward the ground, and Atlas could vaguely make out footprints in the crushed grass. The toes of the feet pointed toward the west, and Atlas followed them for a dozen yards before Stomper stopped him.

"They are headed the wrong way. We don't want to follow them."

Atlas turned to the group and saw them moving the other direction. He walked behind and kept his eyes on the surrounding area. They followed the rock wall until Stomper stopped and scanned their surroundings again.

"So, what is in this dungeon?" Atlas whispered to Shade.

"Don't really know. We only got into the first part and died. Oddly, it was a similar encounter to the trial we did with you. Just a mad rush of mobs."

"Then how do you know it's a secret location? You didn't make it far enough to find anything."

"You'll know as soon as we walk in," the rogue said with a wink.

Stomper ceased his scan and walked to the cliff face. He felt along the edge of a large boulder for a few seconds before looking at the rest of the group and nodding. A soft click sounded and the stone opened up like a doorway. The group shuffled through and he closed it behind him as he entered. As soon as the door clicked shut, a message appeared.

*You've discovered a hidden location! You found Secret Dungeon *#&$*%&#.*

What the hell?

"Uh, is there something wrong with the game?" Atlas asked quietly.

"Saw the message, huh? Yeah, that's how we knew this place was something special. We just needed a healer to get through. I heard Shade tell you we failed before, but we should be fine with you here," Stomper told him.

Instead of pestering the guys with more questions they probably wouldn't have the answers to, he just lifted his staff to a ready position and followed behind.

A stone tunnel was the only path, but there was an ambient light to the place. The odd thing was, there was nothing that showed where the light came from. It almost looked like the soft yellow glow of old incandescent lights back home.

The rest of the party all drew their weapons as they neared the end of the small tunnel. Atlas could see a larger cavern ahead of them through the strange lighting. Just before stepping into the open space, Stomper turned around and looked directly at Atlas.

"This is going to be a strange fight. I want to warn you now because the creatures are both funny and terrifying, assuming the same ones show up. We really don't know. Last time we tried this, chickens swarmed us."

"Chickens? Do I need to throw on my green woodland garb and grab a Hylian shield or something?"

Shade snickered at that but Stomper only smiled and shook his head.

"If only it were so simple. It was a large group of chickens, but they are also six feet tall with blades on their legs and wings."

"Well, that's terrifying," Atlas agreed with a nod.

"That's why I wanted to warn you. It was pretty comical at first when we saw them last time until we noticed the blades and they swarmed us. Even then we almost beat them. Now, let's get this party started."

The group rushed forward into the open area and they formed a loose circle around Atlas. Shade stood on the side near the entrance they'd just come from and quickly vanished into stealth. Loud clucking noises echoed off the stone walls and sent chills down Atlas' spine. When the first one came into sight, he couldn't help but agree with Stomper's assessment.

The creatures were both terrifying and hilarious. Six feet tall white chickens with dark red combs appeared in front of them, emerging from three doorways on the far wall. Light reflected off of metal blades on their feet and from the edges of their wings. As they came closer, Atlas noticed their beaks were serrated on the edge. A quick inspection of them made him chuckle. *Fighting Cocks – Level 19.*

Yep, someone did that on purpose.

He got little time to reflect on that as they crowed in unison and charged. Stomper rushed forward to intercept them with Carhein behind him on his left. His shield met the beak of the first chicken and a crunch echoed through the space.

The fight quickly devolved into craziness. Stomper took turns slamming shields into chickens and slicing with his sword. Carhein was playing things much safer and sticking to the warrior's flank while reaching around the edge of the shield to bury an axe in a neck or shoulder as the opportunity presented itself.

Atlas appreciated his careful approach because it meant he could focus on healing Stomper and not trying to work on multiple people. He cast Harmony to get a rolling heal over time started on the warrior.

You healed FaceStomper55 for 17 HP with Harmony.

Stomper had incredible skill as a tank and did a marvelous job at deflecting most of the damage aimed for him. Naturally little slices and cuts made it through his defense, but he was also fighting multiple enemies at once. It was almost impossible to fight that many and not take damage. Even when he took damage, they were obviously only glancing blows, making Atlas' job much easier.

Harmony continued to tick and restore Stomper's health, leaving Atlas to keep track of the action. Shadows swirled and Shade appeared. He slashed downward, and a wing popped off one bird. It squawked in protest before he reversed his slash and buried a blade in its neck, directly under the beak.

A nearby Fighting Cock tried to attack him, but the rogue threw something down and a puff of dark gray smoke obscured his form. The chicken charged through the dark haze and looked around in confusion when it emerged from the other side without its prey.

Shade appeared again and leaped from the smoke. Both of his blades sunk into the back of the chicken while blood and feathers flew into the air. The rogue jumped off and faded into shadow again as it died.

A loud screeching noise filled the area and the constant smashing of metal on metal drew Atlas' attention back to Stomper. A chicken was on its back, its wings beating furiously as its legs kicked out nonstop. The blades on its wings and legs battered Stomper's shield as he tried to back up and hold his defense against the other enemies. A shimmer of metal flashed in Atlas' view before a piece of a blade buried into his thigh.

*Fighting Cock dealt 20 damage to you with
Death Throes.*

"Damn it, Carhein. We said don't cut their
heads off. Don't you know what happens to
chickens when they flop around dead like
that?"

"My apologies, valiant warrior. The lust of
battle took over. Carhein shall strive to
avoid that in the future," the axe wielding
role-player spouted off.

Atlas swore he heard Shade sigh, even
though the man was stealthed somewhere.
Instead of dwelling on it, he carefully
extracted the blade from his leg and dropped
it to the stone floor with a clatter.

The battering of the dying chicken did more
damage to Stomper than normal, so Atlas cast a
Nurture and refreshed his Harmony spell.

*You healed FaceStomper55 for 17 HP with
Harmony.*
*You healed FaceStomper55 for 38 HP with
Nurture.*

The final three Fighting Cocks went down to
an onslaught from Shade and Carhein while
Stomper held their attention. Quiet filled the
room, but Atlas spotted the notifications for
the experience.

*You gained 2,185 experience for the death
of Fighting Cock. (x23)*

*These guys killed twenty-three of those
crazy things in that short of a span? Hell,
they probably could've beat that fight without
me this time.*

"Looks like our strategy worked better this time. Almost didn't need the druid," Shade called out as he reappeared beside the party.

"The druid has a name," Atlas grumbled as he stuck his tongue out at the rogue. A grin was all he received in response.

"We don't know what else is to come as we," Stomper began, but a rumbling noise stopped him. Three more spaces on the wall opened up. Each of them looked to be about eight feet tall and over thirty feet wide. At the entrance of each stood a row of Fighting Cocks lined up side by side. Noise behind them drew their attention and another set of identical doors appeared, but no chickens sat in these.

The chickens in front of the door on the right squawked and ran diagonally across the room toward a door on the other side. They crossed their wings in front of them and steel poked out as they ran. Atlas felt like he was being charged by a wall of cactus, only they bristled with full size blades and not thorns.

Atlas ran to the side and Shade disappeared. Stomper resumed his defensive stance and Carhein took up his position slightly behind the tank. The birds never even slowed their charge as they closed in with the two fighters. Metal screeched, and both men yelled in pain as blades cut their flesh and tossed them to the side. The birds continued their charge until they stood in front of the door they ran at and turned back to watch the group.

The fighter's health bars each sat in the yellow, and Atlas cast Nurture on Stomper and sent a Harmony spell at Carhein.

You healed FaceStomper55 for 38 HP with Nurture.

As the two were climbing back to their feet, the chickens in front of the middle door squawked and dashed across the room. Stomper tried to brace himself for the charge again when something clicked with Atlas.

It's the plague dance. The birds don't stop charging. We aren't supposed to kill them, just avoid them.

"Stomper! Dodge it. This is an avoidance challenge, not a fighting one!"

Both men glanced at Atlas and nodded before running to the side and narrowly avoiding the chicken closest to the edge. Before this group even made it to their destination, the last group charged forward and ran for the final unoccupied door on the opposite end.

The party raced across the cave until they cleared the path of the birds. Each stopped and looked around in triumph until they heard the first group squawk yet again and dash back across the room toward a different doorway.

The Fighting Cocks seemed to run faster than last time, and the group struggled to keep pace. Each time another group charged, the chickens ran a little faster. Atlas grew frustrated with the increasing speed and shifted to cat form to better keep pace.

The only problem was, they didn't stop coming. There were no signs that anything they were doing was going to end this fight. Shade echoed his sentiment.

"We can't keep this up. We will tire out and we won't be able to move fast enough to avoid the charge. There has to be some way to stop this," the rogue told them.

"I see a glorious butt nugget over there on the small pedestal," Stomper said as he pointed toward a small stone outcropping near the entrance they originally came through. On top of the shelf sat an egg.

Atlas looked around the room. Another charge from the chickens interrupted his search and made him divert his attention. As soon as he was in a space of safety, he continued his search. In the corner, on the opposite wall of the egg, was a nest of woven sticks.

"The nest," Atlas growled in his cat form.

The three party members looked at him and then followed his gaze to see the nest in the corner.

"Take the egg to the nest then?" Stomper asked.

"Only thing I can think of," Shade agreed.

"Shade, can you make that trek while dodging the birds?" Atlas asked.

"I normally could, but my body is slowing down from the nonstop action. Need some time to rest. Not sure I can make it."

"Carhein can retrieve the egg and use his mighty strength and finesse to launch said orb across the room to the waiting arms of one of his companions."

"That's a hard pass. I can guarantee the egg will end up broken and I can only imagine the frenzy that will cause in here," Atlas growled.

The other two nodded agreement.

"Think you can do it in your cat form?" Stomper asked.

Atlas considered it and after looking at the exhausted state of his fellow party members decided it would be the best option.

"I'll do it. After this next rush, I'm
making a dash for the egg. I'm sure the birds
will take a path that tries to block me from
my target so you guys should be safe if you
try to stay far from me as I make this trip."

The group agreed, and the next wave of
chickens ran forward. Atlas dashed straight
for the egg with all speed he could manage.
His feline muscles pumped hard, and he closed
the distance in less than a minute. The
dilemma came when he tried to pick it up. A
lack of thumbs made this impossible. Knowing
he couldn't shift back to elf form and survive
this run, he went with the only available
option and picked the egg up in his mouth.

He turned and ran for the nest. His steps
were much more careful on this run. Too much
jarring could cause him to bite into the egg
and break it. It took multiple stops, and he
even had to run backward once to avoid a rush,
but he finally reached the nest. Resting both
paws in front of him inside the nest, he spat
the egg onto them to cushion the fall.

The egg rolled down his paws and rested
gently into the nest. A chime filled the room,
and the chickens ducked into the closest
doorway. The larger doors all closed one by
one until their original entrance and the
three doors on the opposite wall remained.

*You completed the Secret Dungeon *#&$*%&#.
You are granted 3 attribute points and 1,500
experience.*
Success! You've advanced to Level 20.

Giddy with excitement over both the level and added attribute points, Atlas quickly assigned them where he thought they would be most useful. One went into Agility and Constitution, making them 5 and 16, respectively. Two took their place in Intellect making it 20 and the final one went into Spirit bringing it to 10. More notifications showed up with his added points.

For getting 20 attribute points in Intellect, you have unlocked a bonus. All your spells base power increase by an additional 4.
For getting 10 attribute points in Spirit, you have unlocked a bonus. The base mana cost of all of your spells decrease by 10%.

These bonuses really pack a punch. Cheaper spells and even more damage are both fantastic buffs.

"That can't be the end of the dungeon!" Stomper said in frustration.

"Maybe this isn't the place we thought?" Shade asked.

"No, our contact at Gaia gave us these specific coordinates. They even confirmed something odd was going on here, but couldn't tell us what it was."

"Don't despair, brave warrior. Carhein will help continue this journey until we find our prey."

"Shut the hell up. This isn't time for your role-playing nonsense. This place was supposed to hold actual proof of the corruption of the company. Something we could finally show the world to prove our claims. Most think we are nothing but crazy conspiracy nuts as it is."

"Still plenty of the cave left to explore. Maybe we can find something else here that will lead us to what we need?" Shade reassured.

Atlas ran the conversation over in his head for a few moments before he caught on, "You guys are part of Humanity United, aren't you?"

"You could say that. Technically, Shade and I are the ones in charge of Humanity United," Stomper told him.

"You guys really think there is something strange happening in the game then?"

"We know there is, we just aren't sure exactly what it is. We have a few sources inside the company that tell us there are some odd locations like this with weird anomalies in the logs. The equipment in the pods they use also has far more neural processing power than they need to project images into our minds and to interface with our thoughts. Some of us believe they can use these to alter our memories and insert new thoughts and feelings. This place was supposed to be our first big break with real proof," Shade explained.

"Alright, if you think we have a solid lead here, let's split up and search. I'll admit this place is super weird, and we have seen no loot here other than whatever you guys grab off the chickens. Maybe there's a chest with documents or something," Atlas told them.

The group agreed and Shade went to work looting the birds while the rest of them searched the cave. It didn't take Shade long to comment about the birds.

"Well, add to the list of weird. The chickens just display an error message when I try to loot them."

The group all shook their heads and resumed their search.

They found nothing of interest in the main cavern so Stomper, Carhein, and Atlas each chose one of the three doorways and investigated. He heard Stomper call out that his tunnel was clear and then Carhein confirmed his was shortly after. Atlas continued down his tunnel until he reached the end. Nothing but rough stonework greeted him.

He turned to head back toward the large cavern when a smell drifted to him. The cave itself had a bit of a musty smell about it. Clean and crisp air caught his attention. It reminded him of work. That smell of filtered air in hospitals and clinics.

His nose led him on a merry chase around the cave until he found an area on the side of the tunnel, twenty feet from the end that had a carving on it. The picture itself was small, but it sat around waist height had he been in his elf form. With a thought, he transformed back into elf form and examined the symbol.

"Hey guys, come over here. I think I found something."

Chapter 26

Bodysnatcher

Atlas heard footsteps as the group raced down the tunnel to find him. They all gathered around him and looked toward the wall.

"There's something behind this wall," he told them as he placed his hand on the wall, "I could smell a difference in the air behind it in my cat form and there is a symbol down here."

Atlas pointed toward the symbol, and the group all leaned forward to peer at it.

"Anyone know what that is?" Stomper asked.

"Not sure. Looks vaguely familiar, but I can't quite place it," Shade told them.

"The evil Gloom Elves have marked thine entrance to the cave. Stand back while I ferret out their wickedness," Carhein called.

"Gloom Elves? Are there Gloom Elves in this game?" Atlas asked.

"Haven't met any, and it wasn't a race option," Stomper said with a shake of his head.

"Carhein, what do you mean by Gloom Elves?"

The fighter pointed at the symbol, "They have crossed over from the kingdom of Daratha. The symbol of their kingdom doth shine brightly."

Daratha? That sounds familiar…

"He's right! That's their symbol from Destiny Fall." Stomper said as he leaned closer and brushed the dust off the wall.

"But why would their symbol be here? We haven't seen any mention of their race yet?" Atlas asked.

"Hell if I know, but I'm guessing it's a clue. Look around and see if we find anything else," Shade told them.

The group huddled close to the wall and slowly ran their eyes and hands across the entire surface. Not finding anything in the immediate vicinity, they continued their search outward further down the wall. After covering a forty-foot span, they changed tactics and walked back to the symbol. They turned and checked the opposite wall instead.

As Atlas ran his hand against one spot on the wall, a raised portion in the stone snagged him. He roughly brushed at the area and saw a dial that looked like it was from a padlock. Instead of the large cylinder protruding from it, three small indentions sat on the surface around the disc. They appeared to be finger holes to help spin it. The edge of the disc had a bunch of symbols on them he couldn't discern at first until he realized they were numbers in the Gloom Elf language.

"Anyone good with the Gloom Elf language? I was a big fan of the game and all, but not that hardcore of a fan boy." Atlas said.

"I can't read it, but I dealt with them enough to know the numbers. They only did business in their own numbering system," Stomper explained.

"Well, what are these numbers then?" Atlas asked as he pointed at the dial. Stomper walked over and examined the device.

"Looks like the number one through ninety-nine. Is this a padlock?"

"That's what I thought it was. Anyone know a three number combination it could be?" Atlas asked.

"The symbol of the Gloom Elves and the dial being in their language means it has to be something significant to their culture. Don't know enough about them to even venture a guess," Shade told them.

"I bet those foul creatures chose six, thirty-eight, seventy-seven," Carhein told them.

"Why would that be the combo?" Stomper asked.

"On the thirty-eighth day of Salun, the sixth month, in the year two hundred and seventy-seven, the disparate tribes of Gloom Elves banded together to form their kingdom. That day was also the day that symbol was created," Carhein said as he pointed at the wall with the picture.

"Not that I doubt you, but how do you know all this?" Stomper asked.

"T'was my most glorious of missions to hunt down the infestation of Gloom Elves. I had to learn everything about them to fight them."

"Damn, dude, you could just say you read it in the lore compendium," Shade huffed.

Stomper smiled at Shade's comment but tried the combination Carhein suggested. When the final number reached the top of the dial, a small click echoed in the cavern and rumbling rocks caused everyone to turn their attention to the space with the symbol. A panel on the wall the size of a standard door popped backward a few inches and then gradually slid into a small space in the rock.

The party looked into the new opening and saw a flight of stairs leading down.

"Excellent work, Carhein. Let's go find what we came here for," Stomper said as he clapped the fighter on the shoulder.

Everyone pulled out their weapons and tromped down the stairs. Stomper took lead with Carhein following him. Atlas came next, and Shade brought up the rear.

The sight at the bottom of the stairs caused them all to freeze in their tracks. Glistening steel walls stretched down an expansive corridor. It looked like the stereotypical hideout for an evil mastermind. All they needed now was a team of henchmen to dispatch around the world and steal treasures for them.

A message pulled his attention from daydreaming about a favorite old game of his.

Caution! You have entered Restricted Area A11. Only approved moderators, game masters, and designers are allowed in this zone. Leave now or the Guardian will be activated!

"That could be bad," Shade whispered.

"A guardian sounds like a problem, but this place has to be what we came here to find," Stomper affirmed.

"Let us move with haste and find this evidence before Carhein is forced to destroy the guardian."

"You've got to cool it with that, but you have a point. Let's move quickly. Everyone stay close," Stomper said as he moved forward.

The group walked at a fast pace down the metal corridor until they entered a large, open space. Steel workbenches that looked like they belonged in a science lab lined the walls. Glass vials filled with different color liquids sat in wooden holders next to a large contraption that he could only picture as an alchemy set.

Wooden casks were stacked under one of the table on the left, and a thick black sludge gathered on the top near a cork. Most concerning of all was the thing that stood in the corner of the room. Inside a large metal frame stood a robot. At least, that's what Atlas assumed it was. It really looked like a full suit of plate armor except metallic hoses ran down its arms and legs and he could see metal through the gaps in its armor. A large helmet sat on top with a thin visor slit, but it had eagle wings flaring off of each side in a backward sweep.

They all stared at the contraption in silence.

"I hope that's not the guardian," Shade said, causing everyone to flinch. The game must've thought that was the cue because lights hummed to life on the metal frame and the thick black sludge he noticed on the casks pumped down tubes and entered the main body of the machine.

Guardian Otto activated! Have your identification ready or you will be dispatched.

The two hoses supplying the black liquid popped loose with a hiss and the openings in the armor closed. Its eyes flared with a green light as it walked toward the party.

"Identify yourselves or be executed," its monotone voice rang out.

"Well, damn. Looks like we get to fight," Stomper said and charged the machine.

The robot barely moved as the tank charged forward. Stomper brought his shield around in a powerful blow and it smashed into the side of the guardian's head. A metallic gong rang through the room and the machine remained in the exact same position, its green eyes shining into Stomper's stunned face.

In one quick motion the guardian punched the shield and Stomper flew ten feet through the air before hitting the ground and sliding to a stop. The shield on his arm bent and battered. With a pained expression, he extricated his arm from the leather straps and held it close to his body.

Atlas looked on in horror at the scene until his attention focused on the health bars. Stomper was in the yellow, flirting with red. Snapping out of his fear, he cast Nurture and immediately followed it with Harmony.

You healed FaceStomper55 for 42 HP with Nurture.

You healed FaceStomper55 for 21 HP with Harmony.

The warrior's health bar jumped up at the first cast and then gradually started ticking higher. Movement caught his eye, and he watched as Shade and Carhein attempted to engage the metallic monster.

Their blades sparked and hissed as they
scratched across the armor but didn't even
scuff the plate. Shade ducked below a swipe
from the guardian, but Carhein wasn't as
lucky. He almost dodged the hit, but it
clipped him on the shoulder and sent him
tumbling to the ground. Rings of his chain
mail popped loose and rang across the floor as
they bounced.

Atlas shifted focus and cast Harmony on him
as well.

You healed Carhein for 21 HP with Harmony.

"We can't hurt it!" Shade yelled.

"It seems impervious to our weapons of
steel. Maybe some magic is in order valiant
druid?" Carhein called toward Atlas.

With a nod of agreement, Atlas looked
toward the guardian. Its name and level
quickly flashed up as he finally took the time
to examine it. *Otto Hinden, the Shiny Hell
Instrument of Torture – Level 25.*

Someone definitely had extra time on their
hands to name him that. Instead of trying to
remember it, Atlas decided he would just call
it OH SHIT.

Atlas let instinct take over as he
activated Nature's Wrath. The movements came
to him and his body almost completed the spell
on its own. Two balls of green power launched
forward and punched into the breastplate of
the machine. It rocked back two steps in
surprise before it turned its gaze on Atlas.

*You dealt 34 damage to OH SHIT with
Nature's Wrath.*

Atlas chuckled that the system recognized his name for the creature and adapted.

"Did you hurt it?" Stomper asked.

"Yeah. The spell seemed to do full damage."

"Good. None of my attacks did over one damage," Stomper told him.

"Same," both Carhein and Shade said in unison.

OH SHIT headed for Atlas and he began weaving his next spell. Without realizing it, he cast Entangle. The strange part was, he never activated the ability, just cast the spell by memory. The notification proved it.

You dealt 9 damage to OH SHIT with Entangle.

Rejoice! You mastered Entangle.

You can now cast Entangle without fail or backlash. You unlocked the spell Upgraded Entangle. Master it for additional bonuses.

That's great news. Also meant his spells evolved.

His excitement about mastering the spell lasted only a few more seconds as he heard the ripping of vines. OH SHIT was quickly tearing free of his bindings and trying to move forward. Atlas activated Sunfire and cast the spell. The column of white energy smashed into the contraption and it dropped to a knee under the onslaught.

You dealt 21 damage to OH SHIT with Sunfire.

"I can't keep this up forever. I don't have enough mana to kill him by myself," Atlas told the group, "We need a plan."

"Anyone else have any hidden magic up their sleeves that they've kept quiet?" Shade asked in a sarcastic tone.

"It has to have a weakness. Any ideas?" Atlas asked.

"Machines are usually prone to overheating. Too bad we don't have a fire mage," Stomper grumbled.

"The vials! Maybe try throwing them at the creature?" Atlas called over.

"Great idea unless they emit poisonous fumes or decide to explode. Then we all die." Shade said.

"The black stuff in the kegs! It was pumped into the machine. Is it flammable?" Stomper asked.

Shade dashed to the side and slid under the table to stop near a keg.

"Smells like an oil. It should definitely be flammable."

"Carhein, with me," Stomper said, and they both raced for a barrel.

Atlas turned to see the guardian rip free and continue its warpath directly for him. Instead of casting another spell, Atlas did the next most reasonable thing. He ran. The major downfall of the machine seemed to be it couldn't run, only walk.

It adjusted course and followed Atlas as he ran around the room. Kiting the boss around the space definitely sounded more appealing than trying to fight it face to face, at least until they had a plan on what to do. Stomper and Carhein ran in from the side as Atlas watched, carrying a barrel between them hoisted up on their shoulders.

When within range, they both heaved with a throw that would've made a shot-put coach weep and the barrel spun end over end until it shattered against the guardian. Black liquid ran down the exterior of the machine like syrup.

"Now what?" Atlas yelled to the guys.

"One step at a time! Haven't figured that out yet!" Stomper yelled back.

"Let us show the metallic monster the might of the future!" Carhein said as he ran over and grabbed a small empty vial. He ran back over to the barrels of the thick fluid and filled the tiny glass up. With a quick jerk, he ripped a small piece of cloth from his sleeve and stuffed the end into the liquid.

"How are we going to light it?" Stomper asked the fighter.

"My fire burns bright with the strength of my arm. Carhein the Mighty can handle this task."

"Shut the hell up and quit being stupid. You don't have any way to light it!" Shade yelled at Carhein.

"Give… it… to me," Atlas said through gasps as he tried to catch his breath from constantly running.

Carhein looked at him and nodded. Atlas pointed the direction he was headed and Carhein took a path to intercept. The fighter handed him the vial and kept running to get away from the machine. Atlas looked at the item.

<table>
<tr><td colspan="2" align="center">Item - Vial of Volatile Fury</td></tr>
<tr><td>Requirements: Level 10
Rarity: Uncommon
Quality: Fair</td><td>Durability: 5/5
Weight: 1.0 lbs.
Slot: Chemical

Traits: A small vial filled with volatile liquid. Adding fire will create a disastrous effect.</td></tr>
</table>

Looks like it doesn't register as a weapon or anything since I'm sure it's new in the game.

Atlas activated his Basic Firestarter spell and lit the end of the cloth on fire. Praying this would work, he turned toward the guardian and launched the vial. It tumbled end over end until breaking against the leg of the machine. Fire instantly consumed the thing and black smoke billowed up to the ceiling before slowly filtering up the stairs.

The party coughed and did their best to stay low to the ground and away from the smoke. They looked at each other and smiled in relief.

"Something like that shouldn't exist in a game like this," Stomper grumbled.

"Completely agree but we still took care of it," Shade said with a sigh.

The group huddled on the ground as Atlas continued to suck in deep breaths. Metallic screeching filled the room, and the group turned toward the center of the flames. Their eyes widened as the monster emerged, its armor now stained black with soot. He looked to his notifications.

*You dealt 160 damage to OH SHIT with Vial
of Volatile Fury.*

*The heat of the attack has inflicted
Brittle Armor on OH SHIT. His armor rating has
decreased by 75%.*

*The Brittle Armor effect on OH SHIT has
caused more flexibility in his frame. He gains
a 30% increase to speed.*

"Oh shit," Atlas breathed.

Atlas jumped to his feet and ran. The
machine was still focused only on him and
resumed its pursuit. Unfortunately, it no
longer moved at a fast walk. Instead, it ran.

"Could use some help guys! You should be
able to damage it now. Its armor dropped
seventy-five percent from the fire."

The other three party members were already
on their feet watching the machine chase Atlas
around the room. With his statement, they all
ran forward to engage the guardian.

Stomper swung his sword in a wide arc and
it sunk into the shoulder plate of the
machine. It didn't go in more than an inch,
but any damage was better than what they
achieved before.

Carhein connected with the thigh of the
contraption, and his axe bit deeper than
Stomper's sword. A large rent opened in the
thigh plate. The axe wedged deep in the metal,
preventing Carhein from pulling it free.

Shade didn't have as much luck. His blades
slashed in quick succession across the armor,
but only left scratches. They couldn't
completely break through the metal.

A wild swing from the guardian hit Stomper and sent him tumbling to the ground. Its arms never stopped their flailing attacks while it chased Atlas. Carhein was the next to take a hit from another flailing arm. Both men fell to the ground, their health bars quickly hitting yellow.

"Its attacks do far too much damage. We can't take more than one hit without dying," Stomper moaned as he tried to roll back to his feet.

"Fire seems to be the only thing that works. Can we try the same thing again? Do you two think you can grab another barrel?" Atlas asked.

"It might, but it only seems to make it faster. I don't think another bonfire will kill it, and if it survives, I'm worried its speed boost will let it wipe us out in seconds," Shade told him.

Atlas sucked in air as he ran. His legs were burning from the constant action. Shifting into cat form was an option, but he badly needed to heal his party members. He also didn't want to waste mana he would probably need later.

HP:	180
Mana:	160

"Shade, can you cut one of his hoses? They have metal covering them, but it should be brittle enough for you to break it open."

"I might be able to, but I'd need him to stop running long enough to line up an accurate shot. His movements make a precision strike like that almost impossible."

The rogue dropped low and slid under a swing from the machine before popping back to his feet. Atlas turned the corner and bolted across the room in a diagonal pattern.

"If I can stop him, can you do it?" Atlas asked.

"Yep. Don't get yourself killed trying, though."

"Well, this is going to hurt one way or another. I can't keep running like this. My stamina won't last forever."

Atlas kicked in a burst of speed to gain a little distance on the guardian. When he thought he might have enough distance, he came to a halt and spun to face the machine. He cast Entangle and his hands wove in a quick pattern, but it wasn't fast enough.

A fist connected with his chest right as the last motion released the spell. Atlas fell backward and rolled away as pain erupted in his chest. He was relatively sure it broke at least one rib from the attack. His vision flashed red, and he noticed he only had 15 HP left.

He fished in his bag and pulled out a health potion. Popping the cork off, he drank it down in one quick gulp. The liquid slid down his throat and its magic took over almost instantly. Two bones moved in his chest and he felt a soft pop as they returned to the correct place. The pain quickly subsided, and he jumped to his feet.

It didn't quite top him off, but brought him back to a respectable 140 HP. A grunt of pain drew his attention. Glancing at the guardian showed Shade bringing his blade up and into the armpit of the machine. The knife bit deep into the tube and black sludge ran down the creature's side. The contraption swatted the rogue away, and he landed in a heap, holding his shoulder.

"I have to get close enough to light that stuff on fire, preferably without him killing me. Any ideas on how to immobilize him?" Atlas asked.

"Don't have enough health to keep him occupied for long. He also seems solely focused on you since you have threat."

"Not my fault he's only vulnerable to magic and the elements."

"The valiant Carhein to the rescue!" the warrior bellowed as he glowed with a red haze. His speed increased, and he held his one remaining axe with both hands as he chopped away at the guardian like a lumberjack felling a tree.

"I'll help," Shade called and then he appeared behind the machine in a flash. His form blurred as he constantly vanished and reappeared with double bladed strikes each time. His pattern was random and erratic as he jumped from spot to spot near the back of the machine.

Small punctures and dents appeared as they smashed attack after attack into the metal armor. Its steps caught on damaged pieces of its armor as it moved, causing it to stumble and work to regain its balance. Completely stopping the thing seemed out of the question. All of them were already low on health and trying to light the guardian on fire was as likely to wipe the entire party out right now as anything else. Atlas tried his new big ability. He cast Tranquil Fountain.

The movements were broad and sweeping as his mana gathered in front of him. A final few twirls of his hand and a small pedestal the size of a bird bath formed, made of golden energy. Rays of light extended out and connected with each of his party members.

You healed FaceStomper55 for 43 HP with Tranquil Fountain.
You healed Carhein for 43 HP with Tranquil Fountain.
You healed Shade for 43 HP with Tranquil Fountain.
You healed Yourself for 43 HP with Tranquil Fountain.

Atlas continued to concentrate on the spell, and everyone's health ticked up at an incredible rate. Restoring 43 HP a second on each person was a bit overpowered, but it had the downside of him now being immobile.

OH SHIT continued its trek toward Atlas while still randomly swinging at his party members who ventured too close. Atlas concentrated on the spell. A big dip in Stomper and Shade's health told him the machine hit both again. The spell quickly restored them as he focused on keeping it going.

Atlas hoped his party members could finish the guardian after his death. The machine was only a handful of steps away, and if he dropped the spell, they wouldn't last much longer. As the machine loomed in front of him, he closed his eyes in anticipation of the end.

A loud metal clang sounded through the room, and a grunt followed. Atlas opened his eyes to see Carhein standing between himself and the golem, his body glowing slightly with red light. His axe was buried in the machine's chest and its green eyes were now focused entirely on the fighter.

It reached forward and grabbed Carhein by the neck.

The warrior turned toward Atlas, his face turning a dark shade of red as the guardian squeezed tighter. Without a word, he raised his hand and gave him a thumbs up.

"You'll die if I light it on fire now."

"Carhein the Mighty… has no fear… of death… do it."

Atlas saw Carhein's health drop faster than his spell could heal, so he quickly dropped it, ducked under its arm, and slid to its side. He used his Basic Firestarter spell and the leaking fluid caught fire.

Flames spread quickly as all the exposed liquid burned. Hissing filled the air as fire burst from the different tubes all over the guardian's body.

A minor explosion rocked the space and Atlas tumbled away. He rolled to a stop and saw his health flashing red and burned spots on his leather. It also caught Carhein in the conflagration, and Atlas could only watch as his health bar bottomed out.

Atlas scurried backward and took a resting position near Shade and Stomper. They waited with nervous anticipation, remembering the last time they supposedly won this fight.

"It can't be," Shade breathed.

Everyone followed his line of sight and watched as the machine shambled from the fire, a charred Carhein still held in its hand.

"I've got nothing left," Stomper told them softly.

The machine took three more steps before a loud snapping noise echoed through the room. Its right leg broke free, and it collapsed to the ground, dropping Carhein's body. Determined to carry out its mission, it pulled itself along the floor with its hands. It didn't take much longer for one of them to break at the shoulder, releasing more of the fluid in a quick flood and instantly igniting the area again.

The group watched in silence and held their breath. A string of notifications excited and relieved them.

You dealt 1,180 damage to OH SHIT with Internal Combustion.

OH SHIT died.

You earned 345 experience from killing a Mythic Boss.

You've earned the artifact Steel Hide. With this artifact equipped, your Dire Bear form will gain steel plated armor, reducing your damage taken by 50%.

You've gained 3 attribute points for killing a Mythic Boss.

All members of your party have gained 5 attribute points for being the first party to kill a Mythic Boss in the game.

You've completed a Mythic level Secret Dungeon and earned 6,000 experience, 4,000 skill experience, 100 gold, and 3 attribute points.

You've advanced to Level 21!

The group looked around and rose to their feet.

Holy crap! That is an amazing amount of stuff. A little disappointed there isn't any cool gear but the money, artifact, and bonus attributes more than make up for it.

The party stood in stunned silence until they all looked at each other and smiled before their gaze wandered to Carhein's smoking form.

"We did it, but it wasn't without a loss. Hopefully, his experience penalty isn't too bad." Atlas said in a grim tone.

"The dude is usually pretty annoying, but I'm not gonna lie. That was a baller move to bail you out at the end," Shade said as he looked to the charred remains of Carhein.

"Yeah. I was dead for sure otherwise. I owe him for that. The least I can do is keep him from waiting through that timer."

His attention shifted toward the remains of Carhein, and he fished an item from his pouch. Focus Crystal in hand, he cast Resurgence.

His left hand held the Focus Crystal out while his right wove patterns around it. Magic slowly settled into the gem before a crack appeared and it crumbled to dust. Everything around him took on a deep purple haze and his mind shifted focus to Carhein.

The man sat in a chair, floating above the body on the ground, and tapped away at the classic controller in his hands. Atlas walked over and watched the guy shoot the crazy little pixelated bugs with his white spaceship as they dove toward him in patterns.

"Gotta love classics."

The voice startled the warrior, and he jumped in his seat before turning to look at Atlas.

"How are you here? I'm waiting on respawn."

"Resurrection spell. We still have a mission to complete. It's the least I could do after you saved our butts there. You have some nice surprises waiting on you when you get back. The bonus rewards for that fight are pretty epic, but it didn't drop any neat weapons or anything."

Carhein chuckled, "I guess thou dost need the protection of Carhein the Mighty. Lead the way good druid and we shall return."

Atlas shook his head and grabbed Carhein by the hand. With what amounted to a flick of the wrist, he tossed his spirit back at the dead body. It sunk in and Atlas watched as the body healed itself. With a jolt, he was out of the spirit world and all the colors returned.

Carhein was slowly climbing back to his feet and Atlas took the time to cast Harmony and Nurture on him. Resurgence only brought them back at 10% health.

You healed Carhein for 42 HP with Harmony.

You healed Carhein for 21 HP with Nurture.

Atlas took stock of the situation and noticed he had an astounding 10 attribute points at his disposal from the bonuses for the dungeon. Since his cat and bear form redistributed points for him when he shifted, there was no reason to worry about Strength and Agility. Speed might become important later, but for now he'd forgo Agility. That left him with Constitution, Intellect, and Spirit. He put 4 into Intellect bringing it to 24, 4 into Constitution bringing it to 20, and 2 into Spirit bringing it to 12.

For getting 20 attribute points in Constitution, you have unlocked a bonus. You now regenerate health at 3 HP every 20 seconds when out of combat and get a permanent boost of 30 HP.

"Damn man, didn't know you could resurrect people as well. Looks like we definitely picked the right man for the job." Stomper said with a clap on Atlas' shoulder.

"It's actually the first time I've used that spell. Learned it from a class quest at level ten."

"Your magic is mighty indeed. It prevented the damnable gods of this world from leeching as much of Carhein's battle knowledge as expected. Ten percent is a small price to pay for the death of that abomination," Carhein said as he glared at the husk of the machine.

"I didn't know it reduced the experience penalty. That could prove useful indeed." Atlas said with a smile.

After everyone finished reviewing their notifications and assignments, they all turned to look at the hallway opposite where they'd entered.

"Ready to go find out what this place is hiding?" Stomper asked.

The group nodded in agreement and walked into the passageway. It curved twice, but after one-hundred yards they entered a room that made them shiver. It looked like a modern day jail. Cages lined the walls. Metal bars stretched floor to ceiling.

Atlas stayed rooted in place, but the others continued through the room. They checked in each of the cells but didn't find anyone. When they reached the last one on the right, they stopped. Atlas couldn't tell what they saw, so he slowly crept forward.

"You guys don't look like the crazies I usually see. Are you with Gaia?" A voice called from the cell.

"No. We are here to investigate what's happening," Stomper said.

"Oh, thank God. I've been trapped down here for weeks. I was hoping Atlas would notice me gone, but I haven't seen him yet. You think you could get me out of here? I've got to go find him and warn him something is wrong here."

Atlas heard his name and hurried forward. The voice sounded so familiar, but he couldn't place it.

He turned and looked into the cage to see a male beastkin looking back. His feline eyes narrowed at the sight of Atlas. The dark gray fur looked soft and smooth. A set of basic starter clothes covered his legs and chest.

"What Atlas are you looking for?"

"Nah man… Not an Atlas. I'm looking for my friend IRL. He's actually a nurse. We've been friends practically our whole life." The beastkin told him.

"Keenan?"

The cat's eyes stared at him for a few seconds before they flashed in recognition.

"Atlas! You found me. Why the hell did it take you so long? I'd think my best friend would notice me missing for weeks."

Is this game playing tricks on me? Keenan told me he was a beastkin, but surely this can't be him.

"What do you mean missing for weeks? I talked to you yesterday. You said you were busy with your new position as an executive."

"You okay, bud? What's this nonsense about being an executive?"

"You found a secret in the game and were made an executive. There was a press conference for it and everything. I know. I was there."

"He's right," Shade said as he pointed at Atlas, "I was there when they announced Keenan Hall found one of the hidden secrets and they promoted him to executive."

"I've been trapped here since a couple of dickheads ambushed me and drug me in here. I've seen no one other than some strange Gaia Corporation scientists in here poking and prodding at me. I've been a little lost on the exact time, but I'd imagine it's been at least two weeks, maybe longer."

Can it really be him? He's been acting weird in the real world since they promoted him. The changes in posture, the slips in speech, I just chalked them up to his new lifestyle. Is it possible I've left my real friend trapped down here this whole time?

"It's worse than we thought," Stomper said softly.

"What do you mean?" Atlas asked.

"We've been trying to warn everyone something was off about this game and Gaia Corporation had a more nefarious purpose. We just weren't thinking big enough."

"Is this even possible, though? I've never heard of technology that can do this?" Shade asked.

"It has to be possible. We're seeing the effects here."

"Keenan, who ambushed you?" Atlas asked.

"Some jackasses I met in Nirithan. We partied up, and they trapped me in here. Got around their fancy party agreement because they didn't actually harm me. Some dude named Hercules, and the other was Skullcrusher."

"Damn. I should've told you. Those were the asshats who killed me back when we first started." Atlas said.

"Then we definitely need to hunt them down and kill them slowly. Maybe we can spawn camp them? But first, you need to get me out of here and someone needs to tell me why I can't log out of the game. The option doesn't appear when I lay down, and the button is grayed out when I try to access it through the menu. I've even tried submitting tickets to the game masters but received no response."

Atlas stood there with his mouth slightly open, unsure how to answer.

"Keenan, I'm Stomper. Shade and I," he said while motioning toward the rogue, "are part of a group called Humanity United. We have a few friends inside of Gaia Corporation who tipped us off and warned us that the company was doing something odd. The logs for the game and the immense power of the pods didn't add up for what they needed to just play a game. We thought they were using this upgraded hardware to alter memories or influence the players to do what they wanted. Instead, it's much worse."

"What do you mean? I still don't understand." Keenan said.

Shade looked into the cell and stared into the feline eyes of the beastkin, "Keenan, I don't know how else to say this but someone in Gaia Corporation has stolen your body and is masquerading as you."

End Notes

Thank you for reading Atlas Rising. This book is my first step in expanding the universe I am working diligently to create. Anyone following the Facebook page knows that this story is in the same universe as the main series, The Dimensional Wars. Before you ask, no I won't tell you how, you just have to wait.

The Divine Genesis series will be a trilogy but it won't be the last you see of Atlas. We will leave it at that. Now that this book is done, my attention shifts to Regicide, book 3 of The Dimensional Wars. It will be the next book I release. Keep an eye on the Facebook page and sign up for the newsletter to keep up to date about releases and writing progress. I promise I don't send emails out unless it's an important announcement.

Books by the Author

The Dimensional Wars

Book 1 - Dravincia
Book 2 - Soul Bond
Book 3 - Regicide (Release TBD)

The Dimensional Wars Origins

Book 1 - Rayne

Divine Genesis

Book 1 - Atlas Rising

If you are looking for more book recommendations, or if you feel like chatting about books you have already read. Go to the LitRPG Books group on Facebook.

If you want to see updates on The Dimensional Wars or if you have any questions or comments you wish to share with me let me know on The Dimensional Wars Facebook page. I'm always willing to talk to anyone.

If you want updated news about releases please visit my website http://www.thedimensionalwars.com to subscribe to my mailing list.

To see new releases as well as any LitRPG books that are on sale, visit the LitRPG Releases Facebook Page

Finally, if you're looking for a new book to read but can't decide what to try next, pop on over to the LitRPG Amazon Storefront.

To learn more about LitRPG, talk to authors
including myself, and just have an awesome
time, please join the LitRPG Group.

Final Stat Sheet

Name: Atlas	**Agility:** 5
Class: Druid	**Constitution:** 20
Level: 21	**Intellect:** 24
HP: 260/260	**Strength:** 2
Mana: 280/280	**Spirit:** 12
Experience: 1085/7500	

Combat Skills:
Anticipate
Blade Chase
Charge
Disrupt
Double Slash
Fallback
Pursuit
Triple Threat

Magic Skills:

Transformation:
Dire Bear
Nightstalker

Nature Magic:
Barkskin - Rank 2
Entangle - Rank 2
Harmony - Rank 2
Nature's Wrath - Rank 2
Nurture - Rank 2
Resurgence - Rank 1
Sunfire - Rank 1
Tranquil Fountain - Rank 1

Crafting Skills:

Herbalism: Level 8
Jewelcrafting: 18 (3840/4800)
Leatherworking: Level 19 (445/5300)
Woodworking: Level 27 (15,460/21,000)

Artifacts:
Steel Hide